DARK APPRENTICE

FALL OF MAGIC BOOK ONE

VAL NEIL

LIVING RELIC PRESS

CONTENTS

Editing by The Blue Garret
www.thebluegarret.com

Cover Illustration by Warm Tail
www.pinterest.ru/Marin_Iuri/

Ebook ISBN: 978-1-955075-00-8
Paperback ISBN: 978-1-955075-01-5

PROLOGUE

Medea willed the roots to rise up and pierce the still-warm flesh. No point in transporting this body back to the graveyard—it was already near capacity and she had limited use for corpses these days. Let it replenish the soil.

She'd been reading in the forest when he'd interrupted her—that alone should be a mortal offense, but that's not why she'd killed him. He'd been with her what, three years before initiating the challenge? Apprentices seemed to have grown more impatient these days, yet if they were going to turn on her, she preferred they get it over with. This one had been a half-rate necromancer, barely able to reanimate a squirrel, yet he fancied himself talented enough to best her. The insult still stung.

She picked up her discarded book and sat, propping her back against a tree.

What a waste. Not of his life, but of hers. Immortal she might be, but sometimes she felt like Sisyphus, forever rolling a boulder uphill only to have it slide back at the last moment.

Too many apprentices had gone this way over the last few centuries. There had always been a sizable percentage interested in so-called dark magic, but ever since the Collective's crack-down, it seemed that's all she got. She counted one apprentice in the last eighty years that was interested in anything else—*ONE*—and he'd only sought her out to learn how to combat dark magic. At least *he* hadn't tried to kill her.

The rest though . . .

Bunch of devious, self-centered ingrates. Never mind that she was a grand master healer and fleshweaver. No one came to learn *that* anymore, or nature magic, or summoning, or any of the dozens of other specialties she'd mastered over the years. Hell, these days she spent so much time correcting bad spellwork, apprentices barely scratched the surface before they decided to turn on her. She had half a mind to stop training people.

Belatedly she realized she'd been scanning the same page for ages. She made a frustrated noise and shot a glare at the body, now wrapped in vines.

"You realize you've ruined my whole day."

The glassy eyes stared vacantly at the sky. One barbed tendril snaked into the mouth, which hung open in slight surprise.

She snapped the book shut and stood. "How could you *possibly* fail to see this is how it would end? Do you have any idea how much I hold myself back during sparring matches? And you couldn't even best me *then*." She paced as she spoke, acceler-ating the decay of tissue until little more than clothes and bone remained.

That's it—no more apprentices, not unless they wanted to learn something different. Or maybe not even then, because people would just lie to get accepted. Dark magic practitioners were always liars.

She reached out with her magic, intending to scorch the remains—couldn't have new apprentices stumbling across dead ones—but pulled herself back, though it took far more effort than she wanted to admit. There would *be* no more apprentices, not this time. The skull observed her in quiet admonishment.

"None." She nodded curtly to herself and retreated from the forest.

1

THE LETTER

Ireland, 1955

People could be sorted into two categories: Useful and Useless. Useless people simply existed alongside you. They took up space and there was no benefit to interacting with them. Useful people had things Nikolai wanted. Money. Sex. Influence. A nice apartment.

When he'd first come to Haven seeking training, the good places were already rented. Nikolai could have boarded with someone, but roommates were annoying, so he found a building owned by a middle-aged couple—the Gallaghers—and quickly made friends with the wife. He made friends with her nightly as he fished for information about her tenants.

Nikolai found a satisfactory target—a nervous gentleman who had trouble paying his rent on time but had lived there forever and so the Gallaghers let him stay. Nikolai approached the man and offered to split the rent in exchange for a bed.

Getting rid of him was easy. All Nikolai had to do was drop the social mask at home. For some reason, people found his acerbic remarks and lack of emotional expression unnerving.

Three days later, the man banged on Mr. Gallagher's door, pleading for help removing his new flatmate.

"Afraid? Of *me*?" Nikolai feigned confusion and glanced down the hallway at his flatmate, who ducked out of view behind Mrs. Gallagher. "Did he say why?"

"No, not exactly," said Mr. Gallagher. "Only that you, uh, made him uncomfortable."

Nikolai projected his voice down the hall to his flatmate. "I'm terribly sorry if I caused offense. I'm still learning the local customs." He shook his head with a sigh.

"I'm sure it's nothing," said Mr. Gallagher. "Sometimes these things just don't work out. In any case, Davis has been here longer, so—"

"And here I thought Haven upheld the Collective's rule of welcoming fellow Magi, no matter their nationality." Nikolai met Mr. Gallagher with an icy stare. He had no idea if a formal rule even existed, but it didn't matter. Societal pressure enforced cultural norms better than laws ever could. Mr. Gallagher would be ostracized if word got out. "I guess I was wrong."

Mr. Gallagher blanched. "No, no! It's not like that." He spun, frowning at Nikolai's flatmate. "It's *not* like that, is it Davis?"

The nervous man peeked out from behind Mrs. Gallagher, who edged away from him. "I don't . . . uh . . ."

"Christ, Davis!" Mr. Gallagher spat.

"No! It's . . . he's . . ." Davis' eyes darted between Nikolai, who wore a benign face, and the increasingly concerned Mr. Gallagher. "You don't know what he's like when no one's around!" he finally blurted. "I just . . . I want my place back."

Mr. Gallagher turned away from Davis with a scowl. "I'm sorry, son," he said to Nikolai. "We don't do that here. I can see if another tenant would be willing to—"

"You know, Mr. Gallagher," said Nikolai, as if the thought had just occurred to him. "Davis doesn't strike me as the kind of man who'd be prejudiced. Perhaps it's something else." He glanced sheepishly down the hall, then leaned forward and whispered, "I've seen the picture on the mantle. His son was my age when he died, wasn't he? And we both have dark hair." It was about the only thing they had in common, Nikolai being rakishly handsome and Davis' son stout and homely, but Mr. Gallagher would welcome anything that absolved the prior accusation.

"I suppose you *do* look a little like him." Mr. Gallagher rubbed his chin. "But I can't ask a man to be around someone who pains him."

"Of course not," Nikolai said with feigned concern, "but living estranged from his family hasn't done him any good either. Just yesterday, he received a letter from his daughter begging him to visit. He'll never admit it, but he wants to go. Perhaps it's time he mended that bridge. Lay old ghosts to rest."

Before Mr. Gallagher could ask Davis what he thought, the Useful Mrs. Gallagher bustled forward to throw in her support for Nikolai. Davis was out on his ass that afternoon, ostensibly to visit his daughter. Nikolai got a furnished apartment, and Mrs. Gallagher visited him regularly for sex, which reduced the number of times he had to actively seek it. Fuckable wasn't a strong subcategory of Useful, but it was the most fun.

If only finding a Useful mentor had been as fruitful. Black magic was illegal, and those who practiced it usually weren't the sharing sort. Nikolai had contacted as many as he could prior to graduation, but few responded to his inquiries. Petrov was at the top of a very short list. Nikolai had tracked him to Haven, where he owned an enchantment shop, and exchanged his not-inconsiderable skill as a salesclerk for an apprenticeship. A fortuitous arrangement, or so he thought at the time, but in two years the man had failed to teach him anything of value. Either the man didn't know as much as his history suggested or he'd gone soft.

Nikolai entered Petrov's shop, prepared for another dull shift.

He brewed tea, watered the ficus, and set to work sorting through the stack of orders waiting on the counter. Haven wasn't large enough to support much local trade—most of their business was conducted by mail. An hour into his shift, Nikolai had barely made a dent.

As he sliced through yet another envelope, a wink of blue caught his eye. Nikolai peered at the heap of letters, but nothing stirred. Must have been a trick of the light. This client wanted a Luck bracelet. Thankfully, they had plenty on the display hooks.

Nikolai moved to retrieve one, pivoting at another flash of blue. His hand dove for the source and came back with a letter from the bottom of the pile. Strange blue symbols shimmered across the envelope, which had no name or address. How had it gotten here? Nikolai ran his finger over the letter and the blue symbols shifted to form text:

To Mr. Petrov

He sliced the envelope, but before he could extract the contents, new text appeared at his fingertips:

You're not Mr. Petrov.

Interesting. The spell wasn't one he recognized, but he knew enough to appreciate its complexity. Conditional spells required a degree of talent beyond the reach of most practitioners.

"I am Petrov's apprentice," Nikolai said, not knowing if anyone could hear. "I am authorized to open mail on his behalf."

The letter did not respond. Apparently whatever enchantment lay upon it was not triggered by auditory input. Nikolai removed a folded page from within. More text appeared along the crease.

There is a price for reading another's correspondence. Continue only if you wish to pay it.

That gave Nikolai pause. He placed the letter on the counter and picked up his wand. Petrov had taught him several reveal spells, but they only checked for standard enchantments. A custom curse might not be detectable. He waved his wand over the envelope and spoke the incantations. Nothing.

Nikolai stared at the folded paper. He could give it to Petrov and that would be the end of it, but his curiosity was piqued. What price would it exact if he attempted to read it? Perhaps the threat was merely a bluff to ward off potential snoopers. Then again, whoever sent it was talented. But were they skilled enough to enchant it with something undetectable? The possibility only intensified his desire to read the contents.

He glanced over his shoulder. Petrov's office door was closed while he tackled the ledgers, a task which would keep him occupied for some time. It would be easy enough to reseal the letter, and he could always talk himself out of trouble if discovered. Sorting and opening mail was one of his tasks. It would be an honest mistake if he were to open personal correspondence. Nikolai picked up the letter and unfolded it.

The sheet was blank.

Disappointment stabbed him. He should tear the letter into a hundred pieces. Burn the damned thing. No, that was rash. The message was probably hidden. He would hide the envelope, pretend it never arrived, and plumb its secrets in private. Before he could pocket the letter, words appeared and danced playfully across the page:

I hope you enjoyed reading this.

There was a pause, and then sharp black letters slashed the parchment:

It will be the last thing you ever see.

No sooner had Nikolai's brain registered the words than his sight winked out. He blinked several times and waved his hands in front of his face. Nothing.

Nikolai groped along the countertop for his wand, irritated but not panicked. Anxiety and fear were outside the realm of his experience. As a child, he could never understand why his brothers cried and cowered when the metronome announced another air raid. Nikolai would run to the window, hoping to catch a glimpse of the destruction. Mother always shooed him away, and he had to satisfy himself with picking through the crumbling buildings after the fact. It wasn't until he learned telepathy and dipped into the minds of Mundanes that he saw what fear could do to a person. Until then, he'd half thought people made up the emotions they claimed to display.

Emotions had to be the Useless byproduct of some evolutionary chain, though he couldn't fathom what benefit they were supposed to offer. One didn't require feelings to solve a problem.

Nikolai continued his search of the counter. His hand smacked painfully against the register and sent something long and narrow clattering to the floor. It was too good to hope that was a pen.

He slowed his search of the counter until his fingers found both the letter opener and pen. Damn. Kneeling gingerly so as not to snap his wand, he searched the floor. His fumbling disturbed a fine layer of dust that set him coughing.

At last he felt the wand lying snug against the bottom of the counter, nestled in a crack between the floorboards. He reached for it, but his fingers could not get purchase. Every time he thought he had it, the wand slipped back into the crevice. He cursed and punched the floor. Several minutes passed before he had the sense to grab the letter opener and use it to extricate the wand. Nikolai stood, aimed the wand at his eyes, and spoke the incantation for a counter curse.

Something punched into his face, *hard*.

His eyes pounded in his skull. Rubbing them with his free hand, he tightened his grip on the wand to avoid losing it again. The wand . . . the handle felt wrong. A quick palpation told him it wasn't his. Who knew how long this wand had been hiding under the counter?

"Blyad!" he swore. *Where* was his wand?! He knelt again, this time expanding his search. A few minutes later he found it near the ficus. Triple-checking the feel to make sure it was his, Nikolai set to work casting every counter curse he knew. Either he'd permanently damaged his eyes with the wand misfire, or his counter curses failed to work. As much as he hated to be discovered in this state, he needed assistance. He called loudly to Petrov several times, fighting to keep the irritation from his voice. Eventually he heard some sort of reply followed by shuffling footsteps.

"What're you hollering about, boy? I'm trying to work!"

"I've been blinded—some sort of curse on one of the letters." Nikolai felt around for the letter and thrust it at Petrov. He could almost hear the man recoil.

"Don't give it to me! Put it back on the counter. Good. Now tell me what happened."

Nikolai recounted the events, emphasizing that he was only doing his job as a dutiful employee, conveniently leaving out the initial warning he'd received and ignored. He heard Petrov approach the counter and pick something up, probably the envelope.

"That explains it," Petrov said. "Medea and her bloody integrity . . ." There was the scratching of pen on paper.

"What are you doing?"

"I'm writing the damnable woman. If you're lucky, she'll consent to remove the curse. If not—well, let's just hope she says yes."

Nikolai gripped the counter, jaw clenched. How far had the letter traveled to come here, and how long would it take to return? Would he be blind for days? Weeks? What if she said no? She had better fix it. This was all *her* fault.

"There," said Petrov as the scratching ceased. "I hope for your sake she's listening right now."

"Can she hear us then?" He hoped she hadn't heard his fumbling and cursing.

"I meant listening as in watching for a response to her letter. Whatever I write on this paper comes out on her end, or so she explained to me."

Petrov drummed his fingers on the counter as they waited for a response. Concerned the old man would go back to his ledgers, Nikolai broke the silence.

"Who is she, this Medea?" He mentally added her to his list of people who needed to die.

"You haven't heard of her? Surprising, given your . . . interests. She's the most powerful Magi in the world. Deadly in duels."

"Does she know much black magic then?"

"She would tell you there's no such thing, but yes. If it has to do with magic, Medea knows it. She identifies items for me whenever she's in town—that's what the letter'll be about. Spells fall out of fashion like anything else. She's ancient. If she can't identify something, then no one can."

"How ancient?"

"I dunno . . . five hundred? A thousand? One time I had her identify a brooch for me. It was silver, shaped like a lizard with two ruby eyes. She recognized it, if you can believe that. Belonged to a friend of hers in the 1600s—quite grateful to get it back too."

Immortal *and* skilled in black magic? Nikolai collected every myth and legend he could regarding immortality. Abundant though the stories were, none of them went into detail regarding the method of such a thing. Had she found an ancient relic, like the Holy Grail? Made a bargain with a demon? Located a Fountain of Youth? He had to talk to this woman.

"How does she keep herself alive?"

"Who knows? She refuses to share her secret with anyone."

Nothing a little manipulation, telepathy, and torture couldn't cure. Everyone had their pressure points.

"We're in luck! She's writing back." Petrov paused a moment, made a frustrated noise, then began frantically scribbling. "You're a damn apprentice, not a bloody spy! What's she doing cursing a letter like this anyway?"

The whole thing was intolerable. If Petrov couldn't convince her to release the curse, he'd have to figure it out himself. Every spell had a counter. It might take time, but eventually all would be put to rights, and then he'd make the bitch pay.

"There. She's agreed to lift the spell. Uh, hold on." A pause, then a tearing of paper. "Give me your hand."

Something pressed into his palm. Nikolai closed his fingers around it. "A wad of paper?"

"The bottom third of the letter, yeah. You, uh . . . need to eat it," Petrov said apologetically.

Nikolai shoved the wad into his mouth. Bitterness bloomed and he almost gagged. What kind of ink was this? His mouth filled with saliva as his body rejected the ghastly taste. With great effort, he forced the wad down and the world came into sharp focus. He scanned the room for some way to remove the taste and spotted his morning cup of tea. It would do. He swished the lukewarm liquid and spat it into the ficus. Still the bitterness lingered. He pulled a kerchief from his pocket and proceeded to wipe his tongue. It helped, though not enough.

As he continued to dab, his eyes fell to the remainder of the letter. A new message mocked him from the page:

Repentance is such a bitter pill to swallow. I hope you enjoyed yours.

He froze, mind awhirl. Had she . . . had she made it taste bad on purpose? Had it even been necessary to eat the damned thing? He scowled at the words. He could almost feel her laughter ringing through the parchment.

He was going to *kill* her.

Nikolai grabbed for the pen, but Petrov snatched it up first.

"Whoa there! You don't want to say anything rash. She's not someone to mess with."

"Neither am I!" He made another grab for the pen. Petrov held it out of range and put up a forestalling hand.

"Boy, listen to me. I saw her kill a man once. There was no investigation from the Collective. People just shrugged it off. If anyone discussed it, they used the same tone they would for someone who died of disease. It was sad, but that was life—as if a force of nature killed him, rather than a person. I've never seen anything like it."

"If the old hag is so powerful, how come I've never heard of her?"

"Eh, she's not exactly popular. Given her reputation, I wouldn't be surprised if she's a forbidden topic at the Academy. Besides, she mostly keeps to herself. Shows up in town once in a while, stays a week or two, then vanishes again. Sometimes she won't be seen for decades—long enough for people to forget about her." Petrov scooped up the letter and wagged it at Nikolai. "She's only dangerous if provoked. Don't provoke her."

Nikolai made a conscious effort to relax. She had information he wanted, making her Useful, and Useful people had to be approached with care.

"You said she takes on apprentices?"

"Don't get any ideas," said Petrov. "Most of them don't survive. Besides, you owe me two more years."

"They die from the training? Is it really that dangerous?" Obviously the others hadn't been good enough. A challenge would be welcome after Petrov's lackluster lessons. Anything to hinder the boredom that was Nikolai's constant companion.

"Perhaps some do, but many die afterward. She kills them."

Nikolai frowned. That didn't make sense. Why would she train people only to kill them? Perhaps she took on apprentices because she was lonely, eliminating them when they became too much of a nuisance.

If that were the case, surely he would succeed where others had failed. Lonely women were easy to manipulate. Nikolai knew how to listen, or at least fake it. His passage across Europe had been paid for by a string of wealthy older women. Had he not had greater aspirations, he could have been the consort of a number of them.

Petrov interrupted his reverie. "She'll be here in three days. Given . . . recent events, it might be best if you take that day off."

"No!"

Petrov held up a hand. "I can understand the appeal. Believe me, I can. But I don't want to lose my apprentice because he can't hold his temper."

"I won't. This—I was upset, but that's over now. I have to apologize to her in person. You know how good I am with customers."

"True, but Medea is nothing like my customers. Flattery won't work on her, and if you try telepathy like you do on the Mundane patrons—"

"I know better than to use telepathy on one of our own." Did Petrov think him an idiot? Magi could sense that kind of intrusion, even if they weren't strong enough to repel it. "I'll be careful. You know me. I'll treat her with the utmost courtesy and respect." He flashed a reassuring smile.

Petrov didn't look convinced. He shook his head, but before Nikolai could press his case, he said, "Alright. You can stay. But you must let me do the talking." He went back to his office and shut the door.

Nikolai returned to the letters. Three days was plenty of time to devise a plan to meet with Medea alone.

2

THE ANCIENT ONE

Nikolai peered at his reflection one last time. He smoothed his dark hair and straightened his collar. Nothing could be out of place. First impressions were important, and he did not intend to mess this one up. Medea was to arrive around twelve thirty. Before opening the shop, he posted a small sign reading CLOSING AT NOON TODAY in the window, thinking thirty minutes would be enough to wrap up with any customers. He did not wish to be disturbed.

Rather than trying to persuade Petrov to let him meet with Medea alone and thus making his desires known, Nikolai simply poisoned him. Nothing too serious, of course—just something slipped into his morning and evening meals the day before to loosen his bowels. To avoid suspicion, he first dosed a few other families and spread rumors of illness within the village.

By closing time yesterday, Petrov was pale and weak, and resigned to spending the following day abed. The epitome of concern, Nikolai helped the old man home and tucked him in, even going out of his way to check on him the following morning, where, under the guise of making a restorative tea, he dosed Petrov again. No point in risking him feeling better too soon.

Despite his weakened state, Petrov gave Nikolai firm instructions on how to interact with Medea. He asked for her original letter so he might let her know he would not be there, and as he wrote he attempted to shield the words from view. Not one to be denied, Nikolai hovered a small nearby mirror behind Petrov's shoulder.

Petrov scribbled, "Won't be in tomorrow. Apprentice will show you the items." He paused for a moment and added, "Please don't maim him."

The words disappeared shortly after they were written, and a response appeared. "No promises."

Petrov cautioned Nikolai to be polite, without flattery or useless ceremony. Medea was curt and valued honesty. Under no circumstances was he to compliment her appearance or do anything that could be perceived as flirting. "I know you do well with the ladies, but this one is different. She doesn't like men. She doesn't like anyone really, but amorous men in particular. Just stick to business and you'll do fine."

Easier said than done. True, he laid the charm on thick when he needed to, but often enough he'd done nothing to ingratiate himself with the doughy middle-aged women who seemed enamored of his company. Older women didn't bother him as they did some men—Mrs. Gallagher was in her late fifties—but a woman Medea's age? A shriveled old hag with scraggly grey hair and chipped, yellow teeth? The real question was whether he would acquiesce to a tryst should she show interest. It depended on what knowledge she had to offer.

Nikolai didn't plan to lock the doors at noon, as he wanted Medea to enter unhindered, but would instead politely turn away any customers who happened to wander in. As luck would have it, the shop was unnaturally busy all morning. The news that several families had fallen ill spread rapidly through Haven, and most of the patrons sought disease-warding amulets. Within an hour they sold out. He should've poisoned the villagers ages ago to drum up business and alleviate some of the boredom of working in Petrov's shop. Today, the bustle was inconvenient. Nikolai spent the morning taking orders. Eventually requests for the amulets died down, word having spread that Petrov himself was home sick.

As noon approached, Nikolai found himself with one last customer. A dowdy woman had stomped in and promptly asked for a "gift" for her "no-good cheating husband." Nothing Nikolai suggested seemed good enough. Noon crept ever closer and his patience wore thin. His problem was compounded when another group of customers entered.

He projected his voice to the newcomers—a portly middle-aged man accompanied by an attractive blonde half his age, and an elderly crone dressed all in black. "We will be closing at noon today. We're all out of disease-warding amulets, but I have a list here if you want to be added. If not, please let me know what I can get you."

"Certainly, certainly," said the man, only half listening, "won't be but a moment." He whistled amicably as he moved away from his young companion to peruse the Virility collection.

The crone shuffled across the store, leaning heavily on an intricately carved walking stick. White tufts of hair poked haphazardly from under the rim of her black hat. With gnarled hands, she inspected a number of items around the shop, holding them close to her face and mumbling to herself. Thinking she might be Medea, Nikolai attempted to catch her attention, but she took no notice.

Rebuffed, Nikolai brought his attention back to the scorned woman at the counter, who was now staring daggers at the man's blonde companion. The younger woman wore a floor-length red dress that accentuated her lovely figure, though the effect was somewhat ruined by her sour expression. She wandered idly as her beau shopped.

"Is that your husband?" Nikolai asked the scorned woman, nodding to the portly man.

"What? No." She turned back to him momentarily and hissed, "But he has a ring and *she* doesn't."

He had to get the woman to focus on something else or she'd never leave. "Maybe she's his daughter," Nikolai offered.

"Do these things work?" called out the portly man. He raised a Virility bracelet in the air.

Like he'd say anything if they didn't. "Yes, sir," said Nikolai. "You'll be as potent as a young stallion." No wonder the blonde looked irritable. What did she expect, attaching herself to such an old lover?

The man giggled like a child selecting sweets and chose two bracelets, which he held up for his companion to see. "What do you think?" he asked. The blonde waved at him dismissively and muttered something about function over form.

Across the shop, the crone was now rummaging through the bargain bin. Every so often she would extract an item, cluck her tongue, and put it back. If it was Medea, she seemed a bit addled. No matter. It would make her easier to manipulate.

"I'm sorry about that, ma'am," Nikolai said to the scorned woman, tapping the counter to draw her attention. "This bracelet is a good choice. It will give the wearer boils in a most sensitive location. And this"—he pointed to a locket—"will bring bad luck to whatever target you please. Simply add their picture and a lock of their hair."

The scorned woman paid Nikolai no notice. She looked as if she'd like nothing better than to strangle the blonde with one of the necklaces. "A pretty face," she mumbled to herself. "I gave him years of my life, and he left me for a pretty face."

Time for another tactic. Nikolai leaned in conspiratorially and kept his voice low. "It's not fair, is it?"

"What?" The scorned woman turned slightly, enough that she could listen more closely, but not so much that she couldn't glare at the blonde.

"It's not fair that a man like him gets a woman like that. He should be with a good woman his own age."

The scorned woman leaned closer, and Nikolai knew he had her.

"What does she see in him?" he continued. "There's no accounting for taste, I guess. It's unsightly."

"Indeed! 'Tis disgusting! Men, bah! Oh, I don't mean any offense to you, my dear." She chuckled and patted his hand.

The conversation flowed again, and Nikolai showed her several more selections, none of which pleased her. It was clear that although she was angry with her husband for leaving, she didn't want to harm him. Most of her ire was directed at whoever had "stolen" him away. She ranted about the "no-good harlot," her diatribe intensifying as the blonde approached.

Oblivious to the raving woman beside her, the blonde casually leaned back with her elbows against the counter, a bored expression on her face. The unladylike posture pushed her hips forward and her breasts up. Was she aware of how enticing it was? The scorned woman certainly noticed, for her glare deepened.

Nikolai blinked away the distracting thoughts the blonde conjured and glanced at the clock. It was now a quarter past noon. Where was the old crone? Shit. He couldn't see her anywhere. Had Medea given up and left?

"Please, ma'am," he said. "I'm going to have to ask you to make a selection."

"I just . . . I just don't know." The woman stared at the items on the counter.

The blonde groaned and spun around. *"Non possum diutius*

audire." She pointed to the locket Nikolai had shown his customer earlier. "Hand me that."

"I'm still deciding!" snapped the scorned woman. "I was going to buy it."

"No, you weren't," said the blonde. "None of these items appeal to you because you want your husband back. Why you'd want a man who betrayed you is beyond me . . ." She shook her head. Then, to Nikolai, "The locket." Her hand poised expectantly.

"Don't you dare hand it to that . . . that . . ." The scorned woman seemed incapable of using the word "harlot" to the blonde's face.

"That what? *I'm* not the one who fucked your husband. *He's* the culpable party. If he gave a damn about his vows, he would never have strayed in the first place."

The scorned woman gasped, placing a hand to her chest. "Such language . . . can't believe . . ."

Nikolai froze, unsure how to proceed. On any other day, he would have been delighted to watch their spat unfold—maybe even encouraged it. Today, he needed them gone.

"Fine," said the blonde, and the locket zipped into her hand.

It was Nikolai's turn to gape. Some Magi could perform telekinesis without a wand, but it was erratic—a self-defense mechanism fueled by instinct. This woman used it intentionally.

The blonde cupped the locket in one hand and gestured over it with the other. He could sense magic being performed but couldn't understand how. Enchantments required incantations and wands, not finger wiggling.

When the blonde finished her spell, she grabbed the scorned woman's hand and thrust the locket into it. "Here. Put his picture and a lock of his hair inside, just as the boy said—"

The *boy*? What?

"—then wear it about your neck. Your husband will be impotent as long as you wear the necklace. Take it off, and he'll work just fine for you—if you want that sort of thing." The blonde's face made it clear how little she thought of "wanting that sort of thing."

The scorned woman stared at her hand, flabbergasted. "I . . . uh, he left. I don't have a lock of his hair."

Undeterred, the blonde continued, "Do you have anything of his? Something personal? Something he's touched? Clothing works, but it must be something he alone has worn."

The scorned woman nodded. "Yes, he didn't take all of his clothes when he . . . when he left me."

"That will do. Cut a patch of cloth from an area that gets sweaty. Armpit or groin works best."

"I will." Then, as an afterthought, "Thank you."

The scorned woman turned to go, but the blonde stopped her. "Aren't you forgetting something? Payment perhaps?"

"I . . . oh, yes, I'm so sorry." She turned to Nikolai. "How much do I owe you?"

Nikolai recited the price for the locket, took the woman's money, and watched her leave. It was only then he realized he was alone with the blonde.

"Looks like she scared off your friend," he said.

"Who?" The blonde looked confused.

"The man you were with, I think that lady scared him off." For someone who could cast complicated magic, she seemed a bit slow.

"Oh, him. We didn't come here together. By the way, I saw him pocket a bracelet and sneak out while you were busy."

Nikolai cursed. Petrov would no doubt blame him. Nothing was going right today. He had to get her out of the shop before anything else went wrong. "Thank you for what you did. Unfortunately, I'm going to have to ask you to come back tomorrow. We're closing at noon today, and it's well past."

"I see." The woman remained where she was and gave Nikolai a calculating look. "Why close so early?"

"We have a . . . delivery. A special delivery that's arriving today."

"A delivery? Really?" She smirked. "Seeing as it has not yet arrived, I should be able to conduct my business. It won't take long."

Nikolai bridled. He didn't need to be dealing with customers now. Medea would be arriving any moment, if she hadn't already left. God, he hoped the crone hadn't been her.

"I'm sorry, ma'am, but I'm going to ask that you come back another time. It really isn't—"

"A delivery wouldn't normally require that customers vacate the premises."

Nikolai kept his voice professional. "Once it arrives, I need to catalog the contents. My master is out sick and there is no one else to man the counter."

"Why not just catalog it later?"

"I need to make sure nothing is broken or missing. It's a very important delivery," he said with a tone of finality.

"I see."

Thinking he had finally made her understand, Nikolai walked to the entrance, assuming she would follow. When he glanced back, he saw to his chagrin she hadn't moved. One side of her mouth quirked up into an infuriating smile. Why did the weird ones always show up right at closing?

"You're waiting for someone. Why not just say that? Why the *lie*?" She put a peculiar emphasis on the last word.

Helpful or not, she was being deliberately annoying, and her reference to him as "the boy" still rankled. Sure, she was pretty, but she was too skinny. Her unkempt hair fell lank about her shoulders and, he noticed with distaste, she wore no shoes. The more he looked at her smug face, the more he disliked her.

He abandoned all pretense. If Petrov lost a customer, so be it. "Because people want to feel important! If I said I was waiting for someone, they would feel slighted. Isn't *their* time just as valuable? Isn't *their* money just as good? A delivery is less personal."

She didn't speak for a moment, then ventured, "I suppose that makes sense."

Nikolai relaxed. "I'm sorry, but I do have an important appointment and I need you to leave. Please." He gestured once again to the door.

She sighed. "Very well then." A flick of her hand and the curtains were drawn, the door locked. "Show me what Petrov wants identified." With that, she turned on her heel and walked toward the storeroom, leaving Nikolai standing with his mouth slightly ajar.

He rushed to catch up. "You're Medea?"

"Obviously."

She didn't look much older than his twenty-two years. On closer inspection, her red dress was rather dated, like something from the middle ages. He'd seen similar dresses in plays, often with a zigzag of ribbon across the bodice begging to be pulled, sadly absent here. Long sleeves extended to her wrists. The cuffs, neckline, and waist were trimmed with gold filigree, and she wore a thin leather belt. He could imagine his hands about her slender waist, among other places. A pretty picture, though likely an illusion. God, how he hated illusions.

"Are you using a glamor spell to look like that?" He tried to keep the acid from his voice and failed. Thankfully, Medea didn't seem to notice.

"No. This is how I truly am." She spun to face him with her arms spread wide, walked backward a few paces, then turned around again. The move nearly caused her to walk face-first into a stack of boxes, which she narrowly avoided by jerking her body awkwardly to the side.

Such grace.

"Everyone expects me to look older," she continued. "I don't really see the point in living forever if your body is so decrepit it can't function. Is this the room?"

"Yes. It's the box on top, the one made of metal. How do you stay young?"

"Sheer willpower and spite. I see it."

"Here, I'll have to open it. Petrov taught me the spell to—"

But the box was already unlocking itself. The lid opened, and a parade of objects flew into the air, where they hung suspended for a moment as a nearby table cleared itself. The motley collection of amulets, bracelets, weapons, and a few other items placed themselves neatly upon the table.

"How are you doing that!?"

Medea waved her hands theatrically and smiled. "Magic!" At his expression she amended, "I didn't get to this age by being terrible at what I do."

She touched her belt, which until now had looked purely decorative, and a small brown bag expanded into being. From it she withdrew several sheets of paper and sent them gliding to the table, where they aligned themselves neatly, one next to each object. She clapped her hands together.

"There we go! Nice and organized. I am going to identify each object in turn. A description will be written upon the sheet next to each item. If you wish you may stay, and I will give you a verbal summary as I go, but do not interrupt. Or you can go back up front and reopen the shop, though you seem disinclined to do so. Staying then?"

She'd rattled it off so fast he barely registered when she finished. "I . . . yes, I'm staying." This was not going at all how he'd planned, but there was no way he was leaving now. In the thirty minutes since she'd arrived, he'd witnessed incredibly advanced magic.

Medea gestured to the first row of items. "Most of these are junk. Minor spells that have all but worn off over time. Petrov would do better to dispel their enchantments and start over." She moved on to the second row. "This dagger imbues the holder with incredible speed. This one is cursed. When it inflicts a cut, the wound will bleed endlessly—very nice."

Medea identified half a dozen more items. When she came to a Luck pendant, she offhandedly mentioned the spell was dead. He attempted to ask what she meant, but she sternly reminded him not to interrupt, and by the time she finished, he'd forgotten.

The last item was a tall but slender earthen pot sealed and stamped with wax. Medea placed a hand on it and said, "This is my payment."

Petrov had told him she would choose an item—either from the shop wares or, more likely, from the unidentified items—as payment. It didn't matter what she chose, and he wasn't to question the selection, as it was usually odd or worthless.

"One time it was a pouch of seeds. Another, a book on flowers. She's partial to books and scrolls. I've started including something eccentric and useless each time"—Petrov had laughed—"and she nearly always chooses it. Last time she took a shard of glass. Glass!"

And now she was choosing a pot.

"Can you tell what's inside?" Nikolai asked.

"No. It is obscured with a magic I do not wish to disturb just yet. However, it is stamped with the Ouroboros."

The name was familiar—probably mentioned in one of his classes—but he couldn't recall what it meant. Nikolai moved closer. There was a circular impression in the wax, but age had blurred the details. "What is it?"

"A snake consuming its own tail. The symbol is Egyptian, though it can be found in many other cultures. It represents an endless cycle of death and rebirth."

That was interesting. "Any thoughts on what it contains?"

She shrugged. "Pots such as this were usually storage for foodstuffs, so it could be nothing."

"But it's protected with magic. Whoever sealed it must have hidden something important inside."

"Not necessarily. It could merely be an antitheft measure. What matters to one person may mean little to another. Look at Petrov—he attempts to placate me with what he considers junk so I won't choose something more valuable. The Ouroboros means nothing to him, and so he passes over a potential treasure. It's probably nothing, but it *could* be something. He cares not for books, unless they contain spells he can monetize—not that he could even translate most of what he's offered me—and so he doesn't see their value. All this"—she waved toward the items on the table—"I could easily replicate on my own, had I the need. What use is a dagger of speed to me?"

"I don't know—what if it lets you cast spells faster?"

"Interesting hypothesis." She grabbed the dagger. "Let's test it."

"Now?"

"Yes, now." Medea glanced around and gestured to a wide wooden beam. "There. Pick a low-mana dueling spell. Something basic you've cast before."

Nikolai tried to think of a spell. His dueling repertoire didn't contain anything that basic. Bleed, Pummel, Lance, Amputate, Lightning—these were the kinds of spells he collected. Defensive spells like Gust and Flash didn't have the same appeal, though he did know a few. What did he know that was small?

Ah, Puncture. The spell was a favorite among novices at the Academy, as it did little more than simulate being stuck with a pin. They loved to cast it on one another and unsuspecting instructors.

"Got it." He drew his wand and moved into position.

Medea gave him a look of distaste.

"What?" he asked.

"Nothing. Go ahead."

Something had irked her, but he didn't press the issue. "How will you measure?"

"With my mind. Cast it several times so I can get an average."

He aimed his wand at the beam. *"Punctum, Punctum, Punctum, Punctum, Punctum!"* Tiny puncture marks pocked the wooden beam in rapid succession.

She shook her head. "I already know how this is going to end. No matter. Here is the dagger."

He accepted the golden handle and aimed his wand once more.

"PunctumPunctumPunctumPunctumPunctum!"

He laughed. His hand flew like lightning. The words rattled from his mouth with no breath between. He'd have to figure out how to weasel the dagger away from Petrov. Perhaps he could forge a new document claiming it was worthless. "Definitely faster!" He turned a grin to Medea and was surprised to find the same look of distaste. She must be irate at having chosen the pot. Her loss.

"Yes, well, when you cast spells in the slowest manner possible, anything that increases your speed will improve your performance."

He bristled. "I'll have you know that I was the fastest dueler when I left the Academy."

"That is truly disheartening."

He stepped forward and loomed over her. It wasn't difficult. The top of her head barely came up to his chin. He brandished the dagger in her face and spoke slowly, "You're just upset you didn't pick this."

Her mouth curved into a smirk and she nodded toward the beam, which instantly became pocked with a hundred tiny holes.

He'd felt no spell emanate from her. It was as if the spell began and ended at the wood itself. Petrov's scrawled words rose to the forefront of his mind. *Please don't maim him.*

He took a step back, but she closed the distance between them. Somehow she managed to look down on him from below.

"When you cast spells with word or wand, you only slow yourself." Her voice was low. Not menacing, but careful and measured. "Tell Petrov I said you should keep the dagger. Clearly you could use the extra help."

With that, Medea marched around him toward the door. She paused with her hand upon the knob, then rolled her eyes and stalked back to the table, where she snatched up the earthen pot and muttered, "Forgot this." The bag on her hip expanded and she hastily crammed her prize inside, arm disappearing to the elbow. When she withdrew her hand, it clutched something small. "And this."

She tossed it to Nikolai—one of the Virility bracelets the portly man had been examining.

"I removed it from his coat as soon as I realized he was stealing it," she explained. "If you hadn't been so keen on throwing me out, I would have returned it to you sooner." With that, she marched back out, the door closing with finality behind her.

Nikolai stared at the wooden beam, as punctured as his ego.

3

THE HANGED MAN

W hat an oaf. A powerful, dangerous oaf at that.

Medea pushed through Petrov's shop door and strengthened her invisible shields. Sound, smell, glare—all of it could be reduced to a tolerable level. All but the people. Haven was getting too crowded. She moved to the side of the street with fewer pedestrians. Thankfully, her reputation ensured most of them kept out of her way. Social interactions were exhausting. One or two a day was all she budgeted for, but the boy would seek her out soon enough. There was no way around it.

She should have known when Petrov wrote her about the letter. What kind of person opened another's mail despite multiple warnings? An idiot, that's who. Or someone who thought the rules didn't apply to them. But no, she'd given him the benefit of the doubt. Maybe he'd been distracted and opened it by mistake.

The boy seemed normal enough while helping customers, but what struck her most was the magical power radiating within him. Magic had been slowly dwindling for centuries, and every generation was weaker than the last, if one was talking about averages. More witches, fewer Magi. His very existence was a pleasant surprise.

Apprentices were a good way to alleviate the boredom of immortality, and it had been so long since the last one. The urge to share her wealth of knowledge was overwhelming. She'd tried to stave it off by writing a massive compendium, but it wasn't the same. If the boy had turned out to be decent, or interested in a variety of magics, she might have considered taking him on.

That hope was dashed. After so many apprentices, it had gotten easier to recognize an aspiring dark wizard. She wasn't going through *that* again. Fool her once, shame on them. Fool her a dozen times, and a pattern emerged. Under that polite veneer was someone hungry for power. He probably didn't even know why, but it meant he'd seek her out, and soon. They always did.

At least she had time to mentally prepare for the encounter. Pushing them away rarely worked. If she said "no" nicely, they took it as an opening. If she said "no" curtly, they tried harder. It made no damned sense. Avoiding him would only prolong the inevitable. She'd tried that before. Best get it over with quickly.

A collision against her shield threw her thoughts into disorder, and she almost tripped over a man sprawled on the cobblestones. He must've walked into her. It was a frequent occurrence in Mundane towns, where she'd taken to making her shield more convex so colliders neatly rolled off to the side, allowing her to continue without pause. Satisfied the man wasn't an imminent threat, she stepped around him and attempted to collect her scattered thoughts. It was no good. They'd popped like bubbles.

She hated these excursions away from home. Everything was muted now. Even here in Haven, where most of the population were presumably casters, people barely registered against her senses. Dim, that's what they were, wavering like candles about to go out. All except the boy.

That magic was dying was frightening enough by itself, but what was even more alarming was that no one seemed to notice. Age likely played a role. Who else but an immortal would notice the slow decline? She wasn't even sure there were others left. Immortals were a notoriously solitary lot. The condition required a particular state of mind and strength of character. Boredom was a real problem, as was loneliness.

Those who required consistent company seldom made it beyond a few centuries—watching loved ones die took a toll. The obvious solutions were not to have loved ones in the first place, or to share immortality with them if you did. Sharing was risky. The more people you shared with, the more likely you were to become the target of those who sought such power for themselves.

The Baba Yaga sisters had each other for company, but that was a double-edged sword. Quarrels were frequent. At some point they had a falling out over a lover—a stupid thing to argue about —and one of them struck off on her own. After multiple attempts to mend the bridge, the remaining sister had taken her own life.

Still, very few people could live completely alone. They needed something. Pets were an option, but these died too, and with greater frequency than humans, unless you happened to like tortoises. Many immortals created a familiar, which could live indefinitely and had magical powers of its own. The spell sheared off a piece of the soul to create an animal companion and could only be cast once. After Thomas left, Medea had been desperate enough to try it and got nothing for her trouble. So much for that.

What she really missed was having a peer. There was no one to bounce ideas off of, no one to spar with. God, how she missed a good spar! Dueling had been her favorite pastime for centuries. But she'd gotten too good. She tried handicapping herself by using less common schools of magic or fighting multiple opponents. When that didn't help, she fought without shields, without healing, or restricted herself to one school of magic. Nothing worked.

Apprentices were no help at all. Yes, they alleviated the boredom and gave her an outlet for her desire to share magical knowledge, but few of them lasted. One by one, they either dropped out, claiming her methods were too harsh, or else they turned on her. She couldn't remember the last time she'd had one make it all the way to master rank. The good ones, those with real potential, rarely stayed on more than a year or two.

And now magic was dying out. Soon there'd be no more Magi, let alone peers, and she'd be but one woman alone with the knowledge of what used to be.

Medea turned down a narrow street and knocked on the first door. An elderly woman answered. "You must be the healer! Thank goodness you're here."

"Where's the patient?" Medea entered the small apartment, looking around for someone on a bed. She didn't normally do cases this small, but she had been intercepted by the town council as soon as she had arrived in Haven. At first she feared attack—she was long overdue—but they were only concerned over a recent rash of illness that wasn't responding to magic. She didn't think anyone remembered she knew healing, but apparently someone did, for they'd approached her despite their reservations.

The home smelled overwhelmingly of potpourri. Medea had dropped the aroma-repelling portion of her shield in anticipation of the appointment—some diseases had a distinct odor—but if she stayed here too long, she'd get a headache. What on earth possessed people to scent their homes?

"He's, uh, in the bathroom. Has been for a while now."

"And where is that?"

"Just down the hall. I can let him know you're here, and he can finish up—"

"That's not necessary," Medea said as she walked down the hall.

"Wait!"

"What?" Medea paused. Why did people always have to interrupt?

"He'll be done in a minute."

"Okay." Medea started walking again, the woman huffing behind her. What was her problem? Before Medea reached the door, the woman lurched in front to block it.

"Just give him a minute."

Medea's head swam. Adding aroma-repelling back to her shield would do no good now. Her head was already surrounded with the particles. By the time the shield had pumped out stray scents, it would likely be time to leave. Better make this quick.

She leaned against the wall and expanded her senses into the bathroom, scanning the body within. The woman was saying something, the noises plinking against her brain like tiny stones. Medea tweaked her shield to mute all incoming sound and focused on the body on the other side of the door. Adult male. Arthritis, heart disease, the usual signs of aging, benign tumor clinging to the left lung—ah, there it was.

"He's ingested a laxative. Tell him to drink lots of fluids. He'll be fine." Medea moved to leave. Two stops in one day was one too many. Something touched her arm, and she turned to see the woman mouthing wordlessly. Oops. Better let the sound back in.

"Sorry, I didn't catch that."

"I said, please don't go, he'll just be a minute." The woman banged on the door. "Hurry up, hon! The healer is here!"

"I told you, it's a laxative. I couldn't see any left in his stomach, so it should resolve in a few hours. By the way, the tumor on his lung is nothing to worry about, but I can remove it if you want. I must step outside, though. I can't work with this smell."

———

After Medea left the shop, Nikolai reported briefly to Petrov. The old man was feeling better, though disappointed to hear the current batch of wares only contained a handful of decent items.

Nikolai didn't know how to feel about the dagger. He wanted it badly, and yet Medea's words left him unsettled. He contemplated listing it with the items to be reenchanted, but in the end told Petrov she thought he should have it. Petrov replied that he wasn't running a charity and if Medea wanted him to have the dagger, she could damn well pay for it herself. Nikolai left in a dark mood.

Medea's abilities brought his current master's inadequacies into sharp relief. When he first sought apprenticeship, Petrov seemed the ideal choice. The man spent years lining his pockets by performing forbidden spells until he was discovered and forced to flee Russia. There was talk of wrongful death and even necromancy, and as a fellow countryman, Petrov would be predisposed to favor his new apprentice.

Nikolai had arrived in Haven, hopes high, expecting a talented dark wizard. Instead, he found an old man content to run a shop. Petrov knew many minor curses, but if he had more powerful spells in his arsenal, he'd yet to divulge them. Perhaps exile made him wary of the Collective and their rules.

Don't let the Mundane see your magic, or at least keep it to a level that could be explained away by the skeptical. Don't sell magical items, potions, or spells to the Mundane. And never cast spells that could bring the law to your door—no curses, hexes, or black magic. Dueling, a longstanding tradition for settling disputes, was relegated to a recreational activity with harmless spells.

To hell with that.

What was the point of having magic if you had to strangle your powers? You'd think the war would have made the Collective see sense. Survival was all that mattered, and Nikolai hadn't survived the Nazi invasion by holding back. His Mundane siblings hadn't been so fortunate. Only he had emerged from that hell unscathed.

At age twelve he left Russia and traveled alone, chasing rumors until he reached the fabled Academy, esteemed school and seat of all magical knowledge. Surely there he'd find others who valued survival and tenacity as much as he.

It was not to be.

The cowards at school were as bad as the Collective. Even his classmates shied away from combat spells. How could they? Didn't they understand how vital it was to protect themselves? The war, rather than hardening people and awakening them to the Mundane threat, had done the opposite.

Most students wanted nothing more than to rejoin Mundane society. Sure, there were benefits to technology—planes got you to places faster, telephones were unbeatable for communication, and who didn't enjoy movies? But what was the cost? The loss of their magic, their heritage? The loss of the one thing that allowed them to survive while Mundanes killed each other?

Catering to the next generation of cravens, the Academy focused on assimilation within Mundane communities. Instead of training warriors, they churned out Magi who could hide in plain sight. Stage magicians, soothsayers, and spiritualists—casters who used illusions to dazzle their audience but whose abilities could be chalked up to nonmagical methods and quackery.

Useless, all of them.

Nikolai stayed until graduation, mainly for access to the library. There he searched every available source for stories of black magic practitioners who might take him under their wing, leading him to Petrov, the man who was supposed to be his salvation but who'd taught him nothing of value.

Life was too short to train with someone subpar. If Nikolai wanted to reach his goal of being the most powerful Magi in the world, who better to train him than the person who currently held the title?

Unfortunately, he had made a poor impression on Medea. He

would not make the same mistake again. If he was to secure an apprenticeship, he needed to know everything about her.

The rest of the day was spent carefully teasing information out of people. There was a book dealer, from whom Medea regularly procured rare or ancient texts. "I don't even put the real finds on the market anymore, just send her a letter asking if she's interested, along with the price. She doesn't like to haggle." The potion ingredient supplier turned out to be a dead end, as Medea preferred to collect and process all ingredients herself. The woman was affronted Medea didn't seem to think anyone's supplies were good enough.

But the most Useful information came from a veteran Enforcer at the Spotted Sow. Light had not yet faded from the sky, but the pub was already bustling with activity. Chandeliers bathed the wide room in a honey glow. Warm oak benches encouraged patrons to mingle at long tables, while an open space invited couples to dance. On weekends, a local band played. Today, a woman strummed dulcet tunes on a harp. Mary and Kate, the owner's daughters, weaved through the crowd distributing drinks.

Nikolai's mark, a grizzled man in his seventies, nursed a pint of ale on one of the benches. If Medea was as dangerous as Petrov said, an Enforcer would have something to say about her. Thankfully, the man appeared to be in Kate's section. Mary was a bit of a flirt, and while Nikolai enjoyed her company, he didn't need the distraction today.

Nikolai took a seat next to the Enforcer, intentionally bumping the man's arm and spilling his drink. He apologized profusely and insisted on ordering two more rounds for the gentleman. The next fifteen minutes were spent building trust before he casually dropped that he had helped a very odd customer earlier in the day, a Magi known as Medea.

The Enforcer, in the process of bringing his mug to his mouth, set it down forcefully, taking no notice as ale slopped over the sides. "That bitch in town?"

"Yes. My master warned me to be careful around her."

"Careful. Ha! Yes, everyone is careful. She should've been locked up ages ago."

"Why wasn't she?"

The Enforcer took a long draught of ale and peered at Nikolai. "Yer young. You know yer history? 'Bout how the Collective was formed?"

Nikolai nodded. "After the witch trials, wasn't it?"

Magi hadn't always hidden from view. In the old days, magic was a profession like any other. Most towns had a few open practitioners—a healer here, a midwife there, a witch, and occasionally someone who could solve your problems discreetly without worrying about little things like legality or ethics. Though regarded by some Mundanes with suspicion, Magi were generally left alone.

With Christianity came loathing. More and more Magi hid their true powers, until a rash of witch trials in the sixteenth century changed everything. Fearing accusation by their Mundane neighbors, Magi fled their homes to form new communities consisting of their own kind. Haven was one such place, born of Scottish Magi settled in Ireland, where the Mundane were more likely to blame calamities on mischievous fae rather than witchcraft. It was the new communities that cracked down on the practice of magic in order to avoid detection. The Collective was formed with a representative from each Magi town, and their rules were backed by Enforcers.

"Yeah, after the witch trials." The Enforcer wiped his mouth with the cuff of his shirt. "Medea was in the Americas during the worst of it, though I hear the colonies had their own trouble. When she started coming 'round again, she didn't want to follow the rules. Didn't think we should be hiding."

Neither did Nikolai, but he kept the thought to himself. There was nothing to be gained by disagreeing. "Easy for her to say. What does an immortal have to fear from the Mundane?"

"You get to the meat of it, boy. The Collective sent a delegation to treat with 'er. If she didn't agree to our rules, they were to deal with 'er, one way or another. We can't have rogue Magi, you understand. It endangers us all."

A man sitting further down the table slid close enough to join the conversation. He said nothing but watched the Enforcer over his mug.

"So what happened?" Nikolai asked.

The Enforcer drank again, his face dark. "They didn't want to get 'er back up. Send in a team of Enforcers, and she might kill them all straightaway. That was the thinking anyway. So they only sent one Enforcer. The rest of the delegation were experts in dueling. Only one made it back alive. Dunno if he yielded or she let him go to deliver 'er message."

"What message?"

"Leave 'er alone and she won't kill us."

The man across the table shook his head but offered no comment.

"How many delegates did they send?"

"Twenty."

"Twenty!" The idea was unfathomable. Nikolai was the best dueler in Haven, and his limit was three, maybe four. The top dueler of the century had a record of six. Nineteen had to be an exaggeration. More likely the real number was ten, and it had grown with each retelling. "How did she manage to kill that many?"

"Who knows? It was well over a century ago, and the reports from the survivor make no sense. He raved about exploding heads and the ground swallowing people whole and spells hitting them from every direction. He said she agreed to be discreet, but only when it suited 'er."

"So never. Did they ever try again?"

The Enforcer shook his head. "Nobody wanted to risk it. Today, our orders are not to engage, no matter what she's doing." He gave an apologetic look to the man across the table, one that spoke volumes.

For the first time, Nikolai directed his attention to the silent man. "What did she do to you?"

In response, the man opened his mouth. He had no tongue.

"But why?"

The mute man shrugged, but the Enforcer answered. "He had a mind to flirt with 'er." The Enforcer shook his head. "You sorry sot. I did warn you."

"Do you think she'll come in here?" Nikolai put alarm in his voice and peered around worriedly.

"Nah, she likes the Hanged Man. Prolly the only one who does."

The tongueless man chuckled appreciatively.

The Enforcer continued to rail against Medea for some time, his face reddening with drink and righteousness, until he was boldly asserting that if they'd sent proper Enforcers instead of duelists, things would have turned out differently. "Give me five good Enforcers and I'll have 'er in chains for yeh," he slurred. Nikolai hardly saw a difference between the two—both were trained in combat, although Enforcers had Collective backing—but he commiserated with the man and begged off as the topic had run dry.

Nikolai stepped into the moonlight, donned his hat, and considered what he'd learned. The woman was secretive. Among the townsfolk, she seemed to have no friends. Those who only knew Medea peripherally regarded her with dislike or fear. The few with which she did regular business respected her but also treated her as they would a serpent who could turn on them at the slightest wrong move.

If he'd had any doubts about her prowess in combat, the Enforcer had laid them to rest. Nineteen duelists killed! Exaggeration or not, the idea of that much power made him heady. To be able to cast whatever he wanted, whenever he wanted, free of the Collective's yoke . . . Like him, she understood the necessity of acting without unnecessary restraints, of striking down enemies before they became a true threat. Survival was the only thing that mattered. Petrov didn't understand that. The man took no chances. The future belonged to the bold, and Nikolai planned to have a bright future indeed.

―――――

The following day, Nikolai forwent his usual lunch inside the shop and headed for the seedy inn known as the Hanged Man. Most locals preferred the Spotted Sow for their refreshment and merriment; it could get quite loud and boisterous in the evenings. The Hanged Man was dreary by comparison, but as Medea preferred it, that was where he went.

Haven looked like any other small Irish town. There were the same shops for food and household items (though nothing electric). Citizens dressed in the same tweed suits and linen dresses as the rest of the country. Men donned hats, women scarves—though younger women were beginning to forgo this trend. Nikolai wore only the latest Dublin fashions.

On closer inspection, the subtle differences in Haven became apparent. If you needed to make a phone call, you had to travel to the next town over, for there were no telephones in Haven. Cars were frowned upon. Signs at the edge of Haven prompted visitors to park and make their way on foot. The town was small enough that most people walked wherever they needed to go. For those who needed assistance or were traveling farther, there were horse-drawn carriages. At night, darkness reigned. The town had its streetlamps, but they were gas, not electric, as were all the household lights. Electricity was strictly forbidden, as Mundane technology interfered with magic.

While the population skewed heavily Irish and Scottish, immigrants like Nikolai were not uncommon. Magi were welcome no matter their nationality. Mundanes were not. There was a taboo against renting or selling property to Mundanes, but it happened on occasion. Those who moved to Haven found nothing but bad luck. Their crops died and their homes were fraught with ill omens and supernatural disturbances. They were pushed out of town one way or another. Better to have a Magi neighbor who didn't speak the same language than a Mundane neighbor who did.

Nikolai smiled and greeted people as he passed, mentally sorting them into categories. This one owed him a favor, that one knew all the latest gossip. He carefully avoided anyone who would trap him in conversation. At last, he arrived at the Hanged Man.

The rickety inn stood near the center of town, age evident in every beam, looking as though a stiff breeze would cause the whole place to topple. Medea was indeed brave to board here. The scent of stale beer greeted him upon opening the door. Light from the large front window illuminated dust motes in the air but did little to quench the darkness. Gas lamps situated around the room threw as many shadows as they destroyed.

A rowdy group of men laughing over their drinks took up several tables. On the other side of the room, two women conferred in whispers. An old man in tattered clothes passed him, coughing up something foul. Nikolai wrinkled his nose and moved to the side. It was then he saw Medea at a table in the far corner of the room. She faced the door, her nose in a book and a mug in her hand. Her long blonde hair was tucked behind her ears.

When he got close to her table, the noise of the inn abruptly ceased. He glanced around to see what could have caused it, expecting stares in his direction, but the patrons were still engrossed in conversation as if nothing was amiss. It must be a localized spell. In any event, he appreciated the calm. He hadn't fancied trying to yell over the raucous men. Before he could open his mouth, Medea spoke without looking up.

"No."

He didn't let her reaction throw him. "No, what?"

"No, I won't train you."

He slid into the seat across from her and smiled. "You must be an amazing telepath. I didn't feel you enter my mind."

"It doesn't take telepathy to know what you want." She continued to stare at her book. "You want the same thing they always want. I'm tired of wasting years training apprentices only to watch them die."

"Word has it that you kill them. You *could* let me live."

"The training kills some of them. I do my best to select students with talent enough to survive the challenges I throw before them. Not all of them make it, but that is not of what I speak. I am talking about men like you, who come to me begging for tutelage, only to turn around a few years hence and attempt to slay me."

"Ah, you kill them in self-defense. I had wondered."

"It is hardly self-defense to swat a gnat. You are talented. Of that, I have no doubt. I can feel the potential thrumming inside you. I would not seek to waste my time and yours only to watch you die. Go. Live and learn. Become as powerful as you wish, but not by me. I do not wish to kill you."

"I would not dream of challenging y—"

"Do not lie to me!" She looked up then, daggers in her eyes.

"I know what you are. Do you think I cannot recognize your type after so long? You do not wish to learn magic. You wish to learn *dark* magic." There was distaste in how she uttered the word.

"And if I do? Who better to teach me?"

"That's the rub. My reputation damns me to endure the overtures of men such as yourself." Her gaze fell to her hands. She idly pinched each fingertip from pinky to thumb on one hand before switching to the other. "I train them, even though I know how it will end. Some spend years with me. Always there comes a day when they believe they have learned enough. Not wanting anyone to follow in their footsteps, they seek to destroy that which fashioned them—me."

Her eyes snapped back to him.

"I cannot abide such insolence. As if they could learn in half a dozen years what I spent multiple lifetimes cultivating! I weary of it. Begone." She flicked a wrist in his direction and picked up her book. "Find someone else to teach you."

"I'm going to go order a drink. Can I get you anything?"

She scoffed and shook her head, not as an answer to his question, but at the question itself. He got up and headed to the bar, wincing as a wall of sound assaulted him a few feet from the table. It was as though the world had paused and come rushing back.

"What'll it be?" asked the elderly barman.

"Tea." He did not want to numb his brain just now.

The barman laughed. "You look like you need whiskey after dealing with her." He nodded in the direction of Medea's table.

"Whiskey would be preferable, but just the tea, thank you. I'm afraid she's not too happy with me."

"Don't take it personally, she's rarely happy with anyone."

"You know her well?"

"She's been staying here for generations. Owns the place,

though I doubt she remembers." He picked up a filthy mug and began to wipe it clean.

"How can she own a place and not remember?"

He shrugged. "She's old. Forgets a lot, I imagine. The way the story goes, my great-grandfather was in debt. Had to put the place up for sale, and the man wanting to buy it planned to tear it down. Medea came the next day with a bag of gold and bought it on the condition that we always have a room for her."

The action was oddly philanthropic, given what little he knew of her. There must have been a reason. No one made a purchase like that without expecting something in return.

"The room you keep for her—is it always the same, or does it change?"

"Always the same."

Interesting. Did she stash something there? "How long is she staying?"

The barkeep suddenly looked uncomfortable. "Why do you want to know?"

"I don't plan on provoking her, if that's what you're thinking." Nikolai gave what he hoped was a disarming laugh. "From what I've heard, it wouldn't end well for me. No, I'm trying to persuade her of something and want to know how much time I have."

The barkeep snorted. "Yeah, she gets a few of those. But she hasn't taken an apprentice in some time. Better for business, in my opinion." He set down the mug he'd been wiping. Despite the thorough scrubbing, it didn't look any cleaner, brown streaks mottling the clear glass.

"Why would that make a difference?"

"Because her apprentices usually don't survive, and there's always some hotheaded relative of the deceased trying to pick a fight. At least she kills them outside, but no one's coming in here to buy drinks as long as there's a corpse lying out front."

Nikolai could've told him that wasn't the only issue. The place was a dump. It was surprising they had any customers at all, corpse or no.

"The real problem is if a newer Enforcer is on watch," the man continued. "Then things can get ugly."

"I thought they weren't supposed to engage with her?"

The barkeep picked up another mug, focusing intently on it. "Young men tend to ignore the rules. Think they're more capable than they really are—begging your pardon, sir."

"No offense taken. Is it true she killed nineteen Collective delegates?"

The barkeep shrugged. "She did *something* to make them turn a blind eye. But it's not like she goes around killing people left and right. They probably figure it's better to have one body in the street than half a dozen, so they leave her be and clean up the mess." The barkeep shot a glance at Medea, then leaned toward Nikolai and whispered, "I hear there are other things she does, though, that they don't like so much."

Nikolai scooted closer. "Like what?"

"I hear she kidnaps Mundanes for her experiments."

Nikolai raised an eyebrow. "Surely they'd do something if *that* were true."

"Just what I've heard." The man straightened and his tone became more formal. "But you wanted to know how long she's here. Her room is paid up through next Tuesday. I don't think you'll have much luck, but I'll tell you this—if by some miracle you do manage to convince Medea, don't cross her. I've seen her disembowel men without so much as a wand."

"Her room is paid up, is it? My good man, are you telling me you charge the owner of this fine establishment for room and board?"

The barkeep returned a broad grin. "I told you, she doesn't remember."

Nikolai laughed. "Your secret is safe with me."

The barkeep moved away to greet another customer, returning only to deposit a mug of tea, its dark brown handle worn to pale beige after so much use. The warmth of the mug seeped into Nikolai's hands as he considered the problem. Petrov said Medea sometimes disappeared for years. If she left Haven, he would likely never get another chance to convince her. Time was the enemy, and he only had a week.

Why did Magi have to be sensitive to telepathy? Manipulation was so much easier with the Mundane. He'd have to do this the hard way. Nikolai picked up the mug and made his way back to Medea's table.

4

PERSUASION

D amn, he was coming back. "My answer is still no."

The boy set a mug across from her and sat down like he had every right to intrude.

"Let's start over. I'm Nikolai." When she didn't reply, his eyes strayed to her book, *Tous les hommes sont mortels*. "You speak French?"

"No, I simply enjoy staring at words without comprehension."

For a moment he seemed taken aback and she hoped he might leave, but he plowed ahead. "Can I speak plainly?"

"Probably not, but you can try." No reason to respect someone blatantly disrespectful. Responses to the tactic usually fell into one of two categories. Either they called her all sorts of colorful names and stormed off, which was a definite win, or they eventually cast aside social conventions and gave it back just as harshly, which meant they were finally being their honest selves—also a win.

She had the pleasure of seeing him struggle to remain civil in the face of her unbridled hostility. He recovered quicker than most.

"I know you won't train me, but there is much I could learn from you. All I ask is a bit of your time."

As if time wasn't a precious commodity. She crossed her arms. "I *had* intended to read my book."

"Don't you have plenty of time for books? As an immortal, I mean."

"The thing about books is that people keep writing more of them. While I may have an eternity, I can never quite catch up." It was a common misconception that immortals had unlimited free time. Yes, they didn't have to worry about running out per se, but their days were still consumed by all the small necessities of existing—eating, sleeping, bathing, shitting, chores. There were never enough hours in the day to do all the things you *wanted* to do.

"I'm not asking for an eternity. I'm asking for one hour every day for as long as you're here." He reached into his coat and pulled out something wrapped in brown paper. A sandwich, which he proceeded to eat. Sure, just make yourself at home.

"A few lunchtime conversations. Surely that's not too much to ask? It pales in comparison to the years your apprentices have stolen from you. You don't even have to kill me at the end."

Damn, he was persistent. If she turned him away now, he'd just try something more annoying, like showing up when she was with a client. Needling him *was* moderately entertaining. She could make it work, provided certain conditions were met.

"You're dedicated, I'll give you that. Fine, lunch. But if I tire of you, you will leave without hesitation, is that clear?" Let's see if he could stick to an agreement.

He nodded.

"What is it you wish to know?"

"How did you deaden the sound? It's truly masterful." He looked around them as if to emphasize his point.

Dear god, this was going to be a long week. "I see. Start with a general spell that is in no way dark and attempt to flatter me. I'm not impressed."

He blinked and pressed on. "*Actually*, I wanted to know because I do not wish to be overheard asking anything *illegal.*"

She almost snorted. "I doubt that was your true motive in asking, but nice redirection. It's a modified shield spell. The key is to focus on what you want to keep out, or in. You must be specific. In this case, I want most sound kept out."

He was doing his best to hold back a smile. Smug little shit. She didn't normally tell people the next part, but his ego was begging to be punctured.

"Sounds pertaining directly to me can penetrate the bubble, and those are amplified so I know if someone is talking to me, or about me. Speaking of which, everything the barkeep said about me was true."

The timing was perfect. She got him right as he was drinking from his mug. He choked, slopping tea over himself. She handed him a napkin.

"You have tea on your shirt."

He took the napkin and dabbed at his front. "You heard all that?" he said between coughs.

"Yes. Now, are you going to ask me anything worthwhile?" Please make it a good question. Something interesting.

"What's the most powerful black magic spell you know?"

Goddamnit. Always so predictable, century after century. The worst part was he had potential. Already she could see him wasting his life pursuing dark magic with the same narrow-mindedness as her previous apprentices. Medea picked up her mug and found it empty. She set it resolutely back down.

"Magic is neither black nor white. This is something I have often tried, yet continually failed, to impress upon my students. There is only the caster and their intent."

"And if their intent is to do harm, what is the most powerful spell they would use?"

"In the hands of a master, any spell can be dangerous."

That garnered a flash of youthful irritation, quickly concealed. Chilling to think how much better he'd get at controlling these little tells over time.

"Now I have a question for you." She pierced him with her gaze. "Why do you want this so badly?"

"What do you mean?"

"Surely you must have a reason for wanting to learn so-called 'black' magic."

"Because magic is power, and black magic is the most powerful of all."

Wrong. So wrong that not correcting him was like ignoring a knife twisting in her gut, but she had a point to make, and that was more important. "And why do you want power?"

"Why . . . what?" The confusion on his face spoke volumes. He didn't know. He hadn't even thought about it.

"Why do you want power?"

"I want to improve the lot of Magi. I want to make the world a better—"

"That's not even a *good* lie." She sat back and pinched the bridge of her nose.

Liars were the worst. Habitual liars often couldn't distinguish between reality and their own fabrications, ignoring objectivity for whatever made the best narrative in their heads. How could people live like that?

"It's one thing to lie to me—it's another to lie to yourself. Misunderstanding your own motivations only leads to heartache. Don't answer, just think on it. I believe we're done for today."

She picked up her book and pretended to read, praying he'd at least keep his word to leave when she said so. If he didn't, she'd have to hurt him. After a moment she heard the blessed sound of chair legs scraping across the wooden floor and the sandwich being rewrapped. At least he had that much self-control.

"Until tomorrow," he said.

Medea made a noise to indicate she'd heard, then held her breath until his footsteps abruptly muted upon crossing the sound shield.

Nikolai ruminated on their conversation all the way back to the shop. Tomorrow he'd do better. The rest of the day passed in a blur. Customers came and went, enchantments were cast, orders taken. He scarcely noticed any of it. Medea's question kept popping unbidden into his mind.

Ridiculous question, really. Why *not* have power? There was nothing to be gained by not having it. Power got you things. Money. Sex. Admiration. Fear. It got you across borders that weren't meant to be crossed, in with people who would have turned you away. Power kept you fed when everyone else was starving. No matter how high the bodies piled up, power ensured you weren't one of them. As well ask why he wanted to breathe.

Medea said she didn't expect an answer, but clearly it was important to her, so he had to think of some sort of response. What would other black magic practitioners want? Political influence? Their own country? Wealth? He'd need an answer that was closer to the truth but set him apart from previous applicants.

In the meantime, he had to figure out how to best approach her. She was suspicious, and his questions had clearly offended her somehow. At this rate he'd never convince her before she left Haven.

Best stick with tried and true tactics. Building rapport was as simple as giving people the opportunity to talk. Most experienced happiness or validation when allowed to speak freely about themselves. These positive feelings were inadvertently attributed to the listener. He would provide a sympathetic ear and mine what she divulged for nuggets of interest. Find a person's passion and you had a key to their heart.

Nikolai entered the Hanged Man on Wednesday determined to make a better impression. He greeted Medea warmly and asked if he could sit. Her stony gaze didn't inspire confidence, but he went ahead with his usual strategy of asking open-ended questions.

What brought her to Haven? "Business."

What was her book about? "I'd know if someone stopped interrupting my reading."

Why did she vanish for years at a time? "I get sick of people."

What was the best part of being immortal? "Not dying."

Before he could adjust his technique, she picked up her book and pointed to the door. Discontent festered within him like a rotting tooth as he made his way to the shop. Why couldn't she carry on a conversation like a reasonable person? She was conceited; that was it. Her power had gone to her head. Or, the thought nagged at him, she was purposely trying to drive him away. She would find he did not give up so easily.

Petrov was surprised but pleased to see him back so early. Pale and weak, the man had returned to the shop yesterday afternoon. Today he sat on a stool at the counter. As soon as Nikolai walked in the door, Petrov wobbled to his feet and retired to his office. Well enough. Nikolai wanted time to think.

Perhaps he ought to take an opposite tactic with Medea, but what would that entail? Acting as though he didn't want an apprenticeship? She'd know that for a lie. Insulting her? Disrespecting her? Too risky. He'd already lost two days. He needed advice from someone who knew her.

Petrov was out of the question; Nikolai was not yet ready for his master to know how seriously he sought a replacement. The book dealer didn't seem to know Medea all that well. She was a valued client, but there was no deeper relationship. The only other person he could think of was the barkeep of the Hanged Man.

Petrov went home midafternoon, claiming he still felt weak, leaving Nikolai to close up the shop on his own. He returned to the inn and scanned for Medea. Thankfully, she was absent from the common area. He approached the barkeep and asked for a quick word outside, hoping her auditory spell had a limited range. The barkeep called a young lad over to cover for him and led Nikolai into the alley behind the inn.

"Rejected, eh?" said the barkeep.

"Yes. I don't get it. She seemed insulted by my questions. I have no idea what I'm doing wrong. Any advice?"

"You're not trying to hit on her, are you? Because that's a good way to get yourself killed."

"No, nothing like that. I'm just trying to work up to an apprenticeship, I swear."

"Also a good way to get yourself killed." The man crossed his arms and leaned against the bar door. "Look, you're going about this all wrong. If you want to get Medea talking, ask her about magic."

"I have. She seemed insulted."

"Then you probably asked about black magic. Everyone asks about that. Pick something else. The more obscure the better." The barkeep chuckled to himself. "Just be prepared to sit there all day while she answers."

"I can do that."

"And for god's sake, stop with the idle chatter. Get to the point. She doesn't care much for formality."

"Are you suggesting I just walk up to her and ask about, I don't know, teleportation or something, without so much as a greeting?"

"Yes."

"That sounds rude."

"Does she seem particularly polite to you?"

"No, but—"

"Try it. Look, you came to me, remember?" The barkeep clapped a hand on Nikolai's shoulder and turned to go inside. "Be direct!" he called out as the door swung closed.

Nikolai walked through the alley, rats scurrying from the human intrusion. Here and there, windowsills sported saucers of milk, bread, sometimes wine. More elaborate displays were decorated with flowers or vines. The practice had baffled Nikolai when he'd first arrived. Petrov explained they were offerings for the fae. More like a feast for vermin and a waste of good food. Ridiculous how Magi could be as superstitious as the Mundane.

The barkeep suggested he ask Medea about magic, but what kind? It had to be something that would differentiate him from all previous applicants.

A rat carrying a chunk of bread half the size of its body bolted across Nikolai's shoe. He kicked at it and managed to overset a nearby saucer, which clattered against the cobblestones. A stout woman poked her head out the window to chastise him for bringing bad luck. Didn't he know not to mess with fairies? He apologized and handed her the bowl, which she yanked out of his grasp with a muttering of Gaelic.

Ridiculous. Each saucer he passed flagged the occupants as weak and incompetent. What did Magi have to fear from fae, if they even existed? He doubted Medea would stoop to making such an offering.

There was a thought. He could ask Medea about the fae, couching it as a foreigner's interest in local customs. Given her age, she was bound to know something of how the practice had evolved over time, and it would give her an opportunity to showcase her unique knowledge. Best of all, it was unlikely a previous hopeful had broached the topic.

The following day, he pushed aside his reservations about

appearing rude, slid into the seat across from Medea without so much as a greeting, and asked her what she knew of the fae. At his question, her cold indifference morphed into surprise and then suspicion.

"And this is of interest to you, why?"

"Because I accidentally spilled one of their offerings last night and want to know how much trouble I'm in." His smile made it a jest. "I'm not from here. In Russia we have stories of Leshy and Vodyanoy, but I've never taken them seriously. They sound too much like tales spread by Mundanes who don't understand magic. But in Haven, Magi speak of the fae as if they were real. I just want to separate fact from fiction. I figured if anyone knew it would be you, given how long you've lived and how much you've seen."

The explanation seemed to mollify her, and the flattery slipped by unremarked. The barkeep hadn't been kidding. She launched into a lecture so overly detailed he had difficulty pretending to listen. There were no fae. It was just the regional name for spirits, a form of sentient magic that influenced religion and culture across the globe. On and on she went, from animism, to ancestor worship, to polytheism and monotheism. Her diction, already exceedingly formal, became even more so. She began to gesticulate, her voice rising with her enthusiasm until it was almost a shout. Had it not been for the sound barrier, the whole inn would have been bombarded with her inane minutiae.

She was in full stride on Eastern belief systems with no sign of slowing when he dared check his watch and found he'd been sitting for an hour and a half. It took him fifteen more minutes to politely interject and excuse himself. Her mouth opened and closed several times, as if she could barely contain herself from spouting more information. At least this time she seemed sorry to see him go.

He spared a glance at the barkeep on his way out. The man stifled a laugh.

That night, Nikolai stayed up late contemplating his next move. There was a plethora of questions he wanted to ask Medea. How did she keep herself young? How did she kill the Collective delegation? Where did she get the gold to buy the inn? How did she cast spells without a wand?

All too obvious. Others had come before him, each asking the same questions.

The safest play was to repeat what he'd done today—ask her some general magical question. But greatness didn't come from playing it safe. He had to go beyond distinguishing himself. In every encounter she'd had the upper hand. He needed to subvert her expectations and knock her off balance. On Friday he strolled into the Hanged Man, question at the ready.

"You're immortal . . ." he began. Her body tensed. Good. She thought she knew where he was going with this. "Is there any special wisdom you can impart, something that would normally take several lifetimes to learn?"

Her eyes widened and she leaned back in her chair. She looked to the side for a moment. Had he managed to stump her?

When at last she spoke, her self-assured tone was absent. "I don't know. Everyone learns differently. What might be as natural as breathing to me may take another ages to master. I honestly cannot say if I'm more gifted with magic, or if I'm simply better by nature of my longevity."

"But what of nonmagical wisdom?" This was a gamble. Magic was her strength, and she'd shown disdain for personal questions. The question was peripherally personal, but more than that, it demonstrated his willingness to learn more than magic.

"It's the same problem, isn't it? We all have different lessons to learn." Her mouth curved in a wry smile. "After all these centuries, I still have trouble understanding people."

From what he'd seen that didn't seem to be the case, but he did not contradict her. "How about me then? What's a lesson you think I could learn?"

"Oh, there are many lessons I think you could learn—patience for one." Despite the return of snark, her next words were thoughtful. "There is something, though you probably aren't ready to hear it. Reputation is everything, especially when you're immortal. Are you prone to exaggeration? Quick to anger? Forever running late? Do you borrow items and never return them? Such things follow you."

She paused, brow creasing as she studied the table. "The pursuit of wealth, status, appearance—these things do not matter as much as *who you are*. If hundreds of years ago I gained a reputation as a liar, it would still be following me, even if I'd done nothing but speak truth since. It's more than simple honesty. Integrity matters." Her eyes locked on to his momentarily. "Decide what your principles are and hold to them, no matter what."

Was she unaware of her own reputation as a murderer, or had she intentionally cultivated that persona? It had to have some downsides. Did she wait until she was too powerful to be opposed before letting loose with no regard to consequences? He kept these questions to himself but continued on to general magical topics, making philosophical inquiries whenever he could.

Lunch ran nearly two hours, for he aimed to depart on a positive note. Petrov would be cross, but he'd be leaving the man's service soon enough. Progress with Medea was more important.

On Saturday he hit a snag. Petrov, now feeling better, required him to stay and mind the shop all day while he ran errands. How would Medea interpret his absence? Would she think him inconsiderate? Cowardly for giving up? Worst was the possibility she might not care at all. There was no way to notify her, and it was full dark when Petrov returned to help close the shop. Nikolai left in a sour mood.

He made his way to the Hanged Man on the off-chance Medea was in the common room for dinner. The normally sleepy village was alive with the sound of young men and women out for a good time. Haven, like most Magi towns, had managed to insulate itself somewhat from the country it occupied. While the rest of Ireland faced economic crisis and mass emigration, and Catholicism kept the majority of Irish women subdued, Haven plodded along much as it always had. Citizens were in reasonably good spirits and never lacked for food, and women were treated as equals.

Unfortunately, in recent years this had gained Haven somewhat of a reputation as a place to be. Every Saturday there was an influx of young people from neighboring towns with little else to do but drink their sorrows away and dream of better lives beyond their country's borders. Their coin was good, and locals tolerated them as long as they behaved themselves and did not overstay.

Nikolai took a shortcut down the alley between shops. Drunken laughter erupted from the Spotted Sow—not unusual at this hour, except that it came from behind the pub rather than in front of it. He rounded the building and saw the source. Three young men had cornered Kate, the barkeeper's younger daughter, while she emptied the trash. Two stood in the alley while the third, a huge bulk of a man, blocked the pub door. They loomed over her tiny frame, too close and too familiar. One of them toyed with her red curls as the others probed her with questions.

When did she get off work? Why wouldn't she join them for a drink? They were only looking for a good time; didn't she want to have a good time? Kate deflected with noncommittal answers. She held the trash can in front of her like a shield, her back pressed against the building as if hoping to be absorbed by it.

Fucking amateurs.

Nikolai kept his current trajectory down the alley, straight toward the men. As he passed, he caught his shoulder against that of the nearest man.

"Watch it!" the man snarled.

"My apologies—the stench was so bad I mistook you for one of the trash cans. Although now that I see your face, it's obvious I've gravely insulted trash cans everywhere."

The man blinked without comprehension. Nikolai sighed internally and forced himself to make a crude joke about the man's mother. That, at least, was guaranteed to bring blows. Sure enough, the man stepped forward to take a swing.

Nikolai danced back to the wall, peppering his assailant's face with jabs, and dodged the next punch. The man's fist crunched satisfyingly as it hit the bricks. The other two were closing in fast, girl forgotten. They did not fight as a unit, but as separate, enraged animals more likely to get in each other's way than to land a proper blow.

The smaller man reached Nikolai first and pummeled him in the chest. A normal man might shrink back from such an onslaught. Nikolai leaned into it, closing the gap and bringing up his knee into the man's groin. The man staggered and fell over, whimpering.

Big man was here. It was he who'd been blocking Kate's escape. Now he loomed over Nikolai, biceps bulging against his sleeves. Something collided with Nikolai and sent him sprawling to the ground.

The first man straddled him, striking at his face with one fist, his broken hand cradled against his chest. Stupid. He should have used his injured arm to block.

A punch to the throat and Nikolai was able to roll the man off, directly into the path of his friend. The giant stumbled, inadvertently kicking his own friend in the back of the head and knocking him out cold, but caught himself against the wall. He roared at Nikolai and charged.

Nikolai hastily retreated farther down the alley, dodging boxes and other refuse as he unlocked doors with the wand concealed up his sleeve. Closer. Closer. Come on, get into position. There!

BAM!

The door flung open, slamming the man in the face. He staggered back, clutching his nose, then tripped over a pile of boxes and fell with a crash.

"Collido." The pummel spell hit the man in the back of his head, knocking him out cold.

Nikolai stood grinning, adrenaline coursing through his veins. Dueling was fun, but it didn't compare to the rush of a brawl. It was exactly what he needed after a shitty day. Too bad the feeling wouldn't last.

He stooped to grab his hat. It was sodden with something; he didn't like to imagine what. The commotion had attracted the attention of the locals. Light spilled from several open doors along the alley leading back to the Spotted Sow.

One of them perfectly illuminated Medea's disapproving face.

THE SPOTTED SOW

Medea glared at the unconscious swine. The boy had bloodied them, but not enough. She scanned their bodies. Aside from a few minor injuries and a concussion, they were in perfect health. A nicked blood vessel here, deprivation of oxygen there, severing of the spinal cord, perforation of the intestines, so many ways to kill them . . .

The boy was suddenly at her side. "I know this looks bad, but—"

"Is that all you're going to do?"

"I . . . what?"

"Is that all you're going to do?" She gestured to the bodies. "Surely they deserve more." Some of her more zealous apprentices would have decorated the walls with their guts by now.

"Uh, there's not much more I *can* do. They're not locals. If I hurt them too badly or they go missing, Haven gets investigated by outsiders."

That sounded . . . remarkably rational coming from him. But still, there were ways around the law. Hadn't Petrov taught him anything? Pain was just as good, especially when interspersed with brief periods of relief.

"You could always cast a slow curse," she said, "something that wouldn't take effect until they were home." She had a nice spell that compressed the kidneys in just the right way.

"True." He leaned in and smiled. "Know anyone who could teach me such a thing?"

She rolled her eyes and turned aside. "Walk with me."

At the mouth of the alley, she reached back with her magic. Haven might let such transgressions slip, but she did not. She gave no outward sign of spellcasting as she placed the tracking wards. The last thing the boy needed was more incentive to seek an apprenticeship.

She turned onto the street, trading the packed earth of the alley for cobblestones. The smooth surfaces felt pleasant, if a tad damp. Normally she stepped from stone to stone, avoiding the space between them when she could. With the boy at her side, she endeavored to walk at a more consistent pace. His stride was longer, and he'd have a hard enough time keeping himself from walking ahead without her ambling.

"Did you lose your shoes?"

"I try not to wear shoes unless absolutely necessary," she said. The risk of attack was too high in a place like Haven. Besides, who needed shoes when you had shields? An imperceptible barrier protected her soles from filth but still allowed sensory information through. Shield was her favorite of the basic spells. So versatile and functional!

"What brought you back there? Were you following me?" The boy had a stupid grin on his face.

Did he really think she would follow him? Or was it a jest? When in doubt, assume the person was asking an honest question.

"No, it was the noise of those brutes. I was with a client and heard them through the window." The noise had been a welcome distraction. Potential clients never liked it when you turned them down. No matter how many times she explained she wouldn't remove hexes placed by another, people got mad.

"What client? What were you doing for them?"

"Business with my clients is confidential. Did you know the red-haired girl?" Medea had arrived in time to see the girl bolt through the back door while the boy toyed with her attackers.

"Not well, but yes. Haven't exactly big."

Odd, he didn't seem like the chivalrous type. "Why did you rescue her?"

He paused a little too long. Of course. She should have known. All men were the same.

"I don't know. I was in a bad mood and they irritated me." His tone lacked conviction.

"I see. So it wasn't so she would feel compelled to fuck you later?" Her tone was harsh, her choice of words deliberate. The boy seemed taken aback, and she braced herself for a flurry of excuses.

His reply was matter-of-fact. "No. Kate's a little young for me."

A frown creased his brow, and they walked in silence for a time. Interesting. Maybe he didn't even know the reason he'd saved the girl, acting on impulse with no real thought as to why. She took the opportunity to scan his body.

Healthy male, forebrain still developing, but that was normal for his age. The forebrain was responsible for long-term planning and restraint, and it continued to grow until the midtwenties. It was the reason she'd waited until then before halting her own aging process, though at the time she didn't know what the structure did, only that she should probably allow it to finish growing.

More concerning was his undersized amygdala. He could have been born that way, or it might have been the result of early trauma. It explained some of the behavior she'd seen—getting in her face about the dagger for one. The amygdala processed emotions. Aside from anger, everything he felt—if he felt anything at all—would be muted, fear especially. Too much fear was limiting, but not enough was just as bad, particularly when coupled with an immature forebrain. There was literally nothing holding him back.

As if to emphasize her train of thought, out of nowhere he shot her a knowing smile and said, "I prefer more mature lovers."

Heaven help her. She shook her head and walked faster. Thankfully, he seemed to realize his error, for he slipped back into pensive silence, the best kind. They were almost to the Hanged Man when he spoke again.

"I saw three assholes pawing after *pizda* they didn't deserve because they were too lazy to put any effort into making themselves genuinely desirable. Women choose mates based on qualities that they want to pass on to their offspring—strength, fitness, cunning, the ability to amass resources. It's a contest, and those men know they're losers. They can't even be bothered to try. It just pissed me off."

At least he'd sorted it out for himself. There was hope for him yet, if he could learn to think critically about his actions. That was one benefit to the small amygdala—emotions would have no bearing on his decision-making. He'd do well under pressure . . . if he didn't get himself killed first.

"And I was running late, so it felt good to take it out on someone," he added.

She rolled her eyes. At least he was being honest for once.

"If you keep doing that, your eyes are going to get stuck."

"No, they won't."

"I know. It's a joke. I—never mind."

They reached the Hanged Man and she paused outside. Time to be rid of him.

"Thank you. This was most enlightening."

He frowned. "I was hoping we could have dinner together. I apologize for missing lunch. Petrov kept me busy."

"I'm afraid I have things to attend to." The drunk men were on the move. She'd have to hurry if she wanted to catch up with them without drawing too much attention to herself.

The boy seemed intent on seeing her in. She'd probably have to go inside and walk upstairs, then double back after he'd left.

"I just remembered," he said, "I have an answer to your question—about wanting power."

Two self-reflections in one night? She should congratulate him, or whatever it was people did, but all that came out was a noncommittal, "Hmm?" Brilliant, way to encourage the kid.

"I want to be self-reliant. More than that, I don't want to be beholden to anyone, ever—like you."

Autonomy was certainly something she valued, but the way he said it sent shivers up her spine.

"Ah, but I'm beholden to myself, and my standards are high."

"As are mine."

He said it with such sincerity she almost burst out laughing. As it was, she had to bite the inside of her cheek to keep from betraying herself.

"I will see you on the morrow." This time he took the dismissal. She ducked inside and watched from the window until he vanished from sight, then she left to pursue her quarry.

Nikolai headed back to the Spotted Sow, boots clacking on cobblestones. His mind returned to Medea's question. Why *had* he saved Kate? It's not like he got anything out of it. At fourteen, she wasn't old enough to be of interest. Some men might enjoy that kind of thing. They'd never know the pleasure of having a woman scream out their name in ecstasy because they put all her former lovers to shame. Experience was essential to validating one's abilities.

Now, Kate's older sister Mary, *she* was interesting. An outrageous flirt notorious for turning down every bachelor in town, Mary had rebuffed Nikolai for two years running. She had to be getting it from somewhere, but no one was talking. Saving Kate might win points with Mary, but that hadn't occurred to him when he'd chosen to intervene. So why had he done it?

The answer he'd given Medea was unsatisfactory, but he couldn't pinpoint why. It nagged like an itch he couldn't scratch. What was it about Medea's probing that sent his thoughts spiraling in new directions?

The problem was that all of them—the drunken men and Kate —fell into the Useless category. Yes, Kate had *slightly* more value than the men, being both female and Magi, but uncertain future potential didn't warrant defense. Was it because the drunks were outsiders? No. If anything, he could have attacked Haveners more openly. It had something to do with them being men, he was sure of it.

Men weren't inherently Fuckable, at least not to him, and were therefore Useless by default. Was he missing a category? He considered his brothers and how antagonistic he had been to their arrival. As the eldest, he'd enjoyed a certain level of comfort and attention during his stint as an only child. Each successive birth created yet another rival for attention, for food, for time.

Men were Competition.

Women could be Competition too, if they vied for the same resources, but men were Competition by *default*. Winning meant weakening or eliminating the Competition. That's why he attacked the men—not because he saw any value in Kate, but because it was a convenient excuse to eliminate the men.

Nikolai smiled, satisfied to have sorted out the puzzle.

Bawdy laughter erupted from the Spotted Sow. He stepped

aside for a merry couple and entered the pub, now packed with outsiders, mostly men. Magi women could appreciate pleasure for the sake of it, without romantic entanglements.

Unfortunately, word had spread among the Mundane that Haven women were easy, at least compared to their Catholic counterparts. He doubted they opened their legs for many outsiders, but apparently it happened often enough for young men to flock to Haven for the opportunity.

There were five men for every woman in the pub. The odds didn't bother Nikolai. He never had problems finding a willing partner, but quicker would be better tonight. Aside from regular morning trysts with Mrs. Gallagher, he'd barely gotten laid all week. Nikolai scanned the room for his usual partners.

A gentle touch on his arm, and Mary was there, pushing a pint into his hand. "For my sister," she said.

Nikolai took it with thanks. "How is she?"

"Shaken. Da and I were so busy we didn't notice she was taking too long with the rubbish. She isn't the best with spells and gets flustered easily. Even if she hadn't left her wand behind the bar, she probably would've been too panicked to defend herself."

"I noticed. What happened to the men? I imagine your father had some choice words for them."

"He ran them off. Anyway, I have to get back to work, but drinks are on the house tonight."

Mary sauntered away into the crowd. Nikolai carried his mug to the bar. If ever he had a chance with her, it would be tonight. Might as well stick around and see where things went. Regardless of his intentions for saving her sister, there was no point in letting his recently earned goodwill go to waste.

He had a companionable conversation with her father, a barrel-chested, formidable fellow. Kate made a puffy-eyed appearance around ten. The sight of the packed bar almost caused her to flee back upstairs, but when she spotted Nikolai, she drew herself up and braved the crowd to come thank him. They chatted for a bit, and she inquired if Petrov had any decent protection wares.

The rest of the evening passed slowly. He watched people, engaged with those around him, and got into a debate with a drunk who soon forgot what they were even discussing. Last call came and went, and soon he was chatting with Mary as she wiped down glasses behind the bar. Kate cleared off the tables nearby.

"Tell me," he said, "how is it the Spotted Sow is the only place in town with electric lights? I thought they weren't allowed."

"They're not anymore, thanks to Da. You know him—got a stubborn streak. He figures since they don't bother us, why not have proper lights?"

Everyone knew Mundane technology screwed with magic. Only witches seemed immune to the effects. It gave them an edge in big cities, and they'd expanded into Mundane spaces the way other Magi couldn't. Using electricity in a Magi city was more than rude; it was akin to force-feeding shellfish to someone with a known allergy.

"Nobody complained?"

"Oh, they complained. There were protests and everything, but there was nothing on the books saying he couldn't use electricity, and the elders had to let it go. Afterward, they passed the statute banning electricity from being added to buildings."

"And now everyone drinks here." After visiting the Hanged Man, he could see why.

"Indeed they do. Buncha hypocrites."

Nikolai raised his glass. "To the hypocrites." He'd drunk here several times a week since arriving two years ago. As far as he knew, there were no long-term effects from exposure to Mundane technology. A thought tugged at him. Medea chose to room at the Hanged Man, in the oldest part of town. Was it because she'd hidden something within her room, or because she was avoiding technological interference? Something to ask her tomorrow.

He chatted with Mary until Kate went upstairs, then made his offer. She shot him down yet again.

He sighed and got up to leave. "Tell me this—do I have a chance in hell, ever?"

She shook her head. "Sorry, Nikolai, you're not my type."

"What *is* your type? I don't know a single lad who can claim he's had the pleasure, but I see you flirting with everyone."

She leaned forward conspiratorially. "You're sleeping with Ethne, aren't you?"

Was that her problem? She wanted exclusivity? That would never happen.

He stood straighter. "Ethne *and* Shailyn." And whatever Mundane tail he could get on the weekends in Dublin. "Neither of them is bothered by it. I don't see how it's an issue."

"Oh, but it *is* an issue. You and I have the same type."

"Wait . . . are you implying you fancy Ethne?"

Mary smirked. "I've done more than fancy her. She's a little upset you haven't been to see her all week."

With a single sentence, Mary removed herself from Fuckable and slid into Competition. He was used to competing against women in academics and combat. Despite knowing that some women preferred other women, it never occurred to him that he might be competing with them for sex. Didn't people usually stick with one or the other? This added a whole new dimension to things.

He took a long drink and studied her freckled face. Bitch looked damn smug.

"You fucked my girlfriend?"

Mary laughed. "Since when are any of the women you sleep with 'your girlfriend'? Last I checked, you weren't exclusive with anyone."

"I'm not, but still . . . Why didn't you tell me sooner about liking women? I would've left you alone." And saved what little money he had. For two years he'd been overstaying, drinking far more than he should in the hope Mary might come home with him. So much for that. He plastered a smile on his face. "I always got the impression you were flirting with me, but I guess I was wrong."

"You weren't. Men order more drinks when they think they have a chance."

She'd been conning him too? Definitely Competition.

"Besides," she continued, "even among our kind, there are many who look down on it."

He tilted his head in acknowledgment. "It's a damn shame when Mundane stupidity manages to permeate our culture. Well, thank you for telling me. At least now I can laugh at the poor sots trying."

"No problem. Oh, is the club still meeting tomorrow? Word has it you've been a bit distracted."

Shit. He'd forgotten all about dueling club. A year into his apprenticeship, when it was clear Petrov wasn't the master he'd hoped, he'd sought out sparring partners. Petrov hadn't been keen on the idea, but the younger locals loved it, given there wasn't much else to do in the sleepy village. Soon he had nearly a dozen people that met once a week, and far more spectators.

It would probably be best to cancel tomorrow's match. Tuesday was rapidly approaching, and he needed to put all his efforts into coercing Medea. Then again, maybe if she saw him in action, it would tip the odds in his favor.

"Yes, we're dueling tomorrow." A sudden inspiration hit him. "Bring Kate. I know your Da thinks she's a bit young for it, but given what happened today, I'm sure he'll see the necessity. She can partner with me. I'll see she comes to no harm." It was perfect. He could gift Kate his spare wand holster. Medea would see him at his best—fierce combatant and gracious tutor. Doubtless his prowess in combat would outshine all of her previous apprentices.

Mary smiled. "I think she'd like that."

"Until tomorrow."

"Hold on a moment, I'll walk you out."

She took off her apron and followed him to the exit, thanking him once again. The oaken door closed and the heavy thump of a bar falling into place sounded behind it. The night was thick with fog. Light from a solitary lamppost fought bravely against the curtain of white. Nikolai donned his hat and walked to his apartment, a broad smile on his lips.

6

DUELING CLUB

When Nikolai entered the Hanged Man on Sunday, Medea greeted him with a smile. Or rather, what passed for one. True, she did not greet him by name or say hello, but one corner of her mouth turned up and her usual chilly demeanor thawed considerably. Since her face seemed perpetually stuck in a frown, he called that progress. Had his brawl at the Spotted Sow impressed her? Perhaps she shared his fascination with violence in any form. If so, the duel would give her another opportunity to see him in action.

He brought up the topic as casually as he could. It broke his usual rule of allowing his target to do most of the talking. For once, he had to give her a bit of information about himself, and in a way that wouldn't sound like bragging or false modesty. He'd formed the dueling club and taught most of the members their spells, for when he'd arrived in Haven, there'd been no one with whom to practice.

"Do you kill your members then, or merely enslave them?" she said over her cup. Her tone made it a serious question.

"I . . . no, of course not. It's just for practice."

"Then it's not a dueling club. It's a sparring club."

Semantics again. She often argued over words like this. As old as she was, it was probably difficult for her to accept that colloquial definitions changed over time. "Sparring, yes, though we refer to it as the Dueling Club."

She shook her head at this. "Dueling used to be a serious matter."

"Outlawed, wasn't it?"

"Yes. A shame. There were tiers to dueling, depending on the seriousness of the dispute. At the top was *Servitus aut Mors*, in which the loser is killed or enslaved."

"Enslaved? How? Couldn't they just run away?"

"No, they'd be soul-bound. The loser has no choice in their fate, but death would be preferable."

"Well, while our stakes aren't as high, I would be honored if you came to our match. I'd be very curious to hear what you think of it."

"Would you?" A hint of a smile again.

"Of course. Your prowess in combat is legendary. It's this evening at five, on the outskirts of town. Do you know where the Reid barn is?"

"You battle in a barn?"

"Not my choice. It was a concession with the local Enforcers." Their meetings had originally been in the open. They'd started with drills, then split into teams and spread out, incorporating the terrain as they hunted each other. Villagers complained. Why did he need to teach them *those* spells? Few Haveners sent their kids to the Academy. Family magic could be learned at home. Still, if he was going to teach them spells, why not the nice, Academy-approved set? His choices hearkened too much back to the old days. What if they were seen? It was cancel the club or submit to being muzzled. Nikolai had chosen the muzzle—for now. Haven was but a temporary stop.

"I'm sorry to hear that." She looked it.

"Will you come?"

"I'll consider it."

The rest of their time passed amicably, but he couldn't get a more committed response. Afterward he went to his apartment to prepare. Like most shops in town, Petrov's was closed on Sundays. Some Mundane influences couldn't be helped. In a drawer he found his old wand holster. It would have to be taken in to fit Kate, but she'd be able to hide a wand up her sleeve.

The holster went into the worn bag he carried with him to every match. Back when the club had more freedom, the bag was stocked with potions and powders that could be used to disable opponents or aid allies. Now it contained a few bandages and healing potions—another concession to the Enforcers. They were hardly needed. The club was under too much scrutiny for him to teach or cast any truly dangerous spells.

The cobblestone streets changed to dirt as he reached the edge of town. Sheep grazed sedately in the green pasture. The sight irked him each time. Why any Magi stooped to a lowly profession like farming was beyond his understanding. The Reid family were not strong casters. Their magic pertained mostly to the keeping of animals and tilling of soil. Every full moon they made offerings to some god of hearth and harvest. Their yields were good and their animals were healthy, yet they had lived in the same quaint holding for generations. Didn't they see how much more they could accomplish with their powers?

The road curved toward the Reid barn a half mile down. Sean Reid and a few other members greeted Nikolai as he entered. It was Sean who'd offered up the barn after the village had gotten testy. His family mostly used it for shearing and storage. The dusty air stank of animals. Stacked hay bales lined the walls, doubling as seating for spectators. A variety of mismatched chairs were available as well. The center was relatively large and free of obstructions. Not the most prestigious place to show off his skills to Medea.

The club members attempted to clear the dusty floor with Gust, a spell that created a small burst of wind. Most of them had so little control they merely spread dust from one area of the barn to another. Nikolai shook his head. How quickly they forgot.

Most spells were powered by mana, the magical version of stamina innate in all Magi. Running out meant mana exhaustion, which prevented you from casting spells and made you feel like shit until you'd had a chance to rest. A spell's mana cost was directly proportional to how much energy it took to create the effect. Nudging a pencil across the table was cheaper than punching a hole in a wall. At this rate, the idiots would use up half their mana before the match even started.

"How many times do I have to say it? If you're not a witch, use a broom! Save your mana for the match."

The hay bales crowded with spectators as match time approached. Nikolai scanned the audience for Medea. She had to come. It wasn't like she had anything better to do. Surely an evening of live entertainment was preferable to reading.

Kate and Mary entered the barn together. Kate chose a front seat with her friends, Mary a high seat at the back of the room. Ethne joined her a few minutes later. They didn't touch but leaned close as they conversed. He'd have to do something about that. Whether or not he was dating Ethne was beside the point. Mary had outmaneuvered him and he couldn't let that stand.

It was almost time to start. He took out his wand and twirled it in hand, pacing as he did so. Where was Medea? If she didn't show, he'd have to postpone giving the holster to Kate until he could arrange for their paths to cross again. When he could put it off no longer, he turned and faced the crowd.

"Greetings, friends. Let's get started, shall we? Ronan and Catherine, why don't you go first?"

He'd taught his club members several dueling spells, including Shield, Puncture, and Pummel, while keeping more powerful magic to himself. Allies or opponents, no point in letting them know all you could do.

Participants were encouraged to bring spells from within their homes, ostensibly to share with the group. Did their grandparents know of anything that would be Useful? Had they checked old letters or journals? Much of what they'd brought back was worthless for combat and therefore of little use to Nikolai. A few spells didn't even work. Perhaps they'd been written down incorrectly or required some long-forgotten ingredient.

Ronan and Catherine stood and drew their wands. Less skilled contestants always went first, and this pair was particularly terrible. Neither of them could even cast a shield spell. Ronan cast *Fulgor*, intending to blind Catherine with a flash of light. He put too much power into the spell and blinded not only himself but a good portion of the audience. Catherine used Gust. It was unclear if she was trying to blow dust into Ronan's eyes or move him backward. Either way, her wand only generated a sad puff of air. Nikolai stalked the outskirts, offering encouragement and pointers. Fat lot of good it did.

Catherine tried to conjure something, and a burst of static electricity erupted from her wand. Was she trying to make lightning? Pitiful. Ronan somehow succeeded in igniting his own pant leg. The audience howled with laughter as Ronan frantically slapped at his pants. His girlfriend, seated on the sidelines, helpfully suggested he throw himself in a nearby water trough, advice that he took. When Ronan emerged drenched, Nikolai awarded the match to Catherine. She might be a weak caster but at least she wasn't a complete menace.

"Nice work, you two." He kept his voice measured and kind. "Ronan, I like that you're trying new spells. A bit more practice at home and I'm sure you'll have it."

A flash of red drew Nikolai's eye. Medea entered the barn, looking bored and vaguely irritated as always. She peered around for a moment, then took a seat in one of the chairs and pulled out her book. Why the hell did she come if she was just going to read? She'd better put down the damn book when it was his turn.

Nikolai called the next contestants, two brothers. Like Ronan and Catherine, shields were beyond their capabilities. He couldn't have asked for a worse performance in front of Medea. Their match rapidly devolved into telekinetically flinging cow pies at each other until they dissolved in a fit of giggles and he dismissed them.

Thankfully, they were on to better members. Sean and Briana approached the middle of the barn and conjured their shields. An oblong disk appeared in front of each duelist, yellowish but transparent. The disks moved with them, always hovering about four inches in front of their bodies. Shields protected from head to ankle but weren't so wide one couldn't shoot spells around the sides. Their strength varied from caster to caster. Some only blocked physical attacks or weak spells, but a powerful Magi could push enough power into their shield to make it virtually impenetrable, or so he'd read.

Sean and Briana danced around, shooting Pummel at each other from behind the safety of their shields. Spells like Lightning and Fireball were easy to see, erupting from the tip of a wand and shooting toward wherever the caster aimed. Other projectile spells might be no more than a minor tint in color moving through the air. Those with a lot of force built in, like Pummel, created a ripple effect you could track if you knew what to look for.

After a minute, the combatants' shields began to deteriorate for lack of mana, until both casters were once again unprotected. Neither of them had mana left for Pummel, and they resorted to Puncture—harder to spot and dodge, but also less dangerous. The battle ended when Sean caught Briana's hand with a well-placed

Punctum, causing her to cry out and drop her wand. The audience broke into steady applause and Nikolai took the floor again.

"Excellent disarm, Sean. Kate, would you mind coming up here?"

Nikolai presented the holster to Kate, adjusting the straps to fit her slender forearm and demonstrating how to conceal it up her sleeve. He taught her two spells. The first was Gust, a standard from the Academy. While not harmful, with practice one could increase the power enough to make conversing extremely difficult without shouting. The second was *Vomito*, the nauseating spell—not exactly pleasant if you were standing in the crossfire, but it would be enough to halt most people in their tracks. Both were perfect for Kate, given that she wasn't one for confrontation. The audience laughed and cheered when he insisted Kate test the spells on him. Thankfully, she wasn't yet strong enough to give him more than a minor stomachache.

During the performance he kept an eye on Medea. She hunched over her book, elbows on her knees, legs spread wide like a man. Not once had he seen her look up. Well, this would get her attention. He spread his arms and grinned broadly at the audience.

"Alright, who wants a go at me? How about four of you this time? Mary, Yasar, Grace, I know you're up for it. Who else?"

"I'll take those odds!" Well-muscled and tall, Darby stood with his wand raised.

Nikolai moved to one side of the barn, careful to keep Medea in his peripheral vision, while his challengers lined up opposite. Grace conjured her shield with ease. Darby and Mary, being witches, had a more involved process.

Witches were an odd subset of Magi. Like the Mundane, they were born without the gift of magic. Instead, they relied on the power of a deity to fuel their spells. Had Nikolai been born thus, he probably would have chosen patronage too, no matter how distasteful the idea of being forever shackled to another creature. A man should be free to make his own way.

Darby and Mary chanted softly to themselves, begging the Morrígan, a trio of Irish goddesses, to grant them power for battle. While their gods might not mind granting power for small everyday spells, something this mana-intensive required permission. Nikolai tapped his wand against his leg. Finally, their request was complete and their shields sprang up. About time.

Everyone glanced at Yasar, who remained unprotected.

"No shield?" Nikolai asked.

Yasar grinned. "Thought I'd try something new today. Courtesy of my grandmother." He spun his wand and chanted in Arabic. Dust and debris swirled into a small tornado that encased his body. Impressive.

Nikolai began the countdown. "Everybody ready? Three . . . two—"

"It seems to me that it would be far more challenging if two of your opponents were behind you." Medea's voice carried, though she hadn't looked up from her book. There was a murmur of assent from the audience, and then a few people shouted directions at the other duelists, telling them to spread out, move around him.

"Sure, why not make it interesting?" If that's what they wanted, he'd make do. "Mary and Yasar, you up front. Grace and Darby in the back." Nikolai positioned himself as well as he could, facing the audience, back to a wall. His flanks were exposed on either side. He'd have to pivot his shield to block incoming attacks.

"Three . . ."

Darby was overzealous. He would be the first to attack, hard and quick, without any thought. Grace was slower to cast, with far weaker spells.

"Two . . ."

Mary would pull no punches, regardless of recent events—Competition indeed. Yasar's dust shield begged for testing. Impressive did not mean effective.

"One!"

"Collido!" shouted Darby. Nikolai pivoted to block the pummel spell, then shot his own at Yasar. It hit the swirling dust with a puff. Yasar stumbled, but the dust absorbed most of the impact, which meant spells of force were out. Piercing or elemental might work.

Mary was conjuring a bright ball of light at the tip of her wand. He turned to Darby and Grace. Grace conjured an ethereal serpent around her waist like a belt. Not a good choice, considering she'd have to get right next to Nikolai for it to do anything. Typical of her to go defensive first.

Darby shot another Pummel at Nikolai, easily blocked. Nikolai followed up with three of his own, grinning as he sent the last winging not toward Darby, but at an angle toward Grace. As he expected, Darby thought all three were intended for him and faced his shield accordingly. The pummel spell hit the right side of Grace's shield, sending her lurching into Darby. They fell in a heap of limbs. Darby screamed as the snake's fangs found his flesh.

Medea had to be impressed with that move. But no, she slouched back in her chair, legs tucked under her with the book resting on her lap. Nikolai's grip tightened on his wand.

Pain seared his arm, wrenching his thoughts back to the battle. Yasar and Mary fired on him, Mary with balls of white light, Yasar with painful green bolts. Time to see what Yasar's dust cloud was worth.

"Fulmen!" Lightning arched toward Yasar. The dust lit up as bits of hay ignited. Yasar sprawled backward.

Nikolai itched to cast Lance or something equally damaging, but this was a sparring session, not a real duel. He would quickly lose practice partners if he got a reputation for bloodying people. A Pummel to Yasar's unprotected belly was good enough to be considered a "kill" shot. Nikolai sent several more at Mary, but she dodged them.

He aimed blindly over his shoulder, hoping to hit Darby or Grace. Darby wouldn't give up easily, but Grace was another matter. Soon enough she was calling out, "Yield!" He sent another Pummel at Mary and chanced a look behind him. Darby was lying motionless on the floor, eyes glassy. Grace's snake belt was better than he thought. He'd have to ask her for the spell.

Nikolai turned his full attention to Mary. They danced, trading spells, unable to penetrate each other's shields. She was good for a witch, but not as good as him. Not here and certainly not in the bedroom.

"*Lancea!*" An ethereal spear erupted from his wand. Unblocked, the spell had enough force to punch through bone. CRACK. Her shield held, barely. Fissures radiated across the surface. Mary stopped attacking, focused on repairing her shield.

His eyes found Medea. The bitch still hadn't looked up.

Nikolai stalked the barn, gradually maneuvering Mary between himself and Medea. When they were lined up just right, he aimed low and shouted "*Lancea!*" Mary dodged, clearing the way for his true target—Medea's chair legs. The spell splintered its way through wood, knocking both front and back legs clean off.

The chair should have fallen over. Instead, it hung in space as if supported by invisible pillars. Medea gave no outward sign that anything unusual had happened. After a moment she locked eyes with him, casually licked her finger, and turned the page in her book. The feigned apology he'd planned died on his lips.

Mary continued to assail him with spells, but his heart was no longer in it. He cast Fear at her exposed hand.

The spell's effect was different for everyone, catering to the target's specific anxieties. The few times he'd experienced it at the Academy, he'd begun to atrophy, flesh growing sunken until his hands and arms were skeletal claws. Sores developed on his skin and the air grew thick with flies and the scent of decay. The sores broke open with a splatter of pus to reveal wriggling maggots. What flesh was not consumed by the white worms sloughed off and hit the ground with wet slaps.

An exceptionally realistic hallucination, but a hallucination nonetheless. He'd ignored it. The gasps from his fellow students and his instructor's look of horrified fascination told him his response was unusual. Perhaps they thought he'd seen nothing. He didn't bother to enlighten them but paid close attention to its effects on others, noting each of their insecurities.

He had no such luck with Mary. A shot to the hand wasn't nearly as potent as one to the head. If he'd gotten her head, she would have given him something truly worthwhile, perhaps even betraying herself. Instead, she jerked her hand around and brushed at it frantically while shrieking something about spiders.

"Get them off! Get them off me!"

Pathetic. He never understood how Fear made people so unhinged. Mary's shield vanished with her concentration. A quick Pummel to the chest, harder than it needed to be, brought her down. He thought he heard a rib crack. Good.

The audience stood and cheered. People rushed to clap him on the back and shake his hand. Four opponents! They'd never seen anything like it. Would he be fighting four from now on?

Nikolai smiled absently and assured them he would. Where was Medea? Was she upset with what he'd done? Had he ruined his chances? He caught the back of a blonde head exiting the barn. She turned the corner and vanished from sight.

7

MANIPULATION

Medea stepped into darkness and inhaled the cool night air. The landscape was blanketed in fog. She conjured a ball of light and walked away from the revelry in the barn.

Relief washed over her with each step. Bad enough to be stuck in there with the crowd, the noise, the smells, but to see how far magic had fallen was truly disturbing. True, Haven wasn't a bastion of magical talent, but in the old days there would have been far more duelists. It had taken all her will not to run into the ring and show them how it was done.

That the crowd lauded the boy as some sort of paragon said a lot about the state of things. It was clear he'd been holding back for fear of injuring his opponents, a struggle she knew all too well. The decline in magic didn't account for all she'd seen, though it explained much. Something else was going on.

She'd heard that the Collective had outlawed dueling, but surely that wouldn't make everyone give up combat spells. Didn't they want to defend their homes? The children seemed eager enough to learn, flocking to the boy's teachings like he was a damned prophet.

Again, she'd been struck by how dim they felt. She could

have been in a crowd of Mundanes for all the magic she sensed. The boy alone stood out. Not that his magical energy was incredibly strong, but it was certainly on par with mages of old. With training, it could blossom into something great. He might even be able to reach peer status. With training.

Medea sighed. She'd been down this road too many times. If she trained him, he'd die. That much was certain. His personality wouldn't let him be anything less than the best, and that meant turning on her, which was a death sentence. His magical potential was too precious to waste.

Best to let him continue on his own. He might flounder a bit, but he had Petrov, did he not? Petrov was . . . well, he was acceptable. The man knew his way around a curse, and the boy's own drive should be enough to carry him the rest of the way. He'd be fine. Maybe not as powerful as he could be, but alive.

Nikolai tried in vain to make his way to the exit. Adoring faces pressed in from every side. Any other night he would have basked in the attention—getting drunk with the rest, telling jokes and reveling in his victory, culminating with his head buried between a pair of willing legs. Tonight, he only saw his future slipping through his fingers.

"Excuse me. I do apologize, but I must be going."

Shailyn, one of his regulars, was making a beeline for his position. He had to get out of here. She'd want to know why he hadn't been to see her all week, and then he'd be stuck talking to her for twenty minutes. He backed his way through the crowd. Shailyn's eyes sought his. He pretended not to notice. The edge of the crowd was close. He stepped free and grabbed his coat, tugging it on as he bolted out the barn door.

The nightly fog had rolled in, shrouding the landscape in

blurry darkness. He set out at a brisk jog. When Medea did not come into sight, he broke into a run. He was nearly back to town when he finally spotted her on the road ahead.

"Medea!"

Fog wreathed her as she paused and turned to face him. Her hand clutched a pale blue orb, illuminating the mist with unearthly light. A Mundane would have thought her a will-o'-the-wisp bent on leading him to his doom.

His breath came fast and heavy as he halted. Was he sweating? He raked a hand through his hair in case it had fallen out of place. It was unseemly to approach her so, but he couldn't let her leave angry, not with so little time left. Tomorrow was Monday. Tuesday she would be gone.

"May I"—he took a gulp of air and tried to calm his breathing —"walk with you?"

"I suppose."

"About tonight—"

"Do you always use a wand for sparring?"

"Yes. I—"

"Do the others?"

"Yeah. It's considered the standard."

"Is it?" There was a note of concern in her voice.

"Not for all spells, of course. Potions don't need a wand, or spells that require physical ingredients, but other than that . . ." He shrugged.

"I see." Medea focused on the road ahead and they walked for a time in silence, her face unreadable. What he wouldn't give to be able to see Magi thoughts without being detected.

"Your opponents, they seem rather . . . Is that the standard level of talent around here?"

"Unfortunately, yes. Same for the Academy. Dueling was discouraged, not that many kids in Haven attend the Academy. Most stay at home and learn their family's trade spells. None of it's offensive though—potions, charms, that kind of thing. Some of them didn't even have wands or had hand-me-downs. I had to show them how to craft one, bind it, all that. Otherwise they would have been useless as sparring partners."

Her frown deepened.

"Look, I wanted to apologize—"

"I can't teach you." She seemed to say it to herself as much as him. "You have potential and ambition. You'll do fine on your own. If you trained with me, it would not end well for you. It would be a shame to see you die. Best put the whole thing out of your mind."

She was wavering, he could taste it. The sparring match had worked despite his outburst. He had to press his advantage now.

The most annoying voice in the world sounded behind them.

"*There* you are!"

Shailyn trotted up the path. She threaded her arm through Nikolai's and pressed against him. Only then did she pretend to notice Medea. "Oh, hello. I'm Shailyn. And you are?"

"Leaving," said Medea. She stepped off the path and extinguished her light and his hopes, leaving them in darkness. Somewhere in the distance, a sheep bleated.

"Brrr, it's cold!" Shailyn snuggled against Nikolai's limp arm. If he'd been carrying the dagger, he would have been tempted to stab her.

"It's not cold, and you're dressed for the weather."

She startled at his tone. He freed his arm and strode toward town. She jogged to keep up.

"*Ignis. Ignis. Ignis.*" Fire shot from the tip of his wand, thudding into the dirt every few steps.

"I didn't know you could summon fire! Why don't you use it in duels?"

Because we duel in a barn full of hay, stupid bitch.

"*Ignis. Ignis.*"

"You were great tonight. Everyone was impressed. Not me, though. I always knew you could take on four. I'm just glad everyone else got to see it. You were wonderful, do you know that? Absolutely spectacular. I should take lessons from you." She looked up at him expectantly.

"Ignis. Ignis."

"I'm sure Mary will be alright. Ethne was concerned, but she seemed fine to me. Bruised is all. Have you been to see Ethne this week?" She laughed nervously. "I thought you might have given me up for her. Who was that other woman? She didn't look too happy to see me."

They crested a hill with a lone hawthorn tree. Nikolai envisioned Shailyn and aimed his wand at the trunk.

"Flamma!" A fireball shot from the tip of his wand and winged toward the tree, which blossomed into flame.

Shailyn gasped and covered her mouth with her hands. "Nikolai!"

"You said you were cold." He yanked her close and sought her mouth. That would shut her up. She melted against his chest. Thrice a week for the past year, he'd pleasured her as no man before, and this was how she repaid him? By interrupting what might have been the most important conversation of his life?

He broke the kiss and grabbed her arm, tugging her through the damp grass, heedless of how she stumbled to keep up. At the base of the tree he flung her down. Her eyes danced with excitement and the reflected light of the flames. He fucked her hard as the tree burned, punishment for her transgression, though she seemed to enjoy it more than their usual romps. When he finished, he left her by the smoldering ash and stalked home alone.

Nikolai sat at his desk, head in his hands. He ran his fingers through his dark hair, as if by massaging his scalp he could force a new idea into his brain. Tomorrow was his last meeting with Medea. The following day she would depart.

Motivating people was simple—find out what they wanted and convince them you alone could get it. Everyone wanted something, even if it was intangible. What did Medea value? What could he give her that no one else could? Did Petrov have something he could steal? Did anyone else in this godforsaken town?

He opened the desk drawer and fished out the speed dagger, borrowed on the pretense he'd found a buyer. Twirling lines formed intricate patterns on the golden handle. Even unenchanted, it would have been a fine blade, yet Medea had mocked him for wanting it. What had Petrov said? She always chose books, scrolls, manuscripts—items she couldn't make for herself. Knowledge was what she valued most. Knowledge . . .

He glanced at the shelf above his desk, home to his old textbooks—*Potions of the World*, *History of Dueling*, *Wand Crafting and Use*, *Defensive Spells Vol. 2*, *Illustrious Illusions*. The last had been autographed and given to Nikolai as a joke. *Potions* was a good reference, though he had little use for potions these days. The others he kept to loan to Dueling Club members. How laughable Medea would find these. Even the few books he'd managed to collect on black magic, like Ruggeri's tome on necromancy, were probably child's play compared to . . . to . . .

Nikolai's eyes widened. He had an idea. It was a gamble, but it was the only thing he could think that might work. This was it. It had to be. He grabbed his book on illusions and flipped through it. Yes . . . yes, this would work, he was sure of it. He rifled through his room until he found a large enough sack and stuffed the textbooks inside one by one.

The next day, he strode purposefully into the Hanged Man

with the bag slung over his shoulder. Medea smiled and closed her book, but he remained standing behind his usual chair. She was anticipating one last lunch with him and he needed to deprive her of that. It was important she miss his company.

"I won't be staying today." She looked surprised. Good. "I attended the Academy for several years. I tried to learn everything I could. Unfortunately, their curriculum is quite . . . restrictive. There were no good mentors there, not for the things I wanted to learn. Do you know what their most popular subject is? Illusion, so you can earn a living performing magic in front of the Mundane, because they'll assume you're doing tricks."

Her brow furrowed. So, she didn't know what it was like at the Academy. All the better.

"They sat down with each of us prior to graduation, making career recommendations based on our strengths. For me, they recommended séances or fake soothsaying." He smiled bitterly. "The Mundane pay well for such services, and if money was all I cared about, I could easily have done well in that line of work."

She opened her mouth to speak, but he quickly continued.

"That's not what I want. I want real knowledge. I want to *understand*. Yes, I want power, but that's what knowledge *gives*. I will not settle for anything less. But what are my options? Study on my own? I've tried. Knowledge is scarce. Even the Mundane have public libraries. What do we have? Nothing."

He spoke passionately and without pause, leaving her no gaps with which to graciously interrupt. If she did, he'd have to talk over her as if he hadn't heard. Thankfully, she seemed transfixed by his words.

"The only avenue for advanced study is apprenticeship. I thought Petrov could teach me what I want to know. He can't. I see that now."

Medea sat as if frozen, face impossible to read, but he noted her intake of breath when he mentioned the lack of libraries.

Excellent. He slid the bag off his shoulder and placed it carefully on the table.

"I respect your decision not to teach me. As friendly as we've become these past few days, you owe me nothing." She opened her mouth again, but he pretended not to see. "Yet I have one small favor to ask." He placed his hand on the bag. "These are my textbooks from the Academy. I'd like you to look through them. If you believe I've learned as much as I can, that I can reach my full potential given my current resources, fine. However, if you think I could do better under someone else, I'd appreciate any recommendations you can offer. Petrov was at the top of a very short list. Oh, and here—"

He withdrew an envelope from his pocket and held it out to her. She startled as if poked and took it, her face a mask of confusion.

"My address. I look forward to your letter. Thank you for the company this week. It's been a pleasure."

It wasn't until he turned to go that she finally spoke. There was a delicious note of desperation in her voice. "Are you sure you can't stay? You have to eat after all . . ."

"I'm afraid I must get back to the shop. Petrov is expecting me, and I've taken up too much of your time already." He smiled at her and left.

8

UNINVITED

Nikolai went straight home after his shift ended to wait for Medea, confident his plan would work. Some people had core values, intangible things that spoke to their souls—if you believed in such things—and Medea's was knowledge. By emphasizing his desire for knowledge and demonstrating that his options were limited, he'd effectively thrown the problem at her feet.

Medea could ignore it, but then she'd be preventing him from learning, which was against her values. Whether she wanted to teach him or not was irrelevant. It would chafe in just the right spot. To get relief, she'd have to recommend another teacher or take him on herself. Either way, he'd won.

As he shut the door, he glanced around the small apartment, overwhelmed with the desire to pack. He'd added small embellishments over the last two years, pilfered from Mundane establishments outside of Haven.

A large mirror hung next to the front door. Tasteful artwork, chosen to appeal to female guests, adorned the walls. Silk sheets invited use of the bed, though he preferred nocturnal activities take place elsewhere. Easier to leave someone else's place than convince a woman to go home after sex. On the desk was a picture of a stranger who could pass for his mother if the question of family came up. Aside from clothes and books, he could leave most of these things behind.

The place was simple, clean, functional. Satisfactory but not satisfying. He couldn't afford the opulence he desired on his current salary, and stealing too much would have raised suspicion. One day he'd have a home worthy of him—a sprawling mansion with vaulted ceilings, immaculate gardens, fountains and frescoes, high hedges and iron gates for privacy, and a swimming pool like he'd seen in American movies.

Packing was out of the question. Medea might show up in the middle. He'd caught her off-guard, but she wasn't stupid. Once she'd had a chance to think through their conversation, she'd realize he was trying to play her. His play was good enough it shouldn't matter, but seeing him pack would be a slap in the face.

He moved to the wood-burning stove and put the kettle on just to have something to do. As he waited for the water to boil, he wiped down the already-clean table, nightstand, and desk. The water announced itself with a shrill whistle. His supply of black tea was running low. No need to buy more; he'd be leaving soon. While the tea steeped, he grabbed an empty plate and took out his wand.

"Panem."

A flaky golden *pirog* appeared on the plate. He cut a small square and pushed it to the side of the plate with his fork, then sliced into the center of the pastry. Steam billowed forth, filling the air with the scent of beef and onions. He ate rapidly, mouth open to dispel the heat, tongue shuffling food around to minimize the burns. Soon the plate was clear, save for the piece he'd pushed aside and a scattering of flakes that had stubbornly avoided his fork. He rose and resolutely scraped the last piece into the trash, glancing at the clock.

He hadn't really expected her to show up in time for dinner. She'd probably eat at the inn, then come see him. Or maybe she had her own packing to do. She was leaving tomorrow, after all.

Nikolai looked around the spotless apartment, trying to find something else to tidy. The shelf that had previously held his textbooks now contained gaping holes. He attacked it with gusto, moving books around until it looked neat once more.

A knock sounded. Perfect. He knew she'd come.

"Just a moment!" He took his time crossing the room. It wouldn't do to appear too eager. At the mirror, he paused to smooth his hair and practice a surprised face. A snatch of conversation came from beyond the door. Two voices, both female. Shailyn's high-pitched voice was unmistakable.

He wrenched the door open. Shailyn was taller than her counterpart and looked down on Ethne with a smile that said she would win whatever this was. When she saw Nikolai, she gave him a boisterous greeting and whirled past him without invitation. Ethne remained in the hall, face full of worry.

"I'm sorry, I didn't mean to intrude. I need a private word if that's okay." She glanced past him to Shailyn, who'd already shed her coat and thrown it across the bed and was now helping herself to biscuits in the pantry.

He had to get them out of here before Medea showed up. Ethne was the reasonable one, but whatever she wanted might take longer. "I'll be a minute," he called over his shoulder as he stepped into the hallway with Ethne and closed the door. "This is as private as you're going to get with her in there. What's going on?"

"It's about yesterday . . ."

"What about yesterday?" He glanced down the hallway at a noise, but it was just an aged tenant shuffling downstairs.

Ethne took a deep breath. "You hurt Mary pretty bad."

"Mary! I *knew* I hit her too hard!" He palmed his forehead as he chastised himself. "I had to rush out so fast I completely forgot to check on her. Is she okay?" His eyes pleaded for good news. Sympathy was something he'd practiced extensively in the mirror.

"We think she might've cracked a rib. I gave her a healing draught, but she's still pretty sore. There's no good healer in town since the Dunns moved away, but I think she'll be alright."

"I'm glad she's in your capable hands. Please keep me informed on how she's doing. If there's anything I can do, just let me know. I hate to see any of my duelists injured. Was there anything else?"

She looked down and rubbed one arm. "I thought, maybe . . . you know, I thought you might've done it on purpose . . . because of us."

He placed a hand on her shoulder. "Ethne, how could you even *think* such a thing? Mary is my *friend*. When she told me about your relationship, I was relieved. I'll be leaving Haven shortly, you see, and I was worried you might get lonely with me being gone. I'm so happy you two found each other. She can give you so much more than I can." Except for the one thing he had that Mary didn't. He desperately wanted to ask which one of them was better. Him, obviously, but it would be nice to hear her say it.

"I feel stupid. I should've known, but you left so quickly, I thought you didn't care."

Her eyes were actually getting misty. God, he loved this.

"Of course I care. I'm the one who should be apologizing. I've been so distracted this week, I've let everything else slip. You, Mary—hell, Mary had to remind me about the club meeting, if you can believe that!"

Ethne dabbed her eyes and gave a weak chuckle.

"Listen, I gotta get back to—" He nodded his chin toward the door.

"I'll let you go. Thank you so much, Nikolai." She embraced him and started down the hallway.

He watched her for a moment. Damnit, he had to know. "Hey, Ethne!" She pivoted. "Which one of us is better?" She laughed and shook her head. What the hell did that mean? Compulsively, his mind reached out and brushed hers.

"Nikolai!" She swatted the air at his contact, as if telepathy was a fly buzzing around her head.

"Sorry! Sorry. It was an accident." He tried to shrug it off, but her walk became brisk. One day he'd figure out how to do that without detection, but there was no way to practice without alienating himself from the Magi community.

Her thoughts had been Useless anyway. She hadn't been thinking about his question, just getting back to Mary. Mary Mary Mary. Fuck both of them.

He reentered the apartment with the intention of getting rid of Shailyn as quickly as possible. Instead, he found her naked and enshrined on his bed. She'd blown out all the lamps, leaving only candles on the nightstand. What the hell was she thinking? What if he'd invited Ethne in? Sure, Ethne, come on in, would you like some vagina with your tea? Probably, but that was beside the point. If Medea came now it would be a disaster.

"I waited for you," Shailyn purred.

"You need to leave." He collected her discarded clothes from the floor and tossed them to her. She let them fall and pushed herself up from the bed.

"You've never said no to me before," she pouted.

She'd never been this annoying before. "It's not a good time."

"You haven't been to see me all week. I had to track you down yesterday. It's enough to make a girl think you don't care." Arms were suddenly around him. Greedy lips found his. One of her hands plunged inside his trousers. God, he wanted it, but there wasn't any time. The last thing he needed was for Medea to come by midthrust. Bad enough he'd have to conceal his rising interest. He removed Shailyn's hand and pushed her back. She blinked at him in confusion.

"I mean it. Now isn't a good time. I'm expecting someone."

Her face darkened. "It's that woman you were talking to yesterday, isn't it? Who is she anyway?"

"Someone I'm trying to get an apprenticeship with."

"Do you think I'm stupid?" She put a hand on her bare hip. "You already have an apprenticeship!"

"And I'm trying to get a better one."

"You expect me to believe that?"

"I don't really care if you believe it or not, so long as you get out of my apartment before she gets here." He shouldered past her, grabbed the clothes off the bed, and shoved them against her belly. She made no move to accept them. "If I have to, I'll throw you out as you are."

Shailyn snatched the clothes and began to dress, taking longer than necessary. He moved to the window and glanced out. No sign of Medea, thank god.

"Don't call on me again," she said as she buttoned her blouse, concealing her biggest assets.

"Funny, I was about to tell you the same thing."

On the way out, she slammed the door with such force that the mirror dropped to the ground and shattered. Great. He remained at the window. It would be a stroke of bad luck if she encountered Medea on her way down. Only when Shailyn reappeared below did he abandon his post to clean up the mirror. He tugged the bedding straight again and sat down with a book, dragging the chair closer to the window.

An hour later, he was still waiting. What the hell was taking Medea so long? He could have slept with Shailyn and had plenty of time to spare! Didn't she realize he had things to do? Her behavior was utterly inconsiderate.

The hour grew late. Should he get in his pajamas? Too casual, but if he remained in his day clothes, she would know he'd been waiting for her. Sleep was out of the question. He didn't want to risk missing her knock or waking up groggy and unkempt.

He compromised by dressing for bed and reading in the chair, or trying to. She would come.

Medea snapped the book shut and rubbed the bridge of her nose.

"Find what you were looking for?" the Botanist asked. A former apprentice, and a decent one at that. Too bad he hadn't stuck around to complete his training.

"I don't know."

On the one hand, it was nice to find out the boy hadn't lied. On the other hand, the truth was bleak. The boy was right. There was no way he could train himself, not if this was what passed for magical education these days. Handing him off to someone else would accomplish nothing. The boy was like a vial of nitroglycerin—one wrong bump and he was apt to explode with devastating consequences. He required a steady hand, and if she wanted it done right, she'd have to do it herself.

"Medea?"

"Huh?"

The Botanist stood holding their teacups. He yawned. "I said, is there anything else you needed tonight?"

"No, sorry. Thank you for letting me check your books." She collected the boy's books and left, vaguely registering the "good night" voiced behind her.

There *had* to be a way to train an apprentice without killing them. Well, a dark apprentice anyway. This was never a problem with a *normal* student. Why couldn't they all be like the Botanist? Where had she gone wrong with the others?

Obviously their baser instincts led them to pursue "dark" magic, and for some reason, they always tried to kill her. To what end? They already had access to her library. What else did they want?

Always she'd put the blame on the student, on their character, but perhaps the fault was her own. Was it not the job of the master to train the student? That she excelled at magic did not necessarily make her a good teacher.

She spun around and walked back to the small cottage in the woods, rapping soundly on the door.

The Botanist took a moment to answer. "Forget something?"

"Why do my apprentices keep trying to kill me? Is there something I could be doing differently?"

He leaned heavily against the doorframe. "Yes, you could stop training necromancers and pyromancers and demonologists."

"Those are perfectly acceptable magical schools. You know a bit of demonology yourself!"

"Yes, but I'm not trying to take over the world, am I? Medea, it's a little late for this."

"I'm not going to stop training magic."

"*Dark* magic."

"*Magic.*"

He shook his head and yawned. "Did it ever occur to you that letting students wander free in that library of yours was only encouraging them? They can look up anything, for chrissakes."

"They come to me because they want to *learn*—"

"They want to *learn* how to *kill people*. And you're surprised when they want to kill you?"

She opened her mouth and closed it again. Surprised wasn't the right word. Insulted maybe, that they could be so stupid. Anyone who spent more than five minutes with her should see how impenetrable her defenses were. Killing her was a laughable goal.

"Look," he continued, "part of teaching is knowing when your students are ready for certain information. If you give it to them all at once, they can't make sense of it. Dish it out slowly, when they're ready. *If* they're ready."

"I'll not censor myself."

"Then don't be surprised when things turn out the same as they always do. Good night."

He shut the door before she could think of a retort.

Medea walked down the lane, turning off into the woods at a certain stump that used to be a great tree. Dead now, like everything else she'd ever known. Moss gave it a shaggy coat and conk mushrooms decorated one side. Even in death, the tree still served some purpose. Medea stopped to slice off several conks and add them to the pouch on her hip.

Death was something she'd long since grown accustomed to. It was inevitable. Less inevitable was watching apprentices die. Other masters didn't seem to have this problem. Of course, other masters churned out unprepared students.

Perhaps the fault was with her training, but she couldn't see how. Her students—those who survived and didn't try to kill her —were some of the most powerful Magi she'd ever known. Withholding information felt dirty. Knowledge was the greatest gift one could bestow on another. It was *meant* to be shared.

Then again, not everyone was like her. Many of her students lacked restraint, especially since the Collective had formed and started passing laws against certain types of magic. As abhorrent as it seemed, perhaps limiting the boy's knowledge would be prudent, at least in the beginning. If she could direct him toward other subjects . . .

That was it!

Always, she'd allowed them to pick their specialties from day one. Most of them had such a narrow view of what was possible they picked the first thing that popped into their heads. She'd never argued because it was their decision to make. So, delay the choice. Give the boy a firm grasp of *all* magical schools before allowing him to pick a specialty. She wasn't holding back information per se, simply ensuring he had what he needed to make an informed decision.

Medea opened her pouch and fished around for paper and pen. She needed to jot down the preparations she had to make for the boy's arrival, before they'd slipped from her mind. No time to get to it tonight. He must be informed of her decision. Hopefully it wouldn't be a mistake.

Nikolai's head jerked up. Damn! He'd dozed off. Something had woken him—was it a knock?

"Coming!" He put the book aside and hastily pulled a robe over his clothes. For all he knew, Medea could've been knocking for some time before he'd woken. As he opened the door, he pretended to stifle a yawn.

"Yes? What is it? Medea! It's rather late. What brings you—"

"Stop the act." She barged into the apartment and leaned against his kitchen table, arms crossed, face even more severe than usual.

"Whatever you need, couldn't it have waited until morning?"

"Pfft. As if you haven't been waiting up for me."

"As a matter of fact, you just woke me."

"Oh, really? Tell me, do you normally sleep levitating above a perfectly made bed?" She gestured to his immaculately tucked blankets.

"*Actually*, I fell asleep in a chair while reading."

"You mean the chair conveniently positioned next to your window?"

"The light's better there during the day."

"Is it really that difficult to speak the truth we both know? I can see the scratch marks on your floor from when you moved the chair! Do you always lie compulsively? Never mind, don't answer that."

She took a deep breath and let it out. "Look, if we're going to have a working relationship, you need to be honest. I know you manipulated me today. It's rather disturbing to realize that and know I'm going to acquiesce anyway." She twisted her hands absently and began to pace.

Nikolai smiled and moved to the kitchenette. "I prefer to think I made a compelling argument. Tea?"

She didn't appear to be listening. "Those books . . . I thought they might be fake. I *hoped* they might be fake. I tracked down the few alumni in town and checked their textbooks."

He had a sudden image of the pint-sized blonde woman barging into people's homes demanding to see their schoolbooks.

"They matched yours, so I checked the Academy book dealer, then visited a few people abroad."

"Why?"

"To verify their authenticity, of course."

"You thought I forged my own books *and* everyone else's in town *and* the book dealer's?"

She paused her pacing to look at him. "Well, yes. You're talented and rather desperate to get what you want. I don't know what connections you have or how long you've been planning this."

"I didn't even know the shop here sold Academy textbooks." The Academy was in Turkey. Why would a shop in Ireland carry their books?

She waved a hand dismissively. "It doesn't. I went to Istanbul.

Then Germany to visit a colleague and see his books. I can't believe how little they teach you of the basics, let alone combat or advanced magic . . ."

"How the hell did you get from here to Turkey to Germany and back so fast?"

"See?" Medea stopped pacing and gestured at him with both arms. "*This* is what I'm talking about. You don't even know what's possible! As far as I can tell, all they've taught you is bad habits."

Medea stared at the floor, eyes darting back and forth as if she were reading. "I'll have to undo that. We'll have to start from scratch . . ." She trailed off, speaking inaudibly to herself.

She'd used the phrase "working relationship," but confirmation was needed. When it came to agreements between Magi, wording mattered. Not all pacts were magically binding. For those that were, it was perfectly acceptable to find creative ways around an agreement, but karma or some other force might come down on those who broke their word. Perhaps that too was superstition.

Nikolai cleared his throat. "So, you'll teach me?"

"Huh? Oh, yes. Damn it all, yes. You're right, there's really no one else to teach you. Even if I could recommend a colleague, you'd likely be running circles around them in a year. I do have conditions, though." She straightened, her tone businesslike.

"What conditions?" Not that it mattered, he'd agree to them regardless, but it was important he appear to weigh seriously.

"One, you must be honest with me. I cannot help you if I don't have the information I require. Holding back, for fear of reprisal or exposure or judgment, will only cause your education to be delayed and sidetracked. If you wish to know something, ask. I will do my best to give you a complete and accurate answer, and train you in any magic you desire to learn. That is my vow to you. Is this acceptable?"

"Yes."

"Two, do not attempt to kill me." She sighed and shook her head. "I know you probably will. They always do, and it's such a waste. Just . . . don't make me kill you for such an insult. If you think you can beat me in a duel after all I teach you, then it will prove you have learned nothing. Give me your word. I know you won't mean it, but a vow must be given for it to be broken."

Easy to lie, but she was expecting it. "I thought you wanted me to be honest with you?"

Her mouth opened in surprise. She thought a moment before answering. "Give me . . . whatever honest vow you can."

Generations of apprentices had gone before him and told the same lie. Time to stand out. But what honest vow could he give that wouldn't make her call the whole thing off?

Medea waited as the silence stretched.

"I vow I won't try to kill you until I am certain I can win."

"Thank you for your honesty," she said quietly. "If you are ever certain, check again. But if that is what you truly wish, I will honor your request for a *Servitus aut Mors* duel. Now, what number was I on?"

"Three." Interesting that she thought he'd ever challenge her to a fair fight, or that he needed to outmatch her in magic to kill her. Winning was more about exploiting your opponent's weaknesses than overpowering them.

"Ah, yes! Three, my home, my rules. We will be together for a good long while. I have strict rules regarding my place and my possessions. I expect you to follow them. I promise they are not too strict or out of the ordinary."

A rule for following rules? Seemed redundant and unnecessary. Perhaps her age affected her brain, regardless of how young she looked. He nodded.

"Your vow," she said.

"I will follow your rules."

"Four, your apprenticeship ends when I say it does. It will be long. How long, I cannot say, but it will most certainly be many years before you reach the rank of master. Very few of my apprentices attain this rank. Most leave before their time has been fulfilled, or else attempt to kill me and perish. Know that you are free to leave at any time. I will, however, be forever disappointed by your lack of foresight. There are benefits to becoming a master under me."

"Like what? Aside from the knowledge gained, of course." Unless there was some clear advantage to completion, there was no reason to stick around any longer than necessary to learn what he needed.

"Masters are granted permanent access to my library, my laboratory—all my facilities. You will not understand the significance of this until you've seen them. I also offer a parting gift. It is bound to the individual and cannot be used by anyone else. When they die—*if* they die—the item returns to me."

He'd have to find out what this item was and if it was worth the extra time. "I vow to complete my training and acknowledge that if I choose to leave prior to obtaining the rank of master, I will not be entitled to any of its benefits."

"Five—"

How many rules did this woman have?

"Your apprenticeship will be painful. Of late, my students have described my methods as cruel and barbaric. My vow is to make you stronger—not just in magic, but in mind. I cannot build upon a weak foundation. Some of my tasks will seem pointless or dangerous. Everything I do has a purpose. There is no easy path to power. I will protect you as much as I can, but the training is not without harsh consequences, some of which can be fatal. Do you vow to do as I say, without complaint, for your own benefit?"

"Yes."

"Very well. Take whatever time you need tomorrow, then meet me at the inn when you're ready."

As soon as she was out the door, he began packing his clothes. Everything else could stay. He would meet Medea as early as possible in the morning. No reason to linger. There was no one in Haven he needed to say good-bye to, no one he cared about. All that remained was to get out of his contract with Petrov.

9

PETROV'S SECRET

Nikolai entered the shop in good humor. His new life was about to begin. Petrov muttered behind the counter as his wand moved over an amulet with the characteristic flourish of a protection spell. At his elbow, a pile of mail threatened to fall.

"Good morning!" Nikolai smiled at his mentor but received only a grunt in return. No matter. He opened the shutters, watered the plant, and brought out the till for the register. Petrov was usually chatty in the mornings. Perhaps the poisoning had weakened him. That was well enough. It might make the news of Nikolai's leaving easier to bear. He was just about to bring up the topic when Petrov cleared his throat.

"There's something we need to discuss. You've been neglecting your work."

"I covered for you the whole time you were sick!"

"Aye, and you skived off your duties the rest of the week—taking long lunches, ducking out early, not paying attention. I won't have it."

"Well, you won't have to deal with me any longer. After today I am no longer your apprentice. I've convinced Medea to take me on."

Petrov's face darkened. "Is that so? You owe me two more years, boy, and I'm the one who gets to decide if you're to be released early. I'll not have you gallivanting after that woman just so that you can end up dead in a few years."

"I didn't realize you cared," Nikolai said acidly.

"I care enough not to let you make such a foolish decision."

"It's not foolish, and it's my decision!"

"Is it now?" Petrov barked out a laugh. "You signed a contract, remember? Four years working for me and I'll teach you what I know."

"You haven't taught me anything Useful. All day you keep me cooped up in this shop, handling your customers while you mess around in the back. And what do I have to show for it? A few enchantments and lame curses—nothing I couldn't have learned on my own."

"I've taught you plenty more than that," Petrov growled.

"You've taught me how to lay low like a whipped dog after a little bit of heat from the Collective."

Petrov jammed a finger into his chest. "Don't you dare speak to me that way! You will stay here and finish what you started. I won't discuss it again." With that, he turned his back on Nikolai and busied himself with the items on the counter. Then, more softly, "It's for the best. I don't like to think what would become of you if you went into her care."

Nikolai fumed. Petrov had no right to keep him here. He mentally flipped through the contract. It was a simple arrangement. Work and a modest income in exchange for knowledge. It ended when Petrov said so, or after four years, whichever came first. Nikolai could think of only one other way out of it.

His fingers brushed the speed dagger concealed in his pocket. No. He was not Medea, to get away with such a thing. What if he had to come back here?

The rest of the day, Nikolai was careful to present his usual charming self. It would be difficult enough to pass off Petrov's death as an accident, but he was leaving town that very night and would be a prime suspect if it was undeniably murder. All day he contemplated how best to do it. Should he fake a break-in? Stab the man in the storeroom, then pile boxes of weapons on top of the body to make it look like they had fallen? Poison? They all seemed too obvious. He might have to risk it and change his identity afterward. Medea's apprenticeship was worth the risk.

At closing time, he was still mulling it over. He locked the door and shuttered the windows as Petrov counted the till. It was now or never. He transferred the dagger from his pocket to his sleeve and started toward Petrov, with no more plan than to lure the man into the back. Before he could open his mouth, Petrov spoke.

"You did well today. I'm proud of you. I know you're still angry with me, but you didn't let it impact your work. That takes real control. Come here, there's something I'd like to show you."

Petrov walked halfway to the back and stopped outside his office. Nikolai followed obediently. Maybe he'd earned enough goodwill that the old man had changed his mind.

"I never told you why I left home, did I?"

Nikolai shook his head.

"I'm sure you've heard rumors, but as usual, rumors tend to fall far from the truth. I dabbled in black magic, that much is true, but I never did anything bad. You know how it is—a guy beats his wife, she comes to me, and I curse him for her. I helped maintain the peace and never took advantage of people. Everyone in town knew about my magic, and they respected me for it. Not like here, where you have to hide everything from the Mundane."

Petrov sighed. "I made a terrible mistake. I . . ." He closed his eyes, steeling himself against the memory. "I caught my wife in bed with my brother. I don't know what came over me, but I do know this—if I hadn't known those kinds of spells, I might not have acted so rashly. Maybe I would have talked to them. Not sure what they would have said, but when a man loses his wife and his brother in the same instant, it's bound to make you think of how things could've been different. I was impulsive, and it cost me everything. The worst was after. I couldn't live with what I'd done. I couldn't let it rest . . . let *them* rest."

Nikolai perked up at this. Finally the man was getting to the point. "You resurrected them? I didn't think such a thing was possible." Resurrection was almost as good as immortality. Maybe there was something to be learned from the old man yet. But Petrov was quick to dash his hopes.

"No. Necromancy isn't true resurrection. The bodies reanimated, and they moved, but there was nothing left of my wife or my brother." He shook his head. "I couldn't control them. They ran about like savage beasts, and I put them down like animals. By then, the whole town knew what I'd done. I'd crossed a line. All because of one lapse in judgment. My hasty actions were bad enough, but instead of owning up to my mistake, I tried to fix it and made things worse."

What was the point of all this? Did Petrov seek to placate him with stories of poor necromancy? The sooner he got this over with, the sooner he could be on his way.

"I see a bit of myself in you," Petrov continued. "I was always drawn to the darker magics. But I tell you, boy, they require a certain frame of mind. They require control, and you've an impulsive streak. It's a bad combination. Today you showed me that you can leash your emotions when you've a mind to. If you prove to me that you can hold back, maybe I can teach you a bit of what I know."

Nikolai kept his face impassive even as his temper flared. A bit? The man admitted he'd taught him nothing the past two years, and he expected Nikolai to be fine with it?

Petrov reached a hand toward Nikolai, and for a moment he

thought the old man would pat his shoulder, but it extended past him to the wall. When Petrov's palm touched the wood, it dissolved to reveal a doorway. Petrov flicked his wand several times, and oil lamps blazed to life.

Shelves lined the walls in the room beyond, stocked with black magic artifacts—candles, feathers, bones, and body parts floating in jars. Rats stared with beady eyes from a rusted cage dangling from the ceiling. A grey, pockmarked altar took up most of the back wall. Wooden floor planks changed to smooth stone tiles as Nikolai entered. A summoning circle, at least six feet across, dominated the center of the room. The red paint on the floor drew the eye and pulsed the air with subtle magic. Nikolai stared in disbelief.

Petrov grinned. "Impressive, eh?"

"Indeed." Nikolai forced a smile. Two years. The man had hidden this from him for two years. Why hadn't he thought to cast a revealing spell in the hallway? Because it hadn't occurred to him that Petrov had anything to hide, at least not on this scale. The room, fascinating as it was, was tainted with Petrov's betrayal.

The shelf closest to the door was lined with books—*Treatise of Life and Death*, *Forbidden Funeral Rites*, *The Key of Hell*. He moved further down the shelves, where *Pseudomonarchia Daemonum* was wedged next to *Binding Demons*. Nikolai chose a book on curses and flipped through it. Minor hexes, ill luck charms—there had to be something here he could use.

"Now then, what's something simple I could teach you . . . ah! I have it. How about a séance spell? You lost your family in the war, didn't you? I'm sure you'd like to hear from them again."

Nikolai could think of nothing he'd like less. What did a young man like himself have to say to the ghosts of children? Father went to war and never came back, the same as so many others, and he'd never missed the man. As for his mother, they hadn't spoken since he left Russia—not that she was speaking much to him then. He had no idea how she fared, nor did he care.

The past was something to leave behind. Petrov's casual presumption was insulting, but he found people got choked up about the war and did his best to mimic the expected response.

"Thank you for the offer." Nikolai took a deep breath and continued with a quaver in his voice. "I'm afraid I must decline. It's not something I'm ready for yet. Is there something else you can show me? Something more . . ." He left the thought hanging and gestured vaguely. To say he wanted something more interesting would have been discourteous.

Petrov gave him a sympathetic look and turned to inspect his shelves. "Hmm, something more fun . . ." His fingers trailed over different objects until he came face to face with the cage. "Here we go. Sit down and watch." His manner spoke of a man anxious to show off.

Nikolai sat on the far side of the summoning circle, book open in his lap. He did his best to show interest in Petrov as he scanned the book for spells with backfire potential. The Academy loved to tell cautionary tales of clandestine black magic practitioners who fell victim to their own experiments. Whether or not the tales were true was irrelevant—people believed them. No one would look askance at a man who died in a room with black magic etched on every surface.

Petrov pulled a fat brown rat from the cage. Before the creature could struggle, he neatly snapped its neck and placed the limp body in the center of the circle, withdrawing his wand.

"Seco." Blood welled in the wake of the wand as he traced the cutting spell across his own thumb. He made a fist over the rat. Scarlet dotted the rodent's fur and dripped onto the cold stone floor. Petrov began a low, guttural chant as he ran his wand in complicated movements over the body. The rat twitched and stood up.

By some method Nikolai could not ascertain, Petrov signaled the beast. It capered about the circle, dancing and flipping in an almost comical fashion. Necromancy was a magic so dark it was taboo even among Magi. The rodent's cavorting made it seem no more than a cheap party trick. It was almost insulting to see it used so frivolously. Nikolai feigned laughter at his mentor's eager smile.

"Control is the hardest part of necromancy. When I first started, the rats ran amok biting things."

"Do you have an army of rats then?" Nikolai asked hopefully.

Petrov laughed. "I'm afraid not. I can only control one at a time."

A single rat was underwhelming compared to what Medea had to offer. From her, he could learn immortality as well as necromancy. The opportunity was too good to pass up.

"Can I pick the next spell?"

"I suppose so. What did you have in mind?"

"Can you summon a wraith?" Nikolai held up the book in his lap and turned it toward Petrov. According to the spell, a wraith was a vengeful spirit that could be used to hunt enemies. Give them something to track—bone, blood, hair, or skin—and they would find their target no matter the distance.

"Pass it here," said Petrov. Nikolai reached across the circle to hand him the book. "Hmm. Seems easy enough. Yes, I think I can do this. Move back, out of the circle. Good. It shouldn't do anything without a target, but it doesn't hurt to be cautious. Safety is important when you cast black magic."

Petrov stood and brandished his wand at the circle. His incantations were pitched higher this time. The inside of the circle darkened and something like smoke began to coalesce and take shape. A wretched face came into being and screeched with the ferocity of a banshee. The body was a formless mist except for two taloned hands.

"The circle will keep it contained. Mind the edges."

The creature turned to Petrov and screeched again. Without warning, it slashed his face. Petrov fell back against a table, knocking over several bottles. Angry gashes lined his cheek. When the wraith crossed the boundary of the circle, Petrov's eyes brimmed with fear.

"H-how?" he stammered. The wraith slashed again, this time scoring his belly. Blood soaked his shirt and dripped to the floor. He hastily conjured a shield and shouted at Nikolai to run, save himself.

"Thank you, but I'd rather stay and watch." Nikolai leaned casually against the opposite wall, hands in his pockets. "The book said the wraith should disappear as soon as its target is dead. I'm in no danger. You, on the other hand, left blood in the circle when you reanimated the rat."

"Then help me, boy! There! On the shelf next to you—the grey powder! Dump it on the beast." Petrov pushed all his power into maintaining his shield. The wraith scraped it with increasing fury, pinning him to the table.

Nikolai plucked up the tub of grey powder and walked toward his mentor at a leisurely pace. "It's a shame you didn't see fit to teach me better spells before tonight or let me out of my apprenticeship willingly—"

"What are you doing? Throw the powder at it!"

The wraith ignored Nikolai, who came to stand beside Petrov. Quick as lightning, the golden dagger bit into Petrov's jugular. The man's eyes widened and his shield winked out.

"Then maybe I wouldn't have to kill you." Nikolai jerked the dagger free and stepped back to let the wraith fall upon its unprotected prey. Petrov's scream melted into a faint gurgle as the wraith savaged his face.

When the deed was done, Nikolai made sure the book was placed on the floor near the circle, open to the page with the wraith spell. It took him longer to find the paint that Petrov had used to make the circle on the floor. Ever so carefully, he painted over the hairline scratch he'd made in the circle with his dagger.

Back at home, Nikolai opened his trunk and pulled out a set of clean clothes. Though he'd done his best to keep out of the splatter, he didn't want to take any chances of a missed spot of blood. He penned a quick letter and stowed it in his pocket. Certain he'd packed everything of import, Nikolai gathered his bags, adjusted his hat, and left the small apartment without a backward glance.

The Hanged Man was not his destination. Not yet. There was one last thing he needed to do. At Petrov's place, he spent a good ten minutes pounding loudly on the door until the neighbor woman stuck her head out the window to curtly inform him that maybe Petrov wasn't in.

"Do you know where he went? I tried at the shop and he didn't answer."

She tugged a moth-eaten shawl closer about her shoulders. "Do I look like his secretary?"

"No, ma'am, and I'm sorry to trouble you, but this is urgent. I've accepted a new position, but I have to leave tonight. I wanted to tell Petrov in person. I owe him that much. Perhaps, if it's not too much trouble, can you give him this letter? It's my resignation."

The woman accepted the envelope with much grumbling.

"Thank you kindly. Please give him my best." Nikolai tipped his hat and set off for the Hanged Man.

Medea had foregone her usual table and awaited him at the bar. She eyed him curiously as he approached. Fearing he had a speck of blood on his face, Nikolai feigned a cough and turned sideways to glance in a mirror mounted nearby. Nothing there. He coughed one more time and turned back.

"Excuse me, and good evening. How will we be traveling?"

She said nothing for a moment but continued to study him. Then, "Did Petrov let you out of your contract?"

"Certainly. I explained the situation and he agreed I could learn far more from you."

"I see." She let the silence stretch until even the barman raised an eyebrow.

Nikolai broke it first. "So, uh, do I have time to order a drink or—"

"Tell me, what was my first rule?"

"Don't try to kill you?"

"Be honest with me."

"Ah, yes."

"I dislike liars. To adequately train you, there must be trust between us. Lying destroys that."

She knew. No, that was impossible. There was no physical evidence of what he'd done. Did she suspect then? Yes. That was it. She knew what kind of man he was and was attempting to manipulate him into giving something away.

"I'm not lying. I really do want to know if I have time to order a drink."

She crossed her arms and waited, but eventually a resigned look came over her face. "Fine. I suppose your apprenticeship does not technically begin until you set foot on my island. There will be consequences the next time you lie to me." She walked past him and up the rickety stairs to the rooms, pausing on the landing. "Coming?"

He wasn't sure if he should bring his luggage, but leaving it unattended didn't seem like the best idea. He pulled out his wand and levitated the trunk to the second floor, then shouldered his rucksack and followed. Every step creaked loudly with his passing. Medea had vanished from sight, but he soon found her again down the long hallway. She waited for him at the last room. At the door, she motioned him inside. Perhaps she wanted to grill him further about Petrov and didn't wish to make a scene downstairs.

Cramped and musty, the room offered little in the way of furniture or comfort. The bed was made up with a garish green quilt that would have been at home in a grandmother's house. It didn't seem worthy of someone with her kind of power. Medea followed him in and closed the door. Not sure where she was going, he tried to step aside, but the confined space made it impossible to get completely out of the way. Her body pressed momentarily against his in passing, leaving a familiar tightening in his pants in its wake.

At the closet she raised her palm to the wood. Suddenly the close quarters and her insistence on having this particular room made sense. There was probably a larger suite hidden beyond the closet door, and this first room was a decoy for assassins. Did the innkeeper know about the second room, or had the secret died out over generations? Medea lowered her hand and opened the door.

Beyond lay the ocean.

10

THE ISLAND

I t was an illusion. It had to be. A trick from a paranoid woman to deter would-be killers.

"You first," said Medea.

Nikolai stepped from the warmth of the inn onto the beach and was nearly brought to his knees as he crossed the barrier. His brain struggled to grasp the sensation, to compare it to something familiar—the first breath after being submerged, the slow trickle of warmth spreading through hands numb with cold, the blessed relief of removing a tie at the end of a long day, a bite of food after a long fast. Nothing had ever felt so profound or so right. He gasped, barely registering where—or who—he was.

"Move."

A sharp poke from behind brought his awareness back. Seabirds cried overhead. A chill wind whipped around him, catching his clothes and spraying his face with a fine mist. The beach sloped up a hill covered with swaying grass. If this was an illusion, it was damn impressive. Fooling one sense was easier than several. It even smelled like a real beach.

Nikolai stepped forward and turned to find Medea exiting a

stone archway. In the center of the archway, hung impossibly in space, was a door-shaped view of the bedroom.

"You look surprised," she said. "Never used a gateway before?"

It took a moment for him to process her words. The sensation, whatever it was, still permeated his being. He was whole and happy, and it was wonderful to be here.

"Are you alright?"

"Absolutely!" He beamed despite himself, wiggling his fingers idly at his sides, as though he could stir up whatever was in the air. "I'm sorry, you asked me a question?"

"I asked if you'd ever used a gateway before."

"No, no." The sensation wasn't going away, but he was getting used to it. He took a deep breath and continued. "At first I thought this might be an illusion."

"It's real. This is my island. You won't find it on any map. I've sunk enough ships that sailors know to avoid the area for fear of treacherous waters, and it's heavily warded against trespassers. Did the Academy fail to educate you on gateways?"

"I came across them in my reading, but I've never met anyone who claimed to be able to make one. Some of my professors seemed to think they were no more than stories dreamed up by the Mundane." He laughed at the idea of his former professors seeing this and circled the archway. The inn was only visible from one side. Around back, he could view Medea between the weathered granite columns. The whole thing sat well above the high-water mark, allowing one to come and go without risk of wet feet.

"I see a lot of that lately. Ironic those who should know the most about magic seem to understand it least. The concept is quite simple really, though it takes a great deal of skill and power to perform. Tell me, do you sew?"

"When I need to mend something," he said, returning to the front of the arch. "Usually a loose button."

Medea grabbed the front corner of his coat, pulling it taut. "Pretend this is the world. Space." She pointed to one button. "This is where we are now." Her fingers walked to a second button. "This is Haven. How do you propose we bring the two together?"

"Fold the coat so they touch."

"Yes! We simply pinch the fabric together until the two meet. That is all a gateway is. It's a place where the caster pinches the two locations together."

"That doesn't make any sense. The world doesn't move like that."

"Not that you can see with your eyes. That is why it takes an advanced practitioner. One who can see beyond what is there, to the space between places. Now, this particular spot is not where you will normally exit. The wards do not recognize you, and so they have redirected us to the beach, rather than inside my home. Stand still so I can identify you to the wards." Medea walked around him. As she did so, sand swept out of the way to form a circle with strange symbols within. "State your name."

"Nikolai Fedorov."

Medea placed a hand on his head and mumbled something in another language, along with his name. "There. Follow me." She led him up the beach, bare feet dodging pieces of driftwood and strands of seaweed buzzing with flies.

The stench of seaweed retreated as sand gave way to grass and a narrow path. The few scattered trees were deciduous, which narrowed their location to a temperate zone. As they crested the slope, Nikolai scanned the horizon, trying to gauge the position of the sun in relation to where it had been in Haven. It seemed lower, but given he was distracted when they left, he couldn't be sure.

Up ahead squatted a dilapidated hovel. Beyond that, in the distance, he could make out a forest. The path veered off to the right of the hovel and headed toward the dense cluster of trees—as good a place as any to hide an estate.

Magi towns did their best to prevent Mundane incursion, but they were still public areas that could be located by anyone with a map. Those who lived outside these safe areas were more careful, with fences to block casual access and bushes to obscure the view of passersby. The Academy, which had to hide a large number of practicing students, was built inside a mountain. The rooms were a network of caves, carved and reinforced with magic, the only entrance well hidden. Concealing a home within a forest of trees on a deserted island unknown to man seemed on par with Medea's level of caution.

As they approached the hovel, the ground became more cluttered. Remnants of a stone wall, broken pillars, and the occasional statue littered the left side of the path, as if someone had taken a smattering of fixtures from a Roman temple and unceremoniously dumped them in the field.

Further up the path lay several neglected garden beds. The area was a riot of color. Wildflowers and weeds battled for space inside the beds and everywhere in between. Bees moved purposefully from bloom to bloom. Cracked pots lay stacked and forgotten next to a rain barrel. An assortment of gardening tools were propped haphazardly against the statue of a crowned woman holding a bundle of grain.

The neatness of the area opposite the garden was jarring by contrast. A low wall surrounded a flat area of gravel. Large moss-covered stones poked out of the gravel like islands. The placement looked intentional, although he could discern no pattern. In front of the wall, a rake leaned against a stone bench. Aside from the moss and a single twisted tree, it was devoid of plant life.

The whole area seemed mismatched. Nikolai half expected to see a rusted bicycle or cans littering the ground. He suspected the hovel had housed several generations of servants, each adding something of their own. Perhaps the latest occupant had no need for the garden beds and chose only to keep up the gravel pit, but to what end he could not see.

At the hovel, Nikolai turned to follow the path veering toward the woods. Medea's voice called him back. She stood at the hovel door.

"You can see the forest later. For now, I'd like to show you your quarters."

She expected him to live in this dump? Bullshit! It didn't even look weathertight. Weeds sprouted from the thatched roof, which threatened to cave in, and the whole structure sagged ponderously to one side.

Medea seemed to guess some of what he was thinking. "I know it doesn't look like much, but it's nicer inside. I just never bothered to keep up the exterior. Come." She opened the door and entered.

He didn't move. Harsh training was one thing, but expecting him to live in squalor while she lived in comfort elsewhere? No. He'd lived in poverty before and had no desire to experience it again. A small part of him wanted to storm back to the beach and take the gateway home, if it was even still open. He hesitated a moment longer and then approached the derelict structure. Sometimes one needed to go forward to go back.

He realized a second too late the door was a touch shorter than average. His head struck the frame. He cried out, then narrowly avoided falling as his feet tripped over something—a pile of muddy boots that had been carelessly piled by the door.

Medea kicked the boots out of the way. "Sorry, I, uh, don't usually have guests."

He rubbed his head and looked around. It did *not* look nicer on the inside. To call it quaint would be generous. The room contained no more than a single table pushed against the wall. It was so cluttered with books, papers, and dried plant clippings that he could not see the surface. A thick layer of dust covered every-thing. No bed. Not even a hearth. His eyes fell to a bucket under the table, and he belatedly recalled he'd seen no backhouse outside. Unacceptable. No wonder so many apprentices tried to kill her.

"This way," said Medea, crossing to the opposite side of the cramped room.

"I think I've seen enough."

"Don't be silly. The rest of the house isn't nearly as bad. I don't really keep it up, as I only come through here on my way out. Not that I'm the tidiest person, but the work areas are far more organized. Come. Place your palm here."

Relieved this was not to be his bedroom, Nikolai approached. The wall must hide another gateway for an added level of secu-rity. He should have realized the hovel was a decoy. He placed his palm upon the wall, and she covered it with her own.

"Say your name again. These wards are different."

"Nikolai Fedorov."

The wall grew warm and a section of it vanished. The room beyond was large—too large to be contained in the hovel they'd entered. Two cozy chairs beckoned toward a crackling fire in a hearth. Ornate rugs adorned the stone floor. As they entered, flat crystals embedded in the ceiling sprang to life, casting soft white light over the room. Dark wood lined the walls, with matching bookcases crowding every available space not taken up by door or hearth. Toward the back, a circular iron staircase led to a loft with a single door.

Something felt off—almost patchwork, as if the room beyond had been cobbled together hastily with no real floor plan. Maybe it was the size. He couldn't make sense of it.

"How . . . ?"

"You just place your palm on the wall and it will open for you," said Medea.

"Not that." He stepped through the opening and gestured around the room. "This! Is it invisible from the outside?"

She frowned. "It's just a simple volume-increasing spell."

Impossible. No, not impossible, as she'd clearly done it. Talented Magi could increase the volume of a container to hold far more than normal. He had enchanted his pack to hold a trunk's worth of space. Enlarged rooms were almost unheard of. The larger the container, the more difficult the spell and the less space, comparatively, you could create. At some point you hit a wall, as if the universe itself pushed back at you. Going beyond that point was dangerous. The Academy told them horror stories of wizards who'd taken it too far and been sucked into their own bags, which then collapsed in on themselves and vanished forever. You had to be careful and know your limits.

This . . . this was ridiculous.

"You have two stories here. And I count seven doors leading elsewhere. How did you do it?"

"I thought you were familiar with the mechanics of the spell —I detect it on your bag."

Did she really not understand how unbelievable this was? Or was it simply that easy for her?

"At the Academy—"

"Which we've established isn't very good. Sorry, go on. Did your school tell you there were limits on this?"

"Well, yes. The largest increase they have on record is a room —I don't remember the dimensions—but it wasn't large, and it only increased by about thirty percent."

"I see. I suppose this does look incredible by comparison. Skill plays a role, though maybe I've succeeded because I added rooms gradually over the years as I've needed them. But I can't possibly be the only person to try that." She shrugged, as if it were of no consequence.

The patchwork vibe made sense now. He tried to piece

together the order in which she'd added rooms. "You started with the shack, then added this room, then . . . the stairs?"

"No, that came later. The house outside and the entrance room —that's original. I never saw the point of starting from scratch with a new building. I'd already added so many enchantments, I doubt I'd remember what to cast all over again. And the size of the house made it easier to transport to the island."

Medea began to talk about the order in which the rooms had been created, except she couldn't remember and kept stopping to correct herself. Soon he was sorry he'd asked. After five minutes that seemed like an eternity, she came to a close.

"The stairs were last. I had two bedrooms down here originally, but I pushed the second one upstairs."

"You moved rooms after they'd been created?"

"It's easier if you think of them like separate boxes, or bubbles, or what-have-you." She mimed moving small objects around. "Just push this one over and make a new one in the middle, connecting the two."

It sounded as if she wasn't expanding space so much as creating all-new spaces. In the middle of nothing. Out of nowhere. And then swapping them around. To his knowledge, no one else had ever done such a thing.

"Now what else did I need to show you?" She pulled a scrap of paper out of her pouch and consulted it. "Ah, yes. Work areas on the left. They will remain locked and warded until I've had a chance to go over them. Common areas on the right. That's your room there. Kitchen is this way." She led him to the last door on the right.

A carpet of dust covered every surface. Tendrils of cobwebs speckled with tiny corpses swayed in the draft from the open door. Just standing in the doorway made him want to cough.

As he crossed the threshold, he had the curious sensation of stepping back in time. Most Magi homes lacked modern appliances, but Medea's kitchen looked as though it hadn't been updated in centuries, with its stone oven, hearth with a spit, and low table. Shelves hosted a modest collection of mismatched plates and cups. Pots hung from the ceiling on metal hooks. At the back of the room a larder sat open, old food decomposing inside —no, not food, some sort of rodent's nest.

Medea strode forward and cried out as she walked face-first into a cobweb. After much spitting and flailing, she held her hands out as if clutching an invisible ball. Dust and debris drifted from around the room into the space between her hands. It gathered into a swirling grey sphere. When the particles stopped flying toward her hands, she looked around with a frustrated grimace. "Where did I put the trash? Bah!" She turned her attention to the mass between her hands. It shrank and hardened until it became compact, then abruptly, the ball was gone.

"Where did it go?"

"Outside somewhere." She waved her hand as if it was of no import. "Do you cook? Or can you summon food?"

"I can conjure a variety of breads and pastries filled with fruit, nuts, or meat." His chest swelled with pride. The other Academy students could get only plain loaves or unleavened bread.

"You should be able to get far more, and it's summoning, not conjuring."

"Is there a difference?"

"Yes. You can't *make* something out of nothing." Her tone implied this was obvious. "That's not how magic works."

He stared at her. Wasn't that exactly how magic worked?

She sighed and sat at the table, motioning him to join her. "I suppose the distinction has been lost over time. Observe."

She stretched out a hand, and a wooden spoon flew off the wall into her palm. "*That's* telekinesis. I am magically *moving* something."

She set the spoon on the table and raised her hand. Flames

erupted in her palm. "*That's* conjuring. Shields too. It's—well, I'm not sure how exactly to describe it. Conjuring creates something, but it's not solid. Not in the traditional sense. It's more like . . . playing with energy." She tilted her hand back and forth; the flames curled into a ball and rolled with the motion. "Much of elemental magic is conjuring. The spells you use in dueling—those are mostly conjuring or telekinesis. Understand?"

"I believe so. And summoning?"

She snapped her hand shut and the flames disappeared. "Summoning is different from conjuring. You cannot conjure a *thing*. The physical substance has to come from somewhere. When you say you are conjuring food, what you are really doing is summoning food across space *to you*."

"Wait a minute, are you saying that when I conjure—I mean summon—bread, I'm stealing it off someone else's plate?"

"Probably."

He laughed, longer and harder than he'd laughed in a long time. Oh, he could have fun with that. How much control did one have over the origin? He'd have to learn the favorite dishes of people who irritated him.

"Yes, well. You see the difference now. The distinction matters, because you have to visualize *exactly* what you want. If you are too vague, you may end up with something half-eaten, undercooked, poisoned—yes, poisoned. Or otherwise contaminated. You have no control over where your food is coming from, so be specific."

The thought was concerning, given how frequently he used the spell. Bread wasn't usually enough to live on long-term, not unless it contained other things baked in, as Nikolai's did, but it was enough to keep Haven alive during the Great Famine. Most people could only summon one type of bread. Even if the Collective hadn't put limitations on how often the spell could be cast, the monotony alone meant people didn't use it more than necessary.

"Is there a range on the spell? Like a limit to how far away the food can be?"

"Not to my knowledge, but there have been times when a summoning has failed to work. In my case, it's usually been a side effect of living so long. Plants that were once common are either no longer cultivated or go extinct." She sighed. "One of my favorite teas vanished like that. Dishes may be lost forever when a civilization is wiped out."

A chipped plate drifted from the shelf and landed in front of Nikolai with a gentle tinkle.

"Show me what you can do. Remember to concentrate on *exactly* what you want."

He stared at the empty plate. Food had been heavily rationed when he was growing up. What would he have eaten then if he could've had anything? He pulled out his wand.

"Panem."

A stale loaf of rye appeared on his plate, a far cry from his usual fare, let alone what he was trying to summon.

The corner of Medea's mouth twitched into a half smile. "And that is why I require my students learn Latin."

"That's not what I was going for."

"I imagine it wasn't, but your mind said one thing and your lips said another. Your incantation called for bread. Try again without the wand and words."

"I can't do it without the wand."

She made a dismissive noise. "Yes, you can, but we will tackle wands tomorrow. For now, you may use the wand. Do not say the incantation and think only of what you *want* on the plate."

Ten minutes later he slammed his fist on the table, rattling the empty plate.

"Now, now," said Medea, stilling the plate. "What are you trying to summon?"

"Beef Stroganov."

"And are you very familiar with this dish?"

"I've never had it, but I always wanted to try it."

"Ah, that's the problem. Best start with something you know well. Intimate familiarity is required for summoning, which is why most people can summon food but not other items. They can imagine the smell and taste, how it feels in their mouth. It is a primal thing, food, and social. A dish shared with friends, a grandmother's hands kneading dough, sneaking forbidden sweets with siblings—memories and emotions form connections. They make the thing we are trying to summon feel more real. Try again."

Nikolai stood and retrieved a bowl. It took him three more tries, but at last it filled with *shchi*. He stirred the watery cabbage soup, looking in vain for lumps of meat. Alas, it was as plain as he remembered Mother making. Not his favorite dish, but at least it wasn't bread. Now that he knew what the spell required, he vowed to familiarize himself with as many fine dishes as he could.

"Well done. Here." Medea summoned a meaty dish to the chipped plate and pushed it toward him. Strips of beef lay on a bed of curled egg noodles. The hearty brown sauce covering the dish smelled heavenly.

"Is that—"

"Yes. You will probably need to have it a few more times before you'll be able to summon it on your own."

Nikolai carefully pushed a single piece of beef onto the rim of the plate. The sacrifice wasn't as difficult as it had once been, back when memories of starvation were still fresh, but the ritual seemed important to maintain. He tackled the Stroganov with gusto, suddenly famished. He would have preferred potatoes, but noodles were fine.

"Have you had it much then?" he asked between bites.

"A few times. Enough to get a feel for it, though I had it in America, where it's known as Stroganoff."

He snorted. "A French name for a Russian dish in an English-speaking country."

"English steals much of its vocabulary from neighboring languages. Speaking of which, what language do you prefer for instruction? English or Russian?"

"I speak Turkish too." He dropped the information casually. She might speak several languages, but he doubted she spoke that, especially when it had changed in the 1930s.

"Is that what you prefer? I can probably manage."

His fork clattered against the plate. "You're telling me you speak English, French, Russian, Latin, *and* Turkish?"

"I speak far more than that."

Ridiculous. No one was that good at everything. "How many?"

"I don't *know*. I think you underestimate the benefit of being an academic with unlimited time. For centuries I traveled the globe looking for new spells. I couldn't very well learn from the local populace or read their texts if I didn't pick up their languages. The written word is easier. It doesn't change as rapidly. Speaking, well, I've had some trouble if I haven't visited a country in a long time."

"So you're not fluent then. Let me hear your Turkish." There was no way she spoke modern Turkish. He'd had to relearn it himself after arriving at the Academy.

"Why do you care so much about this?"

"Maybe because you're offering to teach me in a language you don't really know."

She crossed her arms and gave him an appraising look, then spoke, completely mangling a phrase.

He stifled a laugh. "Even for Ottoman Turkish, that's bad."

"I don't see what's so funny. I'd like to see you learn every major language and remember them all with perfect fluency. Just for that, I'm going to make you learn Latin *and* Greek."

He picked up the fork and stabbed a strip of beef. "Let's stick with English. I could use the practice anyway."

"You speak it well. Most Russians have trouble with 'the' and have a much thicker accent."

He spoke between bites. "I went to Dublin on weekends. Watched American movies." Mimicking accents or mimicking expressions—it was all the same to him. His chewing slowed.

Hunger satiated, Nikolai poked through the sauce with his fork. The taste wasn't what he'd expected.

"Something wrong?"

"I thought it was supposed to have onions."

"Oh, that. I don't like onions."

"You don't like onions?"

"No."

"So you didn't summon onions?"

"Or mushrooms. Americans put mushrooms in it."

Had the food she'd summoned been made without mushrooms and onions, or was there a plate somewhere in America devoid of its contents, save for a pile of mushrooms and onions?

"You're responsible for your own meals. I often forget to eat, and more than a few apprentices have accused me of trying to starve them." She chuckled and dug out her slip of paper again, waving it too fast for him to read, though it appeared to be in Latin anyway. "Now I have a list. 'Make sure they can summon food.' So, that's done. You can store food here and cook if you want. Some apprentices like to do that, though I can't imagine why. Really, who has time for that nonsense?"

Her speech had become as rapid as a bird darting through bushes. Before he could swallow his food and say that he concurred, she moved on.

"Do you know any cooling spells?"

He shook his head.

"Then you'll have to use the larder. Don't leave things in there so long they rot. Clean up after yourself. What else? I think that's everything. We start early. An hour past sunrise. Don't be late. Do you have any questions before I retire?"

She stood to leave. He slurped his last noodle quickly and pulled out a handkerchief to dab his face.

"I don't believe so. What time is it here?" He made to pull out his pocket watch and realized it was in the coat he'd worn to work, now packed with all his other things.

"Sundown, I think."

Well, that was helpful . . .

"Anything else?" Despite the question, Medea was already walking toward the door. He had to twist in his seat to look at her.

"I guess not."

"Ah, there it is!" She'd spotted a trash can near the door. "Of course I find it now. Rubbish goes in there."

He couldn't help himself. "Really? Rubbish goes in the rubbish bin?"

She continued as if he'd asked a legitimate question. "Yes, it's emptied once a day."

"By who?"

"By a spell." Again the condescending tone. She left without another word, closing the door neatly behind her. He shook his head and turned back to the table. Odd woman.

Nikolai pushed the tepid soup aside. *Shchi* was boring and he could do better. He aimed his wand at the plate, now clear aside from a single beef strip on the rim, and envisioned *kolbasa*.

His first sausage was raw, as was the second. The third

showed evidence of chewing. He discarded it in the trash along with the beef and retrieved a clean plate. Raw. Burned. Spoiled. Why was this so difficult?

Medea said memories and emotions helped. He tried to recall the first time he had the sausage, before the war, back when they'd had food. It was no good—he couldn't remember the first time. Instead, he closed his eyes and focused on the times he'd eaten it after the war, on the smell and the savory flavor in his mouth.

When he looked at his plate he found not a sausage, but a fat severed finger. Fresh blood welled from the end. Had it come from a sausage-making facility? Did someone lose it there? Into the trash it went, and a new plate was retrieved.

Twenty minutes later he slumped in his seat and stared at a perfect *kolbasa*. Or so it seemed. For all he knew, the inside could be filled with maggots. He picked up a knife with shaking hands that betrayed mana exhaustion and cut into the center. Slice by careful slice he examined the sausage. When it was clear the food wasn't contaminated, he pushed aside a single piece to be discarded and ate the rest.

After cleaning the dishes in a makeshift sink made from a metal trough, he collected his things and made his way to the bedroom, located directly below the upstairs balcony. The door above had to be Medea's. It placed her literally above him—the message couldn't have been more clear. He opened his door and stared in dismay.

While not exactly what he'd envisioned when he first saw the hovel, it was close. What little furniture the small, windowless room contained was old and worn. A backless chair, more like a tall stool, was pushed against a small desk bearing an inkwell and an oil lamp. The bed, little more than a pallet stuffed with straw, squatted in the corner closest the door. On top lay a crumpled bundle of fabric, which turned out to be a single sheet and a thin blanket. At least it lacked the cobwebs and dust of the kitchen. Medea probably had it on her list. "Clean apprentice's room."

He dragged his trunk to the bed and opened it. Where was he supposed to keep his clothes? There were a couple hooks on the wall, but no wardrobe, dresser, or closet. Keeping with the decor of the rest of the house, there were, however, several bookshelves.

As he set out his clothes neatly on the shelves, he vowed to smuggle in a new mattress. He would not spend the next years living in squalor, no matter how good the instruction. When he finished unpacking, he lay down on the mattress, cursing and punching it several times. Damned thing probably had bugs.

Despite the disappointing accommodations, there was no denying he had the opportunity of a lifetime. Who knew what artifacts and books Medea had collected over the centuries? Tomorrow he would ask for a tour, taking note of off-limit areas. He would not permit another master to hold out on him. Willing or not, he would extract every shred of knowledge from Medea and turn it against her. He would surpass her ability. His ego could not conceive of a world in which it was otherwise.

He reached under the mattress and pulled out the golden dagger, idly unsheathing and sheathing it. That Medea had to die was without question. He still owed her for the blinding, after all, and it was important to keep promises made to oneself.

More than that, Medea was the ultimate Competition. The notoriety of killing the world's most powerful Magi was too tempting to pass up. He wouldn't even get in trouble for it. Hell, the Collective would probably give him a medal. Besides, allowing her to live meant allowing her to train future Competition, and he couldn't have that. Her unique and powerful magic would be his and his alone. Killing her ensured no one followed in his footsteps.

Countless others had attempted to kill Medea and failed. He needed to find out how so as not to make the same mistakes.

Immortality was not the same as invulnerability, and Medea's caution implied vulnerability on some level. As he studied magic, so would he study her. Everyone had a weakness to exploit. Nikolai smiled as he drifted off to sleep, dagger clutched in his hand.

11

MALAISE

Nikolai awoke to straw jabbing him in the back, but made no effort to roll over or rise. Why bother? What was the point? Why had he even come here? He recalled fighting so hard to win the apprenticeship, and yet those memories felt like they belonged to a different person, someone capable and cunning. He was neither.

Useless, conniving boy. Why had he ever thought himself talented? Absurd that Medea even consented to teach him. She'd only done so out of pity, or to be rid of his incessant prattling. He was incapable of learning. Worse, he was a backstabbing, lying fraud. He lay motionless on the bed, staring at the wall. A collection of knots in the wood formed a drooping face that mirrored his mood.

Sometime later, a rap sounded on his door. "Get up! How can you be so late to rise, and on your first day?"

He couldn't find the will to respond.

The knocking came again, louder this time, and Medea's voice shouted, "On your head be it. I give you one hour to rise and report or consider us done."

Probably for the best. He struggled to sit up. It wasn't that his body was unresponsive, but that he lacked the mental wherewithal to even try. Eventually he managed to get upright, shivering as the cold stone floor sucked the warmth from his feet. Pulling the blanket over his shoulders was like moving through molasses, and when it slipped off he couldn't find the will to try again. His robe hung on a hook a few paces away; it might as well have been across an infinite chasm. Even the urgency of his bladder wasn't enough to force him into motion.

His eyes roved the room. He had wanted to redecorate—a rug here, a new bed with a soft mattress, a mahogany desk, gilded mirror, wardrobe . . . pointless now. He should be packing, but all he could do was stare at his bags. Everything was too much.

An hour must have passed because the banging came again. "You had better be dead in there!" Before he could respond, or perhaps because he hadn't, Medea swung the door open with a force that sent it crashing against the wall. She stood framed in the doorway, hands on her hips. "What are you doing?"

He simply looked at her.

"Well?" she demanded.

"I should be going. I don't know why I ever came here."

With the effort of a snail climbing Mount Everest, he stood and crossed to the bookshelves. Something clattered from the bed to the floor. It didn't matter what it was. None of it mattered. He gazed at his neatly folded clothes. It would be simplest to swipe everything into his trunk, yet he stood staring at the shelf without taking action.

"Wait," said Medea. She approached and grabbed him by the chin, yanking his face down to her level, and peered into his eyes. No, *past* his eyes. He felt the faint touch of her mind against his. "I see." She released his chin and left without a backward glance.

He kept expecting her to come back and berate him, but she did not. Eventually he moved to lie back down, not to sleep but because standing was too difficult. His foot kicked something on the way back to the bed; the gold dagger skidded across the floor. Something tugged at his subconscious. This didn't feel right. He had really wanted to be here. He'd literally killed for the opportunity to train with Medea. Why was he so desperate to give it all up now? What the hell was he *doing*?

A fog lifted from his mind. He jerked the door open and yelled into the common area. "Medea!" The empty room offered no response.

He cursed and dressed hurriedly, checking his watch—past noon Haven time. Two horrible first impressions, and now this. What kind of student sleeps in on the first day? What on earth had come over him?

The door closest to his room was a bathroom, thankfully more modern. He relieved himself. No time to shower or shave. His hair was probably a mess, but there wasn't a mirror in which to check. He cupped his hands under the faucet and combed his hair with his wet fingers.

He checked the kitchen, not really expecting to find Medea given the layer of dust he'd seen yesterday, and found it empty. The doors on the opposite side of the common room were locked, but one had a note attached. It read simply, "Outside." He wrenched open the antechamber door, narrowly avoided tripping over stray boots, and smacked his head on the low doorframe again.

Medea levitated over the gravel pit adjacent to the garden beds, legs crossed and eyes closed.

"I'm sorry I'm la—"

"This is for you." Eyes still closed, she gestured to the stone bench abutting the pit wall. On it was a small belt pouch similar to her own. "Keep it well-stocked with potions and whatever else you require. One of your daily duties is to create mana and healing potions. I made your allotment for today, as we are already behind schedule, but I will not do so again." Her voice carried a note of warning.

"Thank you. I'm sorry. It won't happen again."

"I seriously doubt that. When it does, I expect you to get up and do your duties regardless." She drifted over the low border and landed next to him.

He bit his tongue and nodded. Anything he said would be seen as an excuse. Earning the apprenticeship was one thing; today he had to show he deserved it.

Medea led him along the path away from the hovel. The day was bright and clear, drastically different from Ireland and its frequent rain. A gentle breeze, pleasantly scented by the ocean, set the meadow grass swaying. When Medea was dead and the island his, he could use it to stage seductive romantic picnics.

About halfway to the forest, she paused and flattened a swath of grass with a single gesture.

"I want you to try to kill me," she said. "You may use your wand this time."

"Pardon?"

"I said you could use your wand." The wind tugged at her blonde hair. She absently tucked it behind her ears.

"Not that—you told me never to try to kill you."

"Sparring is different. I need to see how good you are, which I can only do if you don't hold back. My only caveat is that you stop if I call a time out to explain something. I dislike being interrupted."

"What if I hurt you?" He knew some rather nasty spells.

"You won't."

"But—"

"Tell me, do you ever worry that one of your 'Dueling Club' members will hurt you?"

"No, but they don't know what they're doing."

Her smile turned his own comment against him.

"I know what I'm doing!"

"Compared to them, yes. You and I both suffer a lack of adequate sparring partners. I have not been remotely challenged since the seventeenth century. Fear not. I could pass out drunk on the grass and you could not kill me."

He grinned. "I have some vodka in my room if you care to test that theory."

"Hypothesis, not theory, and I'm not Baldur."

"Who's Baldur?"

"You know, *Baldur*."

He stared at her blankly.

"The Norse god? Killed by mistletoe?" She made an exasperated noise and walked several meters away, the standard dueling distance. "Never mind. The point is, even if something *seems* safe, putting yourself at risk for the amusement of others is stupid."

"No need to get testy because I didn't recognize your obscure reference."

"It's not obscure! You just need to read more."

"I read plenty. *Useful* things like dueling spells. Who was it, this 'adequate' sparring partner who challenged you back in the seventeenth century? Another immortal?" Nikolai rolled his shoulders and stretched his arms.

"A particularly capable apprentice of mine."

"This apprentice have a name?"

She crossed her arms. "Why do you care?"

"I like to know who I'm competing against."

"Competing? How would you be competing with someone from two hundred years ago?"

He shrugged and withdrew his wand, twirling it between his fingers. "I like to be the best. So, who was he? No, wait—who was your *best* apprentice?" No point in worrying about mister "particularly capable."

"They are one and the same. He was with me for seventeen years."

Seventeen years! Most apprenticeships lasted four, perhaps six, but *seventeen*? He'd be thirty-nine if she kept him that long— practically an old man. No wonder she didn't want apprentices asking how long they had left.

"Thomas was a witch from the Massachusetts colony."

"A witch?" Nikolai scoffed. No wonder the guy took seventeen years. Half of that was probably bringing him up to Magi level.

"Religious beliefs aside, he was a talented caster."

"He can't have been that good if he's dead."

"Not everyone desires immortality. In any case, I've not spoken to him since 1686. For all I know, he's still alive."

Not bloody likely. "The parting gift you give your apprentices —the one you said returns to you if they die—did Thomas' return?"

Her jaw momentarily clenched. "Yes, but—"

Nikolai laughed. "Give me enough time and I'll surpass him."

"With the amount of time you waste asking inane questions, I doubt it."

"You could at least pretend to have some confidence in my abilities."

"It is not my job to bolster your ego. Overconfidence can get you killed."

"It doesn't seem to have hurt you."

"I merely have a realistic idea of my own abilities. Now, enough nattering, let's—"

"Lancea!" He launched the lance spell toward her chest. Was it cheating? A little, but she said she was in no danger. It was her own fault if she got hurt.

"Increbesco! Sanguino!" He grinned as his spells winged toward her. The second would spread the injury; the third would

cause her to bleed out. He'd been dying to use them in conjunction. Damn the Collective and their stupid rules. Testing on sheep wasn't the same as dueling someone who could fight back. Medea might get a shield up in time to block the third spell, but he was confident at least the first two would hit.

She casually flicked the spells aside, where they thumped harmlessly into the dirt. Nikolai found himself momentarily suspended in the air like a rag doll. He slammed into the ground, knocking the air from his lungs and the wand from his hand.

"I *said* I don't like being interrupted, but as you're anxious to start we may as well begin."

He rolled onto his side, gasping as he struggled to draw breath. After an eternity, his lungs recovered and he sat up to search for his wand. He could do this. What were the most powerful spells he knew, aside from Lance and Bleed? Lightning, Fireball, Slicing Wind, Fear, Barrage, Pain. She'd said he didn't need to hold back, so he wouldn't.

He launched Fear and Pain back-to-back, hoping at least one of them would hit, buying him time to land damage spells. Fear was parried. Pain was plucked from the air with her bare hand, as if it was the most normal thing to do. She flexed her fingers and shook her wrist, like someone attempting to discard the tingling sensation after sleeping on their arm wrong.

Slicing Wind was met with some sort of pointed barrier that neatly deflected it to either side. Lightning was grounded. Fireball blocked. Barrage rebounded and he had to dive to avoid being bludgeoned.

He lurched to his feet and nearly fell over as his whole body trembled. Mana exhaustion. Never before had he cast so many powerful spells in such a short sequence. He stood with his hands on his knees, panting.

"Your mana reserves are terrible. Take a potion." She nodded at his new pouch.

The drawstring defied his fingers the first several attempts, but soon his hand gripped a thin vial containing a milky white substance.

"Isn't this"—he inhaled sharply and rubbed his temple—"supposed to be yellow?"

"My version is better. Drink. You look ready to pass out."

He obeyed. Most mana potions took some time to work. Not Medea's. The trembling subsided almost immediately and was replaced with a warm, almost euphoric tingling throughout his body. "This is strong!"

"Mine have an initial boost, in addition to the accelerated regeneration effect. Give it, oh, ten minutes and we can begin again." She sat down on the grass and he did the same.

"That fast?"

"You don't have much mana to regenerate. Let's talk about your wand. Do you use it for everything?"

"Of course." Shit, she was going to take it from him. He should've crafted a backup.

"And yet you see I do not use one. I want you to think back to the first time you used magic. What was happening? And before you answer, remember you have sworn to tell me the truth. I do not care how embarrassing the memory is. I cannot help you if I cannot show you what you did right."

He considered this. First-magic stories were a significant glimpse into another's life. At the Academy, some students shared theirs openly; others only told close friends. Magical ability often woke under duress, and while a few stories were humorous—one boy accidentally set his cousin on fire during a spat—more often than not, given the time in which they'd grown up, the stories were bleak.

Harper had accidentally given himself blond hair and blue eyes, an illusion he still maintained. Another boy was the sole survivor when a bomb destroyed his apartment. One hollow-eyed girl spoke of Nazis searching her home; they'd taken her parents but looked right through her as though she wasn't there. Nikolai had listened to each tale before concocting his own, one which garnered sympathy and made him out to be a bit of a hero.

Medea looked at him expectantly, though not impatiently. Saving Kate from the drunks had won him points. There was no reason he couldn't create a new story along those lines. Medea was unlikely to run into his former classmates, and he could always claim the story he'd given her was what really happened.

"Father was drunk again. Mother was making *shchi* and I was playing on the floor nearby. I think I was about five. Father tasted the *shchi* and became angry—he was forever complaining about the way she cooked. He backhanded her, then grabbed her hair and shoved her toward the boiling pot. She was crying and struggling . . ." He paused, closing his eyes as if overwhelmed by the memory.

"And you intervened?"

"Yes, though of course I didn't realize it at the time. He yelped as if his hand burned and released her. Mother froze in place. He hit her again, blaming her for making him burn his hand, then walked by me. Stumbled, actually. He was so drunk he could barely walk, but he saw me and my toys as culpable and made to kick us both out of his way.

"I dodged his boot and focused on his neck. He gasped and choked, clawing at his throat. Mother rushed to his aid. The ungrateful bastard swatted her away and collapsed. I'll never forget how his face turned ashy blue." Nikolai picked at the blades of grass, casually shredding them as if torn over what he'd done. "When he passed out, I released my grip. It was then I knew I'd done something extraordinary."

"You nearly killed a man and you didn't need a wand to do it."

"That was different. More . . . primal. Isn't that how a lot of

Magi first find out their abilities, they get mad and stuff starts flying across the room?" Telekinesis was supposed to be the most basic, instinctual form of magic. Most of his teachers' first-magic stories involved flying objects or things mysteriously falling.

"Yes, but that isn't what you were doing," said Medea. "The dishes weren't flying around the room. You didn't slam your father into a wall. Instead, you focused intently on one thing, and you made it happen. Magic requires three things: mana, will, and focus. Mana gives you the energy to perform the action. Will is something many people have, including the Mundane. Without will there can be no commitment to action. Focus is your ability to see precisely what you want to happen. A Magi that lacks sufficient focus may cause items to fly around when they are upset, but to no purpose."

"I don't see what this has to do with how I cast. I have mana, will, and focus."

"No, you have the first two. The third has been stripped away by *that*." She pointed to his wand. "Like any tool in your arsenal, wands are not inherently bad, but how they're used matters, and what I see in use today is vastly different than the wands of old."

Medea's youthful countenance might disguise her true age, but at heart she was just another old woman. He leaned back on his arms and braced for the obligatory "kids these days" lecture.

"In my day—"

And there it was. If his time with Petrov had taught him anything, it was to act interested whenever an old person rambled on about how good things used to be.

"—wands were imprinted with a single spell. They were not meant to be used for anything and everything."

"Imprinted?"

"If you wanted to cast a spell above your ability, you could buy a wand to cast it for you. The spell utilized your mana, and your will told the wand to cast, but the *focus* was built into the wand itself. You needn't know any of the magical theory—useful if you needed a spell for a particular task. For instance, a family might store a healing wand for a child to use in case a parent was incapacitated. A thief could use a wand of Sleep, Silence, or Unlock."

He abruptly sat up. "What kind of thief doesn't bother to learn spells of his own trade? And how would a child even have the mana for something like that?"

"The Mundane kind, and almost everyone had a degree of mana back then. Of course, some wands had mana built in, but they had limited uses before the wand ran dry."

Clearly she was getting senile. Mundane with mana? *Witches* didn't even have mana, only Magi.

"Wands became more complex later. Instead of single spells, they replaced the focus of the caster. I saw from your textbooks that you were expected to drill extensively with a wand. Is this correct?"

"Yes. An hour a day for each new spell learned until our form was perfect."

Medea snorted. "I'm not opposed to drilling. Some people are easily distracted or flustered in combat. Drilling that often with a wand though . . ." She shook her head. "Current wands bypass focus. They join with the caster, interpreting what you want to do, even if you cannot quite formulate the right thoughts. The burden of focus falls to the wand, not the caster."

"Isn't that a good thing? I know several people who can barely cast *with* a wand."

She waved her hand. "That is due to an unrelated issue. The problem with allowing a wand to do the focusing is you can't cast anything remotely original. Wands like to stick to the book, so to speak, and work best with standard spells. If you've trained a wand to summon bread every time you use a certain movement and say *Panem* . . ."

"You summon bread instead of Beef Stroganov."

She nodded. "Now imagine if, instead of a disappointing meal, it was your life at stake."

He looked down at his wand, the wood worn smooth at the base by frequent handling. The making of a first wand was a rite of passage. Students chose a wood most compatible with the spells they wished to cast, then went in search of a tree during the waxing moon. They placed a palm to the trunk and begged permission from the tree to take a clipping. If the bark felt warm, then permission had been granted.

Nikolai had chosen oak, a masculine wood known for its strength and endurance. Casting had been so much easier since he'd crafted it all those years ago. Could he really give it up? Should he?

"You will not use a wand while you train with me, not without my explicit permission. The potion should have worked by now. Let's try again, this time without the wand."

The removal of choice irked him, but he slid his wand back into its holster without complaint.

Medea stood and picked flecks of grass off her dress. Nikolai attempted to take the sparring stance but couldn't figure out what to do with his wand hand. Holding it empty in front of him felt odd, but allowing it to dangle limply at his side didn't work either, nor did placing it in his pocket. As he experimented with placement, Medea covered her mouth with a fist, holding back a smile.

"You look ridiculous," she said.

"I don't hear you making any suggestions."

"Why should I? This is far more entertaining."

At last he stood with both arms slightly bent at his sides, like some sort of strongman ready to wrestle.

Medea shook her head. "No, that will never do." She fumbled with her hip pouch and withdrew a sad twig of a wand, which she tossed to him.

"You want me to give up my wand and use another?" It hadn't even been sanded or inscribed.

"That's not a wand, it's a stick."

"All wands are sticks."

"Ah, but not all sticks are wands."

"Why do you carry around a stick?"

She shrugged. "Sometimes I pretend to cast using a wand."

"Why?"

"Because then my opponent wastes time trying to disarm me." She grinned.

He chuckled in spite of himself. He'd have to use that one. The look on his opponent's face would be priceless.

"A fake wand will help with the transition," she continued. "You can still go through the movements, but there will be nothing to inhibit your focus. As you gain confidence, we will start by dropping incantations, then wand movements. A few spells require such things, like those which invoke spirits, but most do not."

"Is some movement required? I see you cast spells using your hands and face." Her slight nod back at Petrov's had filled the wooden beam with pockmarks.

"Not really. Some of it is habit—most is for the people around me. If you hadn't seen me move, would you have realized I was the one doing magic?"

"I don't know."

"Well, I do. People stare around stupidly for the source if they don't see you *doing* magic." Her arms waved in an exaggerated casting motion, then she chuckled into her hand like a child about to confess something forbidden. "I, *heh*, I have a couple spells I use when I really want to make an impression."

Medea planted her feet and held her upturned hands in front of her like claws. Wind whipped her hair and dress. The air tingled with electricity. She rose ten feet off the ground, her body taking on an eerie glow. When she spoke, her voice was a booming echo.

"FEEL MY WRATH, MORTALS!"

If he had known nothing of magic, it would've been a stunning sight. Instead, he found himself laughing at the overly dramatic effects.

"Shh! You're making me break character. *Ahem*. BOW BEFORE ME, FOR I AM MEDEA, CONQUEROR OF . . . OF . . . uhhhh, I'm no good at this." She sank back to the ground, straightening her dress and putting on a casual air. "You get the idea."

He grinned. "If you ever get bored being a hermit, you could make a killing entertaining the Mundane."

She shuddered. "Ugh. Why did I even show you that? What were we talking about?"

Definitely senile. It would make manipulating her easier.

"We were discussing wands, and how I'm impotent without one." He frowned at his word choice. Why did he say that? The sunny day was suddenly oppressive and gloomy. Wind cut through his coat and chilled him to the bone. Medea spoke of wands, all noise and no substance.

"Are you even listening?!" Her fingers snapped in front of his face.

He blinked and looked down. "I . . . I'm sorry, I don't feel well."

"You're already behind for today, and I have yet to see how well you perform without a wand."

He found himself unable to care about her irritation. She insisted he try his spells again, but they were impossible to cast without his wand. He was a failure. A fraud. Why did he ever think he was going to succeed?

A slap interrupted his wallowing, but he could do no more than look down at Medea with disinterest.

"You will push past this," she said. "Do you understand? Focus!"

"I'm sorry. This is all my fault."

"Yes, it is."

He bowed his head at that. No matter how she yelled, focus and will eluded him. When her frustration reached a boiling point, she stalked back to the hovel. Nikolai meekly followed.

TAINTED

Nikolai awoke the next morning with a crick in his neck. Damn the mattress. It hadn't been a good night. After he left Medea, he'd returned to his room and lain down, mired in his thoughts. He'd been torn between wanting to pack and wanting to stay. Neither option seemed good, and so he lay awake for hours, past dinner and well into the night. At some point he must have fallen asleep, yet when he woke, it was as if he hadn't rested at all.

He stood and pulled on his robe, making his way to the bathroom for a shower. At least he had that modern amenity. The hot water tap appeared to be for show, for the water that came out was icy even after a sufficient wait. Nothing he wasn't used to. He stepped into the chill water and scrubbed. Halfway through his shower, the water abruptly turned scalding and he nearly fell trying to escape the torturous stream.

Belatedly, he recalled the bathroom didn't have a mirror. How was he supposed to shave? The process took twice as long as usual. Every time he checked his work with his hand, he found more stubble he'd missed.

He dressed in his dueling garb—loose-fitting wool pants and shirt—and strode to the kitchen, determined to have better success with summoning today. He got a decent *kolbasa* on the second try. Summoning black tea resulted in a wet table, which combined with the dust on the towel he grabbed to create a sort of brownish sludge. Back and forth he went from table to sink, rinsing and wiping until at last the table was clean. His second attempt to summon tea took place over the sink, and eventually he found he could control where the liquid arrived by encircling a mug with his hands. By the time he sat down, his sausage was cold, but it didn't matter. He was getting the hang of this.

As he ate, he tried to puzzle out the previous day. The dark moods had struck without warning. He felt fine this morning, and yet there'd been a brief period of lucidity yesterday too. Perhaps gateway travel did not agree with him.

When he returned to his room, he found a note instructing him to seek a blue door. After a quick circuit of the common room, he found a door with a blue rune glowing on its surface. He touched his palm to the symbol and heard the snick of a latch unlocking.

He opened the door to a laboratory larger than his old apartment. Like the common room, it was lit with large flat crystals. A long, sturdy table, scorched and blemished from centuries of use, stood in the middle, providing ample room to brew multiple concoctions simultaneously. Counters at the back boasted a variety of cauldrons, flasks, and alchemy instruments. Shelves of ingredients took up well over half the wall space.

He passed a rack for drying herbs and perused the closest shelf of bottles. There appeared to be quite a few duplicates. No, not duplicates, variations. "Milkweed, *Asclepias incarnata*, marsh, full moon, Aug 17, 1940." And another, "Milkweed, *Asclepias incarnata*, pond, south side, Jan 9, 1936." There were several more for milkweed, including different species, and over a dozen for mandrake. He admired the thoroughness of the labeling, which bordered on obsessive. Many of them contained not only locations, but map coordinates, time stamps, and weather.

"Ah, good, you're up." Medea's voice came from an open cabinet. She stepped into view, arms laden with flasks, and closed the door behind her with one bare foot. She wore the same red dress as always.

Back in Haven he'd figured she was simply traveling light, but now that he knew about the gateway, he realized she hadn't slept in the Hanged Man at all. Yesterday was fuzzy, but he vaguely remembered her wearing the red dress then too. Did she ever change? Did she have twenty identical dresses? One dress kept clean with magic?

"I'm feeling much better today." He gestured to the jars. "Why so many variations?"

"Contrary to what some people believe, the conditions under which ingredients are grown and gathered matters, which is why I collect my own."

Nikolai recalled the slighted potion ingredient merchant back in Haven and smiled.

"Feel free to make use of anything here. The brown cabinet back there contains completed potions. If you need one, take it. Rule One: if you use a potion or ingredient, you must replace it doubly, and as soon as you can. I do not mind apprentices grabbing things in a pinch—it beats waiting a month or more for some longer potions to brew—but I expect that you replace whatever you take, times two."

Great, more rules. "Why times two?"

She sighed and lugged a small cauldron to the sink and began filling it with water. "Because experience has taught me not to trust people. They use a thing, get busy, and forget to replace it. Others are sloppy, buying ingredients with no thought to source, or they take and take without replacing anything. Those apprentices don't last long. I've added the buffer to make up for the inadequacies of others. It's not a perfect system, but it helps."

Nikolai nodded. At the Academy he'd been paired with incompetent partners on more than one occasion, and he shared her irritation with such people.

"Now, first things first. Sit there." He approached the center table. Medea carried the now-full cauldron over and set it before him.

"What are we making?"

"*You* are boiling water."

"Er, okay . . ." He looked around for a burner and made to pick up the cauldron.

Medea slapped his hand away. "Not like that. With your mind."

"You want me to boil water with my mind?"

"Yes. Every morning. That is your first task of the day. Did you cast any spells yet?"

"I summoned breakfast."

She waved a hand. "A minor enough spell that it won't matter. Here, focus on the water. Bring it to a boil, then hold it there as long as you can." She turned away from him and busied herself in one of the cabinets.

He stared into the cauldron. "I'm not sure where to start."

"Anger helps. Pretend it's someone you hate, and you want to boil their brain inside their skull." Medea set a skinny jar of dried plants on the counter. She removed a stalk, sniffed it, then tossed it in a bin and removed another.

He focused on the water and thought of past slights he'd endured but felt nothing. Anger was a fleeting emotion, not something he clung to. When provoked, it came upon him suddenly, raging like a wildfire and threatening to burn all in its path, but it fled just as quickly, leaving only the memory of the event. His desire for retribution was conceptual, not emotional.

"Here, let me help you." Medea slapped the back of his head.

"What the hell?!" He spun to face her, fists balled at his sides.

"Ah-ah!" She snapped her fingers and pointed to the cauldron. "Focus your anger *there*. Pretend it's my head." He glared at her as she walked around the table and settled across from him with her plants. With both Medea and the cauldron in sight, it wasn't difficult to imagine it was her. He let the fury build and focused it all on the cauldron.

Nikolai held his concentration as long as he could, but the task was exceedingly dull and soon his mind drifted. Few of Medea's plants seemed make the cut of her sniff test. Halfway through her inspections, she gave up and dumped the remaining contents in the bin.

A magical shove sent his face into the cauldron. He jerked back, wiping lukewarm water off his nose.

"Focus," said Medea. A jar of plants flew over his shoulder and into her hand.

He wished the water *was* boiling so he could dump it in her lap. He directed his anger at the cauldron, but even with his rage swelling anew it was an eternity before bubbles appeared along the sides. By the time the water began to churn in earnest, his hands trembled.

Medea smiled. "Nice to see I haven't lost my touch for picking the right cauldron size. Maintain the boil as long as you can."

Not a minute later he slumped back in his chair. Shivers ran over his body.

"What was the point of that?" Exhaustion made his voice break. He hid his trembling hands under the table.

"You tell me. What do you think it does?"

"It feels like mana exhaustion, but I wasn't doing anything."

"Yes, you were. Boiling water requires energy. Just as athletes lift weights to gain muscle, so too must we push our magic to the limits to strengthen our abilities. This exercise is designed to increase your mana. Speaking of which . . ."

She pulled out a flask of milky white fluid and passed it to him. He unstoppered it and drank. The trembling stopped.

"I cannot overstate how important mana is in combat," she continued. "A rapid burst of damage may win some duels, but showy spells tend to be expensive, and when fighting an opponent of equal skill, whoever has the most mana will likely win. Every morning, while your mana reserve is full, you are to boil water. Twice daily is better. It will get easier. Don't think of skimping on it. I'll know if you haven't been practicing."

"Can I stop when it gets easy?"

"Of course not, we simply get you a bigger cauldron. Now, on to your second task. Do you remember what I said yesterday about potions?"

"You want me to make a mana and healing potion every day."

"No, I want you to make ten of each."

"Ten?" Apprentices were often used as free labor, but they were usually learning new things in the process, not repeating rudimentary tasks. "Why do you need so many?"

"You really think they're for me?" She smiled and held out a hand. A sheet of paper flew from somewhere in the room and landed in her palm. She slapped it on the table in front of him. "Here are the instructions. Get to it."

"Why can't I use my own recipes?"

"Because they're wrong."

"You haven't even seen them."

"I don't need to." She began sorting through herbs again.

Nikolai rubbed his chin as he read the paper, grimacing when he felt another patch of stubble he'd missed. Most of the ingredients were the same as what he remembered, with slight variations. Medea's mana potions used harp root instead of ginseng, and it had to be collected from a sunny field. This part was underlined several times. Her healing potions used ox's blood instead of sheep's, and there was a scribbled notation to use alpaca when available.

The sheer number of potions meant it took several trips to bring the required supplies to the table. At least he could make a big batch and simply increase the quantity of each ingredient by ten, except for the blood, which she'd already written as 30 cc instead of 3 cc.

As he mixed, Medea swooped in to nitpick over his work. He was adding things in the wrong order. The flame was too high. That root had gone bad, he needed a new one. It was difficult to concentrate with her constant hovering.

"You've forgotten to multiply the blood."

"No I haven't. See?" He held up a small beaker about the size of a shot glass.

"You need 300 cc."

"I think you wrote it down wrong." He slid the paper across the table. Medea peered at it, frowning.

"You're absolutely right. My apologies." A pen flew into her hand, and she added another zero. "There, 300 cc per potion. Carry on."

He chuckled. "Medea, these vials don't even *hold* that much."

"That's because you grabbed the wrong kind. Healing vials are in the drawer over there, and you can find more ox blood in jugs under the counter."

"That's over a cup of blood in every potion."

"And?"

He stared at Medea in consternation. Was she fucking with him? Was this some sort of test to see if he knew the proper quantities?

She sighed. "You don't understand how they work, do you?"

"Uh, I drink them and they heal me?"

"They accelerate the body's natural healing capabilities, but the raw materials have to come from somewhere. If you don't provide them, the body will make do with what it has, consuming itself to make hasty repairs. The blood helps, as do food and rest."

She sat next to him. "It is important you understand how they work. Potions can only do so much. They can't get around curses or diseases that impair healing, and if a wound is filthy or necrotic, using a potion is risky. The wounds will also scar easily. The body only cares about structural repairs. The faster the healing, the worse the scarring."

Nikolai shifted on his seat. He took great pride in his appearance. One scar might not be so bad, or even a couple, provided they were in suitably attractive places that allowed for a good fabricated tale, but she was talking about using ten potions *a day*.

"What kind of injuries will I be treating with the potions? Minor cuts and scrapes?"

She laughed as she got up.

"I ask because I don't want my body disfigured." His voice was deadly calm.

"Scars exist to remind us of our failures, making us less inclined to repeat them."

He made no move to continue his work as she sorted herbs. Eventually she looked over and shook her head. "My training is quite . . . vigorous, and repeated injuries make it harder for the body to do repairs. I usually repair injuries properly a few times a week, depending on how bad the tissue is. If I didn't, my apprentices would be unrecognizable before long. I merely want you to understand the cost of using potions habitually. Far better to learn healing spells so you may guide the body as you see fit."

Nikolai relaxed and went back to brewing. He added ox blood until his cauldron was disgustingly thick with the stuff. Medea was back with more corrections. The flame was too high—he was going to coagulate the blood. It needed more vinegar. No, that was too much, and he had to keep stirring. Her constant interference was suffocating.

An hour and a half later, he was nearly done, and her criticisms ceased. He removed the healing brew from the heat and divvied it into bottles to cool. While the mana brew gently simmered, he rose to stretch his legs and explore the rest of the lab.

Unlike the meticulously labeled ingredient jars, most of the cabinets housed an unorganized assortment of equipment. In one cabinet, tongs were shoved unceremoniously into a beaker, which balanced on top of a set of scales, wedged between a crucible and a telescope. He hastily closed the door before anything could fall and break. Another cabinet was home to wadded balls of fabric. He shook one of them out to reveal dated clothing, which he thrust back into the cabinet.

Medea paid no mind to his casual search of her possessions, until he came to a door stained black. A blue rune glowed on its surface.

"That's the dark room," she said, "for potions and ingredients that wither in light. There are two doors, and one must be closed for the other to open. There's a red crystal on the wall. Touch it when you enter, and it will light the room. I'll unlock it for you now." She didn't look up from her plants, but the rune faded.

One door left, also runed. "And here?"

"That goes to the dungeon."

The dungeon! He watched the blue rune for a moment, but nothing happened. Medea was busy stripping brown leaves off a stem. She must've forgotten. He cleared his throat and tried to keep the excitement from his voice. "Would you mind unlocking the door?"

"Why? Do you have a particular spell that requires testing?"

"No, but I'd still like to see it."

"You would," she mumbled.

The lab was silent, save for the plucking of leaves. He stared at the mocking blue glow, willing it to fade.

"Medea?"

She released an exasperated sigh. "What?"

"Are you going to unlock the door?"

The careful dismemberment of flora ceased, and she looked up, scrutiny in her gaze. Involuntarily, he straightened his shoulders. Her eye contact slid from his, back to her plants.

"No, I don't think so."

He clenched his fists and returned to the potions on the counter. When he was finished, she examined his work, holding up a sample of each to the light and tasting it. He stared past her, refusing to be goaded by the unjustified scrutiny. At last she seemed satisfied, and he packed his potions away into his pouch.

"Now," she said with a smile, "we will see how well you defend yourself."

They emerged from the hovel into bright sunlight. The flowers in the garden swayed in the gentle breeze, and he thought he recognized a few of the ingredients from down in the lab. Sure enough, Medea stopped to point out plants he should be collecting daily to replace those he'd used for potions. The grass covering most of the open land was apparently harp root, a key component in her mana potions. When he asked where he was supposed to find gallons of ox blood, she waved his question away.

"You don't know how to collect it properly. I will supply it for now. I tried keeping beasts here once, but they ate all the plants."

When they reached the area of flattened grass, Medea spun to face him, eyes twinkling. "Now we test your defenses. You may use your wand."

It sprang from his wrist holster into his hand, and she gave him a look.

"What? You said I couldn't use a wand without permission, not that I couldn't have one."

"You might be tempted to use it."

"Or I might need it to save my life."

"Fine. This time you block me."

He centered himself and conjured the most powerful shield he could, strong enough to block physical spells and at least stall things like lightning and fire.

Medea shook her head. "You make this too easy."

Something punched him in the back. He sprawled into the grass, shield winking out. He rolled in time to see a giant boulder falling straight at him. Shield back up without a second to spare. His ears rang as the boulder struck the shield, sending a jolt through his body.

The boulder had him pinned to the grass. He ignored an itch on his cheek, trying to figure out how to get the boulder off his shield without collapsing it in on himself. Levitation proved fruitless. Medea was actively forcing the boulder downward. It twisted and scraped against the shield like a nail on glass.

Twist, grind. A crack appeared in the shield. He pushed mana into it, sealing the fissure. Sweat beaded his brow. He didn't know how much longer he could keep this up. The itch became more insistent, and he absently rubbed his cheek against his shoulder. Maybe he could tilt it off and roll away. He pushed against one side of the shield, but the boulder was too heavy.

Now his legs were itching. He chanced a look and almost lost his concentration on the shield. The grass was alive and winding around his legs. One blade rose in front of his eyes and waved at him in a taunting manner before diving up his nostril. More followed until his sinuses were so packed he could scarcely breathe.

He opened his mouth to speak the slash incantation and grass rushed down his throat. With ever-increasing pressure, the blades wound around and through his head. Darkness loomed. He wasn't good enough. He'd never be good enough. Medea was going to kill him, a just ending to his pathetic life. The shield wavered.

Let go. Death was freedom. Just let go.

An immense weight cracked his chest, and all was black.

13

POWER OVERWHELMING

A slap rang across his face. Nikolai jerked upright and pedaled backward, gasping and coughing. Something tickled his throat. He felt around inside his mouth and tugged out a stalk of grass nearly two feet in length. The remainder of his breakfast came up with it. When the heaving ceased, he fell back on his haunches and blinked. Medea crouched next to the boulder a short distance away, watching him benignly.

"What did we learn?" she asked.

Nikolai got to his feet and spat. The foul taste still polluted his mouth. How he longed for a bit of vodka to cleanse his palate. With trembling fingers, he removed a mana potion from his pouch, took several swigs and spat again.

"Don't waste that," she said. "Here." She pulled a waterskin from her pouch and offered it to him.

He shook his head mutely and finished off his mana potion. The trembling subsided and he turned a darkened face toward Medea.

"You tried to kill me!" Back and forth he paced, hands balled into fists.

"Don't be ridiculous." She stuffed the waterskin back in her pouch. "If I wanted to kill you, you'd be dead."

It was all he could do to keep his temper in check. What happened? The boulder had been challenging and the grass menacing, but that wasn't what troubled him. His thoughts had been clouded, he was sure of it. He prided himself on being able to think critically under pressure, on pushing past challenges long after others had given up, yet something within had insisted he drop the shield. Had he acquiesced? He could still feel the weight of the boulder on his chest, the dry scratchiness of the grass as it entered unbidden . . .

"What did you learn?"

Medea's calm arrogance was infuriating. He didn't trust himself to answer.

"I understand this is difficult for you. It is never pleasant being at the mercy of another."

He flinched as if struck.

"Do you recall what I said when I offered to take you on? My lessons will be harsh. You agreed to it."

Harsh was fine. Danger broke the monotony and quenched his thirst for adrenaline, but something was amiss. Thrice now he'd been tormented by thoughts entirely unlike him. Two times might have been coincidence, but three? Was it Medea? Was she doing something to him?

When he didn't respond, she continued. "I promise you're alright. I understand the limitations of the human body far better than you could imagine. Do you detect anything amiss?"

Her words were a little too close to his line of thinking. Was she a telepath too? If so, she'd entered his mind without his knowledge, something he'd yet to accomplish with other Magi. He attempted to set his suspicions aside in case she was listening to his thoughts.

He stopped pacing and tentatively unbuttoned his shirt, now

caked with dirt and blood. His chest was pink and tender where the rock had crushed him, but otherwise there was no sign of what happened.

"I take care of my students, but adversity is the best teacher. Life is brutal. You can either lay down and die, or rise up and say 'never again.' Here, you have a unique opportunity to fail with minimal repercussions. Now, tell me what you could have done better."

Nikolai buttoned his shirt and considered the fight. He'd been pinned under his own shield and attacked by plants. He saw no easy solution, so he backtracked further in the fight. How had he gotten on the ground in the first place? Somehow, she had struck him from the rear.

"I wasn't expecting to be attacked from behind, so I guess I could have rotated my shield. But that would've left me vulnerable on the other side."

"Why not create a shield encapsulating your entire body?"

He frowned. "I've never tried. We were taught to pivot if we needed to block something."

"A complete sphere is ideal—too many people forget to block their sides, head, and feet."

"Is there really much danger of someone attacking feet?" They were such a small target, easily blocked by a standard shield if you could see it coming. Something else nagged at him about the suggestion, but he had no time to think on it.

"Of course there is. If your opponent is smart, they will strike where you are weak, so do not give them any easy targets—unless you mean to draw them into a trap. Now, tell me why your shield failed."

There was no way he was discussing the dark thoughts that plagued him. Impossible to tell if the shield had collapsed when his concentration broke or if he'd listened to the nagging doubts and let it go.

"The force was too great. I had to drain all my mana to keep it intact."

"What could you have done instead?"

"If I knew, I would have done it."

"Why not change the shape, diverting the rock to one side and rolling out from under it?"

He blinked. "Change the shape?"

"That explains much." A yellowish oblong disk sprang to life in front of her. "You recognize this?"

He nodded. "It's a sparring shield. Blocks physical attacks and magic."

"At their heart, spells are shortcuts that enable you to perform magic quickly, without thought. Anyone can create a spell. Incantations, chants, rituals—these triggers allow others to use the spell without understanding what the magic does. It's like . . ." She paused an inordinate amount of time before continuing. "Light switches. I don't know how precisely they work, and I'd imagine most Mundanes don't either, but we can still flip the switch and get light. With me so far?"

"Yes." The Mundane comparison was troubling, though he couldn't say why.

"Standard spells are fine, they have their uses. The problem with becoming overly reliant on them is that you fail to customize. Your shield looks and behaves like everyone else's. Watch closely."

The yellow tint of Medea's shield changed to rosy pink and then periwinkle blue before vanishing completely.

"It's still there," she said, as if reading his thoughts. "Shields are naturally invisible. When competitive sparring became popular, judges created the so-called 'sparring shield' so they could be easily seen. That's what happens when you use spells created for someone else's purpose. Masters customize their magic and use spells with intent."

The shield reappeared and changed from disk to flat plane, then bent down the middle to form an angle like a roof. Tapered like that, the boulder would have slid right off, allowing him to roll away. The shield expanded, enclosing Medea in a full sphere.

Impressive as it was, he immediately grasped the problem that had troubled him earlier. "How am I supposed to attack from in there?"

"What do you mean?"

"Everything will rebound and hit me." It was a little sad she could miss something so obvious. A complete sphere seemed Useful enough for cowards who wanted nothing more than to avoid being hit, but for someone fighting back, a partial shield was required. Without any kind of gap, you'd have to take down the sphere every time you wanted to attack, which meant conjuring a new shield each time. It might not matter to someone like Medea, but it would drain most people's mana in short order.

He tried to explain the problem as gently as he could. She didn't take it well, placing a fist to her brow and sinking to the grass, where she breathed deeply as if steeling herself against his words.

"That was illuminating," she said when he was finished.

"I'm happy to help in any way I can." He sat down next to her, placing his hand comfortingly on her shoulder. Steely eyes greeted his, then dropped to the hand, which he hastily removed.

"To think," she said, "all these years I've been approaching the problem wrong. I thought my apprentices dense. Some people are set in their ways and there's no help for it."

He stretched out and leaned back on his arms. Few things were more pleasurable than being proved right. "It's not your fault. Sometimes these things require a fresh perspective."

She didn't appear to hear him. "Even before wands, I remember students who struggled with the concept. Obviously, wands have made it worse, but this? I never expected . . ."

He wasn't sure what wands had to do with full-body shields, but he nodded and muttered something supportive. It was good he was building rapport. A few more conversations like this and he might even be able to bring up immortality again.

Medea began to laugh, the intensity steadily increasing until she struggled to breathe. Nikolai joined her, doing his best to sound sincere. People liked it when you shared their emotions. Slowly she regained control, but not without periodic giggles. At last, she leaned back in the grass and took a deep breath.

"Centuries of apprentices, and it never occurred to me." Another chuckle escaped. "To think, all this time you believed spells originated from your person."

Wait, what? She hopped to her feet and he jerked himself upright. What was she talking about? She caught sight of his face and the laughter began anew.

"Don't worry," she said with a smile, "we'll get past this mental block you've manufactured." Medea spun around, looking for something, and ran to tap the boulder. "Ah! Here, we'll use this. Hmm, it will probably be easier if you start from the same general direction. Come stand next to it."

"What are you going on about?"

Either she didn't hear him or chose to ignore the question. Her countenance, normally stoic, took on a frantic energy that was borderline manic. In her haste, she magically yanked Nikolai to the boulder and spun him to face the forest.

"There. Don't move!" Her blonde hair trailed behind her as she flew through the air and landed several paces away. "I want you to hit me with a projectile spell. Something small—hmm, how about Puncture? No wand! This time, I want you to focus on generating the spell *from the rock*. Got it? Go!"

She might have been speaking Latin for all the sense she made. "You want me to do *what*?"

"I want you to cast Puncture, not from your wand, but from

the rock, and send it toward me." She spoke slowly, as if he were feebleminded, and pointed from the boulder to herself.

"What? I can't do that. No one—" He stopped, suddenly recalling his conversation with the retired Enforcer. The lone survivor of the Collective's diplomatic mission had said something about spells hitting from every direction, he was sure of it, and she had opened this duel by striking him in the back. At the time, he'd thought it a rock thrown with telekinesis. "Did you hit me in the back with a *spell*?"

"I'm a mage. What else would I hit you with?"

He stared at her, dumbfounded. She was serious. If this really worked . . . "Sorry, I'm just—I'm having trouble understanding the technique. How do you do it?"

Medea opened her mouth and froze, her face going through an odd parade of expressions before at last she blurted out, "I don't *know*, but it's no different than any other spell." She pointed at the ground. "There. Can you grab a blade of grass with your mind?"

"Of course I can." He said it with confidence, and yet it was difficult without the wand. It took several tries, but at last a stalk of grass floated into the air.

"See? You did it, and you boiled water this morning without a wand. How is *Punctum* any different?"

"It just is."

"Can you ignite a fire from across the room?"

"I can spark a flame."

"But you can't shoot a fireball?"

"That's the key word—shoot."

"Ah, so you believe projectile spells originate from your wand."

"They do!"

"And yet nothing else does. A wand is not a pen, to dispense magic from within like ink from a well. You decide where the magic happens. Your focus."

As she spoke, a fireball erupted from the rock—no, *in front of* the rock—and shot toward the sea, flames trailing behind it. He leapt back as heat kissed his chest. A second fireball blazed before him, roiling in place for a moment before launching at the boulder and igniting the surrounding grass. Medea approached. Her hand made a fist, quelling the fire. He couldn't tell if the heat he felt was the warmth of her breath or something leftover from the spell.

"Souls have a bit of self-preservation in them. They provide modest protection against spells being cast directly inside the body." Her head tilted as she studied his chest. "But if your opponent is unshielded, and significantly weaker than yourself . . ." She looked up at him and smirked.

The implication was horrifyingly seductive. No wonder she crushed anyone who'd ever challenged her. With that kind of power, he could do anything. A world of possibilities unfurled.

"I . . . I want to learn it."

"I'm glad you've finally consented to learn something I already told you to try. Go ahead then."

———

Nikolai kicked a clump of dirt, his dreams of easy power snuffed out like Medea's flames. Initiating a spell from a random location had quickly been abandoned, as it required casting without a wand, something he was unable to accomplish consistently.

Instead, Medea tasked him with conjuring a shield without a wand. He could stick with the incantation and circular wrist movement if they helped him focus. It was like trying to write calligraphy with his toes. Technically he had the necessary equipment, but none of the parts were accustomed to operating in such a way. Twice he saw a shield begin to form, but it disappeared before stabilizing. After two hours he'd barely made any progress.

"I believe that's enough for today," said Medea. "You may stay and practice if you wish, but I'm afraid I must retire."

After she'd gone he checked his watch, still set to Haven time. Noon. Here the sun was relatively high in the sky, early afternoon maybe. This morning he'd asked Medea again for the time, and she'd shrugged off his question. Irritating not to know. He toyed with the idea of moving his watch ahead by two or three hours, but in the end kept it set to Haven rather than changing it to a possibly incorrect time.

He sat in the clearing and summoned lunch, *pirog* again. Options were limited when summoning without a plate. As it was, he had to trade hands frequently until the pastry cooled. Before finishing, he tore off a corner and flicked it into the grass.

As he ate, he considered the puzzle before him. Something was messing with his head, that much was clear, but what, and how? He tallied the incidents: yesterday morning, yesterday afternoon, today. What did they have in common? Medea's mana potions were the obvious culprit, but she'd only given them twice and they didn't explain the first occurrence. This did not mean Medea was innocent, only that she must be observed more carefully.

The *pirog* turned out to be the fruit-filled variety, and soon his hands were sticky with red goo. Nikolai returned to the garden by the hovel. There he found what he was looking for behind an old statue—a crank water pump. Hands clean, he set out to explore.

On the far side of the hovel he found a graveyard. Weeds ran rampant between the simple flat stones acting as grave markers. There was no sign that names or dates had ever been etched into the well-weathered stones. If not for a single small mausoleum, he would have mistaken it for yet another curious collection of rocks.

He continued on, picking his way through the tall grass interspersed with the occasional cypress tree, until the land terminated in a sheer cliff. Waves pounded the rocks below in a casual display of eternal power, its beauty intoxicating.

Something tugged at his awareness, little more than a breath of a feeling. As he followed the coastline, it grew stronger. The cliff here was too steep to climb, but further on it sloped to a rocky shore. Nikolai picked his way down between rocks and backtracked along the coast, a hound on the scent.

At the base of the cliff was a wide-open cavern. Humidity greeted him at the entrance. Clouds of steam obscured his view. He made his way carefully, boots threatening to slip on stones slick with slime. Soon his shirt was plastered to his back.

Inside was a natural hot spring. Rivulets of water connected several small pools. Gingerly he tested each with his hand. They grew successively warmer as he approached the back of the cavern. Second to last was scalding, and he dared not touch the final pool.

The cave pulsed with subtle energy, like the immense heart of a sleeping giant, but it was strongest here. A succession of reveal spells found no identifiable enchantments. He'd have to come back when he was more prepared. For now, he might as well make use of the pools.

He chose one a little more than halfway back, stripped, and sank gratefully into the warm water. The tension eased from his muscles. One hand moved back and forth, in time with the thrumming sensation. Small rings rippled out from his hand and moved slowly across the pool.

The more he thought on it, the more convinced he became that Medea was dosing him. The concoction was designed to make him tractable, to prevent him from exploring the island or gaining power too fast. Her feigned anger at his convalescence was an interesting ploy. He would have chosen sympathy, as he had when he was poisoning Petrov, but then she seemed to have a better read on him than he did of her. That would have to change.

Tomorrow he would ask to see the library. Would she bar access, as she had to the dungeon? If everything appeared available, it was a sure sign she had a stash elsewhere. No, that was a certainty. Immortality was one secret she did not share. At the very least, her notes on immortality would be hidden.

When light began to fade, Nikolai exited the pool and dressed in damp clothes. Pink tinged the horizon as he walked back to the hovel. Wind combined with the sound of the ocean to turn the rippling grass into a sea of its own. At the hovel he stooped to avoid the low frame and made his way to the kitchen.

An hour later, he'd managed to summon a very particular style of shepherd's pie. Mary always did love to garnish her favorite meal with a sprig of rosemary. He took a single bite, savoring the flavor of triumph, then dumped the pie in the trash and summoned *golubtsy* for himself.

When he'd finished eating, he washed the dish and returned it to the shelf, right next to a familiar chipped plate. He knew the pattern well, given how much he'd stared at its emptiness before Medea had summoned Stroganov. So, that's how Medea dosed him the first time.

Clever to not always use the same source. She could have used a different concentration the first time, delaying the initial onset of symptoms. He would have suspected poison sooner if he'd taken ill shortly after dinner. By morning, he'd forgotten.

He couldn't let on he knew about the mana potions or she'd find a new way to dose him. The two she'd given him had been premade, but he was expected to make his own from now on, which meant she would tamper with the brew. She probably already had, given her close "inspection" of the potions he'd made today. One by one he took them from his pouch and poured them down the drain.

Nikolai peeked into the common room. Shadows danced on the walls from the crackling fire. He crossed to the lab, praying it would be just as empty. Luck was with him. He could make potions now and Medea would be none the wiser.

Brewing went much faster, as he no longer had to contend with her constant interruptions. He searched drawers until he found a grease pencil and placed a small dot on each of the vials, marking them as safe for consumption. Potions stowed in his pouch, he crept back to his room. Let's see the bitch dose him now.

14

THE LIBRARY

Nikolai awoke refreshed and ready for the day. After several sets of push-ups and sit-ups, he showered and took care of himself, longing for one of Mrs. Gallagher's morning blowjobs. Difficult going without sex for so long. Shaving without a mirror remained a challenge, but he was getting the hang of it. Less stubble today. A hearty breakfast later, he bounded into the lab and offered Medea a cheerful greeting.

"Mmm." She didn't look up from what she was doing but waved in the general direction of the cauldrons, already set out for him and probably already contaminated with her drug of choice.

He smiled and set to work. Boiling water proved a nuisance. His good mood meant Medea had to strike him repeatedly to get him in the proper mind-set. Potion-making went smoothly. He was careful to take longer than necessary so as not to seem overly familiar with the lab. When they were finished brewing, he poured them out and watched as Medea began her careful inspections. He could detect no sleight of hand. Either she was that good, or the cauldrons had definitely been pretreated.

He was just about to ask about the library when she said, "No practical lesson today. I want to show you the library. Collect your potions and follow me." Medea left via the door to the common area, leaving him to stopper the bottles alone. He'd discard them later.

Definitely a telepath. She wasn't even being subtle about it, but then telepaths were exceedingly rare. Most Magi could sense the intrusion. How was she getting into him without detection? How deep could she go? Nikolai could only pick up surface thoughts. If she could delve deeper, he might be in trouble.

Nikolai deposited his vials in his pouch and went to catch up. Medea stood in front of a door opposite the entrance to the hovel. On the same wall, closer to the kitchen, was a second door he'd yet to enter.

Medea looked at him levelly. "Before we go in, I'd like to discuss the rules."

Of course she did. "Replace everything times two?" he teased.

"No." Her perpetual frown deepened. "Many of the manuscripts here are irreplaceable. Food and drink are not permitted. Hands must be clean. Do your palms sweat?"

"No."

She grabbed one of his hands, rubbed the palm while peering at it intensely, then dropped it again just as suddenly. "Everything must be placed back exactly where you found it, though you can leave books out in designated areas if you have longer projects that require multiple consultations. Nothing leaves the library without my permission."

"Okay." Nikolai started toward the door.

Medea refused to budge and pierced him with her gaze. "Failure to follow the rules will mean your expulsion from my island—possibly worse. I do not take damage or theft lightly."

The severity of her expression was almost comical. It was all he could do not to needle her. "I understand."

She scanned his face as though expecting to catch him in a lie, then turned to open the door. His gaze wandered to the other locked door.

"What's through there?"

"What? Oh. That's the gateway room." Again the dismissive wave.

"Can you unlock it for me?"

"I told you, everything remains locked until I've had a chance to explain it." As if gateways needed explaining and it wasn't completely suspicious to keep the only exit locked. In her words, not even a good lie.

"Great! You can show it to me now." Feigning studious interest, he walked over to the other door.

Medea stood rooted, mouth a thin line. *"Today we're doing the library."*

"Oh, alright then. Maybe you can show me afterward." He affected a nervous laugh as he came back to her side. "Boy, I'd sure hate to be stuck here if something happened to you."

"We won't have time later, and nothing is going to happen to me." She preceded him through the door.

Her volume-expanding spellwork, already impressive beyond imagining in the common area and its attached rooms, had nothing on the library. The place was a cathedral. He couldn't even *see* the back.

Dark wood framed the vaulted ceiling, which was painted to look like the sky. Closest to the entrance, pink-suffused clouds and shafts of golden light mimicked sunrise. Tufts of white broke up the blue farther back, which eventually darkened into a midnight sky dotted with constellations.

On either side of the central archway were alcoves with bookshelves towering to the ceiling. There were three levels, though he could see no ladders for accessing the upper reaches. Each alcove was labeled with a type of magic. The left side seemed completely devoted to Healing. On the right, he could make out

Nature, then Summoning. Unlike the rest of her home, the furniture in the library was abundant and reasonably modern, or at least better maintained. Tables were polished to a shine and every alcove sported a comfortable chair for reading.

Immense as it was, the library managed to have a quality every other room thus far had lacked—it was welcoming. He smiled with genuine pride to have pegged her so right. Here was a place of worship, where Medea knelt at the altar of knowledge. He couldn't wait to see her section on black magic.

She led him to the fifth alcove. Instead of bookshelves, it contained a raised dais with a podium. A huge magnifying glass attached to a tall metal arm sprouted from a small table in front of the podium. They walked around to the front of the podium, which held a massive book. Medea opened it and motioned Nikolai next to her. The pages were blank.

"This is my master grimoire. It can be used to access books within the library. Well, some of them anyway. Not everything is cataloged. As you may have noticed, I have quite a few books. It takes time to get them all tagged."

"Tagged?"

"A spell connecting individual books with the grimoire. Watch." She flipped to the first page. Blue runes shimmered across and formed into words. What was it with her and blue runes?

What knowledge do you seek?

Medea retrieved a fountain pen from a nook in the podium. "Let's say you want to call lightning. You write on the first page and the first page *only*."

Nikolai nodded and Medea wrote 'lightning' in a clear, strong hand. The runes moved, filling the page with a list of books and their location within the library.

"Handy."

"It gets better." She flipped through the book. The once-empty pages were now filled with excerpts from other works, in all different languages and styles of writing.

Impressive. He could find anything here, though he'd probably have to learn a few more languages.

"Do you have translations for any of these?"

Medea sighed. "I *had* begun writing a compendium of my own, containing all of this—" She gestured vaguely to the entire library. "But there's so much here, and magical theory changes. I would complete a chapter and a few centuries later it would be out of date. It's a work in progress. In the meantime you can use this."

She pulled the magnifying glass over, adjusting the arm so it was suspended over the page. Nikolai peered through. What had previously been Greek was now Russian, albeit a very garbled version.

"It's a translation disk. I have a few others stashed in the desks around the library. They're not perfect, as you can see. Language is a complicated thing, full of double meanings, connotations, and unspoken assumptions." She closed the book and walked on.

The tour seemed to go on forever. Medea spoke at length about her collection and the work to amass it. With distaste, he saw the largest section by far appeared to be Healing. Elemental and Nature were also quite extensive. Botany at least made some sense, considering how often plants were used in potions, but he had to cough to avoid laughing when they passed several alcoves devoted to music.

The further they walked into the library, the more his disappointment grew. Of curses he saw nothing. Demonology and Necromancy had comparatively small sections, at least two-thirds of which was blocked off. Only the ground floor, she explained, was available to novices. Journeymen and masters had access to the second and third floors, and levitation was required to reach them. It would have been simple enough to bypass if she hadn't also warded them with an invisible barrier barring anyone of insufficient rank. Several other sections, most notably Healing, had no such barriers.

They arrived at one alcove that appeared to be more anthropological than magical. The library was a lot less impressive when one factored in these Mundane texts. As Medea enumerated her difficulties in sorting the regional magics of various peoples, Nikolai seized the opportunity to interrupt her.

"Where is the section on black magic?"

"I've told you, there's no such thing as 'black' magic. There is only the caster and their intent. As I was saying, here we have the Tohunga section, native to New Zealand, which contains a variety of magics, including healing, fortune-telling, astronomy, tattoo . . ."

It would have been funny if it hadn't been so frustrating. He'd been dying to get Medea as a mentor, and here she was rambling about tattoos and tribes, and her magical library had a section on music.

"But certainly there are spells designed only for harm? Bleed, Fear, Flay . . ."

"Yes, there are some spells that have more limited applications, but these should not be the focus of your studies."

"But it's my choice though, isn't it? I didn't come here to learn about astronomy and music."

The gaze that met his was stony. "I was hoping to forestall this conversation a while longer, but I suppose it's best to get it over with."

Medea took him back to the front of the library, to an alcove with two armchairs. When they were both seated, she steepled her fingers and leaned back. "What do you hope to accomplish here?"

"I want to become the most powerful dark Magi in the world. I'll leave the title of most powerful overall to you." He smiled.

Medea's face remained impassive. "And you wish to do this how? By learning nothing but offensive spells?"

"The best defense is a good offense. Opponents should be crushed quickly and without mercy." Unless they were significantly weaker than you, in which case it was more amusing to watch them squirm.

"On that we agree. But there is more to combat than offense. The best defense is an unbreakable defense. You *will* encounter opponents who cannot be dispatched quickly." She rubbed her forehead. "For the first few years I will teach you the basics. There are also things you must unlearn."

"My wand, I know."

"Yes, the wand, among other things. Once I see you making strides in the basics, I will allow you to choose your first specialty. I teach an assortment of magic, but specializing will allow you to reach the rank of master or grand master in your chosen school."

"I'd like to choose now."

She continued as if she hadn't heard him. "Given that your life is comparatively short, I recommend no more than two specialties, possibly three."

"Great, I choose—"

She raised her voice. "You have not even been exposed to all the magical schools yet. How could you possibly know which will be the best fit?"

"I've known for a long time."

"I bet you have. Bear in mind that children are fascinated by flashy things, and steel is more functional than gold. One moment." A sheet of paper and pen flew around the alcove wall and landed in front of Medea. She scribbled something, folded the paper, and handed it to him. "Don't open that yet. First let me hear your selections."

"Necromancy, of course, curses, and, hmm . . . probably demonology."

"Okay, now read the paper."

He unfolded the sheet and glanced down.

You will pick one or more of these:
Curses, "death spells"/necromancy, demonology, voodoo

Definitely a telepath. Her previous apprentices had no doubt been suitably impressed. He smiled and pretended to chuckle. "I forgot about voodoo. Looks like you know me pretty well."

"You and every other Magi with delusions of grandeur and a taste for 'black magic.' They all pick these!" She gestured testily at the paper, obviously upset he knew her secret.

"That's where the best spells are."

Medea sighed and leaned back, running a palm over her face. "No, they're not. Tell me, what is the largest section in my library? You must have noticed."

"Healing, but it's not like I can heal my opponent to death."

The look she gave him was so serious that he burst out laughing. Why did she persist with this ruse? She must know it wasn't working. And yet she plowed on despite his chuckling. "With healing spells, I can outlast any opponent. I can also ravage their body with things like cancer—"

He laughed even harder and mimed speaking with someone else. "Excuse me, sir, I know we're in the middle of a duel, but would you mind taking a break for six months so my cancer spell can work?"

"Your comments belie your ignorance. You do not even know what a curse is."

His temper flared. "Of course I do! And if you can't teach me anything of interest, I might as well leave now." He moved to get up. Fuck her and her bullshit excuses. This was a mistake.

A force slapped him back into the chair so hard it nearly overset. Medea was suddenly in front of him, eyes blazing.

"You admit I am more skilled than you, then have the audacity to insult my knowledge and abilities?" She stalked around his chair like a hungry tiger, glowering down at him, though even while standing she wasn't much taller than him sitting in the chair.

He glared back at her, seething.

"This is why I stopped taking apprentices. Why do you even need me if you already know everything? *Don't answer that*," she snapped, grabbing the paper back from him. "This"—she brandished the list—"is ridiculous! First of all, 'curses' are not a magical school. It's a generic term. Every magical school contains curses. If you curse someone to spontaneously combust, you are using a *fire* spell. If you curse someone to be pursued by crows, you are using a *nature* spell. And if you curse someone to bleed to death, you are using a *healing* spell."

Semantics. She was arguing semantics. At least now he knew the library did contain curses. They were simply buried alongside Useless spells.

"Okay, I can't specialize in curses," he said in a calm voice, "but the rest are still valid. I could summon dead bodies, great demons, and—"

"Are you going to run around town with a pack of dead bodies at your side?" She had her hands on her hips, and for a moment she was his mother, scolding him for getting into trouble again.

"Of course not." He could, but that would draw a lot of attention. The Mundane would go nuts, Enforcers would be sent in . . .

"If someone attacks you in the middle of a city, where are you going to get bodies for your little army?"

Everywhere. The bodies were literally everywhere—frozen in

the streets surrounded by rubble, crouched in doorways, piled up in ditches, abandoned on children's sleds when it no longer seemed a reasonable trade to burn precious calories moving them. You couldn't even tell if they were male or female. Mother hadn't wanted him to see, but he'd never been a good listener.

Nikolai yanked his thoughts away, hand on a hot stove. Had Medea read his thoughts, or had she somehow dredged them from the depths?

He turned his mind back to her question. Most cities didn't have an abundance of corpses. He could kill bystanders, provided there were bystanders to kill, but that would definitely draw unwanted attention. How long did it take to reanimate a corpse? What did it take? Okay, maybe the logistics were a little fuzzy, but it would still be incredible to command an army of the dead.

But then he'd have to house them somewhere. If they had a limited shelf life, that could be a problem. Would they smell? How long did they last? Necromancy began to look a lot less attractive.

Medea relaxed and sat down. "You see the problem. Good."

"What about demonology?" No storage needed. Probably smelled better too.

"That requires a special circle. It's easy enough to paint on a large cloth, which can be folded and carried in your pouch."

"Okay, I pick demonology."

"It also requires candles, sometimes a sacrificial offering . . ."

Annoying, but still doable. She could be lying about all of it. At the very least, she was spinning his favored magical schools in a negative light. Probably trying to drive him to something less powerful.

"The real problem with demonology," Medea continued, "is that you cannot summon anything more powerful than yourself. Technically you *can*, but it would be unwise."

That definitely sounded like a lie. The whole point of

demonology was to summon something with ridiculous abilities to do your fighting for you. "Why?"

"Imagine this. You call forth an archdaemon. It towers over you, immense in power. What does it do?"

"Whatever I tell it. The summoning binds it to my will."

"Yes, but your power is what keeps it in bondage. If you are less powerful than the archdaemon . . ." She gestured expectantly with her hand.

Oh. "It will break the bond and kill me." There had to be a way around that. Surely demonology was Useful for something. She would shoot down his last option, but he asked anyway. "What about voodoo? I suppose that's worthless too?"

"No, actually, voodoo is quite useful—"

Finally!

"—but it's a religion, not a magical school, with its own set of spells and beliefs, most of which aren't designed to hurt people. I can get you a list of gods and you can decide which you'd like to pledge service to."

"You know damn well I have no interest in that."

She shrugged. "Doesn't hurt to ask. You don't have to pick a specialty today. I recommend you take time to learn each school so you can make an informed decision, especially since they complement one another. If they're too similar, it will put you at a disadvantage. Your first choice should be something based off your natural strengths." She moved to get up.

"Telepathy. That's my first specialty."

Medea froze halfway out of the chair, then sank down heavily. "Telepathy?"

"Yes. Is there a problem?"

"No, I just . . . you realize it's incredibly difficult to learn, let alone master? It could take decades. Unless you're born with the skill, the odds of success are—"

"I was. Born with it, I mean." He studied her face for anger, fear, anything, but she continued in the same tone she used when talking about potion ingredients.

"Interesting. Natural telepaths are quite rare. Usually they spring up when a child with latent magical proclivities has a desperate need to understand those around them. I always found it odd that it was not the case for me."

"You didn't want to understand people?"

"That's just it—I did. In fact, when I was a child, I thought everyone was telepathic except me. They understood each other with such ease, whereas I found them baffling, and they me. It wasn't until I got older that I realized they were reading other cues."

"And that's when you decided to learn telepathy?" If he was natural-born and she wasn't, he likely had an edge.

"Oh, that came much later. In truth I put it off for a long time. I'm . . . I've met enough people to know that their minds are something I'd rather not see. But magic is magic, and so I learned it eventually, or enough to keep people out of my own mind. I don't consider myself proficient."

"You seem perfectly capable to me." He smiled.

"What do you mean?"

"I mean I've never felt your intrusions. I'll admit I'm jealous. I've never been able to get into other Magi undetected."

Color rose in her cheeks. "You felt nothing because I've never used telepathy on you. It would be exceptionally rude."

"Uh-huh."

Medea's hands began to shake, and her words came out clipped. "You—I would *never* . . . What do you take me for?" Her voice broke on the final question, almost as if she were fighting back tears.

He had to admire her feigned indignation, even if it was annoying that she refused to drop the act. The performance was spot-on.

"I'm ever so sorry. I didn't mean to offend."

But Medea wasn't looking at him. She stared off to the side, brow furrowed and breath short. Abruptly, she stood. "Telepathy is on the . . ." She paused an inordinate length of time, eyes downcast, then gestured angrily to the right side of the library. "There! Other specialties will have to wait. Now, if you'll excuse me." She left in a flurry of red.

Talk about dramatic. He could have given a better performance in his sleep. Nikolai smiled and walked toward the Telepathy section. Time to see how much fun he could have with his natural gift.

He made it four alcoves before his sense of purpose fled and he sank to the floor.

15

MAGIC SIGHT

Medea stumbled up the staircase, feet moving too fast to land where they should. Rushing always made her clumsy, but speed was necessary. She had to get to her room. Her hands gripped the iron railing, as if by holding on to something physical she could keep herself from flying apart. After what seemed like an eternity, she arrived at her door.

The knob defied her hands. She clenched her jaw, willing back tears as she struggled with what should have been a simple mechanism. How hard could it be to twist something? She resisted the urge to blast it open. A gaping hole wasn't conducive to privacy, and she desperately needed privacy just now.

At last she was through. Sound shield in place? Yes. She took a shuddering breath and sank against the door, hands running over her face.

A sob erupted. One after another after another. The tears that had been trying so desperately to break free were at last given free rein. Medea flung her head back against the door, but the pain did nothing to silence her frantic mind, nor did the fingernails biting into her palms. The shallow breaths deprived her of oxygen. She knew this too, but one can know a thing and be unable to stop it. Emotion was the enemy of logic.

The accusation ran around in her brain like a mad dog. It didn't matter that it was untrue, or that it had been made by a boy who knew nothing about her. The very idea that she would read his mind . . .

Thoughts were private. They deserved to stay private. Using telepathy on an enemy was one thing—even a stranger was acceptable, if you had need and few other options—but someone you knew? Especially in a professional relationship! Insulting beyond belief. It was the ultimate breach of trust. What kind of person does such a thing?

Of course she knew exactly what kind of person did such things, and he was downstairs right now, no doubt learning how to do it better. The thought bled some of the toxins from her mind. There was something new to focus on, troublesome in a different way. The hound inside latched on and worried it.

A natural-born telepath.

Medea sat up—when had she slumped over?—and wiped her eyes with the back of her hand. She should have agreed to start him on necromancy, but it was too late now. Telepathy! Unsettling that it even existed. Still, telepathy was a form of magic, and magic was what she taught. Knowledge was meant to be shared. What her students did with it was no concern of hers. If they stepped too far out of line, the universe would correct them. It always did.

But still . . . *telepathy*.

The training would be difficult for both of them. She knew far more about blocking intrusion, about projecting thoughts into others for the sake of communication, than invading minds. And it meant they'd have to leave the island, go out into the world, and encounter *people*.

She toyed with the idea of taking him someplace where he didn't speak the language. At least that way when he entered minds, the thoughts would stay private. She shook her head. No. Anything worth doing was worth doing right, and as his master she had a duty to uphold.

Maybe she could at least put off the training for a few years. He was, what, early twenties? At twenty-five his forebrain should be finished growing and he'd hopefully have a modicum of self-control. By then he might choose a different specialty. In the meantime, she'd have to brush up on the magical school.

Medea stood and straightened her dress, then went to find her telepathy notes.

Nikolai's ass hurt. His legs cramped too. The next time his brain decided to have a pity party, he needed to make sure he was near a nice chair, not standing on a hard floor. He stood with a groan and checked his watch. Midnight. The episode had lasted nearly twelve hours. He ignored the grumbling of his stomach and stormed toward the front of the library.

What the hell happened? He'd taken one potion earlier to replenish his mana after boiling water, but it was one of his own making, he was sure of it. He ducked into an alcove with a table and fished out his potions. Nine marked, ten unmarked. It didn't make any sense, unless the ingredients themselves had been tampered with. He mentally went through the list of ingredients for the mana potions. Everything he needed was in the garden outside the hovel, or growing wild nearby.

He retrieved the lamp from his room and headed outside. Collecting plants by lamplight was harder than he'd thought. He was about to pocket a bunch of garlic stalks when he realized they were actually deathcamas. Who planted innocuous species right next to their extremely toxic look-alikes? He shoved the death-camas into his breast pocket—you never knew when poison would come in handy—and redoubled his search for garlic.

A half hour later he had all the ingredients he needed, save harp root. Nikolai waded into the golden sea of grass, shining the lamp on the stalks to discern them. He tilted his head, staring curiously at the plants. Harp root was the only nonstandard ingredient in Medea's potions. It had one of those names that sounded familiar, but now that he thought on it, he couldn't recall ever having heard of it before.

He left the grass behind. Back in the lab, he brewed potions once more, grateful that Medea wasn't a night owl. He used the traditional ginseng in place of harp root. Unfortunately, his potions were now obviously different—yellow as opposed to milky white. Perhaps he could palm the vials in such a way that Medea wouldn't notice. Nikolai practiced grasping a vial until he was certain he could drink it while keeping the glass concealed, then went back to his room and toppled into bed.

A fireball slammed into Nikolai's shield, the heat so intense he could've sworn his eyebrows were singed. He shot back with lightning. The freedom of being able to cast whatever he wanted was immensely satisfying. All his life he'd had to hold back for fear of harming sparring partners. Now he could cast anything. Anything!

The lightning arched from his fingertips and crackled the air on its way to Medea, who redirected it to the ground at her feet. That was the downside to sparring with her. Nothing ever hit unless she wanted it to, as she'd done that first time with Pain, simply to see how potent it was. Despite the exhilaration of casting any spell in his repertoire, the results were anticlimactic. He desperately wanted to see something break.

He launched Contagion and Fear, aiming for her head. A clean shot of Fear could tell him a lot. As usual, she blocked it. Contagion was caught in a swirl of green and disseminated. The grass nearby wilted, and Medea paused to burn the patch before it could spread across her precious field of harp root.

It had been four days since he'd stopped using it in his potions, and the results spoke for themselves. He hadn't had a single episode. Moreover, his training was going well. Without the malaise holding him back, he threw himself headlong into his studies, practicing long after their afternoon training sessions ended. He could now cast most of his spell repertoire without a wand.

Medea didn't suspect a thing. He'd been careful to keep up appearances, faking the malady toward the end of every training session. That was another thing he enjoyed—control. If Medea was blathering on about something unimportant, he'd simply pretend the malaise had struck and the lesson was brought to an abrupt halt. No more boring lectures.

Something tickled his ankle. The grass was alive again, snaking up his legs. Casting spells from an origin other than his body remained above his ability, and so he'd made do with partial shielding. This was Medea's way of reminding him he was still exposed.

He sliced the air with his hand, severing the grass at the base of the shaft. Blades fell limply back to the ground.

"Flamma!" He said the incantation out of habit. The grass at his feet blazed orange. Something slammed into his shield and he flew through the air, landing heavily fifteen feet away. Medea's payback, either for using the incantation or for burning her plants. He'd been trying to destroy a swath of it every lesson.

He sat up and brushed the dust from his shirt. Medea held her hand out and made a fist. His flames were extinguished.

"Must you burn my grass?"

"You keep using it against me, so yeah." His stomach growled, which meant it was past noon, almost time to give his theatrical performance. Medea beat him to it.

"Let's stop here for today. You're doing well. Remarkably well, given your . . . condition."

Shit. He'd have to do worse in practical lessons or his performances would be worthless.

"Soon we'll be meeting in the forest. I'd like to try something new. For today, keep practicing as long as you're able."

That didn't bode well. Maybe she already knew. What else would she do to slow him down?

"I will." He waited until she disappeared into the hovel before pulling out his wand and making his way to the garden.

Now was the perfect time to search the island. Only once had he spotted Medea outside her room after she'd retired. He'd been in the garden collecting plants. She'd looked startled to see him and made a hasty retreat back inside. Having a clear head and plenty of unsupervised time allowed him to practice spells unhindered, as well as peruse the library for hours every night.

Medea's master grimoire was less Useful than he'd hoped, but considering she was hiding things from him, it was to be expected. When he searched it for spells, necromancy and demonology came up with almost nothing. He tried other categories and found a strong bias toward healing and nature magic. But there was one Useful spell he managed to find, one he would soon employ.

Nikolai arrived at the hovel. Bees buzzed merrily in the garden beds while a dragonfly searched for easy prey. A shrill call drew his attention to the roof, where a green bird gleefully tugged at the weeds growing there. Not just any bird—a parrot. The island had to be someplace reasonably warm, even if it wasn't tropical. He tried to memorize how the bird looked so he could research its range, but aside from a red beak it had no distinguishing characteristics. The parrot flew off and he turned back to the task at hand.

Unlike Petrov's reveal spells, which searched for specific enchantments, Magic Sight cast a wide net, allowing him to detect *any* nearby magic. Once he'd located areas of interest, he could come back with more advanced spells. Nikolai touched the wand to his brow and whispered the incantation.

"Shit, fuck!"

It was like being woken up in the dead of night by someone flicking on the lights. He instinctively threw up his arm to block the view, but there was no shielding himself from the assault of magic. The spell affected his mind, not his eyes.

Everything was enchanted—the garden beds, the pump, the statues, even the goddamned bees. The hovel blazed like a beacon. He stepped back and kept going until his perception of the structure dimmed. At fifty paces it was tolerable, and he could make out a morass of spells upon the building.

Early in human history, the color blue was so rare that it didn't exist to humans as a concept. They didn't have a word for it, nor did they even see it. Their brains processed blue in terms of what they knew—ancient Greeks called the sky wine-dark. Only the Egyptians, who had access to the deep blue stone lapis lazuli, created a word for blue.

Nikolai lacked the words to interpret what he was experiencing, and so his brain defaulted to color, texture, mood. There was no way for him to tell what the spells did, only that they felt very different against his senses. This one was yellow and smooth, that one smoky grey and wispy, still another was all hard edges and angry. Dozens of spells, all intertwined, wrapped the surface of the hovel.

The garden was different. Everything had a faint magical glow, but there was no order to it. Only a few things stood out. There was a rectangular pattern beneath the garden beds suggestive of irrigation pipes. The water pump had a sort of white honeycomb mesh running through it.

Nikolai walked along the path toward the beach where he'd first arrived. The same faint magical glow permeated everything from the dirt at his feet to the plants bordering the path. He ran his hand over the tall grass, causing the magic to ripple pleasantly against his senses. There was nothing of note until he reached the beach.

The archway through which he'd arrived was all sharp crystal lines in the shape of a doorway. When he looked at it head-on the view was innocuous, but as he moved around the arch to examine it further, the world spun dizzyingly fast. He toppled to the ground, grasping vainly at the sand like a drunk to steady himself, but now he was falling fast into an infinite chasm of space and stars.

Logic warred with sensation. This was no different than the illusions Fear created. He just had to find a way to break free. The firm press of sand against his chest provided an anchor to reality. He rolled away from the arch. When an upward slope impeded his progress, he scooped at the sand like a sea turtle making its slow progress across the beach. The spinning slowed, and abruptly it was gone.

He stood and shook the sand from his hair, then walked the length of the beach. It would take him longer to get to the cave this way, but the search needed to be systematic or he might miss something. He could check the graveyard on his way back.

Sand changed to gravel. The surf beat against rocks jutting out of the water like black teeth. Everywhere, the same magical glow.

What enchantment did she have over the entirety of the island? Was it the wards, or something else?

Perception of the cave long preceded Nikolai's view of it. He picked his way between the rocks, relying on sensation as much as sight. The inexplicable pulsing of magic grew stronger with every step. By the time he could see the cave, it was almost overwhelming. He approached slowly, acclimating himself to the intensity, a frog sitting in water as it slowly came to a boil.

It was impossible not to squint as he entered the cave, little good that it did. He continued doggedly against the power threatening to knock him senseless. When he reached the back he paused, hoping to acclimate again. No good. There were no specific spells he could see, no colors or textures that stood out. At this range, all he could feel was the ceaseless pulsing of magic, though curiously it seemed to be coming from below him, within the rock itself.

Nikolai stripped and got into the hottest pool he could stand. He inched in slowly, giving his body time to adjust to the sweltering water, lungs protesting against the thick, steamy air. When the water was up to his chin, he closed his eyes and sank. Ignoring the screaming protest of his face against the heat, he pressed his palms to the smooth rock at the bottom of the pool. Pulse. Pulse. Definitely stronger here, but even more so toward the next pool over.

He hauled himself out, gravity tugging against his wet body, and walked to the scalding final pool. Could he empty it? Telekinesis was easy enough with solid objects. Nikolai retrieved his wand from his discarded clothes and made swishing motions across the water. A few drops splattered on the surface, like he'd skimmed it with a stick.

Might as well give Medea's method a try. He set down the wand, cupped his hands, and willed the water to move. The results were marginally better. A bucket-sized scoop of water flung itself into the next pool over, losing half its contents on the way, as if the bucket was full of holes. He kept at it, but the pool was so large it made no difference. The water had to be coming through the ground from somewhere, and until he could empty the pool faster than it could fill, the exercise was fruitless.

He stooped and grabbed his clothes, dressing again quickly and heading to the front of the cave. Time to move on and see what the graveyard held.

Maybe Medea had a space for him there.

Nikolai froze at the errant thought. No, it couldn't be. Even as he thought it, his body was already sinking to its knees beside a pool of lukewarm water. He'd replaced the harp root. He'd fixed this! Obviously not. Why did he ever think he could outsmart someone like Medea? She was better than him at everything. He was stupid and worthless and—

NO!

—Useless. Pretty to look at, but if anyone peered too close, they'd see there was nothing there. No substance. Nothing of value.

As the black cloud descended, Nikolai clutched his head, fingernails scraping scalp. He thrashed from side to side and toppled into the pool. The logical part of his mind remarked this would kill his pocket watch. The less logical side took note that water worked just as well for killing people. Nikolai fought against the desire to let go, but his will slipped away like a greased bar, impossible to hold. Down to the bottom of the pool. *Thunk.* Tepid water permeated his clothes and lungs with equal measure.

Something tugged at his midsection, pulling him upward, and then he was beside the pool again, diaphragm working automatically to purge the liquid from his body. He choked and gasped, still in the grip of the malaise. Nothing mattered. Why couldn't he just die? Better for everyone if he'd never been born.

He caught sight of a bare foot and followed the view up. Medea glared at him, fists clenched at her sides, breathing at the steady pace of someone barely containing their anger. "Don't *DO* that." Contempt dripped from her words. "Don't ever make me do that!" She looked on the cusp of saying something more, then she was gone in a swirl of red.

16

DISJOINTED

He was going to die on this godforsaken island. At least that's what Nikolai's brain told him during the dark moods. The pattern, so clearly linked to the potions before, was gone. All that remained was the unrelenting sameness that was Medea's training schedule.

Up early, then to the lab where Medea was already waiting, nose in a book. She rarely looked up at his entrance. Some vestigial reflex made him greet her every time. She either grunted, didn't respond, or launched without preamble into a briefing on what they'd be doing that day.

The water-boiling exercise was frustratingly difficult. Medea was quick to "help" with a cuff to the back of his head. He often wondered if boiling really did build mana or if it was a habit she'd latched on to and refused to let die. A search in the library revealed that the practice started in antiquity as a purification ritual before making potions.

"From there it expanded to cooking and drinking water," he said when he brought his findings to Medea. "That's probably why ancient Magi lived longer than everyone else—they were killing water-borne pathogens without realizing it."

Medea looked skyward with a groan. "I *know*. Don't you think I know? I was *there*. In case you hadn't noticed, those are my notes you're paraphrasing. Mana-building is still a benefit, and you must practice daily if you wish to improve."

That day he'd needed no external help getting angry enough to boil water.

As soon as the potions were finished, it was outside for practical lessons. Medea stalked around him, making corrections as she saw fit. Some of the things she told him didn't make any sense, either due to her inability to accurately put her thoughts into words, as if her very concept of magic defied explanation, or because she couldn't recall a word itself, rattling off variations in different languages until she found something satisfactory.

"Not that spell," she said one day as they sparred in the meadow. "The one you cast before."

"Which one?" He'd cast half a dozen in the last round.

"The, uh"—she held a fist to her forehead for a good twenty seconds—"the boom-strike spell."

"The *boom-strike* spell?" Half the time he thought she was fucking with him. He'd once made the mistake of offering to read her mind. The look she'd given him had managed to be both affronted and murderous. "Could you be a little more specific?"

"Yes, with the forky things." She splayed her fingers out in front of her.

He peered at her curiously. "You mean Lightning?"

"Yes, that."

At noon, they broke for lunch. Nikolai sat and ate while Medea fiddled with a stalk of grass and continued to lecture. She never summoned anything for herself, doubtless so she could blather on unhindered. After lunch they moved to the library, where she helped him select books for study and drilled him in Latin for an hour before retiring to her room for the rest of the day.

That's how it went on a good day, anyway.

Thanks to the affliction, his reality was a fragmented blur. There was no consistency in the timing or duration of his episodes, and periods of lucidity were tainted by the knowledge that at any moment he could be robbed of his faculties. He lost track of time. Some days he awoke a prisoner of his own mind, incapable of rising from his bed. Other times it struck in the middle of a lesson, often when he was on the cusp of grasping one of Medea's lectures. Whenever his brain filled with doubt and self-loathing, Medea grew increasingly bad-tempered. She'd clench her jaw and insist he push through it. When it became clear he could not, she'd storm off, acting for all the world as if it were his fault for interrupting her instruction.

Every uncorrupted waking moment had to be maximized. Food was summoned directly in hand and consumed on the go. Showers were a luxury he could rarely afford. The bouts of malaise left him feeling more drained than a day brimming with work, yet he forwent sleep and pushed himself to the point of exhaustion, drilling ceaselessly or spending hours in the library, only to wake with his head on the table, cheek in a puddle of drool. Medea took on a manic energy of her own when he was feeling well, trying to cram as much as she could into whatever time she was given, but she refused to make any changes to her schedule.

One week the affliction kept him bedridden past noon every day. Medea's dogged insistence that they begin in the lab meant they had no time for practical lessons, for she still retired midafternoon.

"Why do we always have to start here?" he finally demanded. Medea stood at the sink with her back to him, filling a cauldron with water. "Why can't we start with sparring?"

"You need to make your potion allotment for the day."

"What for? It's not like I'll have a chance to use them."

"We've been over this. Potions first. I don't want you to run out."

"Run out? Are you *kidding* me?" He shoved his hand in his pouch and started pulling out potions. One by one he set them on the center worktable.

"Why are some of those the wrong color? I told you to use harp root."

He ignored the question, punctuating his words with vials. "I. Don't. Need. Any. More. Potions." Soon the table was half-covered.

"Stop. You've made your point."

He ignored her, digging out more potions. On and on they came. Once the worktable was covered, he moved to the back counter and started unloading them there. Laid out like this, it was amazing she hadn't run out of empty vials yet.

"I said you could stop." Medea watched him with an ever-deepening frown. In the sink behind her, water ran over the sides of the forgotten cauldron as the faucet continued its deluge. "Really now, this is ridiculous."

"Yes, it is. It's ridiculous you're still demanding I make potions. It's ridiculous we don't spar while we can. It's ridiculous that I have to waste an hour on a good day learning Latin." He set the last potion on the counter with flourish and upended the pouch, jiggling it for emphasis, then leaned against the counter with his arms crossed.

"There's more to learning magic than simply sparring." Medea turned back to the sink and swore, hastily cutting off the water. She dumped the excess out of the cauldron and waved a hand. His potions began to parade back inside the pouch. When a space had cleared on the worktable, she set the cauldron down.

He glared at it.

"We can't skip the lab, *but*," she said firmly as he opened his mouth, "you can forego making potions until you've run through most of your current supply. I trust you to keep track of what you need. And make any new potions with harp root."

It wasn't much, but it was better than nothing. Maybe he could press further. He relaxed his expression and pulled up a stool in front of the cauldron. "Thank you. This hasn't been easy for me. I'm doing the best I can. Instead of retiring early every day, would you mind working with me later in the afternoons? Maybe an evening or two?"

Her body immediately tensed. You'd think he was asking the world of her.

"I'll work as late as I can," she finally said.

The victory was short lived. Medea would stay with him for an extra hour, two at most. As the day stretched on, she either ceased to follow the conversation, as though she'd mentally wilted, or else she grew increasingly irritable, snapping both verbally and magically.

It crossed his mind that she might be draining him to keep herself young and that he'd interrupted some sort of afternoon replenishment ritual. Many cultures had legends of ancient beings who fed upon youth to extend their own lives. While he was not strictly opposed to the idea—whatever kept him alive would be worth it—he did not want to fall prey to such a spell himself. From what he'd seen with Magic Sight, the whole island was enchanted. There was no way of escaping it, save through the gateway door, which Medea kept locked and warded.

He had to get out of here, if just for a time, and see if the affliction wore off. But how to get Medea to unlock the gateway room? Could he say he missed family? She wouldn't buy that. He could say he just needed a day off to take care of some things, but after so many hours lost wallowing in bed, she would accuse him of being lazy.

He was still mulling over the problem one day as they practiced in the meadow. The malaise had not yet struck, and Medea was in a good mood. She was teaching him about shields, a topic she thoroughly enjoyed, evidenced by the animated way in which she spoke of them.

"People have no idea how versatile they can be! I use them for everything—blocking out sound, in place of shoes, preventing unwanted physical contact—they're just so . . ."

Her brain was doing it again, struggling to find the word, and her hand struck an expectant pose.

"Wonderful?" he offered.

"I was going to say functional, but that doesn't quite encompass it. Multifaceted? Anyway, today I'm going to show you how to create shields that block specific things. Generic shields are too light." She made a slashing motion with her arm. "To be really effective, you need a shield that blocks a few things *very* well—usually physical blows or magical damage. Of course there are different *types* of magical damage, but for the most part you're blocking energy. You need one shield that blocks magic. And farther from your body, you need one that blocks physical blows—"

"Are you saying I should have multiple shields?"

"Absolutely! Layers are essential. One shield is worthless. Make ten, and layer them with a space in between, like so." She gestured to herself, as if he could see her invisible shields.

"A moment," he said, and cast Magic Sight. She probably already knew he could cast it, and it would give him a better glimpse of her defenses, or so he hoped.

"Ah!" Nikolai cried out despite himself. Medea was worse than the hovel had been. It was like looking into the sun, if the sun was standing six feet away.

"I'm glad you've learned that spell. It does take some getting used to though. Try to have it on at all times."

"On?" As before, he found himself squinting. Hard to concentrate with her blazing right there.

"You're not quite ready for it yet, as you don't have the mana to sustain constant spells, but further into your training I will school you in which spells to maintain at all times. They're mostly defensive. Magic Sight is one of them, though with practice you can sense magic perfectly fine without it."

A memory clicked into place. "Is that why you didn't watch my duel—er, sparring match back in Haven?"

The corner of her mouth twisted into a smile. "Is *that* why you destroyed my chair? You didn't think I was paying attention?"

"That was an accident."

She palmed her face. "Again with the lies."

A magical blow to his gut made him double over. "Do you always have to do that?" he said between gritted teeth.

"Yes. I'm trying to build an association between lies and pain, although I'll admit it's not working very well. Usually it only takes a couple days before apprentices start flinching whenever they lie."

"Maybe I was telling the truth."

"You expect me to believe you send lethal spells at your sparring partners?"

"When I know they can dodge them."

Medea shook her head, resigned, and Nikolai realized he was killing her good mood. If he wanted her to unlock the damned gateway door, he was going about it all wrong.

"Yes, I was aiming for your chair. You had your nose in a book the whole time, and I thought you weren't watching me. I got pissed. Sorry." The apology felt lame and stupid.

"Well, I was. I can sense spells just fine without my eyes. Now, back to shields."

Medea pointed to the boulder and bid him watch. One by one, she cast shields over it in layers so sheer they were difficult to discern against the backdrop of the island glow.

Nikolai bent to examine them closer. "Why the gaps?" She'd left about an inch of space between them.

"They're imperative for blocking high-velocity projectiles. Bullets have a lot of kinetic energy for their size and can easily break through a standard shield if it's not strong enough. Using multiple shields, with a cushion of air in between, slows their advance."

"Can't you just push more mana into the shield?"

"Yes, but it's not very efficient. Since you don't know where the bullet will strike, your mana has to be evenly distributed over a larger area, which makes the cost exponentially greater. Bullets can be dealt with in other ways, but that's another lesson for another time. For now, I want you to focus on crafting a shield that repels magical attacks. We'll add more shields later."

He conjured a shield, and a bubble sprang to life. Unlike Medea's shields, which had been barely visible with Magic Sight, his was completely opaque. "I can't see shit in here."

"Dismiss Magic Sight."

"How?"

"Will it to stop. Or just focus on something else. It's all in your head, not your eyes. Try to look at me."

And suddenly he could. If he focused on Medea, he would "see" her in all her blazing glory, but if he wanted, he could switch back to the shield. "This is . . ." But he couldn't think of what it was.

"It takes some getting used to. Ready?"

He nodded.

Medea launched one spell after another at his shield. Smaller fire spells, then larger fireballs. Each time she would have him tweak the shield slightly so that the next round could be blocked better. Eventually Medea dubbed his shield "satisfactory," which was high praise coming from her, and switched to lightning spells.

Her good mood had returned. Casting seemed to bring that out in her, or maybe it was the act of throwing potentially deadly spells at him. He could sympathize with that. Sometimes you just needed to punch something. Nikolai took a breath to ask her about the locked door.

"Oh, before I forget," said Medea, "remind me tomorrow to show you the gateway room, if you're not . . . indisposed. It's past time you had a day off. Both of us, actually. Every day you're well I feel like we have to make up for lost time. I'm afraid I've been working you too hard."

"Thank you. I appreciate that," he said. Lightning slammed into his shield, forking into a dozen tiny paths leading off in every direction.

Fucking telepath. Making the first move allowed her to deflect blame when he inevitably became ill and couldn't go. "How *dare* you accuse me of sabotaging your trip," she'd say. "It was my idea!" The move was so goddamned transparent he was insulted she'd used it. Well, he'd drag his ass through the gateway one way or another.

17

GATEWAYS

Nikolai lay down to sleep, certain the next morning he would wake to find his mind clouded. It would be the perfect excuse for Medea to keep him here. She would shake her head and tell him that he couldn't possibly go out in such a state, but don't worry, rest, she could teach him how to use the gateways another day. Perhaps that was why he woke so early.

He had no way of telling the time, but the lab and library were empty, and it was dark when he peeked outside. Nikolai dressed quickly and summoned breakfast, eating hastily in the common room. A quick tug on the gateway door revealed it was still locked. He hadn't really expected it to be open but felt compelled to check.

Reluctant to leave the common area, he perused the bookshelves. Mundane works, mostly fiction published within the last several years. He snorted at *Animal Farm*. No need to read that shit—he'd lived it. Amusing that capitalist countries believed their politicians didn't use the same tactics. He grabbed a random book and sat down to read, though his mind was too occupied to concentrate on the words.

Would Medea really let him go? Unlikely. But what to do

then? He'd have to figure out a way to get past her wards. There had to be something in the library, but it would be like finding a needle in a haystack. Did the wards respond to touch or presence? If it was the latter, he could maneuver Medea to stand near the door one day, tricking it into thinking she was the person to open it. Maybe the door itself could be blasted open. The damage would be obvious, but at least he'd be through.

The sound of a door opening drew his attention. Medea emerged on the landing above. "It takes a day off to get you up this early?"

"I couldn't sleep. Thought I'd get a bit of reading in." He raised the book in his lap.

"How is it?"

"You mean there's a book in this place you haven't read?"

That earned him a chuckle. "Those are my to-read shelves. I read fast, but not fast enough."

She descended the spiral staircase. He replaced the book and joined her at the warded door. It opened to reveal a circular room. A round table with an ornate box sat in the center, but otherwise it was devoid of furniture. On the opposite wall, blue runes framed a doorway.

Nikolai entered and turned in place. The walls were covered floor-to-ceiling with maps spanning the globe. There was no consistent size or style to any of them. It took him a moment to realize the room itself was one large map of the world constructed of dozens of smaller maps. A decorative border of tiles circled the wall above the maps, just below the ceiling.

Tiny lights twinkled on the maps in green, red, white, and flashing yellow. Sometimes they marked cities, other times they marked locations of no obvious significance. A trail of lights followed the Silk Road from the Mediterranean Sea all the way to China.

Europe was overwhelmingly represented and contained the

most lights. Its maps were disproportionately larger and more detailed. In the East, lights were mostly restricted to large inland or coastal cities, probably following some long-ago trade route. The United States had the second-most dense collection of lights, with a higher concentration on the East Coast. Except for Antarctica, each continent had at least one light.

"Every light you see is a gateway I've made. Teleportation, though possible, is rife with problems. Gateways are a far more effective means of transportation."

He approached the map of Russia. It contained few lights, many of which were red. Closer examination of the lights revealed them to be small, luminescent holes.

"What do the colors mean?"

"Red is hazardous. Unfortunately, the world changes over time. I tried to make my gateways where they might last, but it's difficult to predict how the world around them will change."

"Like the Hanged Man going bankrupt?" He grinned. No wonder she'd bought the place and insisted they keep her room clear of other guests.

"Yes, like that. At least there I could do something. It would have been awkward if they'd demolished the place."

"Would that destroy the gateway? Or could you move it by prying off the doorframe?"

"Most people tie the spell to a particular object like that. I don't. The last thing I need is someone stealing a gateway. Mine are tied to a specific relative location. Trickier to accomplish because if you don't get it right, the gateway will open up into space as soon as the planet rotates."

Now there was a thought. "Is that purely theoretical or has it actually happened to someone?"

"Oh it's happened, though I'm not sure people understood what they were seeing. I found old accounts of apprentices watching their masters walk into what they thought was some sort of ethereal paradise, only to fly off into oblivion, never to be seen again.

"My gateways are anchored to their location in relation to Earth, so no matter how the world moves, the gateway moves with it. Some of my older portals have shifted by a few inches or so, but nothing severe."

"So if the Hanged Man was torn down, the gateway would just float in the air where the inn used to be?"

"Yes. So be careful with red. It means the exit has been compromised. In that annoying war a few years ago, many of my gateways became obstructed with rubble, or the buildings housing them were destroyed." Her tone was that of someone who'd planned a nice evening out, only to find their chosen venue closed.

He scanned the maps of Europe. Sure enough, cities that had been the target of Nazi bombings contained more red lights. The war that had shaped his childhood was no more than a minor inconvenience to her. It spoke to her ability that massive world events meant so little.

He shelved the thought. The faster he got through this lesson, the sooner he could get out of here.

"And the other colors?"

"White is functional, with no known threats. Green is gardens. Flashing yellow means the wards have caught an intruder."

"How do you keep people from getting in? They get dumped on the beach?"

"The gateways are warded. They won't open unless they recognize the person entering or hear the password."

"And the password is . . . ?"

"None of your business." She gave him a look. "If someone tries repeatedly to get through, or if they threaten the gateway itself, the wards will neutralize them."

"Kill them?"

"No. They're frozen in midair and paralyzed. That way I can ask why they're trying to break into my home. Of course, sometimes I forget to check and they're dead by the time I arrive."

"Uh, wouldn't a dead body attract attention?"

She crossed her arms. "I *have* been doing this for a while, you know. The wards detect death and dissolve the body. I am not an amateur."

"Of course. I meant no offense. So how do I make a selection?"

Medea took out a small peg from the ornate box on the table and held it up. "With this." She moved to the map of Ireland and stuck the peg in a white hole marked HAVEN, then moved to the runed door and placed a flat palm on the surface. "Make a habit of checking your surroundings before opening the door. *Specto.*"

Oh sure, *she* got to use an incantation, but when *he* did it, it was wrong.

A rectangular area surrounding her palm became translucent. He approached and peered through. Beyond the gateway was the bedroom at the Hanged Man.

"Clear enough." Medea opened the door and passed through. He didn't follow. Would the gateway seal if he moved the peg? Could he lock her out? It hadn't sounded like it. Probably best not to tempt fate until he understood more, but the idea was heartening.

"Now that you've been identified to the wards, you'll be taken back to the Gateway Room when you cross the threshold. You may use the gateways at your leisure. Don't let anyone see you pass through. If someone manages to cross with you, you'll both be deposited onto the beach. If possible, leave them alive for questioning, unless of course you already know why you were being followed. In that case, just kill them."

The offhand way she said this made his heart leap. A mentor

that understood the necessity of killing! It was too bad she was withholding magic and making him sick.

"Did you want Haven, or someplace else?"

It was tempting to bolt before he lost his chance, but Haven was too small for all the things he needed to do. He needed a large city where he spoke the language. Turkey was a mess last he'd heard, and he had no desire to ever return to Russia. That left Dublin, Glasgow, and London. Dublin was familiar, but London was larger and had better clubs.

"London, please."

Medea stepped through the gateway, closing the door behind her. Would it open again? She moved to place the peg.

"No, wait!" He was an idiot, trapped in the mind-set that he had to stay in Europe. The gateways could go anywhere.

"Can I go to New York?"

"You can go anywhere you see a gateway, but it's the middle of the night there. If you're unsure, check the sun strip." She pointed to the row of tiles over the maps, where someone might normally stick clocks of varying time zones. Above the East Coast of America they were dark blue, almost black. As they crossed over the Atlantic they grew lighter, until at last they were yellow.

New York was tempting. The city probably had quite the night life, and he'd always wanted to see America. Unfortunately, he had things to do that required normal business hours.

"What's wrong with you?" Medea gestured at him with the peg. "I've never seen you so indecisive. It's not like you can't go someplace else next week."

"I didn't expect to have so many choices."

"You're picking a destination, not naming your firstborn! Here."

She slapped the peg against his abdomen, and he fumbled to grab it before it fell.

"When you're ready to return, simply walk through the gateway. The wards will recognize you and do the rest."

The door snapped closed behind her. Nikolai turned the peg in his hands. Being allowed to leave at all seemed wrong. What was she playing at?

Only one way to find out. He inserted the peg into London and opened the gateway door.

GOLDILOCKS

Nikolai peered through the door but didn't step across the threshold yet. The dim alley beyond wasn't exactly inviting, but then Medea probably hid her gateways in less-trafficked areas. He cast Magic Sight to check for any additional enchantments she might have layered on, confident that this time he could cancel the effect if the world started spinning. Sharp crystal lines framed the door, just like the beach portal—he didn't sense any other magic at play. Nikolai stepped through the gateway.

Immediately, his body was drenched with an overwhelming sense of wrongness. His palm slapped against the brick side of the building. He heaved, adding to the bouquet of fetid aromas already present in the alley. Canceling Magic Sight wouldn't work, but he did it anyway.

This was different from the spinning he'd felt at the archway. Whatever caused the giddiness the first day he'd set foot on the island, this was the opposite. He was a fish pulled from the depths of the ocean into the world above, suffering the double shock of pressure change and lack of water. Medea's island was a rushing river teeming with life; the real world was a dried creek bed, cracked and dead.

Empty. This world was empty.

He leaned against the brick wall and slid to the ground. NO. The real world was fine. Medea was fucking with him. She'd already admitted to trying to pair pain with lies. This was no different. There was probably some spell embedded into all her gateways. That's why he hadn't noticed anything out of place with Magic Sight. It made you feel wonderful when heading in the direction of the island, and terrible when leaving. No doubt when he returned, he'd have another sweeping sense of euphoria.

Like the Fear spell, it was something to ignore. Physical sensations, uncomfortable as they might be, could be overcome with a strong enough will. He stood, fighting the desire to retch again, and buttoned his coat. Time to get shit done.

The alley opened to a busy street. Noise struck him like an anvil. Voices, cars thrumming by, and people, so many people! Odd that he could miss such a thing. He drank it all in, a sailor finally come home to port, then set off to get directions.

There were several things he wished to accomplish. First and foremost, he needed to find out if the malaise plaguing him would strike while he was away from the island. One day might not be long enough to tell—there were rare stretches where he went for days without incident, lulling him into a false sense of security.

Second, he wanted to better furnish his room. His trunk, bag, and pouch all had volume-expanding enchantments, but none of them had an opening wide enough to get a mattress through. He'd stayed up late ripping apart old clothes and cobbling together a new bag with a comically large drawstring mouth. With luck, he'd be able to get bedding and a clock in there too.

Last but not least, he wanted to get laid. Taking care of himself hadn't improved his mood. It didn't help that Medea was attractive, in a scrawny sort of way. As she was the only woman for miles around, he'd taken to staring longingly at her ass whenever her back was turned, and she fueled most of his fantasies these days, with the occasional ménage à trois with Shailyn. Hell, he chuckled, maybe *that* was the source of the malaise.

He stopped short. Blue balls might not be the cause of his issues, but it would be just like Medea to make a curse like that. She *had* blinded him just for reading a letter. He'd tried to avoid risqué thoughts in her presence, but as a telepath with unknown abilities, she probably knew. It would certainly explain why she was so damned irritable every time the affliction hit.

He searched his memory of the malaise, trying to see if it coincided with any of the times he'd pleasured himself with Medea in mind. It was no good. There were too many times.

It was her own damn fault for keeping him on a deserted island! What did she expect? He was only human. What went on inside his head was his business. His brain helpfully supplied a vision of Medea on her knees begging for forgiveness while tugging insistently at his belt. NO! Not helpful! He shoved the thought aside and tried to focus on something else.

Ah, here was a store where he could find a bed. A clean bed for a clean mind. He spent an inordinate amount of time picking out a mattress and several blankets, which would help conceal the bed from casual glance should Medea decide to enter his room. No doubt she would be irritated at him for redecorating, given how particular she was about her possessions.

When the clerk was occupied with other customers, Nikolai pulled out his wide-mouthed bag and slipped it over the corners of the mattress. Slowly, he edged the bag up the sides until the mattress disappeared. Even with the drawstring, the mouth of the bag was a bit snug and the process took longer than he liked, but as no one expected a mattress to be shoplifted, the clerk paid no mind to what was happening in the far corner.

At another shop, Nikolai picked out a clock and a pocket watch, setting both to London time. A rug and a few wall coverings would give the place a bit more color. Next trip, he'd have to grab a wardrobe.

On a whim, he ducked into a bookstore and searched for anything that might upset Medea. Nothing jumped out, but he overheard a conversation between two women about a novel in which book burning was a central theme. Good enough. He asked them the name of the book and stole a copy.

By midday he'd finished collecting essentials, along with wallets from a few passersby who seemed particularly distracted. Nikolai strolled down the street looking for anything else that might come in handy. His sparring clothes were rapidly wearing out. Haven sold replacements, but Mundane clothing might do as a temporary fix if he could magically reinforce them somehow. Medea probably had a spell for that, given her unchanging outfit. A tailor across the street looked promising.

An energetic man with tousled blond hair bumped into Nikolai on his way out of the shop. "Pardon me, sir," said the man, looking up briefly to reveal a familiar face that held not a trace of recognition.

Nikolai stared after Harper. If he lived to be a hundred, he would be content never to set eyes on his former classmates again, but Harper had always been an exception. When he first arrived at the Academy at age twelve, Nikolai managed to get off on the wrong foot immediately. Mundanes never noticed his casual telepathic probes; he had no reason to suspect it would be otherwise among Magi. To his chagrin, virtually everyone could feel his clumsy attempts and became hostile. Students were suspicious; staff were firm in their stance that that kind of magic was not tolerated.

He had always credited his persuasiveness to charm and good looks. It wasn't until he was denied use of telepathy that he realized how often he used it to supplement conversations. How else was he supposed to gather information, skirt troublesome topics, and know exactly how to respond? Suddenly nothing he said was right, and he went from endearing to pariah.

Companionship he could live without, but it was intolerable being socially ostracized. Life was measurably better when you were popular. Girls showed you their breasts. People did favors for you. They shared information and possessions. They looked the other way and were more willing to do things that ran counter to their own interests. Despite his attractive exterior, he became no more than "that rude Russian kid." No friends, no allies.

Harper changed everything. A year ahead of Nikolai, he was well loved by faculty and students alike for being affable, good natured, and eager to dazzle. He was forever conjuring illusions to entertain or simply to liven up the drab decor.

At first Nikolai had observed Harper from afar, trying to puzzle out what made him so endearing. If he could replicate it, he might regain some of the ground he'd lost. When he was alone, he practiced mimicking Harper's expressions in front of a mirror.

One day he was discovered by another student. The boy laughed and ran straight to tell Harper. Nikolai followed with blood on his mind. He caught up shortly after the boy reached Harper. To Nikolai's surprise, Harper did not find it at all funny and scolded the boy, making him swear not to tell anyone else.

From that day on, Harper spent an hour before breakfast every morning helping Nikolai crack the code to winning friends, which involved silly things such as being interested in others, smiling, praising instead of criticizing, and listening without constantly trying to interject your own ideas.

Harper's motivations made little sense, but his methods worked—and gave Nikolai significantly more advanced tools for his repertoire. He considered these lessons as important as his lessons in magic, if not more so, and was able to climb the social ladder despite his inner animosity toward just about everyone else at the Academy.

Every day he expected Harper to turn around and insist on recompense of some kind. Why else would he be helping? Unable to stand the suspense, one night he crept into Harper's dorm and attempted to access his unguarded mind.

Harper awoke and asked what Nikolai was doing. There was an awkward misunderstanding about the nature of his visit, and Nikolai demanded to know why Harper was helping him. The boy gave him a pitying look and then offered up his mind, just like that.

He dove into Harper's mind greedily, searching for evidence of betrayal. What he found shocked him. Harper had no ulterior motives. As bizarre as it seemed, Harper's interest in others was genuine. Helping people was something he *enjoyed*, and he could think of no greater accomplishment than making others happy.

Nikolai occasionally glimpsed Mundane minds such as this but couldn't fathom why a skilled Magi had such lowly ambitions. When he asked, Harper said, "I saw enough atrocities during the war. Things no one should ever have to see. Why wouldn't I want to bring light and happiness into the world?"

"Because the world eats itself, and if you're not careful, it will eat you too."

Harper shook his head and chuckled sadly. "You're lucky. You got to ride out the war in Turkey with your mother's family. You didn't have to see the horrible things the rest of us saw. If you had . . ." He shrugged lamely. "It gives you a new perspective on life and what matters most."

That was as close as Nikolai ever came to telling the truth about his time during the war, not out of a desire to share his experience but to prove Harper wrong. The boy had learned exactly the wrong lesson from his tribulations. One didn't face up to predators by becoming prey.

From that night on, Nikolai had observed Harper like a naturalist studying some rare creature. It would have been easy to manipulate Harper. Something always held Nikolai back—a nagging thread of loyalty. Harper had helped him when he'd needed it and asked nothing in return. He was Useful, yes, but in a subcategory Nikolai had yet to decipher, which he dubbed Friend for lack of a better word.

What surprised Nikolai even more than his own reluctance to control Harper was his determination to protect the boy from his own idiotic ideals. That Harper always saw the best in people, Nikolai included, was a clear sign he lacked proper judgment. Nikolai kept Harper's inner circle free of other predators. Bad luck befell those who interfered with his friend, the worst being a broken arm in exchange for a broken heart.

When Harper graduated ahead of Nikolai and joined the Mundane sector as a professional magician, they kept in touch with letters. Nikolai told himself it was prudent to maintain contact with such a talented and well-liked individual.

And now the fucker had walked right past him.

"Hey, *Goldilocks*."

The blond man spun and peered at Nikolai in confusion. After a moment his eyes widened in recognition. "Comrade!"

Nikolai shot him a genuine smile and they embraced.

"You forgot what I look like? It's only been two years."

"No, I—" Harper paused and seemed to collect himself. "I was just heading to lunch. Do you have time to join me?"

"I always have time for you," Nikolai said, and found that he meant it.

Harper led them down the boulevard, periodically stealing nervous glances at Nikolai. Even stranger, when they approached the short flight of stairs leading to the restaurant's entrance, he proffered his arm. Nikolai gave him a questioning look.

"Sorry, you look . . . never mind."

A waiter greeted Harper by name and showed them to what

was apparently his regular table. Once they were seated, Harper leaned forward and beamed at Nikolai.

"What have you been up to? Apprenticeship going well? Learning lots of curses?" His tone made the last question a jest.

The man was dapper as usual. Nikolai was suddenly conscious of his own appearance. It was Harper who'd taught him how to dress and groom properly. Half of his teenage conquests were no doubt due to Harper's insistence that Nikolai make himself more presentable.

Nikolai rubbed absently at the beard that had grown in. When was the last time he'd shaved? He'd have to pick up a mirror or two while he was here. Looks mattered. Everyone liked to pretend they didn't, but they did. Whether you asked for the time or sought a quick fuck, people judged you by your appearance first. He'd let things slip since the malaise had encroached on his life. Exercise and grooming had become afterthoughts, if he thought of them at all.

"Nikolai? Are you alright?"

"I'm fine. I just—a lot has happened. I moved and changed mentors. Sorry I haven't been able to send word."

"I was a bit worried when my last letter returned unopened." It was so like Harper, only bringing up a potentially uncomfortable topic after the other person mentioned it first.

"I'm afraid I've been cut off," said Nikolai. "I had to leave abruptly, and my new home is rather isolated. This is the first I've been able to get away."

"Ah. You know, there's a decent barber not far from here."

"How bad do I look?"

Harper winced. "Not as bad as when we first met but headed in the wrong direction. The beard would look decent if you shaped it, but your face is too nice to hide behind hair."

The waiter came by with tea and took their orders. Harper insisted on paying, which was good, given the exorbitant prices on the menu. He must be doing well for himself if he was a regular. Nikolai chose the most expensive dish available. Might as well get the most out of his time here.

After the waiter left, Harper continued. "So, who's your new mentor? Don't tell me you've gone and tracked down Baba Yaga herself."

Nikolai smiled. "Close enough. Have you heard of Medea?"

"No!"

"Yes."

"I was only joking about Baba Yaga. Medea? *Really?*" He frowned. "I thought she teaches nothing but black magic. I knew you had a taste for the odd and archaic, but really . . ."

Nikolai shrugged noncommittally. Harper had always fooled himself into believing Nikolai's interests were little more than morbid curiosity. It wasn't a notion he sought to change.

"What *is* she teaching you?"

"Latin. A bit of Greek. She constantly rails on the Academy. Apparently, everything we learned there is wrong. My daily chores include making ten healing potions, ten mana potions, and boiling a pot of water." He saw no reason to share Medea's emphasis on wandless magic or custom shields. Harper knew too many people and might go blabbing about it. If Medea's methods gave him a tactical advantage, he wanted to keep it that way.

Harper laughed and shook his head. "Maybe she's gone batty in her old age. So, you're not learning anything good? Why stay then?"

"For one thing, she's immortal. I want to at least learn that."

"I heard she doesn't share the method with anyone."

"She doesn't. But maybe if I train there long enough, I can dig something up."

"Be careful with that. Really. I know I said she's batty, but from what I've heard she's really dangerous." Nikolai could see something click into place, and Harper's eyes widened. "Doesn't she *kill* her apprentices?"

"Don't worry about me, I can handle one old lady."

"Nikolai, um, I didn't want to say anything, but you don't look well."

"I've been sick, that's all. Everything's fine. Nothing I can't fix on my own."

Harper looked unconvinced. Best change topics. Nikolai peppered his friend with questions until Harper was firmly on track to talk about himself. He did regular performances in London and had a two-bedroom flat. Stage magician was a popular choice for Magi wanting to make a living in big Mundane cities, but few did anything to differentiate themselves from their Mundane counterparts, who used optical illusions instead of real magic.

Harper was a master of illusion. When his audience first sat, they were put in mind of a movie theater. A large white screen displayed a scene, and Harper told them to join him on a journey. The "movie" would begin, and Harper would immerse the audience in his own memories. From the safety of their seats they could climb a mountain, cross a desert, or raft down a raging river. Audiences were astounded at how real everything felt, swearing they could smell the snow in the air, feel the icy kiss of wind on their skin, or taste the salt on their tongues. Harper traveled extensively, collecting as many new and exciting experiences as he could to share with his audiences. His shows were now in demand in several other countries.

Lunch arrived, and Nikolai portioned off his customary amount of food before eating.

Harper gestured with his fork. "You're still doing that, huh?"

"And you're still blond."

Harper shrugged. "It's my signature look now. You know, you can eat it all. And you probably should."

"What's that supposed to mean?" But he suspected he knew. When he dressed that morning in his nicer town clothes, they hung loosely. The bouts of malaise killed his appetite. Eating was now something he did hurriedly on the way to something else. Was this why Harper hadn't recognized him? How much weight had he lost?

Harper coughed. "You look a bit peaked."

"I'll order dessert."

Harper laughed. "You still keeping bread in your room?"

Damnit. Why did he have to bring that up? If anyone else had discovered him like that, he would have killed them. But it was Harper, and so he had to factor the cost of losing a friend against offing someone who'd seen him in a vulnerable state.

"There's a single loaf in my trunk that I change out once a week." Come to think of it, he probably hadn't done that in a while. Damn, he needed a calendar too. He didn't even know what day it was.

"I still remember that time—"

"Look, if it's all the same to you, I'd rather not discuss the bread incident." Nikolai stabbed errantly at his food. True to his word, he ordered dessert, and when that came, he portioned out a bit of it too. Harper shook his head but said nothing.

After lunch, they visited the barber. Nikolai barely recognized the wild-haired, gaunt figure staring back at him in the mirror. The shave exposed his handsome face, but it was sunken and angular—not as bad as when he was a kid, but it brought back memories he'd just as soon forget.

Harper was free the rest of the afternoon, and Nikolai enlisted his help in picking out new suits. The man was always ahead of the curve when it came to fashion trends. Nikolai, having been stuck in Haven for the better part of two years, wanted to ensure a favorable impression on the London ladies. He ordered several new suits and bought one that fit reasonably well for that evening, along with a stylish new hat.

When the clerk's back was turned, he stole a calendar off the counter, surprised to see it had been months since he'd left Haven. He still had to get a few mirrors, and managed to get two in his pouch before Harper noticed and scolded him, insisting he either put them back or add the cost to his tab. He'd have to ask Medea how she'd come up with all that money to buy the Hanged Man. She probably just stole it, but if she had spells that could make money, he wanted to know.

They parted ways in late afternoon. Harper had a show to prepare for, and Nikolai was looking to satisfy a different hunger. Harper had let slip that he allowed some of his friends to use his flat for late-night trysts, but for some reason he was reluctant to extend Nikolai the same courtesy.

"It's different for you!" Harper protested. "The alternatives here are . . . well, they're not pleasant for men such as myself. Russell Square has nothing on four walls and a roof."

Nikolai laid the guilt on thick. Didn't their friendship matter? Sure, they'd grown apart since the Academy, but he'd thought they were still close. Harper was someone he could count on, but he supposed he was wrong. It was so nice spending time together today, but apparently Harper didn't feel the same. On and on he went until Harper relented and told Nikolai where to find the spare key.

"Hang a tie on the door and stick to the bedroom on the right. That's the spare."

Nikolai thanked Harper and took the tube to Soho, satisfied grin on his face.

INTERFERENCE

Now here was a place for debauchery. The clubs were alive with music and dance and liquor. Nikolai swaggered down the street, dressed to kill, pretending not to notice how he drew many a casual glance. Emaciated he might be, but he was still better looking than most of the sad fucks out here looking to score, and his confidence closed the gap between him and the rest of the Competition.

Nikolai chose a suitable club, ordered a drink, and watched people dance as he scanned minds. Choosing the right target was important. He could only read surface-level thoughts, but they told him much—if someone was having a bad day, feeling neglected, or looking for fun. A nervous woman would take too long to warm up. Experienced women had preferences, which made them more decisive.

Impatient for a quick lay, today he searched for the odd woman out. Most friend groups had at least one member who was less attractive than the rest. Such women were used to being ignored by men and watching their friends get asked to dance. Each time they were slighted, they grew more restless and desperate. They gobbled up compliments with gusto, and usually other things too, as they were often more eager to please than their attractive counterparts.

Nikolai tested the waters with a few different ladies, but they weren't buying what he was selling and so he continued his search. Most guys got flustered or upset by rejection. Nikolai shrugged it off. Sex was a numbers game. If you wanted to get laid, you had to find someone willing, and rejection was a sign she wasn't interested, so why bother? Barking up the wrong tree wasn't going to get you what you wanted, and it wasted time better spent working on someone more agreeable.

He found a prime target in short order. She was plain of face and accompanied by a stunning brunette who already had a small ring of admirers. He scoffed at the stupidity of this. Did they not realize the intense competition for such a prize? The brunette was basking in their attention, oblivious to her friend's discomfort. She would take all night choosing, if she chose at all. To the brunette, the attention was enough by itself. It showed her she was loved. Her friend wanted the same, and some small part of her died whenever she tried to interject herself in the conversation and failed.

Nikolai seated himself beside the Plain Jane and waited for just the right opening. As her friend peeled away to dance without so much as a backward glance, the young woman fell into despair. Careful to affect the right accent, he leaned over and asked her a question, then struck up a conversation. It was amusing to watch the flurry of thoughts that came with such an interaction: Shock. Wow, he's handsome. Is he talking to me? Why is he talking to *me*?

Most men made the mistake of talking at length about themselves. They spoke in great detail of their jobs, their hopes and dreams, and expected women to sit entranced, as if everything they said was fascinating. Nikolai asked the woman plenty of open-ended questions, skimming her mind and directing the flow of conversation to topics of interest to her, dropping compliments here and there.

Precision mattered. Telling a woman she was beautiful was stupid. If the woman had low self-esteem, she wouldn't believe you. If she knew she was beautiful, then you were an idiot for stating the obvious. It also put you in the same camp as every other schmuck who used the line.

"I love the way you've styled your hair," on the other hand, acknowledged something she'd done, as well as her appearance. Women used clothing and makeup to emphasize their strong points and to hide what they felt were their flaws. An observant man could make use of that.

Nikolai had the added benefit of telepathy, and so he complimented her dress, which he knew she'd sewn herself but feared made her look dumpy. It validated her hard work and her estimation of him immediately rose. Of himself he said little, except that he was in town for business.

Things were going well until the woman frowned over his shoulder. Ah, her friend was coming back. Plain Jane knew he would ignore her as soon as he caught sight of her friend. She tugged his arm, suggesting they dance, but he remained seated, saying he much preferred their conversation.

The brunette returned wearing a saccharine smile, which she flashed between them, asking for an introduction. Nikolai gave it, then turned back to Plain Jane, as if she were the most interesting person in the world. Several times the brunette cut in on their conversation. Nikolai responded with polite disinterest, and Plain Jane responded beautifully.

The brunette grew increasingly agitated. A peek into her mind revealed an insecure woman flabbergasted by his behavior and resentful that her "ugly" friend was getting all the attention. She tried her best to catch Nikolai's eye, laughing at everything he said and touching him. It was all very entertaining. He countered by complimenting Plain Jane's earrings, and when she turned her head to better show them, he leaned in to lightly touch her earlobe, then her neck. The thoughts that ran through her mind were tantalizing.

When he rested his hand on the small of her back and whispered into her ear, the brunette loudly announced she thought it was best they both be going. Sealing the deal was always a delicate affair. Nikolai preferred to let the woman broach the subject first, as it made him seem more trustworthy. The brunette's sudden declaration spurred Plain Jane to ask where he was staying. He said he was staying with a friend who was out for the evening.

A cab ride later they were in front of Harper's flat, the door thankfully free of ties. The place was suitably impressive, spotless and tastefully decorated. Harper was doing very well for himself indeed.

Nikolai continued his carefully crafted performance for a time. No sense in rushing things. It gave him a chance to bask in Plain Jane's thoughts of adulation. He was too good for her. Smart and funny and oh-so-handsome! What did he want with a girl like her? How had she gotten this lucky? She'd wake up at any moment, she knew it.

Finally, she placed a tentative hand on his thigh and kissed him. The first barrier broken, he took the lead and fell upon her with the appetite of a starved animal. Her body wasn't bad looking really, even if her face was as bland as oatmeal. He never understood why some men were so picky. Yes, it was nice when they were more attractive, but it's not like it made much difference once you were inside them. Besides, neglected women often tried harder and were more open to suggestion.

Nikolai took his time. Pleasuring a woman was a competitive "fuck you" to any man who came after. Would his lovers long for him every time their future husbands flopped on top of them for thirty seconds? He hoped so. Let the world be filled with women longing for Nikolai. He was a master musician, and she was his instrument. He played her until she sang, though she stubbornly called out God's name instead of his. As if God had anything to do with this.

He was approaching completion when the thoughts snaked unbidden into his mind. He'd picked an easy target because he knew he deserved nothing better. She wasn't really that into him. It was a pity fuck. Why would anyone want him?

Nikolai found himself wilting inside her. He thrust harder in an attempt to make up for it. She gave him a quizzical look, and he dared not read her mind.

No good. It was no good. He pulled himself out and roared in frustration. The woman shrank back, then approached cautiously and told him it was okay, she didn't mind, these things happen. Her gentle assurances only fueled his despair. Reflexively, stupidly, he glanced into her mind. She thought this was why such a nice, handsome man had been interested in someone like her. He couldn't take it anymore. He grabbed his clothes and fled without a word.

Medea sat in the common area and waited. When the wards notified her that the boy left the island, she breathed a sigh of relief. Finally, he was gone!

The past few weeks—months?—had been brutal. It was difficult to share her home with apprentices for years on end. She'd considered the idea of making separate living quarters for them but in the end decided against it. They needed to live on the island and have access to her library and other facilities. Having separate barracks wouldn't solve the issue of casually running into them outside of lessons. It was a sacrifice she'd long ago decided to make.

But the damned curse complicated things. It had kicked in far sooner than she thought it would and made lessons nearly impossible to complete. Rather than giving her new novice the customary one day off a week, she'd pushed them both to make up for lost time. To his credit, the boy tackled his studies with appropriate fervor whenever he felt well.

Still, it was going to be a very long ten years. Probably longer than ten. Fast learner though he was, at this rate she'd be lucky to get him out the door in twenty. The idea of sharing her home for that long made her shudder.

Removing the curse was out of the question. That would be interference. No, he'd just have to deal with it on his own. The curse wove through him in a way that would almost certainly result in death if not removed with expert precision. He might one day be able to extract it himself, but for now it lay beyond his capabilities.

As much as she wanted this one to live, she'd vowed to protect him from her training, not his own stupidity. Actions had consequences, and some consequences led to death. She wouldn't break her own rules to help him.

Dragging him from the water had been a monumental error. When she'd detected his health failing and found him in the cave pool, her first thought was that he'd slipped and hit his head. It was only after saving him and seeing the apathetic expression on his face that she realized the curse was in effect. Accidental or not, she'd broken her rule.

She'd been furious. Furious at herself for interfering. Furious at the boy for putting himself in a situation where the curse might be fatal. Furious for not realizing sooner and leaving him be. Furious at being relieved she didn't have to sit by and watch him die. That couldn't happen again. Interference was against her rules.

Of course, a part of her nagged, she had already broken her rules by restricting the boy's access to certain information and areas. No matter how many times she told herself it was for his own good, that he would get all the information he wanted in due time, it didn't feel right.

She couldn't help him with the curse—not directly—but perhaps she could nudge him in the right direction. Healing was something she attempted to teach all her apprentices. The practicality of the magical school was almost unparalleled, yet for some reason students of the dark variety shied away from it. The boy was no different. Why he didn't think to look in the healing or potion sections of the library for ways to mitigate his symptoms was beyond her.

That said, even if he was looking, it would take him a long time to stumble upon the answer. Both sections in the library were immense. She couldn't just *give* him the books he needed to solve his problem—that would be interfering—but she *could* leave them out in places where he might see them, mixed in with other selections.

Medea stood and raised her hand. The bedroom door at the top of the stairs swung open.

"Tino!" she called.

A mottled blur leapt from the open door onto the landing, changing color and texture as soon as it hit the stair railing. It scurried down, then launched itself into Medea's waiting palm, where its skin changed from smooth iron grey to a semblance of lichen. The gecko turned its head and gazed at her with string-of-pearl pupils. Medea rubbed it affectionately under the chin.

"Sorry you've been cooped up. You want outside?"

"I'll stay with you," the lizard answered in the masculine voice of its long-dead human master. Well, one of them. Unlike most familiars, Concertino had been spawned by not one wizard soul but two. The creature had no voice of its own but could replicate any sound it heard. It nosed under Medea's hair, its tummy cool against her neck.

Hearing the voice was a painful blessing. Valerio had been a good friend all those centuries ago. Part of him lived on in Tino, but he was dead now, and the constant reminder stung. Sometimes she told Tino to use a different voice. Other times she took comfort in Valerio's raucous laughter.

"We've a bit of work to do in the library," said Medea. "Mind a bit of singing?"

Nikolai stumbled away from Harper's flat. Dark thoughts swirled all around, pressing their weight against him. He collapsed not far from the building and sobbed until a policeman came by. Pummel would make quick work of him. Nikolai pulled his wand and muttered *"Collido."*

Nothing happened, and the policeman laughed at his seemingly drunken antics. He was a failure. Couldn't even cast a basic spell with a wand. What little remained of his logical mind tried to argue. It was the city. Everyone knew Mundane technology affected spells. The affliction countered that if he was a remotely decent wizard, it wouldn't matter.

A firm grip on his bicep snapped Nikolai back to attention. He punched the policeman in the one place guaranteed to bring the man to his knees, then ran. Half the night was gone by the time he managed to stumble back through the gateway.

As he suspected, the return trip was more pleasurable than his departure. Medea had definitely woven a spell into the gateway that made it more desirable to return than to leave. Even with the affliction drowning him in despair, he had a moment of purest exhilaration the moment he crossed through. The two sensations warred with one another. He was whole again and everything felt wonderful. No, he was a failure and he'd never amount to anything.

Drawing as much strength as he could from the euphoric sensation, he entered the common area and lurched toward his room. He just needed to make it to his bed before the feeling faded and he was left alone with the dark thoughts. Something whispered behind him.

Nikolai halted, ears straining. Medea was never up this late. She rarely even left her room in the afternoons. He moved to the library door and pressed his ear to the wood. Faint music, almost operatic. Abruptly, it stopped.

Nikolai wrenched open the door and ran down the center aisle. A dozen rows down, he found Medea. She was reading in an armchair, not an unusual sight by itself, but everything here screamed wrongness. Medea had three reading postures. Relaxed, she curled her feet under her body like a cat. Sometimes she leaned back and propped her legs on a cushion. If a book really had her interest, she hunched over it like a miser and devoured it.

Medea sat now with her legs demurely crossed, back rigid. The thick book in her hands was held up, a position one couldn't maintain long with a text of that size. Both her hair and her dress looked as though they had been arranged rather than being allowed to fall naturally.

"Good evening," Medea said. "How was your day off?" Asking about his day was another thing she never did.

"Fine. I bumped into an old friend from the Academy." The residual euphoria from the gateway was fading. Nikolai clung to it like a life raft.

"That's nice." Her tone suggested she hadn't listened to his response, nor did she care to.

What alcove was this? He'd have to remember it, come back and check. Potions.

Medea rose and set her book on top of the rather large stack already on the table. "You know, it would do you good to freshen up on potions. And healing. Such wonderful things to be learned from healing! I'm off to bed."

Nikolai sank into the armchair and closed his eyes. If he had to ride out the affliction, he might as well do it in comfort.

SAY IT

Nikolai grinned even as pain lanced through his foot. The carpet of leaf litter on the forest floor offered no solace from Medea's attacks. His senses strained, trying to determine when the shoots would erupt next, ready to dodge at a second's notice. Challenge with a dash of danger—just how he liked it. So much better than endless drilling or boring lectures.

Another shoot sliced through his heel, causing him to stumble. He jumped, grabbing on to a low-hanging branch, then swung deftly to land on a fallen log. Her attacks would have to come where he could see them now. He danced along the log, careful to keep turning so his back wasn't always facing the same way.

"You know that's not how this works." Medea sat cross-legged on a stump, long blonde hair gleaming in the sunlight. "You're supposed to *sense* them, not see them."

The bark rippled like a wave. Nikolai toppled to the forest floor, where he was stabbed twice more in the back. He attempted to roll over with some difficulty. The plant shoots embedded in his flesh were still attached to their root systems, and reluctant to budge. One tugged loose, but the other broke off under his skin and clung there like the world's most uncomfortable splinter.

"Am I going too fast for you?"

"I'm fine," he said, even though he couldn't sense shit. Errant leaves clung to his shirt. Nikolai brushed them off, wincing as his muscles tugged the shoot stuck in his back. He twisted to see if he could reach it and found he couldn't. "Can you get this fucking thing out of me?"

Medea smiled. "Certainly."

Momentary pain, followed by a blessedly dull ache.

Two months had passed since his first trip to London. True to her word, Medea let him have a day off every week. Each yielded similar results. The malaise struck with the same irregular frequency as it did on the island. One day, after a particularly prolonged episode that lasted almost a full day, he asked Medea for a week off, claiming a friend desperately needed help. She hadn't been happy but consented to the break. He timed it with one of Harper's numerous tours out of town, giving him a week alone at the London flat. The change in scenery didn't help. Dark thoughts plucked at him the whole time, and he was forced to admit that the island could not be the cause.

It had to be Medea herself. Either she'd followed him to London, or the reach of her abilities was extreme. Didn't voodoo dolls allow you to do that? It was difficult to counter her spell without knowing the method of it.

He'd searched the library for spells matching his symptoms. While there were many that addled the brain, causing fear or apathy, nothing quite matched. His affliction had a draining quality that killed his appetite and made him tired but unable to rest. Still, it was a start, and he'd begun to experiment with potions that claimed to solve self-deprecation and apathy.

For his initial attempts at treatment, he chose potions containing commonly available plants—St. John's wort, English lavender, and Roman chamomile. Even without Medea's insistence that ingredients be replaced doubly, he wanted potions that could be made with ease. Rare and exotic wasn't helpful when you needed round-the-clock prevention.

In the supply cabinet, he found that someone had helpfully made a catalog of every ingredient and where it could be found, along with any gateways that were relatively close to collection sites. The penmanship was elegant and graceful, not at all like Medea's chicken scratches, which adorned the pages in the form of corrections.

It seemed that in recent years she'd had to cross out many of the gateways. Usually a replacement was written underneath, but not always. All three of his chosen plants were common and readily accessible near gateways. It only took him a few days to gather enough to replace Medea's stock, as well as build up a nice supply for himself, which he stashed in his room.

With the plants, he crafted several potions of varying concentrations. So far, none of them prevented his shifts in mood. Only the Roman chamomile remained. If that failed, he'd have to try rarer plants or concede that whatever was affecting him could not be solved with a simple potion.

Practical lessons had become more intense. Medea graduated him from repetitive wandless casting to various training exercises, and he soon understood why apprentices found her methods cruel. For his first exercise, she bade him lay on his back in the field. He was to conjure a shield no larger than his head and deflect small stones falling from above.

The task proved to be more difficult than he'd anticipated. At first he kept summoning a full body shield, which blocked the stones but earned him a magical slap. When he was finally able to get the size right, he never seemed to summon it in the right position in time. Soon he was bloody and bruised.

That was when the shitstorm began, literally. Medea declared he lacked sufficient motivation. She summoned feces from god knew where and rained them down from above. He rapidly improved, but not before taking half a dozen hits.

Not all her exercises were that grotesque. Most of the time, Medea simply picked a magical school for her own attacks and tasked him with surviving the onslaught. The injuries were near-constant, and he worked through his collection of healing potions in short order. Despite the pain, he enjoyed these lessons, the adrenaline rush satisfying some primal craving.

For a week now, they'd been working on the current lesson, which took place not in the meadow but in the forest, a place he had yet to explore on his own. He arrived early, ahead of Medea, and cast Magic Sight before entering. As usual, the whole of the island held a faint glow of magic. The trees themselves held even more, and the largest were bright against his senses.

Unlike the rest of the island, which was dotted with pine and wind-battered cypress, here the trees were mostly deciduous—tall and already changing into their fall colors. Shafts of sunlight broke through the canopy, dappling the forest floor. He found some semblance of a path, barely a game trail, and followed it through dense overgrowth.

Light dimmed as the leaves thickened overhead. Soon the air grew chilly. Moss blanketed trunks and branches. Every so often he caught a whisper of something in the distance or saw a light just outside his field of vision. Like the details of a dream fading upon waking, so too did the sights and sounds vanish as soon as he turned toward them.

The path led to a clearing dotted with fallen logs and scattered boulders. Magic Sight turned up no enchantments, and yet he couldn't shake the feeling he was being watched. He stretched out on one of the logs and waited.

The forest was silent until Medea's arrival. She tiptoed barefoot over the leaves and took a seat on the log a few feet away.

"They haven't bothered you, have they?"

His head jerked up. "Who?"

"The spirits who dwell here. This is a sanctuary of sorts. Not all of them come. Many choose to make a last stand where they are, but others find this form of exile preferable to the alternatives."

That explained the lights and odd sounds. He put his head back down. "Huh. I didn't think spirits were real."

"Of course they're real. Didn't you listen to a word I said when we talked about the fae?"

"When *you* talked about the fae."

"You didn't, did you?" She made a disgusted noise and got up. "It's a shame, because they're as worried as I am about the current state of the world. Not only that, you've got a target on your back. Soul like yours—they'd be eager to have it. I've forbidden them to talk to you. For your own safety. If they try, let me know straightaway and make no oaths or bargains. Spirits are —well, they're tricky to deal with."

Was she trying to bait him? She had to be, as she'd brought up the topic and he never would have guessed spirits were on the island. But to what end? He set the thought aside as Medea started explaining the day's lesson, which involved anticipating magical attacks.

Spells could be felt as ripples in the ether. Bare skin helped, which explained her distaste for footwear. It was the reason so many nature-casters of old ran naked through the woods, giving rise to stories of nymphs and dryads. Nikolai enthusiastically suggested they strip for the lesson, which earned him a rap on the head and a stern warning that he was to remove his socks and boots *only*.

The object was to stand, feet grounded, and dodge the plant shoots Medea sent at him through the forest floor. Her attacks came in rapid succession, no doubt due to his colorful comment, and within the first ten minutes both his feet were bleeding profusely. Never had he needed to take a healing potion so fast.

Even after she slowed her attacks, he had difficulty sensing anything in time to dodge. An hour later, his feet were raw from so many regrowths of skin. It went like that all week. Yesterday the buildup of scar tissue had been so thick he could barely walk, and she had to halt the lesson to do a proper healing.

"Shall we go again?" Medea still wore a smile. She did nothing to disguise how much she enjoyed hurting him during their little lessons.

Nikolai gestured for her to wait and downed a healing potion. The dull ache in his back subsided, replaced by the tightness of fresh scar tissue. He'd have to get her to fix that. A look in the mirror this morning had revealed skin heavily marred by such spots. At least he'd gained a bit of weight back. Now that he knew the malaise was affecting him that badly, he'd taken to eating twice as much on his good days. It left him feeling bloated and ill, but what else was he to do?

"Ready."

Medea studied him for a moment. "Let's try something different."

Great. He'd probably have to dodge feces again.

"Sit down with your back to that tree, firmly against the trunk. Good. Now close your eyes."

Nikolai did as he was told, nose primed for the stray scent of shit. The bark rubbed unpleasantly on his recently healed back.

"This exercise is designed to calm your body and clear your mind."

Medea had him relax his muscles, one by one, and focus on his senses. Wind brought the scent of the ocean and rustled the leaves overhead. Birds chirped. Water bubbled in a nearby stream.

"Let the magic of the grove flow through you. Open your

mind to it. Allow yourself to reach beyond what your physical senses can detect."

At first he felt nothing, then a slow trickle of information began to flow. A beetle larva chewed through the bark of a tree. Leaves reached up in reverence toward the sun. An earthworm worked steadily to tug a leaf underground. A pocket of fungus pushed against the soil; tonight, it would erupt as mushrooms. Even the soil itself was a living thing composed of microorganisms. And there something else . . . something sinister, hovering before him.

His eyes shot open. A plant pod the size of a dinner plate halted a breath away from his face. He jerked back and slammed his head against the trunk. He tilted to one side, trying to slip around the tree, but something prevented him from moving. His entire body was wrapped in vines.

Beyond the giant pod, Medea's grinning face tilted into view, mimicking his sideways lean. "Took you long enough to notice it."

The pod eased forward. He struggled against the vines. Why did she have to aim it at his face? Feet were one thing, but his face? He slashed the vines erratically with telekinesis, scoring flesh in the process. Once freed, he started to stand until new vines wrapped him once more.

"Oh, come *on*!"

"No. You can do better. Think. What goes on around you?"

What the hell was she getting at? There was no time to speculate, for the pod opened to reveal rows of sharp toothlike protrusions. The stench of rotting meat emanated from its gaping maw. Its stem bunched up, poised and ready to strike.

He lurched to the side, offering his shoulder, which exploded in pain as the teeth found their mark. Something larger stabbed him and the pod pulsed sickeningly. His shoulder tingled and went numb.

"Dodging won't solve your problem."

She obviously didn't want him using telekinesis. His hand strained against the vines, still accustomed to making wand movements, even without the wand. Time to try without. He concentrated on the base of the stem.

"Lancea!"

The Lance spell erupted from his hand only to reverberate loudly an inch from its target. Medea had shielded the damned plant.

"Attack better."

Attack better? What kind of advice was that? If she couldn't be helpful, she needed to shut up. He tried Ignite instead of Pummel, aiming for the base of the pod, though the pod itself blocked much of his view. Something sizzled and the air filled with the heavenly scent of cooking meat.

"You just burned a nice chunk of your shoulder."

Fuck. At least whatever numbing agent the plant used kept him from feeling that.

"I grow weary of this," said Medea. "Look around you. What can you use?"

"Could you be any less clear? You obviously want me to do something in particular, so why not just tell me what that is?"

"What I want is for you to—" She stopped and swore in Latin. He couldn't understand the words, but the intonation was clear.

"As I was saying, I want you to feel around—" Her voice was oddly muffled. He shifted to get a better look.

"Are you eating a fucking kebab?"

She froze midsentence, looking to the skewered meat in her hand as if she'd only just realized it was there. "Yes?"

"Why?" He'd last seen her eat weeks ago, sitting in the grass during their noon repast. She'd summoned a scone and dunked it in her tea.

"I needed something I could hold."

"Was popcorn unavailable?" He laced the comment with sarcasm, but she seemed to take it as a serious question.

"Popcorn isn't really a meal. Why are you looking at me like that?"

"I don't know, *why are you eating a kebab?*"

"Because my spell has been pestering me all day."

"Your spell?"

"It reminds me to eat. The spell gets increasingly irksome the longer I ignore it. I can make it stop, but that would defeat the purpose." She waved the kebab at him. "Sustenance!"

No wonder she was so slender. Did fasting tie into her immortality somehow? No one just forgot to eat. The body reminded you, as he well knew, and with much insistence.

Her gaze slid past him and she muttered, "Shit."

His back warmed and he twisted toward the new threat. Twenty feet behind him, the brush was engulfed in flames. The heat had to be intense to travel this far, and he soon saw why.

Nestled in the center, plants running right through it, was a human skeleton. It rapidly dissolved into ash, blown away by unnatural wind.

"Who was that?"

"Oh, don't worry about him," Medea said with feigned nonchalance.

Uh huh.

A tingling in his fingers reminded him of the pod, still pumping away at his shoulder. The numbness now extended down his arm and was slowly crawling across his chest.

"So, you want me to use something around me, but you won't tell me what that is."

"What I *want* is for you to solve the problem creatively. What is happening all around you? I know you sensed it."

"Sensed what? Bugs? Leaves?"

"Some necromancer you'll make." She made a large sweeping

gesture with the kebab. "Life and death are all around us. Let nature inspire you!"

"I don't know any necromancy spells—"

"Stop thinking in such restrictive terms! *Feel* what goes on below you. Are all the roots strong and healthy, or do some wither and decay? What process takes place?" As she spoke, a green stalk elongated in front of him. The end bulged into a second pod. "Best hurry, this one *will* hit your face."

He shot her a glare, then focused on the soil below, trying to find what she was talking about. Most of the roots grew strong, but those of one plant withered with fungus. What did she expect him to do, transfer spores to the vines and then wait days for them to take effect? Probably. Who knew how the hell her mind worked? He focused on the spores and willed them to move toward the vines entangling him.

"There's no need for that," she said. "Feel the process. *Focus* on mimicking it. Will the *effect* onto the vines and use your mana to spread it."

Nikolai leaned his head against the trunk and closed his eyes, going back into the meditative state. There were the blighted roots, in a moist patch of soil across the clearing. And over here was the healthy root system which fed the plants attacking him. But how the hell to get them together?

He focused on the blighted roots, building a clear picture in his mind, then he targeted the healthy roots and attempted to overlap his perception of the two. The images kept slipping. He couldn't focus on both sets of roots at the same time, and no matter how hard he willed necrosis onto the healthy plants, it failed to manifest.

His head drooped forward as the world blurred, his lungs working like bellows. The mana exhaustion had come without warning.

"Your will is strong, but your focus needs work. We are done for today."

"Try . . . again . . ." He gasped for air in between words. Sweat trickled down his brow. "Just need . . . mana."

"I think not. You were at it for nearly an hour."

An hour? The vines snaked away from his body. At his shoulder, the pod loosened but did not fall. He fumbled at his pouch. Medea held out a potion of her own, face impassive. After a moment's hesitation he took it. The potion theory was ludicrous in hindsight. Medea's magic required no wand, no words—no outward sign of anything. She could be cursing him right now and he'd never know. By those standards, poison seemed downright pedestrian. Warmth flooded his body as the mana potion took effect.

He set to work removing the pod with his one working hand. His shoulder was slick with sweat and blood, and the pod resisted his efforts to remove it. He reached over to the back, wedged his fingers between the pod and his skin, and wrenched. It came off with a sickening sucking.

Numbness had concealed the damage. His shirt was completely dissolved underneath, the skin puffy and blistered. Blood trickled from wounds left by the plant's teeth. In the center, some sort of plant stalk remained anchored in his flesh. He yanked until it came free with a trail of white fluid. Pain returned with a vengeance.

This time his pouch opened with ease. The healing potion tasted god-awful, but his wounds knitted themselves closed and he lurched to his feet.

"Tomorrow I will assign you a new task," said Medea. "One designed to strengthen your focus."

"Does it involve freezing water?"

The sarcasm escaped her and she considered it a moment. "No . . . but it *would* work for that. My current method is superior, but that's definitely an exercise I could add." She beamed at him. "Thank you, boy."

He bristled. Medea rarely referred to him as anything at all, but "boy" was worse than nothing. Perhaps because she looked his age, it rankled in a way it hadn't with Petrov.

"Boy?" It was an accusation.

A flurry of emotions crossed her face. Confusion. Realization. Concentration. Finally, the consternation of *almost* recalling something and repeatedly failing. "Ni—uh . . ."

"Don't you dare guess and botch it." She didn't even know his name. How could she not know his name, after all these months, after all the effort he'd put into making an impression in Haven?

She had the decency to look abashed. "I'm sorry. The world— it's so full of people and they all die in the end. I don't bother with names. After a time, they all blur together."

"You remember Thomas just fine."

"Yes, well, he was exceptional."

He crossed his arms. "You're digging yourself in deeper here."

"What? He *was*! You're—"

"Don't."

"—sufficient."

"Stop."

"I mean the *potential* is there." She gestured to him.

Anger bubbled beneath the surface, but something else too. A chance to correct. To control. And that required calm.

"How is it that you're a billion years old and haven't learned a modicum of diplomacy?"

Medea considered this. "I understand the importance most people place on cultural customs. I just don't see the point." If someone couldn't talk straight, they were hardly worth talking to. The boy at least had learned to forgo many of the frivolities of communication when in her presence.

"You think you're being pragmatic. You're not. Diplomacy can get you pretty far."

"No, I don't think so. When I was young, I traded knowledge for knowledge. And now . . ." She shrugged. "I can overpower anything."

"Sometimes a diplomatic approach is best."

She burst out laughing. This coming from the boy who'd killed his previous master to get out of a contract. "You? *You* of all people are lecturing me about restraint?"

"I'm not talking restraint, I'm talking strategic use of manners to get what you want. Like with the Collective delegation—"

Not this again. She was sick of hearing about it. They'd invaded her home, Jacques' damned cronies. He couldn't defeat her on his own, so he'd gained the support of the newly formed Collective, convincing them she was an imminent threat. Half a hundred of them had poured onto her beach. When they lost, Jacques spun stories that she'd murdered a small, peaceful delegation, though from Nikolai's conversation in the Hanged Man, it appeared the number had grown in retellings.

"That was an assassination attempt! As I recall, you were rather impressed with how I handled them."

"I was—I am—but that doesn't change the fact that it had unintended consequences."

That was true enough. The event sparked a wave of you-killed-my-brother/cousin/mother/uncle/grandfather dueling challenges and assassination attempts that lasted for generations. Like a hydra's head, every challenger she dealt with seemed to spawn two more. But that probably wasn't what the boy was referring to. "What do you mean?"

"There was no mention of you at the Academy. No one uses

your magical methods, and no one teaches them either. You've been blacklisted. So while you may complain about how little I know and how terrible magic is these days, you helped bring that about."

Ridiculous. Enemies were the best people to learn from! "It's not my fault if they ignore how magic really works."

"People don't care about *truth*. They only care how you make them *feel*. You complain only dark wizards seek training with you. Who else would come? You're the one who lectured me on the ramifications of reputation. No decent person wants to train with a murderer. If you're polite, if you make people feel good, they let you get away with a lot more. They say to themselves, 'He can't be that bad, he's such a nice fellow.'"

Maybe he was right. Jacques might have been a subpar wizard, but he was immensely popular. Popular enough to get scores of idiots to die for him. He and the boy were cut from the same cloth, now that she thought about it. Past experience told her he was probably being manipulative, but she couldn't see how. Her brain circled back.

"All this, just to get me to use your name. Fine, *discipulus*, give it to me again."

"Nikolai."

The name passed through her like a sieve. She nodded and began to walk away.

"Say it." The boy stood with his arms crossed, patient yet unyielding.

"What? Why?"

"You've already forgotten it, haven't you?"

She crossed her own arms. "I know it begins with an *N*."

"Say it three times. It'll help you remember. Nikolai."

What the hell was this? Names held power—was he working a spell? No, she would have felt magic being performed. Besides, he wasn't that good yet. He just stood there, with a too-calm expression that told her nothing. Fine. She'd say his name if it would get him to shut up and leave her alone.

"Nikolai, Nikolai, Nikolai," she mumbled. There. She turned to go.

"Say it clearly."

She spun to confront him. "I am your *master*!" By what right did a novice have to lecture their master?

"And *I* am trying to teach you a valuable skill. This is what *I'm* good at. Say it again. *Clearly*."

His voice was frustratingly patient. The constant sass and irritability were preferable to this. She glared at him, but he didn't flinch.

"Nikolai." She tried to make it an insult.

"Thank you. One more thing, if you really want to remember it, try pairing it with something familiar—another person, object, event. It helps with recall."

"Anything else? Shall I wait for my own apprentice to dismiss me?"

"No, and I apologize if I came across as impertinent. Names are important to me. It's a sign of respect. I know I have no right to demand your respect, so all I ask is this common courtesy."

She hated when he slipped into formality like this. Formality was a lie dressed up, courtesy a shackle people applied to themselves.

"One day I hope to distinguish myself enough that you won't need tricks to recall it." His tone was deferential, pleading. "I want to be like Thomas, not all the nameless apprentices before or since. If I can't reach that level, what's the point?"

Ah, that at least made sense. He did seem rather competitive. So this was less about the name and more about being good enough to be remembered. His desire for recognition had just been a little overzealous. She could sympathize with overzealousness, if not the reason.

"Get good enough, and the name will follow. I have no doubt you can reach that level if you apply yourself. As for your . . . outburst, it is forgivable to come on strong when one seeks to make a point." She paused a moment, then said, "We both have that problem. It demonstrates a passion—for the subject."

He bowed his head. No doubt a calculated move, but she'd take what she could get.

"Good work today, Nikolai."

21

FOCUS

Nikolai stared in consternation at his reflection the next morning. He looked slightly better than he had in London, having made a point to eat and take care of his appearance whenever he felt well enough to do so, yet he was still losing muscle tone.

The healing potion yesterday had done its work but left his skin marred. He counted over a dozen blemishes on his torso and limbs, and then there was his shoulder, which boasted a large circular scar enclosed by two neat rows of small ellipses. He'd have to ask Medea to remove the scars before his day off. The ladies didn't need to see this mess.

Finding willing partners was easier than ever, now that he had access to Medea's gateways, but the malaise was a perpetual nuisance. It didn't strike *every* time he had sex, but it certainly felt that way. He often stayed regardless. Easy enough to convince women that his sudden lack of interest was due to something ridiculous like losing his one true love. That lie in particular tended to earn him pity fellatio, but it wasn't the same as nailing them to a wall with his dick or hearing them scream at him to never stop.

Sometimes he was able to release. Just as often he was not. The black cloud robbed him of the ability to care either way. It wasn't until afterward, when the fog lifted, that his anger at the situation returned. He was better than this! His conquests were supposed to pine for him, not recall him as that pathetic guy who couldn't get it up.

Nikolai ran his hand over the scars on his shoulder. Ghastly. The sooner Medea fixed them, the better. Then again, it might be fun to see how he could use the scars, at least for a night. He could let his accent slip through and claim he'd won a wrestling match with a bear.

"Is true!" he told the mirror. "I von wrestling match with bear! I can prov to you." Nikolai practiced half a dozen scenarios and their accompanying facial expressions before pulling on his shirt and fixing his hair.

The bedroom looked considerably better. In addition to the mirror and mattress, he'd procured an armoire, several wall hangings, a rug, a bigger desk, and a real chair. The gateways offered unlimited potential for thievery. For once, he could be as grandiose as he wanted.

At first he feared Medea might barge in and yell at him for redecorating, but she'd yet to knock on his door since that first day. An unspoken understanding existed between them that if he didn't show up to lessons on time, he was bedridden with the affliction.

The only items he took care to hide were the clock and calendar. Let Medea think she was still messing with his sense of time. Stupid of her to give him access off the island if she wanted to play that game.

He ate breakfast in the kitchen, at the table, with proper plates and cutlery, like a civilized fucking human being. That too, was a thing he'd decided upon returning. The affliction might be sucking away his time, but he'd be damned if he would let it reduce him to the creature he'd seen in the mirror in London. Unlike Medea, he had *manners*.

Medea sat at the counter when he entered the lab, sipping tea and reading a book. If she'd discovered the book he'd planted in her to-read section, she'd yet to mention it, though if she had, it explained why she'd taken to leaving books for him in overly conspicuous places. They were always on healing or botany. He'd ignored the passive-aggressive move.

Medea cleared her throat. "Good morning, Nikolai."

He froze. Not only had she greeted him, she'd used his name. Victory! He forced himself to continue to the cabinets as if nothing were amiss. When he placed his ingredients on the table, he kept his face carefully neutral. Gloating now would spook her into foregoing the habit.

"Good morning, Medea." He allowed himself a polite smile.

She looked down at her tea and took a deep breath. Oh god, she was winding up for something. He placed the cauldron in the sink and began to fill it, hoping the water would drown out the impending lecture.

"I thought about what you said, and you're right."

He turned the water to a slow trickle.

"I have been lax. I used to learn names. They were quite important, actually. At one time, it was traditional for mages to discard their given names in favor of something that suited them better." She gave him a sidelong glance. "As you may have already guessed, Medea is not my given name."

"I thought maybe you were the Magi from Greek legend."

Medea laughed. "I'm not *that* old. I was familiar with her story, and it spoke to me. Never had I seen a woman represented with so much . . . *agency*. She was feminine, and yet her actions were so far from what was expected of women that she was villainized. When it came time to take a name, I knew exactly which to choose."

She grew pensive. "Over time, names became less important to me. It's not pleasant to lose people you care about, generation after generation. Easier not to get attached. Let them blend together. And then once my apprentices kept trying to kill me . . ." She shook her head. "There was little point in learning their names. Sometimes I forget that each person sees their life as important, even if it's brief compared to my own. If I have offended you, I am sorry."

A greeting, his name, *and* an apology? He was on a roll. But her lamentations didn't make sense. Why not make her loved ones immortal? He opened his mouth to ask, but she stood brusquely, all business again.

"Today you will be learning something new. When you are done with your morning tasks, come see me outside." With that, she left.

Too abrupt, even for her. Normally, she hung around the lab and they both went outside together. Had he stumbled onto a sensitive topic? At some point she had cared about people— mildly surprising, but then most people cared about others, or at least those closest to them. It hurt her enough that she'd seen the wisdom in setting aside that nonsense. Still, that she had the capacity to care made her vulnerable. It was something he could use.

Of course it was also possible she'd left to avoid discussing immortality. Maybe her method was something that couldn't be shared, like an artifact. If so, all the more reason to kill her and steal it. The sooner he mastered telepathy, the sooner he could get into her head and find out.

Unfortunately, the ground floor of her library, that which was accessible to him, had been less than helpful. It was painfully clear most of the authors weren't natural telepaths and had a shaky understanding of the magic. Journal entries described the lengthy processes these Magi had required to master a fraction of what he could do as a boy.

The only Useful things he found were exercises for repelling attacks. The most promising suggested visualizing a physical barrier and attempting to hold the image in your mind throughout the day. With practice, it would become subconscious, creating an ever-present magical obstacle, the properties of which depended on what you'd imagined.

He had thought carefully about what kind of barrier would be most effective. A brick wall would provide strong protection, but a swirling mist could confound and trap your attacker. A curtain of water was best for alerts; when disturbed, you'd feel the ripples. He finally settled on imagining a solid sheet of ice—as with the wall, it required force to break through, but even the slightest crack should alert him to an attack.

Incredible that Medea allowed him to learn that much. She'd stormed off so fast the day he accused her of telepathy that she probably forgot to remove any Useful books. For someone of her intellect, she seemed remarkably scatter-brained. Then again, if she was like him, as he suspected she was, then the disorganization was all an act.

In any case, her promise to teach him the specialty had gone unfulfilled. He'd have to press her for lessons, test her abilities, and find a way to access the books he needed on his own.

He dumped the half-filled cauldron and put it back. No sense doing the boiling exercise if Medea wasn't there to see. He quickly made his potion allotment and exited the hovel.

Medea perched atop the largest rock in the gravel pit across from the garden with her eyes closed. The wind tugged playfully at her hair and dress, momentarily revealing a braided leather anklet contrasting sharply with her pale skin. There was voyeuristic plea-sure in catching sight of something normally hidden. Her red dress, though delightfully form-fitting, left little flesh exposed. Was this how it had been in ages past, when women covered themselves so completely that an ankle was considered risqué?

The wavy lines raked into the gravel showed no evidence of tracks. Nikolai paused at the border and cleared his throat. "Can I step on it?"

"You can't levitate?"

"Levitate, yes. Fly, no."

"They're not much different, but that's a lesson for another day."

If he had a coin for every time she said *that*.

An invisible force wrapped his body, and Nikolai rose into the air. He savored the idea that she touched him, even if she wasn't *touching* him. He floated across the gap, landing gently on the rock across from her.

"Sit," she said. "You will need to concentrate for this. The exercise I'm going to show you needs to be completed daily. Save it for the afternoons, when your other lessons are finished, provided you are not . . . indisposed."

"What is this place?"

"It is called a *karesansui*, or dry landscape. I came across them in my travels to Japan. They are used for meditation. Before I created this garden, I did most of my focus exercises on the beach. It is not impossible there, but the wind and fine sand add a challenge. Gravel is not as apt to blow away."

A single grey stone rose into the air between them. "The task is deceptively simple," she said. "Raise a bit of gravel into the air and hold it thus with your mind."

Nikolai began to levitate a stone and she halted him.

"No. Not like that. Telekinesis only. No spells that will allow it to remain airborne without thought. You must *consciously* hold it there until the task becomes *unconscious*."

He tried again, miming with his hand and focusing on the gravel to keep it airborne.

"Good. Now raise another, but do not lose your grip on the first."

Easier said than done. Every time his mind grasped the second piece of gravel and brought it up, the first dropped to the ground. Again and again he tried. Sometimes the stone made it halfway before falling. At one point he tried to bring two up together. Medea corrected him and said it must be one at a time. Fucking impossible. What was the point of this Useless exercise?

After what felt like an hour he finally succeeded. Sweat beaded his brow and his face screwed up in concentration as he hovered two stones side by side. They wobbled precariously.

"Good," said Medea. "Try to relax. Hold them steady. When you feel comfortable, pick up a third."

There was no way to respond without losing focus. It took all he had just to keep the two stones aloft. He reached for a third, then sagged forward in defeat as the other two fell. What was the point of all this?

"What's the goal here? How many do I have to hold?"

"The goal is to build your focus. There is no set number that you need to reach. The object should always be to add yet another stone. That is how you measure your success—one more stone." He glanced down at the gravel pit. So many stones. He looked at Medea.

"How many could Thomas do?"

"At the rank of master, I believe he could hold around thirty."

So he'd have to get at least thirty-one. Forty would be even better. "How many can you do?"

"I do not think it wise that I tell you. It will only make you think of how much further you have to go."

As if he wasn't doing that already.

"Please," he pleaded, "let me see what a grand master is capable of."

Thinly veiled as the ploy was, it seemed to work, for Medea sighed and raised the gravel, one by one, stone by stone. They assembled into neat lines overhead.

"This is harder than it should be," she said. "You're sitting where many of my stones need to go."

"I can move."

"No, I can make do."

Stones continued to rise, an impossible number, yet still they came, marching on like soldiers. They radiated out in a three-dimensional pattern.

"What are you making?"

Medea did not respond. Her brow knit as she focused on the stones above. It was staggering. On and on they came, until the ground below was half-empty. At last the stones slowed, and no new stones rose. She held the pattern for a time, then gasped and allowed the gravel to fall. The surface of the pit smoothed out. A rake rose from nearby and traced wavy lines in the substrate.

"That was incredible." And daunting. Thomas, her best student, hadn't even come close. He could pass Thomas if he worked hard enough, but this? It didn't seem possible.

Which meant it likely wasn't. There had to be some trick to it, a trick she failed to share. That or she cheated and used levitation to hold them without breaking her concentration. The display was designed to be impressive.

Medea shrugged. "It took a long time to get to this point. As you progress, you will be tempted to create a shelf of sorts in the air to keep your pieces suspended. Do not. Use yourself as an anchor. Your body naturally senses where it is in space and attempts to orient the world around it based on itself. Use that sense. Pick a spot in relation to your body, and always begin at that spot."

A single stone rose and hovered in front of her face, an inch off center from her nose. "Build out from there. In time, laying the first stone will be as easy as touching your nose with your eyes closed." A second stone joined the first, this one an inch off center on the opposite side.

"I have found that patterns help. If you frame your stones the same way each time, eventually it becomes automatic. Less concentration is required—like hanging a coat you have hung a dozen times before. When you get to that point, you can trust your mind to hold them in place and focus on adding new stones. I recommend keeping a bit of sand in your room for practice. Gravel is nice, but sand may be easier for you to hold."

"Thank you, I will."

She straightened her back. "There is another matter we need to discuss."

Ugh, what now? "Yes?"

"Have you been boiling water every day?"

As far as she knew, he was. He was careful to do it whenever she was in the lab, but if she was out, or if the malaise kept him bedridden until she had moved on to other things in the afternoon, then no, he hadn't bothered. He hardly saw the point in continuing an exercise designed purely for purification purposes.

Without a trace of guilt or remorse, he answered, "Of course."

A force like a slap rang across his face.

"Do not lie to me."

He held his cheek and stared at her accusingly. "I'm not lyi—"

Pain tore through his back. He gasped and clutched at it in agony, the intensity such that he almost vomited. Just as suddenly, it was gone. He shot her a murderous look.

"That was your kidneys," she said, voice hard. "Next time it will be your scrotum. I told you I would know if you hadn't been doing it. Your mana reserves are far below what they should be by now."

"Fine! No, I don't do it every day. I don't see the point."

"Whether or not you see the point is irrelevant. You are my apprentice, and you will obey me when it comes to your training, or else you will forfeit your position here. Do I make myself clear?"

"Yes."

"Give me your oath that you will perform your duties."

"I swear I will boil water and perform any other Useless exercises you assign me, but only if you fulfill your end of the bargain."

That got her attention. "What do you mean?"

"Telepathy. You've yet to teach me anything."

"You have the library—"

"And you've blocked off the books that would be of any use. The lower level is worthless to someone like me and you know it."

Her face flushed. "When you master the basics—"

"If you mean never, just say never."

"After you master the basics, I will teach you whatever you want."

"Even immortality?"

"No. That is the one subject I do not explicitly teach. Given the stakes of such a thing, it is imperative that a person figure it out for themselves."

"So your vow means nothing."

"I vowed to answer your questions. I never said you would like my answers."

"You haven't answered me at all!" He slid from the rock and paced, heedless of the destruction he wrought to her careful patterns in the substrate. Fuck her *kare*-whatever-the-fuck garden.

Medea watched him impassively. "Then I will explain further.

Death fuels life. You saw that yesterday. It is the same for humanity. For a society to grow and change, each generation must die, and their values with them. New generations are only able to shape their future because those who would have previously opposed them no longer exist. That is how cultures change over time."

"What does culture have to do with anything?"

"It is unethical for an immortal to interfere with the affairs of mortals. It forces the Present to live in the Past. I know my values differ from many societies today. Even in my own time, I was a bit of an outlier. Would it be fair of me to impose my own standards of morality upon others?"

He wheeled on her. "But you *do*. You kill people—"

She waved a hand dismissively. "A few individuals make no difference in the grand scheme of things. I do not seek to influence the world at large, and I will not grant immortality to any who might abuse it. If someone reaches that height on their own, so be it, but I will not place them there."

A waste of talent. That's what she was. So this was why she'd sequestered herself away on a deserted island. This was why, despite all her power, she wasn't ruling the world. Ridiculous! What was the point of having power if you didn't wield it? What higher calling was there, if not to shape the world as you saw fit?

"Is that why you didn't involve yourself in the last war? Because if you had, it probably would have lasted five seconds."

"Do you have any idea how many wars I've seen? They say nothing is certain but death and taxes. I say with certainty that there is always a war going on *somewhere*. I do not involve myself. It's unethical for me to take sides."

What the hell was wrong with her? How could she sit by and do *nothing*? It was disgusting. No—worse than that—it was a dereliction of duty. Like all the damned countries that sat on their hands while the Nazis marched across Europe. Countries that remained "neutral." Neutrality was for the spineless. It accomplished nothing, and by the time some nations chose to get involved, millions had already died.

He was only eight when the Germans arrived on their doorstep, yet he'd used his fledgling magic to save himself and the only person who mattered to him. If he'd had Medea's power, he could have broken through enemy lines, raised an undead army, and slaughtered all who threatened him.

Medea had been here the whole time, reading her books while the world tore itself apart.

"I can see I've upset you—"

He laughed bitterly.

Medea floated from the rock to the low wall bordering the garden. "Your mind is in no state for learning. Take the rest of the day off."

He watched her reenter the hovel, then hopped the low wall and stormed off toward the sea.

Why did she have to be so stubborn? Couldn't she see that her abilities could be put to much better use? What did it matter if she toppled Mundane governments? It was like she said—they were constantly killing each other anyway. Their own paltry attempt at unifying the world was laughable. They needed a firm hand.

With the right spells, government might even become unnecessary. Magic could be used to keep people in line. Why had no one ever tried it? Probably because Magi were too few, and the scope of their power limited. Medea was living proof that more was possible. If he could acquire her level of skill, if he could convince others to join him, he might be able to change the course of history for the better.

Nikolai arrived at the cliffs and made his way down to the cave. He couldn't find the entrance, and for a second he thought he'd gone the wrong way. He backed up to the water and faced the sheer cliff, orienting himself by the sloped path to his left.

There was no mistaking it—solid rock blocked the cave entrance.

He cast Magic Sight, hoping the blockage was merely an illusion. It wasn't. The rock had no magical properties. As ever, something magical pulsed inside the cave. He might be able to blast it open, but the damage would be obvious. Better to come back another time when he was prepared. Nikolai climbed the path to the top of the cliffs and paused to admire the view.

Waves crashed mercilessly against the rocks, as he would crash mercilessly against any who opposed him. For a moment the thrill of raw power held his fascination, then he began to see the folly of it all. The rocks were impenetrable. They took no more note of the waves beating against them than the birds overhead. Foolish to think he could make any headway against systems that had been in place for thousands of years. He was little more than a mangy cur yapping at the heels of fate and kicked aside just as easily.

With a twinge, he recognized the encroaching thoughts weren't his own, and yet he couldn't stop them. They overwhelmed his mind, stripping him of every last shred of confidence. He would do nothing and become nothing. He would die and be forgotten. Medea had been right not to learn his name. Who was he to insist anyone take notice of him?

Nikolai sank to his knees and a dry sob erupted. No point in going on. He was Useless; he understood that now. Better to tumble onto the rocks below than continue his miserable existence. He groped toward the edge, hands grasping dried grass. One second and it would all be over.

Pain shot through his index finger. Nikolai yelped and pulled back his hand. Something green came with it, clamped on like a vise with a serrated red edge. He shook his hand violently and watched the green thing flutter. A bird.

The parrot released his hand only to fly at his face. He swatted at it, but the damned thing kept coming. Claws scratched and wings pummeled his eyes. Nikolai shielded his face with one arm and scrambled backward until the attack ceased.

He sat panting in the grass several meters from the cliff edge. The bird landed on the ground and glared at him with pinpointed eyes. Had he disturbed a nest? When he moved, it opened its mouth and lunged. He looked around for a rock to throw but there were none, and the malaise, which had momentarily retreated, crept back.

Couldn't even defend himself against a bird. Worthless, stupid . . .

Nikolai got up and stumbled toward the hovel. He probably wouldn't make it, but at least he could put some distance between himself and the cliff's tantalizing promise of release.

22

THE DUNGEON

Medea stepped into the crisp evening air and made her way to the graveyard. Dark nights were perfect for scraping lichen off tombstones. When she first moved to the island, she'd seeded it with as many useful plants as would grow in the natural climate. She knelt in the damp grass by the mausoleum and pulled out her collection tools. A moan interrupted her gentle scraping.

Around the corner of the mausoleum she found Nikolai sprawled in the grass; the ambient magic of the island must have concealed his presence from her senses. Dew soaked through his clothes, causing him to shiver in his sleep. Had he spent all night out here? She'd blocked off the cave to keep him from drowning, a gesture that seemed pointless now. The curse could just as easily drown him in the bathtub or cause him to die of exposure. Maybe not here, but elsewhere certainly. Without treatment, it would hang over him the rest of his life. Nikolai's leg twitched and he shuddered. Even though he deserved this punishment, it was difficult to see him so.

Medea scanned his brain and found the curse dormant; the least she could do was wake him up. She conjured a ball of light and nudged Nikolai with her foot. He didn't stir, so she knelt and gripped his shoulder, giving it a vigorous shake. His eyes fluttered open and he glanced about, disoriented.

"What are you doing out here?" she asked, berating herself for the stupidity of asking a question to which they both knew the answer.

"Oh, you know, just chatting with the dead." He sat up and patted the mausoleum wall. "You won't teach me necromancy, so I thought I'd go to the source."

There was an edge to his words. Was he serious? She couldn't tell. Who knew what they taught at the Academy? She erred on the side of caution. "You can't learn necromancy that way."

"I know." He rose stiffly and straightened his jacket. "It's this new thing called a *joke*. You might've come across them in your reading."

"I know what a joke is." She paused and grinned, adding her own. "I work with one every day."

Attempting to puncture Nikolai's overinflated ego had become one of her favorite pastimes. He could do to learn a little humility. Alas, his ego proved to be as impenetrable as her shields, and he brushed aside her casual barbs and jests like they were nothing.

Until now.

Fury flashed across his face. Her smile faltered and she took an involuntary step back. What had she done? Fear paralyzed her, not the fear of facing an enemy of great skill, but something even worse, something she hadn't felt since she'd last had friends—the fear of causing irreparable damage to a relationship.

"Sorry . . . I didn't mean—"

"Yes you did."

"No, I . . ." She scrambled to find the words to make everything better, to assure him she didn't think him a joke. He needed something. There had to be a magic word or phrase that could fix this, but such a skill had always lain beyond her capabilities. If she'd upset anyone else, she could have asked him for advice on what to say, but as he was the upset party . . .

The sight of blood on his jacket momentarily distracted her. "What happened to your hand?" she blurted out. Physical wounds were something she could fix.

"Nothing," he said stiffly.

Nikolai walked toward the hovel, leaving her alone with her guilt.

Nikolai slammed the hovel door and strode to his room. Blood splattered his jacket—probably ruined—and his clothes stank of sweat. With his good hand, he grabbed a set of clean clothes from his armoire and went to the bathroom. He turned on the shower, stripped, and examined the throbbing, ruddy mess that was his bitten hand. The sink tinged pink as he ran it under the tap, reigniting stinging pain. The wound was superficial; nothing a potion couldn't heal. He retrieved one from his pouch and took a sip, testing the shower water as the wound closed—still cold. Despite the modern plumbing, the water always took forever to warm.

He gazed at his reflection as he waited. He tried to keep himself in good condition, well muscled without being too bulky. His mother's Turkish heritage blessed him with the appearance of a slight natural tan. Even with his efforts to eat more when feeling well, his ribs and cheekbones were too prominent, and his skin had taken on a sallow cast. Still handsome, but that was beside the point—he wasn't in top form, and his health continued to be affected by the malaise.

The Roman chamomile—his last hope for a potion remedy—had failed, and he'd nearly killed himself on the cliffs. Not only that, a pattern was making itself painfully clear—the malaise tended to strike when he was doing well, making big plans, or enjoying himself. It didn't always strike at those times, but it *never* struck when he was doing something boring or unimportant, and the effect seemed proportionally worse the better he was doing, ranging from general apathy and lack of energy to predilections for suicide.

Conditional spells—magic that only activated under set conditions—could do that, and Medea had already demonstrated her prowess with them. The letter addressed to Petrov had been enchanted not only to blind anyone beside the addressee reading it but also to give multiple warnings. If he hadn't been so pissed off at being on the receiving end, he would have admired the spell for the work of art that it was. Shame Medea wasn't teaching him that instead of making him boil water and levitate stones.

The spell afflicting him now seemed no less complex. He had to hand it to her, it was a pretty good way to keep apprentices in line. But the long-term ramifications were unacceptable. What if it struck when he was about to make a discovery? While he was giving a speech? Fighting an enemy? Any time he made any headway, the spell could activate and bring him to a staggering halt.

Given his appearance, the spell likely did more than squelch his spirit. The malaise left him weak and weary. Either she was draining his youth, or she was transferring her age onto him. She'd see how much of a "joke" he was when he killed her.

Steam billowed from the shower. Nikolai stepped inside and considered the problem before him. What he needed was information. If Medea had any living apprentices, he needed to speak with them and find out what they knew about the affliction. It was a fair bet she had one or two ex-apprentices stashed in the dungeon. Why else keep it locked? To get in, he'd have to learn ward-breaking.

In the meantime, he would probe Medea for more names. The woman had a weakness for lectures. Her conceit drove her to talk ad nauseam when asked about magic, but the same didn't hold true for other topics. If he could find a way to phrase the question just right, he might be able to get her talking about people she'd trained. If there were none living, he'd have to settle for dead. From what he could recall from the Academy, contacting the dead was tricky. He'd have to check the library for a séance spell.

It was past time he checked Medea for vulnerabilities. A direct attack would be suicide. He was a damn good duelist, but not that good, not yet. Poison might give him an edge, but someone else must have tried it by now. He needed a susceptibility test. Not on the island—she'd suspect him immediately— but perhaps in a Magi town, where an assassination attempt was more likely to come from someone else.

When he did kill her, he desperately hoped there'd be an opportunity to tell her before she died, as he had with Petrov, when she no longer had a chance to stop it. He wanted to see the look in her eyes when she found out it was him. That after a millennium of countless assassination attempts, it was he, Nikolai Fedorov, who'd bested her.

———

Nikolai studied the blue rune on the dungeon door and cast Magic Sight. A slender golden tendril appeared, running from the rune to the door handle. The ward was too simple, almost like Medea expected him to be able to break it. All he'd have to do is sever the magical golden line.

He placed his cheek flat against the door, searching for hidden traces of magic. There. A transparent thread, finer than spider's silk, ran from the rune all the way across the lab and through the opposite door, probably to Medea. If he cut the obvious golden tendril and opened the door, the clear thread would notify Medea. The only way to bypass the clear thread without triggering it was to use a counter spell.

For once, Medea's library had been Useful in that regard. He'd come across an ungodly number of books devoted to the technique in his search for ward breaking. Counter spells used something called resonance, which involved hitting a spell with identical-yet-stronger magic. Somehow this would disrupt the spell and cause it to fall apart.

Due to their nature, counter spells were virtually impossible to create on the fly, as each only targeted one thing. The counter spell for Pummel couldn't be used for Fireball. Not only that, individual Magi could have slightly different variations to their spells, so what worked for Harry might not work for Jane. This was especially true if they didn't use "standard" spells or wands. Medea's insistence on wandless magic made a lot more sense in this context. No one could counter her spells if they were unique.

Technically, he could counter her ward, given that it was sitting there, not winging toward him mid-duel. But that could take hours of careful observation as he tried to piece together the nature of the spell, and a single failed attempt would no doubt alert Medea.

Nikolai traced the golden tendril with his finger, trying to sense what exactly the ward did. On closer inspection, it disappeared into the locking mechanism. At some signal from Medea, it would unlock. The clear thread would be triggered if the door was unlocked, or if the handle compressed enough to indicate the door had been opened.

The hinges, on the other hand, were free of magic.

After a bit of oil and telekinetic coaxing, he managed to remove the pins holding the door hinges in place. He wiggled the door slowly out of its frame—thankfully age had warped the wood, leaving a bit of a gap for his fingers—and propped it against the wall, ward undisturbed.

A circular flight of stairs vanished into darkness. He summoned a bit of flame into his hand and crossed the threshold. The momentary reflection of light was his only warning. On the second step, at knee height, a black thread glistened. Trap or alert system, he couldn't tell. He stepped over it and carefully descended, straining to make out other threads.

As the stairs curved away from the light of the doorway above, crystals embedded in the ceiling sprang to life, emitting a faint glow that extended the reach of his own flickering flame. Halfway down he found another thread of magic, this one at chest height. He ducked under it and continued. The air grew chilly and the stairwell seemed to muffle every sound. At the base of the stairs was another thread at neck height. Their placement was puzzling. Together, all three threads could have formed a reasonable barrier, but placed separately as they were, he had no trouble avoiding each.

The stairs opened to a cavernous room walled with stone. Crystals above glowed as Nikolai entered. It smelled like a cellar, stale and dusty, with a hint of something else, something intangible.

Misery.

An indented stone table lay front and center. Leather restraints dangled from its sides. The surface was pocked with strategic holes leading to a collection trough below. He caressed the cool stone and drank in the rest of the room.

Worktables. Wooden and clean, though worn from centuries of use. Shackles. A rack sporting knives and other cruel instruments. Rectangular doors, as one might see in a morgue for storing bodies, and just beyond them, a large oven. It was beautiful. The things he could do here . . .

Despite Medea's obvious talent, she always scoffed at his

interest in dark magic. He'd almost begun to think she didn't use it. This proved her hypocrisy. Her craft was hidden down here, far from prying eyes.

Shadows stirred to life at the far end of the room. Nikolai grinned and hastened toward a row of cells. He was right, she *did* have apprentices down here. Iron bars framed each cage, supplemented with an invisible barrier to keep the occupants from reaching out. He approached and peered inside. No beds, no furniture of any kind, not even a bucket for them to shit in.

All the occupants were male, save one. A pitiful lot, most sat with vacant expressions, but a few mumbled or cried. Some appeared quite old. How long had they been here? Or had Medea's draining spell made them appear older than they were?

The last two cells on the left shone brightly against his senses. Enchantments wove through the bars themselves, the stones lining the walls, everything. Whoever was in there, Medea wanted to make damn sure they didn't escape.

He rapped the bars on the second to last cell. "Hey. You in there. Are you a former apprentice?"

The man's head jerked up. His eyes narrowed and he spat in Nikolai's direction.

"Come now. That's rude. I'm just here to talk." He tried the next cell over, but the prisoner just shook his head and turned away.

A cackle came from one of the less enchanted cells.

Nikolai followed the sound to cell number four. "What's so funny?"

Prisoner number four had long, scraggly white hair and piercing blue eyes. He wagged a finger at Nikolai. "You're not supposed to be down here."

"How do you know?"

"Because she hasn't given you the grand tour yet."

Nikolai nodded to the last two cells. "Why won't they talk to me?"

"Can't." The man leaned forward and nonchalantly propped his arms against the bars, as if he were conversing with a stranger at a bar instead of from inside a cage. "She cut out their tongues. Doesn't want them castin' any spells."

"And you?"

"I ain't no wizard."

"Then why are you here?"

"Who the fuck knows?"

Nikolai peered into his mind. It was calm like a pool of still water. Overwhelming boredom. Annoyance at being held captive. Hope that he could manipulate the kid into releasing him, or at least into killing Medea. That would be funny.

"How long have you been here?"

"Too goddamned long." He didn't know, but he'd been much younger when he'd woken up in the cell one day. His hatred of Medea was so intense it ran cold.

"How many apprentices have you met?"

Three. "I'll tell you if you get rid of this." The man pressed his palm to the invisible barrier between the bars, unaware that his mind had unknowingly given Nikolai the answer.

"I'll consider it. What I'd really like to know is if any of them are in these cells."

No. "Yes. Remove the spell and I'll tell you which."

Shit. He'd hoped to find at least one down here. Looks like Medea really did kill them. "It's not important. What does she do with you all?"

Images of spell experimentation. Occasional blood-draining and harvesting of body parts. Medea did all this without any obvious pleasure, just clinical detachment.

The man sensed he was losing Nikolai's interest and switched to martyr. "She tortures us! Please. You have to help me!" All a performance, just as Nikolai performed for others. The hatred was real, as was the desire to get out, but the prisoner wasn't remotely afraid. A man not unlike himself. It took a moment, then the prisoner recognized it too and stopped his pleading. The men assessed each other, one predator to another.

"I'm not removing the shield," said Nikolai. "You can't see it, but I can. Which means so can she. Now, if you'll excuse me . . ."

The prisoner spoke to his back. "She's gonna to kill you." Speculation based on information he'd gleaned from one chatty, sadistic apprentice. He had no memories of his own to back up the statement. Wherever Medea killed her apprentices, it wasn't down here.

"She can try."

"You want an edge, let me out and I'll help you bring her down."

As if he needed Mundane help. "I'll consider it."

Nikolai walked back to the stairs. On his way, he paused at the rectangular doors set into the stone, presumably to house bodies. He pulled one of them open.

On the cold metal tray was a young man about Nikolai's age, so well-preserved that he could have been sleeping. The face below a thatch of sandy hair was purple with bruises. Something about him was familiar. Was he a fellow student at the Academy? Was this one of Medea's former apprentices? Nikolai placed his hand on another drawer.

Before he could open it, the man sat up.

23

NECESSARY CONDITIONS

The man gasped, loud and deep, like someone who'd been holding their breath for a long time. He looked around, spotted the rack of knives, and promptly fell off the tray with a yelp.

Who was this guy? Nikolai couldn't shake the feeling that he knew him. Better not use telepathy just yet. If the man were Magi, he would feel the intrusion and possibly conceal what he knew. "Hey, buddy, it's okay. You're safe now," Nikolai said in his most reassuring voice.

The man spun, eyes widening at the sight of Nikolai. He dashed for the knives, grabbing the largest he could find, an unwieldy thing, and pointed it at Nikolai's chest.

Nikolai put up his hands. "I'm only here to help, friend." He nodded toward the drawer. "I just opened that and found you inside. What's your name? How did you get in here?" He belatedly recalled how many languages Medea spoke. If this were a former apprentice, there was a good chance their languages wouldn't overlap.

"Ed—Eddie. Don't remember. Got ossified with the mates.

Some fecker jumped us. Got home and . . ." He pressed his fist to his face, straining to remember.

Irish accent, bruises on the face—this was one of the drunks who'd accosted Kate back at the Spotted Sow. So that's why Medea had ditched him that night. She was probably rounding the three of them up. No doubt the other two were also in drawers. Damnit, why couldn't Medea have anyone Useful stashed down here!

Nikolai dipped into the man's mind. It was a hazy mess, almost as if he were still drunk. He didn't recognize Nikolai as the man who'd given him the bruises. Hopefully that would make it easier to get him back into the drawer, where the sleep spell or whatever had kept him unconscious would take effect again.

Nikolai switched to an Irish accent. "It's okay, Eddie. I think someone's codding ya. Your mates, were they a big fella and a bloke with red hair?"

"Yeah."

"I heard them talking about giving someone a good fright."

"Those wankers!"

"Look, why don't you lie back down here." He patted the metal tray. "I'll go get them. When they open the drawer, you can holler and scare them." If this didn't work, he'd have to use force.

Thankfully, the guy seemed the suggestible sort of drunk and ambled over. "You sure about this?"

"They're the ones that put you in a drawer. Feckers deserve to have the piss taken out of them. You want me to hold that?" Nikolai indicated the knife.

"Wouldn't it be better if I held this up?" He brandished the knife and made a roaring noise.

"It's a little big though. Might get caught on the inside there."

"RUN! GET OUT NOW!" The call came from number four's cell. Motherfucker. The other inmates picked up the cue and began chanting.

Eddie looked from the cells to Nikolai. His eyes hardened, and he raised the knife. Nikolai barely managed to get a shield up in time. Eddie hammered at the shield with savage ferocity. A telekinetic push sent him stumbling backward.

Nikolai summoned a fireball into his hand. "Get inside the drawer or get roasted."

"Fuck you!" Eddie spat. He charged at Nikolai.

Nikolai blew him backward with the gust spell and grinned. "I can do this all night."

"That fireball in his hand don't mean SHIT. He can't hurt you without gettin' caught!" Prisoner four again.

None of the spells in his repertoire were designed to subdue, only harm. Bleed, Amputate, Fireball, Lightning, Pummel—all would leave evidence. All but Fear. Nikolai dispelled his fireball and sent Fear rippling through the air, striking Eddie in the temple.

"Head shot!" Nikolai called out in jubilation.

Eddie screamed. His hands clutched at his head, eyes rolling around in terror. Then he bolted for the stairs.

Shit! Nikolai tore after him, tackling him a hair's breadth away from the damned black thread guarding the stairwell. Eddie thrashed against his grip, little more than a panicked animal. Nikolai punched his face. A few more bruises would go unnoticed there.

Still Eddie screamed. This close to the stairwell, the sound no doubt reached up to the lab. Nikolai made a grab at the man's ankles, but he was flailing so much Nikolai almost lost him again.

Nikolai hooked one leg under his arm and hauled the man toward the drawer. If he could get to the weapon rack, he could knock the guy unconscious. As they passed one of the worktables, Eddie made a desperate grab.

"Let go, you stubborn piece of shit!" Nikolai made to kick Eddie's hand, when suddenly the man whipped out of his grasp and stumbled to the stairs. His head passed below the first thread, but the second was at waist height, much harder to miss.

Nikolai ran after him, shooting Pummel as he went. Fuck evidence. At this point he just had to get the man subdued.

Despite his drunken state, Eddie flew ahead, turning out of sight with every curve of the stairs. The black thread loomed across the stairwell. Nikolai shot Pummel at Eddie's legs.

The spell hit, but too late. As Eddie crumpled to the floor, his hand passed through the black line. An invisible force slammed Eddie flat against the wall. His body moved upward, until he hung suspended with his arms and legs splayed, skin weeping blood. A scream erupted, like nothing Nikolai had heard before. He approached, fascinated. Eddie's skin peeled off in strips, flayed alive. He needed that spell!

"What are you doing down here?" Medea appeared on the stairs.

———

Medea didn't know which was more disturbing, the idea that a subject had gotten out or the reality that Nikolai had broken into the dungeon and was now eyeing the results of her security spell with avid interest.

"I thought the wards were to notify you if anyone came down here," he said, eyes never leaving the carnage beside him, "but I was wrong, wasn't I? They were designed to prevent escapes."

"What are you doing? You know you're not permitted in the dungeon yet." She tried to keep her voice level, but it wasn't cooperating.

Nikolai finally turned his eyes toward her. There wasn't the faintest trace of guilt in his expression. "You keep them for experimentation, correct? To test out spells?"

She didn't answer. The sound shield around her head blocked

the screams of the subject, but the thrashing was distracting. She canceled the ward with a wave of her hand, and his head slumped forward.

"Heal him," she said to Nikolai, nodding to the subject.

"Why?"

"You break it, you mend it. First rule of the dungeon. Which you'd know if you'd bothered to wait." She sent the broken subject levitating down the stairwell, forcing Nikolai to retreat or get bled on. He gave ground, and when she shifted the body onto one of the worktables, she saw a healing potion in his hand.

"Healing potions are inadequate for true healing. You want to cut something up, use livestock. That is not"—she gestured about the dungeon—"what we do here."

"I had no intention of 'cutting him up.' And I did my best to keep him from tripping the wards."

"Out of self-interest!"

"Yes, out of self-interest!" He returned her glare. "I didn't want to get caught, but you left me little choice."

"You could have waited—"

"I've *been* waiting! You said I could learn telepathy but refused to teach me. So I've done what I've always had to do— learn on my own. Except you blocked access to the books I need."

Her stomach knotted. Heat rose in her cheeks at his accusations, all true. He had every right to be angry.

"I need Magi to practice on. Where do you expect me to do that? Haven? Unlike you, I'd rather not make enemies all over the Magi world. I knew there were bound to be Magi down here, so yes, I broke in."

This wasn't going at all how she'd planned. He was supposed to learn the basics, a variety of magical schools. She didn't expect him to turn away from darker magics completely, if that's what he really wanted, but he had to realize there was more out there, so much more. She couldn't think of a single thing to say in her defense and stood mutely as he took a step closer.

He unstoppered his healing potion and dumped it over the flayed subject. "There! If that doesn't fix him, I'm sorry, but it's the best I can do. But I'm not sorry I came down here. I won't be held back—not by Petrov, not by you, not by anyone!" He slammed the empty vial on the table and turned to leave.

She wanted to say something, but the words wouldn't come. Why did she always freeze when it came to human interactions? She never froze during duels.

He was almost to the stairwell. She could block his exit, but that would only enrage him further. Better to let him go, give herself time to get her thoughts in order.

She set to fixing the battered test subject. This, at least, she could do. Reading the physical components of a person was easier than reading their behaviors. The human body was incredible—so many microscopic parts working in concert to make a whole. A whole that was, for the most part, completely unaware of its smaller units, unless something broke.

She willed the skin to fold back and knit together, sealed up severed capillaries, and moved cells around as needed to get the job done. Healing like this she could do in her sleep. Hard to say if it came to her naturally or not, having grown up under a healer, but in all her years, she'd never met another with the same gift for manipulating the human form. Fleshweaving, as she called it, was her biggest strength.

And Nikolai's was telepathy.

Every apprentice she'd ever trained, she'd encouraged to tap into their natural strengths. Yet here she was, blocking access to books and refusing to train Nikolai properly, just because telepathy made her uncomfortable. He'd broken into the dungeon, not to torture the test subjects or try out new curses, but to prac- tice. Had she been any different, sneaking into her master's study and reading scrolls without permission? What Nikolai had done was not only excusable, it was commendable.

Maybe she could start his telepathy training now . . .

But he had so much catching up to do! And the curse wasn't all to blame. Nikolai neglected anything he didn't see a use for. His mana pool remained abysmally small. Whatever he might claim, it was clear he wasn't doing the boiling exercise. He continued to treat all his wounds with potions rather than learn healing. Somehow, she'd have to break through his ingrained biases there.

At least his work in the forest had gotten better, but then it was combat, something Nikolai seemed to enjoy. He could now sense most of her roots and dodge them before they struck. Conjuring blight was still beyond his capabilities, though not for lack of trying.

Maybe there was a way to satisfy his curiosity about telepathy. One lesson a week couldn't hurt. When he had a firm grasp of the basics, then and only then would she allow him to learn whatever he wanted.

She finished with the test subject and placed him back in the drawer, refreshing the stasis spell, then went to her room. There she spent hours painstakingly crafting a letter. Over and over again, she laid out the reasoning behind her decision, each revision more verbose than the last. Her desk became littered with false starts, until at last she scrapped it all and settled for something containing none of the emotional baggage she'd worked through so meticulously on paper. *I will teach you telepathy—* simple and to the point.

She tiptoed downstairs with the letter, but hesitated at Nikolai's door. Was it right to give in? She'd wanted to try something different with him, to see if postponing access to information reduced the odds of students trying to kill her. Flexibility was all well and good in personal matters, but this was science, where variables had to be minimized. If she gave in on this small thing, it could alter the results of her experiment. A dull ache permeated her stomach. Maybe she should go back upstairs . . .

The bathroom door opened and Nikolai exited, wearing only a towel about his waist. He rubbed a second towel over his dark hair. Water droplets flecked his bare chest. Had he lost muscle mass? Irrelevant. The towel at his waist was concerning. A precarious barrier between her and his weapon. She took an involuntary step back.

Nikolai noticed, and there was some subtle shift in his demeanor. He smiled and began to dry his chest with slow pats, then casually draped the towel over his shoulders and moved to open his door. She clenched her jaw and crossed her arms. His arm brushed against her. She stood her ground and tried not to flinch. Close. He was far too close. Knowing he couldn't hurt her didn't stop the reflexive dump of adrenaline into her system.

"So," he said, casually leaning against the doorframe, "to what do I owe the pleasure?"

"I . . ." Damnit. This was why she'd written the letter. Conversations, like experiments, were only good when one could control the variables. Her eyes slid past him, searching for something else to latch on to.

"You've redecorated." What the hell was she saying? This wasn't why she was here. She could just hand him the letter and leave, but he might open it in front of her, and then she'd have to deal with the gloating.

He hooked his thumbs in the towel. "I did. Does that bother you?" For some inexplicable reason, he made it sound like a challenge.

"Why would that bother me?"

"You look . . . uncomfortable." He smiled as he said it.

Uncomfortable was an understatement. His thumbs. His thumbs! The added pressure they exerted on the towel would surely cause it to fall. Run. NO. Fight. Always fight. Nothing could touch her. She was invincible.

". . . silk sheets and everything." Apparently he'd been talking.

"I should be going," she muttered.

"Nonsense! Come in, have a look around." He backed away from the door and smiled at her invitingly.

She squelched the age-old fear and entered, prepared to battle.

Had he known Medea would react so well to his body, he would have taken his shirt off ages ago. It seemed as though Petrov's warning not to flirt with her was bullshit. The old girl was *hungry*. Her eyes drank in his well-muscled chest and scanned downward, lingering a little too long on his crotch. She was so into him she didn't know what to do with herself. The woman stood awkwardly and tried to look away, but every few seconds, her eyes betrayed her interest.

If she was willing, fucking her might solve a lot of his problems. He was skilled enough to make her beg for more. Withholding would be a nice way to exert control. He could get her to lift the curse, teach whatever he wanted, share immortality . . .

He crossed his arms and leaned against the desk, hoping his biceps bulged nicely. Medea examined the room with a certain trepidation.

"Nice, uh, color," she said in reference to the bed. "I suppose after a few hundred years it was time for a new one."

He'd stashed the old mattress in the back of the room. He suddenly wanted to burn it, thinking of hundreds of years of other men's sweat and secretions.

"I, uh, best be going. Are the accommodations alright? Do you, uh, need anything?"

She'd never been so nervous. He had to get her to relax. What better way than to give her an opportunity to show off?

"What about a window? Can you do that?"

Instantly her face changed. There was the confident woman he knew. "Not a true window, no, but I can make an illusion of one."

"How does it work?"

"It's a bit like the gateway, but not exactly. I draw out an area on a surface where light hits, and sort of transfer the image here."

"Can the image come from anywhere?"

"Anywhere with a wall or solid surface."

"Can you get me the view inside Shailyn's bedroom?" he joked, hoping to make her jealous.

He slammed into the cold stone floor. Every inch of him felt like it was on fire.

Medea loomed, eyes blazing.

"Didn't . . . mean it." He gritted his teeth against the pain.

"What *did* you mean?" She'd never looked so cold, and yet the temperature in the room seemed to be rising.

"It was . . . joke."

"You think it's funny to spy on women without their permission?"

"No—Medea, *please*."

The pain abruptly ceased, and she made to storm out.

"Wait!" He reached out to her as she stepped around him, hand grasping at the hem of her dress.

"Don't touch me!" She wrenched her dress away and kicked at his face. Her bare foot didn't connect, but it was as though metal collided with his temple. Pins of light dotted his vision.

"I'm sorry." His brain worked furiously. There was more here than pure anger. There was contempt. He'd only seen her show it once before, back at the Spotted Sow. Somehow he'd slipped dangerously close to a category of humans she despised, humans now residing in drawers in the dungeon. Lies wouldn't save him.

"I fucked up," he blurted out.

She paused.

"You know how sometimes your brain goes to a place . . . you don't mean it, and you'd never *do* it, but the instinct is still there, and you keep it hidden from everyone because if they knew they'd hate you, but then sometimes it slips out . . ." God, truth was hard. How did people do this?

"My brain would never go to a place like that."

"Mine does. All the time. It's my . . . default." He sat up but dared not stand. "Actions are what make us. We can have all the horrible thoughts in the world, but it's what we do about them, or don't do, that matters. I'll admit I miss seeing Shailyn naked, and so I made a joke—a *bad* joke—but I'd never actually do that to her. It's not a line I'm willing to cross. I may be immoral, but I do have morals."

"You realize the definition of immoral means—"

"I know what it means!" The outburst almost got her going again. He took a breath. Anger wouldn't help, not here. "What I'm trying to say is—"

"I understand the sentiment of what you are saying." Back to her formal diction. After an uncomfortably long silence, she said, "What view would you prefer?"

He didn't have to think twice. "The ocean by the cave with the hot pools. I like watching the waves crash against the rocks."

Medea nodded. "I'll take care of it tomorrow."

He couldn't let her leave, not like this. "What did you want to see me about?"

"Huh?" She fingered her hip pouch. "Nothing. Nothing at all." Medea left and he rose to close the door. Across the common room, she threw something into the fireplace on her way to the library.

24

THE GIFT

Medea bit her lip and tried not to cry. When she'd found the book on the shelf, she hadn't recognized it, but then she bought so many books it could be difficult to remember those she hadn't read yet.

An unread book was just a cover—a promise of ideas or emotions. Like people, they introduced themselves and tried to put their best foot forward. It wasn't until you spent time with them that you got to know their true nature.

Nikolai had been like that. On the surface, he seemed like the rest of her dark apprentices—completely driven, with no thought of others—and yet at times he showed a new facet of himself. Behind the Spotted Sow he'd saved that girl. He might not have understood why, but he was still compelled to do the right thing.

And now, he'd given her a book that was both a connection to her soul and a slap in the face. There were overarching themes of people becoming disconnected from each other, as she was, but at the heart was a story of censorship.

For the first time ever, she was censoring her teaching, and now Nikolai had thrown down the gauntlet. He'd chosen the medium she valued most, probably combing through hundreds of books to find one with the perfect message. He knew exactly what she was doing, and he thought it was wrong.

It *was* wrong. Restricting information—this wasn't her. Who was she becoming?

With shaking hands, she set the book down. She had to do something for Nikolai. Such an auspicious gift demanded something in return. But what?

Of course! She would show him her gardens. There he would find the ingredients he needed to control the curse that chipped away at his life. Not that she could explicitly point out the plants he needed—that would be interfering—but she could give him an assignment that would lead him to the answer he sought. It was an assignment she gave most of her apprentices anyway, so it wasn't as if she was doing anything different with him. She wasn't breaking her rules. She was simply moving the lesson up in the queue.

Medea picked up the book and went to find Nikolai.

The distant creaking of stairs alerted Nikolai to Medea's impending approach. He pocketed the list of poisons he'd been making and began to fill a cauldron with water before she got on him about the boiling exercise again.

"Nikolai?"

His back was to the door when it opened, but when Medea spoke, he could hear something off in her voice. Did she know about his late-night excursion to the cave? He'd spent hours scanning the cliffs with Magic Sight to no avail. There were no other entrances he could find, and no wards. If rock magic existed, he'd have to learn it next. Though he hadn't seen any wards that would alert her to his trespass, it was possible he'd missed one in the dark.

He turned around, expecting to see fury. Instead, Medea's face was strained, her eyes puffy. Had she been crying? He'd never seen her so upset.

"This . . . what you . . ." She held out a book, *Fahrenheit 451*.

It took a moment to register what he was even looking at, and then it clicked—this was the novel he'd procured in London, the one about book burnings. He'd placed it on her to-read shelf ages ago. His book had made her cry—wonderful!

He sat and put on a concerned face while Medea searched for the words to express whatever the hell she was trying to say. "Didn't you like it? The bookseller said—"

"Thank you." She clasped the book to her chest like a treasure.

What? She'd *liked* it? It was supposed to make her upset! But then why was she crying?

"You're right." Medea shook her head. "I . . . you're right."

Normally a phrase he loved to hear, but in this case, he had no idea what the context was. "You're welcome." What the hell was in that book?

She smiled at him wistfully. "I want to show you my gardens. We will be collecting plant specimens—"

What the fuck? Her mind made the most bizarre leaps.

"—your job will be to prepare and catalog all the plants." Medea said this like it was a wonderful gift she bestowed on him rather than yet another boring task.

"Come." She beckoned him toward the door.

Now? Since when did she alter their schedule on the spur of the moment? What the hell was in that book? He probably should have read it first.

She led him to the gateway room and pointed to the green lights on the maps. "Each of these is a garden. Familiarize yourself with which plants grow where, so you can replace potion ingredients as needed."

He tuned out as she lectured about climate, only listening again when she brought up her security spells. The gardens were protected by a progressively harsh ring of wards.

The outermost wards induced hallucinations and a nagging sense of being hunted or watched, designed to scare people away. The second group of wards caused injury.

Here Medea sighed and crossed her arms. "Many people make the mistake of causing serious injury to feet or legs. You *want* trespassers to be able to get away. The wound should be bad enough that they turn around and seek help, but not so grave that they die and attract attention or can't leave at all."

The final wards killed and dissolved the body.

"You do all this, just to protect plants?"

"Not all the gardens, no. But the Mundane are encroaching everywhere. It's a good way to scare people away from building in a particular area. They think it's haunted or patrolled by dangerous creatures."

How many mythological creatures had sprung up from Magi using such spells? Both the Scottish kelpie and Slavic rusalka fit the profile. People saw a creature, ignored the warnings, and then vanished, never to be heard from again.

Medea grabbed the peg and made a show of placing it somewhere in southern Mexico. "This is where we're going today."

As if he cared.

The door opened to a hallway of stone and Nikolai stepped through. Warm, moist air threatened to smother him. He took several steps before he realized the sense of wrongness that assaulted him whenever he left the island was absent. He cast Magic Sight. The hallway glowed with the same yellow as Medea's island, only fainter. What was this place?

Medea led him along the corridor until it opened to a stone platform surrounded by lush jungle. Colorful parrots screeched overhead and alighted in the trees, where they vanished in the mass of green. The platform was part of a large stone structure, though it was impossible to make out much from their vantage point.

"People once came here to worship," she said. "The very structure is permeated with their magic. Not a bad place to cast spells that need an extra push."

They walked down a flight of stairs that seemed to go on forever, periodically broken up by more platforms. He looked behind them. From here he could finally recognize the shape—a great stone pyramid.

"Did you know the people who lived here?"

"No. I got here after they'd been wiped out. The New World was so vast, and I could only be in so many places at once." Medea shook her head. "Tragic. All that knowledge lost."

"But the gateway?"

"Ah." She turned to him and smiled. "You can only create gateways on location, and gaining passage to the New World was damnably difficult as a woman."

"Couldn't you just . . . ?" Nikolai waved his hands theatrically as Medea had done during their first interaction. "Magic!"

"Those ships were close quarters. Bullying my way onto one wasn't in anyone's best interest. In the end, money won out. It always does." There was a note of derision in the last statement.

Trees created a corridor over the stairs at the base of the pyramid and vines crept up to meet them. Under the canopy, the world dimmed as the foliage blocked out the sky. Stone changed to a thick carpet of leaves and roots, the yellow glow viewed through Magic Sight dimming fractionally.

Medea paused and looked about as if considering something, her bare toes flexing against the forest floor. Eventually she pointed vaguely to the right. "That way, I think."

Was she guessing? How far would they have to travel across the jungle? If he thought the heat was unbearable when he first exited the gateway, it was nothing compared to now. Sweat soaked through his shirt in the brief time it took them to descend. Insects clamored for attention on every bare patch of skin.

Medea conjured a propeller-like blade and sent it spinning along the path in front of them, slashing apart the dense growth. They hiked for what seemed like hours. She took no discernible path, sometimes veering off in another direction without a word to show him a plant she'd spotted, at which point he was required to collect samples.

She flew gracefully from ground to root to tree, balancing on bare feet and steadying herself with one hand against a trunk. When a larger obstacle blocked their way, she simply flew over it. Nikolai attempted to levitate, but controlling his body while in motion was an awkward process. He ended up too far in one direction or another or went too fast and smacked into whatever they were trying to pass.

On the other side, Medea would be waiting patiently, suspended in the air, offering neither criticism nor help. After the third time, he snapped and asked why she wasn't instructing him in an obviously Useful skill, and she replied that it wasn't why they were there.

"Besides, you'll remember the way much better if you walk it."

Like he would ever willingly come back here.

Eventually he got a system down where he levitated straight up, then manually pulled himself forward using vines and lower branches before settling back to the ground.

At midday, he suggested they break for lunch and Medea informed him they were almost there. He'd begun to doubt she even knew where she was going. Fifteen minutes later, she stopped at the base of a large tree and beckoned him.

She pointed to the canopy and spent a good fifteen minutes detailing the life cycle of moss. Just when she seemed to be winding down, she tapped a cluster of leaves protruding from the bark of a nearby tree and launched into *another* lecture. He tried his best to pretend to listen, though he could think of little else beyond the oppressive humidity and the collection of bug bites begging to be scratched.

"Since you can't fly up there, I'll collect the moss and you can do the Bromeliads."

Oh good, she'd finally stopped.

"The cuttings must be taken from the center, near the base. You see how the leaves make a little cup in the middle? Look inside."

He peered inside the plant. The dense shade made it difficult to see anything, so he illuminated his hand and tried again—water and little black dots floating in gelatinous spheres.

"What am I supposed to be looking at?"

"Frog eggs, remember? They increase the potency of the leaves. Make sure you collect samples from plants that have them, but don't harm the eggs." Medea looked around the ground for something. "Here!" She pointed to a section of root that had broken apart at the top and now contained a shallow pool of water. "Slide any eggs you find into there." Her hand disappeared into her pouch and returned with a pair of pruning shears. "Keep these on you at all times."

Medea rose into the canopy and began scraping moss off the tree limbs. The ground below her soon became littered with moss she found unacceptable for whatever reason. Pluck, sniff, throw. She was careful never to levitate directly above his position. Probably scared he'd look up and see the cobwebs between her legs.

"Try to get as close to the base as you can," she called. "That's where it's the most potent."

Repeating herself again. When he was immortal, he'd take steps to ensure he didn't become just as senile. He sliced neatly through another leaf. Plants. He came to her for curses and necromancy, and she made him cut up plants—it was Petrov all over again. The sooner he discovered her angle, the better. The dungeon had been a dead end. If he wanted to know what became of her apprentices, he'd have to find out from the source. But how to do it without arousing suspicion?

"A lot of your lessons revolve around plants," he called up. "Do you ever get apprentices specializing in nature magic?"

"No, sadly." A clump of moss landed below Medea's tree.

"Well, that's a shame. All that knowledge gone to waste." The gentle scrapes above ceased, and Nikolai chanced a look up.

Medea peered at him curiously, tool poised in her hand. "Thinking of studying nature magic?"

Lying would be too obvious. "No, I'm just curious. You said most of your apprentices are like me. In my experience, people recall the bad easier than the good."

"You think my perception of these apprentices has colored my memory."

"I'm sorry, I didn't mean to offend—"

She barked out a laugh. "No offense taken. It's a good point. Logical. Of course, in *my* experience, people also remember things as being better than they actually were." She tapped the blunt tool against her chin. "Let's see, in the past few hundred years or so, there was a necromancer, a demonologist, a pyromancer—"

Names. He needed names. But as usual, she had none. This was how she thought of people, how she'd thought of him prior to learning his name, if she even remembered it.

"And what's my name?" he asked.

Her recitation continued without pause. "—another necromancer, Nikolai—" At least she remembered *him* properly. "—that guy who was *really* into blood—I think he wanted to become a vampire—"

He paused his leaf clipping. "Is that a real thing?"

"No. You know much blood goes into a decent healing potion. Easy to see how the legend started. That didn't stop him from trying. Got himself stabbed in a brothel in France, I think. Or was that . . . ? No, wrong century. Then there was the Botanist. He loved this place." She waved her tool around. "Lots of rare plants."

"You said you didn't have any nature apprentices lately."

"I only call him 'the Botanist' for his love of plants. Nature wasn't his specialty. No school was. A bit of necromancy, a bit of demonology. A *lot* of defensive spells. Mostly, he wanted to sharpen his skill in combat. He was a decent student. I was sorry to lose him after only three years." Her gentle scraping started back up.

Something wasn't right. She'd briefly referred to the Botanist in the present tense. "He challenged you?"

"Not at all. Was applying for a job and figured he had all"— her voice strained as she yanked persistently on a vine—"he need-ed." It came free suddenly and she flew back several feet into an adjacent tree. She coiled the vine about her hand and deposited it in her pouch before resuming scraping.

"What job?"

"Collective Enforcer."

Nikolai's head jerked up, his pruner catching an entire plant rather than a single leaf. The plant tumbled to the ground, a frog with it, neatly severed in two. *"What?"*

She smirked, evidently delighted to share this tidbit. "I told him he'd be blacklisted if he trained with me, but he wanted to try anyway. Apparently, he got the job."

"Really? Where's he stationed?"

"Oh, he's retired now. Moved back to Germany."

He resumed clipping. She'd given him enough to go on. The Collective was bound to have records of their past Enforcers. All he had to do was lean on Harper to ask his contacts within the organization.

They worked for a time in silence, the air an oppressive blanket of moisture. Sweat ran in rivulets down his face and back. He mopped his brow with a kerchief, for all the good it did in the humidity. As well try to dry himself off in the middle of a shower.

"Have we collected enough yet?" he asked.

"Nearly. I'm almost done." She floated down and landed on a root while he stowed the last of the leaves in his pouch.

"Your turn," she said. "Find the temple."

"Excuse me?"

Medea spread her arms wide. "Look at where we are! This is the perfect place to practice your magical perception. Cast your senses wide, locate the temple, and return to it."

She couldn't be serious. He scanned her face to be sure. She was.

He thought back to her lessons in the forest and tried to regain that meditative state.

"Excellent!" she said. "Don't take too long. It rains in the afternoons here. I'll see you at home." Medea zipped toward the canopy. The branches moved to allow her to pass and then she was gone.

Ditched. In the middle of the fucking *jungle*.

He whipped out his speed dagger and wand, taking aim at a nearby tree and pretending it was Medea.

"IgnisIgnisIgnisIgnisIgnis." The flames erupted so fast they stabilized into a solid beam. He scored the tree and half a dozen others. The clusters of plants he'd been collecting sizzled and popped as they ignited along with their amphibian occupants. Birds cried out and fled the raging inferno. Only mana exhaustion forced Nikolai to stop.

The sky opened and assaulted him with a torrential downpour, dousing the remaining fires. His attempts to conjure a shield failed for lack of mana. He fished around in his pouch for a potion, but the first few turned out to be healing. By the time he'd gotten a mana potion and downed it, he was already soaked.

He leaned against a smoldering tree and closed his eyes, trying to sense the magic of the temple. Faint, but there it was. He struck out through the dense overgrowth, sloshing through mud as he made a beeline for the gateway.

25

SERVITUS AUT MORS

Medea regretted stopping for lunch. Even sitting this far from the kitchen, the incessant whirring of machines grated against her nerves. Nikolai studied his reflection in the window, making what appeared to be a series of practice smiles, and straightened his hair with his fingers. If he ever created a familiar, it would probably be a peacock.

A waitress came to take their order. Nikolai used her name, asked how her shift was going, and made some poor excuse for a joke. The waitress laughed and playfully touched his shoulder. This had to be some sort of mating ritual. Definitely a peacock.

Medea drummed her fingers on the table. If this went on any longer, she'd have to summon her own food.

"What can I get you today?"

Finally! Medea gave her order and stared out the window. The past week she'd taken Nikolai to a different garden each day. Today was a patch of brightweed just outside of Safe Harbor, an English Magi town. Unlike Haven, which managed to remain somewhat secluded, the Mundane world had built up around Safe Harbor, suffusing it with Mundane culture. Elders fought the influx of technology as long as they could, complaining it interfered with their magic, but eventually gave up and moved to the country.

Now, most of Safe Harbor's residents were indistinguishable from Mundanes. At least in Mundane cities, she could pretend magic existed somewhere. But here, in a supposed Magi town, the lack of true practitioners was a stark reminder of all the world had lost. She would have preferred to go straight home, but Nikolai had insisted they stop for lunch, saying he'd never been to a place where Mundanes and Magi mixed so openly. She couldn't bear to tell him the truth—that they were the only two Magi here.

"You're awfully quiet," said Nikolai.

"I'm just thinking of how much this place has changed."

"The townspeople seemed to recognize you. How long has it been?"

"Not long. Unfortunately, brightweed quickly loses potency so I'm continually replenishing my stock. But I don't stay long." Medea shrugged. She really didn't want to talk about it. A couple of Safe Harbor's brightest stars were apparently in the Collective "delegation" she'd killed. Even after all this time, the townsfolk weren't fond of her.

"Are there any places you recommend I visit while we're here?"

Ugh, this was torture. Already chatty, Nikolai was particularly verbose of late, as though silence were an enemy to be vanquished. If he'd asked about magic it would have been fine, but these days his questions served no purpose.

"I have no idea," she said, hoping he'd take the hint.

"What did your other apprentices enjoy?"

The food couldn't come fast enough. What did he want from her, a grand tour? An idea bloomed and she leaned forward with a smile. "Thomas' favorite place was the bookstore." Nikolai always had a curious reaction to her old apprentice. If she accidentally mentioned Thomas during a lesson, Nikolai became irritable but suddenly tried harder. Maybe he would take this as a challenge to read more.

Instead, Nikolai smirked. "I *knew* he was a bookworm." His face grew serious and he caught her eye. "What I don't understand is how your best apprentice could be a witch."

"Definitions change over time. These days witches are known for their lack of mana. In the past, the term was used more loosely, sometimes as a slur, other times to denote a female caster. Thomas grew up a Puritan. In his society, all magic was witchcraft and practitioners were in league with the devil. When he embraced magic, he embraced the name as well."

"How does a Puritan get into witchcraft, let alone train with you?"

Medea sat back and clasped her hands in her lap. People got upset when you shared too much about them, and Thomas' story wasn't hers to tell. She'd have to leave out specifics. "When he was a young man, an incident caused him to question his faith. Well, it was more than questioning actually. It's safe to say that he hated God."

"And he saw witchcraft as a way to get back at him."

Medea nodded. "Thomas was already magically strong, although he didn't know it yet. He trained with another for a few years before his master saw his potential and passed him along to me. I was in the Americas for research and not accepting students, but the apprenticeship fee was good, and there was something about him . . ."

She looked up to find Nikolai watching her with an odd expression. Before she could ask why, the waitress returned to inform them their food would be out soon. Medea tried not to roll her eyes. Either it was here, or it wasn't. And if it was going to be out soon, why bother telling them? Why not just bring it when it was ready? When the waitress started batting her eyes at Nikolai, it dawned on Medea that the intrusion might be intentional. She wasn't going to watch that again.

Medea excused herself to the restroom, where she levitated against the wall and pulled out a book. A chapter later she judged it safe to return and was happily surprised to find her food waiting.

"There you are!" said Nikolai. "I thought you'd left me for good."

"I was reading."

"Of course you were."

Medea sat and dug into her mashed potatoes, then took a sip of tea. The mix was halfway down her throat when she felt the spell take effect.

Over the rim of his mug, Nikolai pretended to watch the waitress make her rounds, circumspectly observing Medea out of the corner of his eye. The wolf's bane in her tea was a small enough dose to cause problems without being lethal. As Safe Harbor was a Magi town, Medea would have plenty of suspects besides him. Oddly enough, the townsfolk did seem antagonistic toward her, shooting dark glances at her back and speaking in hushed tones after she'd passed.

All week she'd been dragging him to her gardens. Medea was making him prepare all the samples, drying some, creating tinctures of others, and labeling them all with absolute precision. There were so many plants sitting on the laboratory counter right now that it would take him a month to get through them all. At least it had given him ample opportunity to quiz her on her previous apprentices. He carefully buried his true questions in a mountain of small talk. Aside from the botanist lead, which he'd already passed along to Harper, he hadn't gotten anything concrete besides Thomas.

Medea shoveled food into her mouth and took a swig of tea. An odd expression crossed her face. Without warning, she slapped the mug from Nikolai's hands, spraying tea all over his coat and pants.

"What the *fuck*, Medea?!"

But Medea wasn't listening. She stood, palms braced on the table, and proceeded to make loud retching sounds. Nearby patrons swiveled their heads to look at the commotion.

Nikolai stared in fascination. Had he overshot? He hadn't wanted to kill her just yet, but he'd take the win.

The waitress came by in alarm. "Ma'am, are you okay?" Then, to Nikolai, "Is she choking? Quick, somebody do something!"

Nobody moved, reluctant to aid a Magi with a reputation for murder. The waitress, seeing she had no takers, attempted to pat Medea on the back, but her hand smacked into an invisible shield. Medea glared about the restaurant as she heaved, searching for something, or more likely someone. A patron tried to leave but found the doors warded.

The retching continued, until at last Medea heaved like a cat with a hairball and spat a small round object onto her plate. A second later, the waitress was suspended in the air, arms trapped at her sides.

Medea's eyes blazed. "Who tampered with my food?"

"I . . . no one."

"Someone must have." She pointed at the spit-covered ball on the plate. "See that? Poison!"

"I don't know!" the waitress wailed.

"Medea, you're hurting her," Nikolai said with mock concern.

Medea snapped her fingers at him. "Is she telling the truth?"

Why the hell didn't Medea check for herself? Maybe her telepathy had limits. She couldn't maintain other spells and use telepathy. He pretended to check the waitress.

"She doesn't know anything."

Medea let the waitress go. The woman crumpled to the floor. Nikolai helped her up, putting his arms protectively around her and asking if she was okay. She buried her face in his shoulder as he caressed her back. The poisoning may not have worked, but he could still work on getting laid.

"Check the others," said Medea.

"Check them yourself," he snarled over the waitress' head.

Medea's jaw clenched. She really did want him to check them. But why? Did she need a potion or something to do telepathy?

"Fine," he said. "But they'll feel it."

"I don't care."

"I apologize, everyone," he loudly told the room. He quickly glanced in every head, just to sell it. They were pissed, confused, terrified of Medea. The older patrons had heard stories about her. "No assassins here. Whoever it was, they probably already left."

Medea nodded and strode to the door, pausing long enough to call him.

He tilted the waitress' chin up. "I have to go, love. Can I come back and see you later?" She nodded weakly. Definitely getting laid tonight. He kissed the top of her head, left money on the table, and joined Medea at the door.

Medea crossed the street, and fellow pedestrians parted before her. Word spread fast. On the other side, she plopped down on a bench. He slid next to her.

"Does that happen often?"

"Not as often as it used to." She looked older.

"How did you do that? With the poison?"

"It's a spell. Detects anything that has the potential to be fatal, within certain parameters, and encapsulates the offending particles so they can be expelled." She shook her head and gave a weak chuckle. "I learned to protect myself quite early from such attacks, though usually they came from apprentices. Still, whoever tried wasn't all that serious."

"What makes you say that?"

"The dose was too low to be lethal. Stupid, really. It doesn't take that much wolf's bane to be lethal. Unless they were only trying to weaken me. Besides, if they had wanted to kill me, they'd just say—"

"Medea! I challenge you to *Servitus aut Mors*!" A middle-aged man stood in front of them with a surprised look on his face.

"That. They'd say that." She stood. "So, you're my wayward assassin. Let's hear it. Which ancestor are you here to avenge? I probably don't remember them, but I understand it's cathartic to say." Her manner and phrasing indicated the encounter was not only expected but something that happened often enough for her to tire of it.

What had the barkeeper at the Hanged Man said? Relatives of the deceased were forever seeking revenge on Medea. Despite this, Nikolai had always considered her obsessive caution to be no more than paranoia. Maybe it was justified after all.

The would-be assassin looked unsure of himself. "I . . . my brother! You killed my brother!" He fished around in his pants. After a moment, he withdrew a wand. It clattered to the cobblestones, along with some change and several slips of paper. He fumbled to grab his possessions, looking up apprehensively at Medea. When he'd stowed the change safely in his pockets, the man pointed the wand at her.

This had to be the least-prepared assassin in history. Why the hell didn't he have his wand up before making a challenge? The idiot was a dead man.

Townsfolk gave the man a wide berth. They clustered in groups at a safe distance. One woman took her children inside with a "no, you can't watch!" Nikolai leaned forward on the bench, a nice front row seat to whatever carnage would follow.

"You understand the terms of the *Servitus aut Mors*?" said Medea. "The challenged picks the dueling ground. Whoever loses is killed or enslaved. I don't take slaves. If you fight me, you will die. Are you certain you want to fight me?"

The man looked as though this was the first time he'd heard any of this, and he was getting increasingly worried about the prospect of dueling the world's most powerful Magi. He glanced nervously at the gathered crowd, unsure if walking away would save him face.

Medea continued, "I will ignore this insult and refuse the challenge, but only if you give me your word to drop your grievances and never seek to harm me again. What say you?"

"I . . ." The man's body trembled, and he lowered his wand. "I swear to set this aside and never harm you."

Damnit! Nikolai was dying to see what Medea could do. Then, inexplicably, she handed him the reins.

"Is he telling the truth?"

Nikolai didn't hesitate. "No."

He half expected Medea to call him on the lie. Anyone watching could see the man had no fight left, but Medea simply sighed and said, "Very well. I accept your challenge."

The man's eyes widened. "What? No!" But he raised his wand again, and that was all Medea needed to confirm the man's intent. His head exploded in a blossom of red.

Nikolai shot out of his seat before the body had even fallen, drinking in the scene. Blood gushed from the remains of the neck. Flecks of brain and skull littered the cobblestones. Glorious. Why couldn't Medea teach him to do *that*? He grinned at Medea, but her face was solemn. What the hell was the matter with her?

"Come," she said. "It's time to go." The crowd of villagers scattered as she made her way toward the alley that held the gateway.

As soon as they entered the common room, Medea slumped into the chair next to the fireplace and fished around her hip pouch. Where was her brandy? Nikolai sat across from her, concern on his face. At last she pulled forth a bottle of amber liquid. She called two glasses from the kitchen and poured them each a measure. The brandy burned as it went down. Better than the dull ache she'd felt since killing the man.

Belatedly, she'd realized Nikolai might have lied about the man's intent, but she'd been so focused on her attacker she hadn't had time to think things through, and Nikolai had been so helpful earlier that day, and alarmed at her treatment of the waitress— sometimes it was enough to make her forget what kind of person he really was. His reaction to the man's death though . . .

She shook her head and drank. Maybe it was nothing. Nikolai was a dark mage, after all. Fascination with death was to be expected. It didn't mean he'd lied.

Then again, he lied a *lot*.

If Nikolai hadn't been there, would she have erred on the side of caution? Difficult to say. Enemies had to be eliminated. Leaving them alive only made them more desperate. She'd learned that the hard way.

She drained her glass, the burning sensation in her throat pulling her attention away from the memory of a blood-splattered corpse. She filled her glass again.

Killing assassins never used to bother her. But now, with

magic dying out and mages becoming scarcer than ever, she'd begun to reconsider her position. Was she part of the problem? What if magic was in decline *because* she'd killed off so many magical bloodlines? Every action had consequences. She tried not to interfere with mortals, not on a large scale, but what if her little actions over the centuries had compounded to make this mess? Should she isolate herself further? Kill herself? No, not that. She could make gateways inside a hundred bookstores, then just take what she needed and never talk or interact with anyone ever again—

"Medea? Are you alright?"

Nikolai's concerned voice jarred her. She hadn't realized he was still there. Why didn't he just go away? Couldn't he see she wanted to be left alone? Alone, alone . . .

"Medea?"

"What?"

"Are you okay?" He really did look concerned.

"Not really, no. I don't like killing our own, at least not anymore." She took another sip of brandy and coughed.

"The man had it coming. He challenged you, didn't he? And he wasn't even prepared!" Nikolai chuckled.

Should she tell him? Would it make a difference in whether or not he one day tried to kill her? Yes. She'd tell him. Knowledge was always better than ignorance. If he was going to challenge her one day, he should at least know what he stood to lose.

She looked at him pointedly. "He didn't have a choice. Years ago, I got sick of all the assassination attempts. I can deflect them, yes, but"—she waved a hand—"it was constant. And they were getting more and more underhanded—poison, as you saw, trying to stab me in the back, trying to shoot me in the head from fifty paces. I got tired of it."

She drained the glass and studied the smooth surface. Even this glass had once been tainted by an apprentice who lacked the spine to face her honorably. They all thought they were being so creative, as if they were the first to ever conceive of poisoning her. At least Nikolai hadn't proved that stupid, not yet.

"What do you mean, he had no choice?"

"I placed a spell on myself. Anyone who wants to kill me will be compelled to vocalize a *Servitus aut Mors* challenge."

His eyes widened, and she had to force back a laugh. Didn't count on that, did you, apprentice?

"Of course, they have to be serious and committed. Passing thoughts won't trigger it, only a true and immediate desire to end my life." She laughed. "Otherwise I'd never have any apprentices." The brandy was working. Already she could feel herself relaxing.

Nikolai was entirely too pensive. Probably trying to figure out a way to kill her without declaring his intent. Disappointing, though not unexpected. She awaited the inevitable follow-up question.

"But you can choose not to accept the challenge, right? Today, you offered that man a chance to walk away."

"Yes, but there is a cost. You have to understand, dueling —*real* dueling, not this sparring you do—is all about honor. If you have a grievance, you have a right to challenge someone. But if they decline, it means you challenged them without just cause, and it reflects poorly on your honor. Now I know what you're going to say—who cares about honor? That is the point of the *Servitus aut Mors*. It's a serious challenge, one that is magically binding. The winner can choose to kill or enslave the loser, but if the challenged refuses to fight at all, there is a penalty to the challenger."

"What kind of penalty?"

"A loss of power. The *Servitus aut Mors* is a form of soul magic, and it takes the penalty from there."

He leaned forward. "Meaning what, *precisely*?" Oh, Nikolai.

His interest betrayed that he was indeed considering the ramifications.

"Your magical power stems from your soul. It would drain much of that. Enough that you'd probably become Mundane. So you see, even if I had let the man walk away, he would never have been the same."

26

THE BOTANIST

Nikolai checked his reflection, then knocked on the door. Every window boasted a flower box filled with yellow and purple blooms, suffusing the air with their heady scent. Several well-tended garden beds sat adjacent to the cottage, while honeysuckle vines crawled lazily up the chimney. Like many Magi homes, it was off the beaten path and relatively hidden from view. Medea's closest gateway had dumped Nikolai in the woods not far from a small Mundane village.

Tracking down the occupant of the cottage had taken some time, but Harper's connections had eventually come through with a list of former German Enforcers. Nikolai checked their service records and ages against Medea's hazy recollections. Günter Bergmann served before the First World War and quickly rose through the ranks, owing to his unique spell repertoire and ferocity in combat.

The door opened to reveal a burly man with a thick white mustache and beard. "Ah! Hello! You must be Nikolai. Do come in."

"Thank you so much for taking the time to meet with me, Herr Bergmann."

"Not at all, not at all."

Nikolai followed Bergmann inside. Potted plants scattered about gave the small home a claustrophobic quality. Next to the kitchen sink, where one might normally find a drying rack, were a variety of orchids; one lay with its roots bare next to a bag of vermiculite, as though Nikolai had interrupted a repotting. A window box in the living room held an assortment of medicinal plants. It took a moment for Nikolai to even spot the other windows, as they were so crowded with plant leaves that nearly all the sunlight was blocked. The plants appeared to be thriving regardless, owing to several of Medea's light crystals that hung overhead.

Botanist indeed. Nikolai had prepared well for this meeting, spending several evenings in the library studying plants and, based on an offhand remark Bergmann had made in their letter exchange, making a small excursion to one of Medea's gardens to find a suitable gift.

"You have quite a collection here," he said, making a show of admiring the plants. "Is this fairy lace? I didn't realize it could be cultivated indoors."

The man swelled with pride. "Yes. I had to borrow a few of Medea's sun stones to do it, but my plants have managed well. Many of these were taken from her gardens. Has she shown you the gardens yet?"

Too goddamned many. "Yes. She has such a fascinating variety of plants!"

"Her collection is extraordinary. Oh, I do miss having access—"

"That reminds me . . ." Nikolai opened his pouch and carefully extracted an oblong mass of brown paper tied with string. "You mentioned looking for one of these."

He handed the parcel to Bergmann, who set it gently on the coffee table and began to unwrap it. Nikolai watched impassively as the man's excitement grew. Bergmann let out a small gasp when an orchid emerged.

"Oh, dear," said Nikolai with feigned concern. "Did I collect the wrong one?"

"It's . . . no, it's the right one. Do you have any idea how difficult these are to obtain? This is really too much."

"Not at all. Happy to help." Nikolai chuckled. "What's the point of having access to Medea's gateways if I don't make good use of them?" The man owed him now, even if he didn't realize it.

"Thank you. Please, sit. I'll make us tea." Bergmann walked away, the orchid cradled in his arms.

Nikolai made his way to a faded sofa draped with crocheted blanket. The coffee table was littered with horticultural publications. He pretended to read one of the periodicals until Bergmann returned with a tray, at which point he made a show of stacking the magazines carefully to one side of the table to make room. Bergmann settled into an armchair, and for a time they spoke of nothing but plants, Nikolai asking questions that would allow Bergmann to show off his breadth of knowledge. When the man's body language signaled he was thoroughly relaxed, Nikolai judged it time to press forward.

"You said you no longer have access to Medea's gardens. I thought her former apprentices were free to use the gateways."

"They are, but only if they graduate. I never made it to master rank. So, how is the old girl?"

"Well enough, I suppose. I don't really have much to compare to. Was she always irritable?"

Bergmann laughed. "Yes. It takes her a few years to warm up to people. Seems like she was just getting used to me when I decided to leave."

"Why did you leave? The gardens alone are worth staying for."

"Not for me they weren't." He frowned and absently rubbed

his arm. "The training was a bit much for my taste. Necessary, of course, but three years was enough for me to learn what I needed."

"I didn't think Enforcers liked Medea much."

"They don't, but she causes far fewer problems than the Magi who come sniffing after her for training. Attracts a lot of dark wizards, that one. Teaches any magic you please, but people don't go to her for the nice stuff. What's your specialty, if you don't mind my asking?"

Illusion was the most respectable answer, but also the least believable. No one in their right mind would go to Medea for illusion when the Academy had a perfectly acceptable program. Nikolai didn't know enough about healing or nature to fake expertise, and he certainly wasn't going to mention that necromancy was his true goal. In this case, the truth might be more fun. He smiled and laid the trap.

"Telepathy."

"Really?" The man's voice was too casual as he poured more tea. "Don't see many of those. How exactly do you intend to use your skill? It could be quite lucrative, if used on unsuspecting Mundanes." He nailed Nikolai with a stony gaze.

Time to put the man in his place. Nikolai put a quiet anger into his voice. "You know, it may have been a decade since my countrymen took your capital, but we still remember what was inflicted on us. My brothers will never be the same. *I* will never be the same." He glared at Bergmann, adding a quaver to his voice for authenticity. "I attended the Academy after the war. It wasn't unusual to see students crying in the hallways. Every night someone woke, screaming from the nightmares. Children of war, all of us. You want to know what I intend to do?"

Nikolai slammed his fist on the table, causing both the kettle and Bergmann to jump. "Heal minds! I don't believe in an almighty god, but if I did, I would thank him every day for giving

me a gift to ease the suffering of my brethren." There, that should
do it.

"I . . . of course—I . . . I'm so sorry."

Pain and guilt warred in the man's eyes—delightfully entertaining. The stupid fool owed him twice over now, once for the
gift and twice for the insult. Given Bergmann's connections and
gullibility, he might be Useful long-term.

"Yes, yes—skilled enough, telepathy could help a great deal
with that. I meant no offense, you understand. I am an Enforcer—
we see lawbreakers everywhere. Puts us in a certain frame of
mind. I do apologize."

Nikolai looked down and sighed. "Thank you. I'm sorry for
the outburst. I want to help others, but fear makes telepaths ostracized. Medea was the only one both willing and able to train me
in my gift."

"Of course, of course. It's a very noble endeavor. But what
can I do for you?"

"In truth, I came for advice. The training is—well, you know
what it's like. I was hoping you could offer me some tips. As I
understand it, apprentices don't often make it through the process.
You were the only one in recent years who survived. What's the
secret?"

"Recent years, ha! I wish." He leaned back, hands entwined
over his belly. "I can't say that there's any trick to it. Keep your
head down, follow directions, don't talk back. She's really not as
bad as they say. I got a lot of flak for training with her. The
Collective almost turned my application down, until they saw
what I could do. Her training is like nothing else, that's for sure.
But I see no reason to worry you won't make it through. Despite
the, uh, injuries, she's careful not to kill her students."

"I see. Do you have any idea how long training usually lasts?
She said I'm not to ask her."

"No, she hates that question. Makes you look impatient. I did ask after I left though. Ten years was the average, I believe. Of course, some people may take more or less time, depending on their talent."

"Ever heard of someone going longer, like seventeen years?"

"That seems excessive. Was the student a bit dim?"

"No, she said he was her best."

"Hmpf. Maybe he stayed for extended study. She'll release you at master level, but you can always try for grand master."

"I suppose." Nikolai took a sip of tea. Now was the moment. "I wanted to ask you, did you ever feel like your life was in danger while you were there?"

A booming laugh erupted from Bergmann. "You mean besides *all the time*?"

"I meant outside of lessons."

"Well, sure." He shrugged. "She's pretty intimidating. Always seems so angry . . ."

Was he being purposely obtuse? Candidness was risky. What if Bergmann told Medea his concerns? She *claimed* not to remember the man's name, indicating they weren't close, but maybe she was trying to hide the only man who could give him answers. Fuck it. He needed to know.

"Did you ever find yourself afflicted? Morose without cause? Unable to rise or do anything at all?"

"What? During training?"

"Yes. Since setting foot on the island."

Bergmann frowned. "No, can't say I ever experienced that. Have you spoken with her about it?"

"She's aware but refuses to tell me anything."

"Really? That's unlike her. Are you sure the problem is magical? If it were magical, you'd be hard-pressed to get her to stop talking about it."

"I've encountered that. This is different. I can tell she knows something, but she's been evasive." Nikolai leaned forward. "I think she might be causing it."

"Any chance it might be"—Bergmann tapped his head—"all up here? There's no shame to it. As you said, many people came out of the war with—well, they were never quite the same."

As if he didn't know the difference! The man clearly had no idea what he was talking about. Nikolai sat back. He kept his voice carefully controlled. "Positive. I never experienced it until I began training with her."

"Strange . . . strange. Has she told you anything? Anything at all?"

"No, but she becomes very angry whenever it happens. She acts as if it's all my fault."

Bergmann's frown deepened. "That doesn't sound like her at all. She's nothing if not fair. I can't see her blaming you for anything you had no control over." Clearly the man had experienced a very different relationship with Medea.

Then it hit him. Of course! It was no coincidence that Bergmann alone had survived the training. Who didn't want an Enforcer in their pocket? The Collective hated Medea. Why not work to gain a valuable ally on the inside? She would have done her best to maintain a respectable face. It was a sound investment, really, but unfortunately, it didn't help him any.

Nikolai turned the conversation back to safer topics.

Thomas—that's who he needed to talk to. But the man was dead, or should be. Medea had been circumspect on that point too. He had been her greatest apprentice, staying with her an unheard-of seventeen years.

Did Thomas linger, not to study but to find out how Medea maintained her youth? She said they'd had a falling out. Maybe he'd succeeded, causing her to craft a spell to rob future apprentices of their ambitions. There was only one way to find out.

27

SÉANCE

Nikolai sat at his desk and took out his most recent purchase, *Mediums for Mundanes*, cringing at the title. The séance spell was covered at the Academy, but as he had no interest in contacting the dead back then, he hadn't bothered to learn it. He did know it was a simple spell any Magi could cast.

So it was telling when he searched for the spell in Medea's master grimoire and it came back restricted, filed away under Soul Magic. Silly thing for her to hide. He simply took the gateway to Istanbul and bought a copy of the Academy's beginner guide to communing with the dead.

On the surface, the séance spell was relatively simple—all it required was a few candles and the right frame of mind—but it came with dire warnings. If the desired soul was unable to be reached, it was possible for other souls and spirits to answer the call and haunt the caster. Nikolai shrugged this off. What did he have to fear from the dead?

There was a list of caveats. Not all souls could return to speak. Okay, that wasn't great. The recently deceased were easier to contact. That wasn't good. If Thomas were dead, he likely passed a couple centuries ago.

The guidelines also stated that a connection was required, preferably an emotional bond. Barring a close family member or friend, a physical object could be used. Body parts worked best for this—hair, nail clippings, and the like. Medea's hasty incineration of the skeleton in the forest suddenly made a lot more sense. Whoever it had been, she'd ensured he'd never speak to them.

Personal possessions were less reliable. The best was an item they had an emotional attachment to. Barring that, it had to be something they used every day—probably working off skin cells or bodily fluids, as Medea's locket enchantment back in Haven had done. With each degree of removal from the person, the chance of success decreased. Nikolai set the book down and leaned back in his chair.

Therein lay the problem. He didn't know Thomas personally, and it was doubtful he'd find the man's hair lying around after two hundred years. It wasn't as if he could ask Medea to identify objects Thomas had used.

There had to be something around here that would work. Medea didn't seem to get rid of anything. The desk alone had probably been here for centuries.

That was it!

He walked to the back wall, pushing aside one of the tapestries he'd purchased to liven up the place. Hidden behind was the straw pallet included with his room. Medea said it hadn't been replaced in centuries.

He grabbed his drawstring pouch and shoved the mattress inside, then headed to the laboratory for candles. In the gateway room, he chose the gateway for the temple in the jungle. If ever he needed a magical boost, it was today.

Humidity smacked him as soon as he crossed the threshold. Not the most comfortable place for a séance, but it would do. He didn't intend to take all day. Finally, he was going to get answers!

Nikolai cleared a few branches that had blown over the stone platform and upended his pouch, depositing the straw mattress. At each corner he lit a candle, then he sat facing north with the séance book in his lap.

The chant had to be as specific as possible. Thankfully, Medea never hesitated to talk about Thomas. Given her adulatory ravings during their lessons, he suspected she had an intellectual hard-on for the guy. He withdrew a list from his breast pocket—god, he was turning into Medea—and reviewed his notes.

He took a deep breath and intoned, "I call thee, Thomas, former apprentice of the great mage Medea. Thomas, who once slept on this very bed. Thomas, witch from Massachusetts. Thomas, who turned his back on the Christian god that wronged him. I call thee. I bind thee. Answer my call." It would be enough.

Nothing happened. He repeated the chant. Again, nothing.

Was he missing something? It did say that some souls were incapable of being called back. Was Thomas one of them? He thought for certain a caster that powerful would hasten to the call.

He scanned the book. Séances worked better when there was emotional attachment involved. He'd make one, damnit. An angry soul was better than none at all.

He stood and shouted into the jungle. "I call thee, Thomas, former apprentice of that bitch-mage Medea. BEST apprentice according to her, even though she is CLEARLY showing FAVORITISM. You couldn't have been THAT good or you never would have DIED. Some apprentice you were, Thomas who had a falling out with Medea in"—he glanced down at his notes—"1686. What'd you do, try to fuck her and get shot down? You give up like the pussy you are? How could you be her best, when you turned away and RAN? Coward. Come here and answer my call, Thomas! I'll have words with you!"

Still nothing.

"I don't think he's coming."

Nikolai spun. "Who said that?"

"If you don't blow out those candles soon, something far nastier than me is going to come through. We get bored, you know. Nothing passes the time like messing with mortals."

Nikolai spun in a circle but saw nothing. "Who are you? Where are you?"

A small creature appeared, almost like a fox except its bushy tail was ringed. Black fur glistened with flecks of silver like stars in the night sky. The creature approached with catlike grace to stare up at him with amber eyes.

"Who are you? *What* are you?"

"A god of old, one whose people have long since died out."

Just some mangy spirit creature then. "I was expecting someone else."

"No doubt. However, you seemed to have grabbed the attention of another. I'd put out those candles if I were you."

"I'm not finished yet. I still haven't spoken with—"

The light dimmed. Birds rose squawking from the trees and the fox-thing vanished. Spirits, always so dramatic. He didn't recall much from Medea's lecture on spirits and the fae, but he did remember that. Their power came from impressing enough humans to part with their souls. It wouldn't work on him.

He paced around the mattress. Clearly, he needed more of Thomas to make this work—more information, more physical connections. Who knew how many apprentices had slept on the bed between Thomas and himself? No wonder it hadn't worked, with so many physical ties to others.

He picked up the candles one by one and began to blow them out.

Creeping Darkness was a spell he had a passing familiarity with. He'd come across it in one of his textbooks, and the name had piqued his interest, but he'd turned the book aside in disgust when he realized it was only an illusion spell.

Illusion spells didn't actually *do* anything; they simply

convinced people that something significant was happening—parlor tricks for lesser wizards. When the jungle disappeared from sight, and the pyramid too, he recognized the illusion for what it was.

Did the spirit really think it could scare him? He held up the last candle. The flame only managed to illuminate a tiny area near his hand. Darkness pushed steadily against it. Soon, even it would be obscured.

"Ah, yes, terrifying." He nudged his foot around until it found the straw mattress. He bent to pick it up and shoved it back into his pouch.

There went the candle. He left it. No point in getting turned around in the dark looking for something replaceable.

He conjured a small light in his hand, but it didn't extend far enough to get his bearings. Great. He'd have to fumble around until he chanced upon the gateway. A wrong step would send him falling over the side of the pyramid. He edged forward a step at a time in what he thought was the right direction.

The light in his hand winked out. A chill shot up his leg and dashed toward his heart, ice pumping through his veins.

Something clutched his ankle. He couldn't see his own hands, let alone his leg. He reached toward the thing that grasped him.

Whatever it was, some of it was soft and yielding. The moist substance parted before his fingers, until they struck something solid. Bone? A hand?

He straightened up and kicked at it. An inhuman shriek erupted from the ground at his feet, then something scrabbled up his chest, clawing as it went.

Warm, hot breath hit his face. The stench of it was like rotting flesh. He pushed and something bit into his hand.

Whatever it was, it must not reach his face. Teeth clacked near his cheek. He feigned yielding, then ducked below it and pushed out with his magic in every direction.

A scream flew back and landed with a sickening wet slap not far away. He conjured a full-body shield and a small light, making it as bright as he could. The light took more mana than it should to fight back the darkness, but he needed to see what he faced.

Something slammed into his shield, scratching and howling. Nikolai fell and rolled dangerously close to the edge of the pyramid. He reached out to halt his progress, grabbing at vines and rock.

The thing pushing him was rotting flesh on a skeletal frame. Not quite a wraith; not quite a ghoul. Something in between. Solid, yet semi-ethereal. It wore the tattered remains of wizard training garb. A medallion hung from its neck—some sort of Celtic symbol—which meant it wasn't Thomas. Still, any of Medea's previous apprentices would do.

"Hey! Heeeeeey!" He waved his hand in front of the creature's face, trying to gain its attention. "I'd like to ask you a few questions about Medea's training." The creature roared and bit at his shield.

"It doesn't have enough of a mind left to answer you." There was the fox-spirit again. It waltzed out of the darkness, illuminated by its own light, and sat on its haunches nearby. "Souls aren't meant to come back. Most can't hold themselves together after death. This"—it indicated the creature—"is just a walking mass of bitterness and loathing. You pissed it off. That's the only reason it's here."

Nikolai studied the dead-eyed creature in front of him. "Any tips on how to get rid of it?"

The fox-spirit grinned, tongue lolling. "A smart wizard would have learned a banishing spell *before* trying to summon the dead."

Useless spirit. He ignored it and focused on his shield. In a blink, it shrank from bubble to disk. He tilted it up, sending the creature sliding over the edge of the pyramid. The darkness went with it. He stood and brushed himself off. "Fat lot of help you are, spirit."

Its grin widened.

A scream emanated from below. The creature was back, flying through the air, howling like a banshee.

"Fuck it." He retrieved his wand from his belt pouch. Medea wasn't here to complain. *"Flamma! Apscido!"* A fireball shot from his wand and hit the creature square in the chest. All four of its limbs were severed from its body, which fell to the ground.

Nikolai twirled his wand with a smirk and holstered it. God he loved being a Magi. It was good to feel competent at something besides telepathy again. Medea made him feel like a child groping after concepts far beyond his comprehension. Pretentious—that's what she was. Why neglect wands and incantations when they were direct and effective?

"It's coming back, you know," chirped the fox-spirit.

Sure enough, the flames had extinguished. Limbs rose and reattached to the body. Not only that, the damn thing was now casting at him.

He flung himself sideways as a black bolt landed inches from his feet, corroding the stone. He reconjured his shield and returned in kind. *"Fulmen! Lancea!"* Lightning forked from his wand, singeing the creature's robes, as the lance spell scored its chest. It took no notice of either.

"Sanguino!"

"Bleed?" The fox-spirit cackled. "You really expect to kill something made of pure magic and will with *Bleed*?"

"Then how do I kill it?" he yelled, sending a few more spells winging toward the creature. None seemed to have any lasting effect.

"You don't," the fox-spirit replied cheerily.

The undead creature maneuvered itself in front of the gateway and fired several green bolts. One hit his shield, cracking it. He repaired the damage and considered his options.

His training pouch with all his potions was at home—it's not like he'd anticipated a battle—and he hadn't thought to throw any in the wide-mouthed bag. At this rate, he would rapidly deplete his mana and then he would be defenseless.

"I can give you a hint," said the fox-spirit, "if you do something for me."

"I'm not giving you my soul!"

A spiraling green light slammed into his shield and began to drill through it. He dispelled the shield and ran, flinging broken branches at the creature as it flew after him. Maybe if he ran all the way around the top of the pyramid, he could make it back to the gateway before the creature caught up with him.

He turned a corner and slammed into a wall, staggering back and rubbing his nose. The stone had crumbled and fallen long ago, blocking his path forward. Time to levitate.

The creature bore down on him just as he cleared the stone. It grasped his boot and once again the icy chill of death spread through him. He kicked the creature in the face and tugged himself free.

There were loose stones here—chunks of the old temple that had weathered down over the years. He used telekinesis to fling them at the creature, knocking it backward, and ran on.

The fox-spirit ran beside him, leaping deftly from stone to stone. "Not your soul. Take me with you when you leave."

"And why would I do that?"

"Because it's dull here, and you seem to lead an interesting life." It grinned at him.

A spell flew past his left shoulder, exploding rock and spraying his face with debris. It cost nothing to bring the spirit to Medea's island, though it might betray what he'd been doing here.

Were spirits bound by their word? He vaguely remembered something like that.

"Give me your oath you won't betray me to my master, or tell her anything of what went on here, then give me your advice. If it helps me defeat the creature, I'll take you with me."

"I, Yoxtl, do swear not to betray you to your master, nor speak aught of what happened here."

Nikolai willed a huge swath of rocks and stone to fly at the creature. Still, it kept coming.

"What's your advice?" He conjured his shield anew, keeping careful watch for the drilling spell that had threatened it before.

"First of all, stop doing *that*. You're using all your mana moving this stuff around. Just hold still and keep your shield up."

"How am I supposed to kill it if I just stand here?"

"It's *dead*. You can't kill it. Banish it, sure, but you would've done that if you knew how. Souls get more powerful the longer they're alive, especially if they belong to a mage, but they can't regenerate mana after they die. Every spell it casts whittles away what it has left. Even maintaining a corporeal form costs it. All you have to do is wait it out."

"So when it runs out of mana it will just disappear?"

"Yup."

Nikolai stopped running. He stood, chest heaving, as the undead mage sent spell after spell at his shield. How long could this thing keep going? Was the spirit trying to trick him into giving up? "I'm getting low on mana. I don't think I can outlast it."

"Then get it to cast some *really* big stuff so it drains itself faster. Try making it mad."

That *definitely* sounded like a trick, but it beat standing around doing nothing. If he couldn't cast spells, words would do.

The undead mage wore a Celtic medallion, making him Irish

or Scottish. All he had to do was insinuate the guy was British.
He took a deep breath and hollered at the creature.

"Hey! Yah Tommy! Yah Tan! You—"

A force flung Nikolai high. He crashed into a boulder, head
rattling against the inside of his shield before it winked out. Fuck.
He hadn't even gotten going yet. Magi usually had far less
national pride. That was a Mundane-level response.

He stood, wobbling, and conjured his shield again, now thin
and brittle. He couldn't take another hit like that.

"So? Why'd she kill you anyway? Got tired of yet another
necromancer? Did she curse you too? Drain your body to keep
herself young? Just think back to all those times she beat you in a
duel. How long did you last, when you challenged her? Five
minutes?"

The creature screamed, unnaturally high pitched, and wind
buffeted Nikolai. The scream and rushing wind merged into a
crescendo to form a whirling vortex in front of the deceased
mage. Dust and rocks rose into the air, tearing away the last
vestiges of his shield.

He didn't wait for the tornado to pick up steam. Magic
crackled in the air around him as he tore down the side of the
pyramid.

Still the creature screamed, but the sound stabilized—it hadn't
followed him. He couldn't say the same for the rushing wind.
Already the trees swayed with the force of it.

He dove into the jungle, heedless of where he headed. The
muddy ground sucked greedily at his boots. It gave way suddenly
and he sank to his knees in dark brown sludge. He hauled himself
out, pushed along by biting wind.

Plants blocked him at every turn, but he lacked the mana to
cut through them. Branches snapped behind him. One struck the
back of his head, momentarily stunning him as debris whirled
past his shoulders. Unable to escape the rushing wind, he curled

up behind a great tree and covered his head. An eternity later, the gale stopped.

Nikolai stood. Twigs and leaves plastered his coat. He tried to take it off and pain shot through his arm. A stick, thick as a broom handle, jutted from his bicep. He yanked it out with a roar.

Damned spirit. Just wait it out, it said. Taunt it some more, it said. Some help it turned out to be.

He followed the path of destruction, which increased the closer he got to the pyramid. Stripped leaves and small branches turned to limbs as thick as his thighs. By the time he reached the stone steps, many of the trees had been upended or snapped in half.

He conjured a weak shield and crept toward the gateway, unsure if the mage was still around. The top of the pyramid appeared to be empty. He ducked into the arch for the gateway and found the fox-spirit lounging on the floor.

"There you are!" it said brightly. "I half thought you dead."

"I almost was, no thanks to you."

"What do you mean, 'no thanks to me'? My advice worked, didn't it?"

"I didn't have the mana to withstand an attack like that and you knew it!"

"Pfft. You seemed to do fine." It grinned.

"Fine. After you." He gestured to the gateway. After seeing what Medea's wards did to a mortal, he was curious to see their effects on a spirit.

"You think I'm stupid enough to fall for that? It's warded to hell and back. You'll have to carry me through."

He made to move around the spirit, but it scrambled in front of him.

"We had a deal," it said.

"I don't like your idea of help."

"And I don't like mortals who renege on their word. Leave me here and you'll be twice cursed."

The phrasing caught him off guard. He peered curiously at the spirit. "What do you mean, twice cursed?"

"I mean you're already cursed, and I would add another. One plus one is two. I know mortals are dim, but I thought they knew basic arithmetic."

So he was right. It *was* a curse. Damn Medea! "You can see it?"

The smile that broke out on the spirit's face was far too eager. "And *you* can't. Pity that. It's quite impressive. You must have pissed off someone *really* powerful."

He crouched next to the spirit. "Can you see what it does? Tell me how to remove it?"

"Why should I help you?" it said haughtily. "You didn't seem to like my advice last time."

"Please." He cast around for something he could offer the spirit. What did spirits want apart from souls? He wouldn't give it that. "What do you want?"

"For now, I want you to remain true to our bargain. We can discuss your curse later."

Not a bad idea. It was best to enter negotiations knowing more than your opponent. Medea's library was bound to have information on spirits, and it didn't appear to be a topic she was opposed to discussing.

He lifted the spirit into his arms. It was light and amazingly soft. On closer inspection, its body put him more in mind of a cat than a canid. Warmth radiated from it like an ethereal purr. A trick, no doubt, to get mortals to care about it. He was immune to that nonsense.

The spirit looked up at him and smirked as they passed through the gateway to Medea's beach.

SPIRITS

"WHERE IS THE INTRUDER?!" Medea barreled down the path to the beach.

The spirit gazed at her with the longing of a starved man suddenly presented with a buffet. "Oh, look at that soul!" it muttered.

Medea lurched to a halt in front of them. She looked from the spirit to Nikolai and back. When they said nothing, she demanded, *"Well?"*

"Nice to see you too," Nikolai said acidly. "I heard you like spirits, so I brought you one." He dumped the fox-spirit unceremoniously at her feet.

She looked down at it with distaste, then back at him, finally taking in his roughened appearance. "What happened to you?"

"Nothing I want to talk about."

"You, trickster!" She snapped a finger at the spirit. "I don't tolerate shenanigans on my island. Spirits who stay must abide by my rules."

"Certainly!" It beamed at her.

"What's your name?"

"Yoxtl."

The spirit squawked and went rigid. Medea intoned, "I bind thee, Yoxtl, to obey my rules regarding my island. You will not interfere with the training of my apprentice, Nikolai."

Yoxtl relaxed and stood panting. "Did you just *geas* me?!" It looked aghast.

"Yes."

"You shouldn't be able to *do* that!" it said with horrified wonder.

"I hear that a lot."

"What's a geas?" asked Nikolai.

Medea opened her mouth to give what would no doubt have been a tedious lecture, but Yoxtl interrupted, bouncing up and down like an annoying puppy.

"It binds the soul!" it yipped. "You have to do what the geas says, or it tears the very fabric of your soul apart!" The spirit stopped and looked up at Medea. "I don't have a soul. How'd you do it to *me*?"

"Would you like me to demonstrate again?" she said coolly. "I can always add more conditions to your stay."

"No, no. I . . . wow. I can see why you don't want to make her angry." It looked at Nikolai, and Medea shot him a glare.

Great, just great. If the spirit caused any trouble, he was sure to be blamed. "I'm off to bed," Nikolai announced.

"No, first you need to deposit that thing in the forest. Then you may do as you like. And next time, ask me before you bring home any strays." Medea marched up the path to the hovel.

Yoxtl stared after her longingly.

Nikolai nudged the wistful spirit with his foot. "What's with you?"

"Her soul. It's *incredible*."

"Didn't you say souls got more powerful with age? Medea is —I don't know how old exactly. A thousand?"

"It doesn't explain *that*. The magic—it's . . . she's . . . there's more raw power there than most spirits have these days! I wish you could see it. It's beautiful."

Now that the spirit mentioned it, he probably had. Did Magic Sight show souls? It would explain why Medea was blindingly bright when he had the spell active.

"Come on. Forest is this way."

He walked up the path. A thin strip of pink bordered the horizon as night approached. Wind flapped the edges of his coat, but Yoxtl's fur remained eerily still as it hurried to catch up. In the dim light of dusk, it took on a silvery sheen.

"Why are you so obsessed with her soul anyway?" asked Nikolai. "She's not going to give it to you."

"Ha! You're male. Do you not appreciate certain female forms regardless of their interest in you? We covet what we desire. Souls are magic, power. There's not enough to go around these days. I lost my source of souls when my people died out. Whatever magic I have left, that's it. Oh, I won't disintegrate if I use magic—not like that thing in the jungle—but my power has dwindled to the point where I can't do much."

"What could you do before?"

"Lots of stuff. I could endow my priests with the power to perform miracles. I could protect them, in a roundabout way. I could create illusions to dazzle the eye and instill loyalty in my followers."

Yoxtl grew pensive. "My reach was never that great, but for a time, I had a dedicated group of humans who worshiped me. They praised me for bringing the sunrise, for blessing them with good harvest, and keeping disease at bay."

"In other words, you took credit for natural phenomena. Not a bad racket. What happened?"

"My people were wiped out by a mightier empire—killed, enslaved, or sacrificed to other gods."

They approached Medea's collection of rubble. Yoxtl fell silent as they passed the crumbling pillars and statues of dead gods littering the side of the path. What did it look like to the spirit? A graveyard? Is that why Medea had transported them here? Did her resident spirits insist on bringing some piece of home with them?

Yoxtl didn't speak until the remnants of old civilizations were behind them. "My name faded and was finally forgotten, as the few who remained converted to the religion of their masters."

"Christians?"

Yoxtl snorted. "They're the obvious culprits, aren't they? No, not the followers of YHWH. Christians came later, to kill those who killed my people. I was happy of that, at the time. It seemed like justice."

As they passed the rock garden, Yoxtl leapt up and trotted along the edge. It gave the garden a curious glance but said nothing.

"So who did kill your people?" asked Nikolai as they veered toward the forest. The path had sharpened since his arrival, owing to its now daily use. Blackened patches of harp grass dotted the meadow on either side where he'd scorched them during lessons.

"The Tenochca, a polytheistic people."

"Polytheistic? Why didn't you join them?"

Yoxtl smiled bitterly. "I was never popular with neighboring spirits. 'Too small.' They refused to let me in on their religion. I had to go it alone, but monotheism didn't have the same reach. Everyone knew pooling resources was the way to go." Its ears twitched. "Then YHWH came on the scene. He's a juggernaut, that one. Rules three major religions, all by himself! Can you believe that?"

"Three? How do you figure?" There had to be scores of Christian denominations.

"Judaism, Christianity, Islam—the Abrahamic religions. All his. Polytheistic spirits used to laugh at guys like that, like me. Now his followers are everywhere, and other spirits grow small."

Nikolai halted on the path as swaying trees loomed before them. "You may find some of them here. Medea has several, but I've never met them. She's forbidden them to speak with me."

"Don't I feel special. Until we meet again, mortal." Yoxtl grinned and bounded into the forest.

Nikolai pulled his coat tighter against the breeze and walked to the hovel. A bargain would have to be made if he wanted to learn what Yoxtl knew of the curse. Time to see what information the library held on spirits.

Medea rolled out of bed and stretched. Last night she dreamt she'd forgotten something, which was probably her brain's way of telling her she had. There was something she needed to do—but what? What day was it?

The spell that reminded her to eat pulsed annoyingly against her senses. A few centuries ago she figured out how to summon nutrients directly into her body from the surrounding environment, eliminating the need to eat. Unfortunately, going too long without solid food meant her digestive tract shut down, causing a host of smaller problems. Better to eat once a day and keep things in proper working order.

Medea conjured fruit and cheese at her desk. Concertino scurried over and she absently passed the lizard half a grape. She ate mechanically as she flipped through her journal, trying to find the date. No good. All the recent dates had question marks scribbled after them.

She moved to a stack of papers piled high on a nearby table

and dug through. Notes. List of spells. More notes. Map. Ah, there they were! She tugged out several calendars marked with magical astrological events. Damn. They were at least fifty years out of date.

She looked at Tino. "I don't suppose *you* remember the date, do you?"

The lizard licked its eye and said nothing.

"You're no help." A shame Tino only repeated back sounds. "Hey, have I ever exclaimed over forgetting something, on a day like today?"

In her own voice, the lizard said, "I left the brew in the lab!"

"That's not it. Try another. Something more obscure."

"Shit, did I feed the apprentice?"

Medea shook her head. "I fixed that one. They feed themselves now."

"I missed the eclipse!"

She frowned. "No, but I think you're on the right track."

Tino recited a string of Latin curses, followed by, "I forgot Xiao's comet again!"

Medea gasped. "Xiao's comet!" She let out a litany of curses, not unlike those she'd just heard, and began frantically calculating the comet's next appearance based on when it last showed up on her calendar. When she had a date, she bolted for the door, nearly slipping down the stairs as she made her way to the gateway room. After popping into the Hanged Man to confirm the date, she went to the laboratory and got to work.

———

A thud startled Nikolai awake. He glanced down to find the book that had been in his lap was now on the floor. He sat up and rubbed the sleep from his eyes. All night he'd searched the library for information on spirits. For once, the grimoire had been helpful in locating books. Unfortunately, the information was scattered over hundreds of books in dozens of sections, and none of it made any sense. All he'd found were descriptions of religions and local legends, nothing on what spirits were or what they could do.

A book floated by. He peeked out of his alcove to find Medea making her way down the center aisle. A second book levitated in front of her.

"No lessons today," she said in passing.

Might as well ask the walking encyclopedia herself. "Do you have a minute?"

She gave him a look that said she very much did *not* have a minute but halted anyway. "What is it?"

"I wanted to know more about spirits."

"I told you all about them back at the Hanged Man, or weren't you paying attention?"

"I was," he lied. "I just didn't have any context until now. I was trying to look up information, but none of the books have anything concrete. Do you have any recommendations?"

"You won't find anything. Everything I know is extrapolated from centuries of research. Unfortunately, I haven't had a chance to write it all down yet. Now, if you'll excuse me." She walked away.

"Give me the short version," he said when he'd caught up. "What are they? What powers do they have? What do they want?" Considering how distracted she was, he might get the short version today.

Medea sighed. "They're sentient magic. I don't know how, they just are. As for powers, illusion magic is common. They can teleport to known areas, or unknown areas if they have something familiar to latch on to. Their communication is odd—they don't make sound waves, nor do they seem to use telepathy. They just speak and your brain understands, interpreting it like you would sound, and vice versa."

He thought back to his conversations with Yoxtl. What language had it been speaking? He couldn't recall. "That's amazing. It was so seamless I didn't even stop to think that I was talking to a spirit who's spent its whole life—or whatever—in Mexico." He turned to her with a grin. "Maybe you should ask your spirits how to make a better translation disk."

"Don't think I haven't tried. Spirits have more to gain from humans not having access to universal communication. At some point they figured out mortals had souls, and ever since they've been convincing humans to part with them. They're the face behind every deity."

"But they can give magic to mortals, can't they? Isn't that how witches cast spells, with the help of a patron?"

"Yes, but in return, the spirit gets their soul upon death." She halted at the library door. "Look, I'm busy, so I will be blunt. If that thing promised you immortality, it's a lie. They want souls, and they can't collect a soul unless you die."

"But they can bargain for other things, yes?"

"Any bargain you make will not be in your own best interest. Your soul is . . . precious. That's why I've forbidden the others to talk to you." She took a step forward, her expression and tone full of warning, "Spirits without a following are particularly desperate. It's your life, but I would advise against trusting the spirit. Perhaps it would be best if I kicked it off the island."

Shit. This was exactly what he didn't want. How could he get her to keep Yoxtl around?

"The spirit knew the people who lived in that pyramid. Think of how much it must have learned! Their culture, their spells—all the knowledge that was wiped out before you got there—you have a chance to resurrect it."

She rubbed her chin; her eyes took on a faraway look. "You're right. But spirits are notoriously tight lipped. I'm not sure it will—"

"Leave it to me. I'll tell Yoxtl it's a condition of staying here."

"Alright."

Medea grabbed her books and headed to the lab. He followed, curious to see what would make her distracted enough to put off lessons.

Every inch of available counter space was being used. The plant samples he had yet to catalog were shoved as far to one side as possible, and new ingredients sat haphazardly in their place. Five cauldrons bubbled cheerfully on the rear counter. Medea added her books to the center table, next to several rolled wooden mats. She chose a mat and unrolled it to reveal vertical script painted on the wooden slats. Chinese? Japanese? He didn't know enough to say.

"What're you making?" he asked.

"A little of this, a little of that. Xiao's comet comes into range in about fifteen hours. While the comet may be visible for a week or so, there are potions that can only be created properly when it first arrives."

"How on earth does a comet affect potions?"

"I really have no idea, but I've tried to make the potions at other times and they don't have the potency. It's the same for plant collection. Some ingredients work best if gathered in the light of the full moon, or during an eclipse, or at a certain time of night. I've found these things out through trial and error, and meticulous record-keeping. Here"—she gestured to the books— "see if anything interests you."

Fat chance of that, given he couldn't read them, but he stood and walked the counter, scanning for illustrations. Nothing jumped out, except . . . He pulled a small red-backed book closer. A man stood proud as enemies closed in from all sides. Broken weapons lay at his feet.

"What's this?" He passed the book to Medea. She didn't take it, nor did she look up from the text she studied.

"Learn Chinese or go get a translation disk. I don't have time to read every entry to you."

"Just tell me what it does. I don't want to go to the library and back if it's not worth making."

Medea made a frustrated noise but glanced down. "Invulnerability Potion. Makes the imbiber immune to most damage for approximately an hour."

"Most? Approximately?"

"Translations can be difficult without cultural context. Invulnerability potions are usually specific. They may protect against physical blows, but not poison or magic. The text doesn't say, but this compendium is for magic applicable to soldiers, so my guess is it protects against external physical damage."

"I see. And how long would it last?"

"There were no watches or mechanical clocks when this was written. They might have been using candles or oil lamps to gauge time passing, but the increments would have been different than today. I estimate anywhere between twenty minutes to two hours. It may also depend on how the potion works. This note here says the potion is for mages only."

"I'm a mage, so it should work just fine for me."

"Yes, but if it requires a mage, then it must use something only a mage would have."

"Mana."

"That is my suspicion. Like a shield, it will use mana to maintain the effect and disappear when your mana runs out. The more damage it absorbs, the faster it will fade." She gave him a sidelong glance. "Have you been doing your water-boiling exercises? If not, you will have little time indeed."

He half listened. Invulnerability! Caveats aside, it was worth brewing. He ran to retrieve a translation disk from the library. The text maintained the vertical alignment under the disk, making it hard to read, but he eventually found the list of ingredients. Several minutes later, he had almost everything he needed placed neatly on the counter. There was only one thing missing—a fresh human finger.

29

PATIENCE OR SACRIFICE

T he dungeon door opened. Without looking up from her potion brew, Medea asked the obvious question.

"What do you think you're doing?"

Nikolai paused. "I need a fresh finger."

Not long after the dungeon debacle, she'd taken him back down to briefly explain the rules. Test subjects were for spell experimentation and ingredient harvesting only. And while he was welcome to use them, they had to be returned to their original state afterward. Considering how little interest he'd shown in healing magic, she doubted he'd taken the time to learn what was required.

"Can you replace the finger once it has been removed?"

"No."

"Then you have your answer." She added a sprig of rosemary to the cauldron.

"*You* could regrow the finger."

The opportunity to teach him a lesson was too valuable to pass up. He'd be angry, but perhaps he'd finally see the value in spells outside his area of interest. "I could, but you are here to learn. You learn nothing if I bypass your struggles." She paused, then added, "There is an easy solution. Use your own finger."

She could almost feel the temperature in the room drop.

"My own finger? You expect me to cut off my *own* finger?"

How could someone so anxious to hurt others be so squeamish? "I *expect* you to do what is necessary. How badly do you want this potion?"

Nikolai returned to the counter with what was clearly feigned nonchalance. "I'll just wait until the comet comes around again."

"You will be waiting for quite some time. It's on a nineteen-year cycle."

"Nineteen years! I'll be old by then!"

So melodramatic. "Please. You'll be what, forty? Hardly old."

"To *you* maybe. That's half my life!" His face twisted with barely concealed rage.

She almost hated to do this to him, but it was the only way he'd ever learn. The ability to heal oneself was an integral part of combat. One way or another, she'd make him see sense.

"Look," she said, "you have two choices. Either you wait for a more convenient time—"

"That's not convenient!"

"OR you use your own finger."

"This isn't fair. You didn't give me any time to prepare!"

"You think *I* had time to prepare? It's a miracle I even remembered this cycle. You've known about this potion for what, fifteen minutes? It meant nothing to you yesterday."

"I know about it now. Please, just let me take a finger from downstairs. It's not like they need all ten."

God, he was whiny when he begged. "It is far more important that you learn appropriate lessons than have that potion." What the hell did he plan to do with it anyway? With his tiny mana pool, the effect would probably last two minutes. "Patience or Sacrifice—both are things you must learn. The choice is yours."

"You're supposed to be teaching me magic, not giving me character-building lessons!"

She straightened and put a finality in her tone. "I told you exactly how I teach. My goal is to make you stronger. Just because you don't see the value of a lesson doesn't make it worthless. You have a choice to make. I will hear nothing more on the matter."

He glared at her, then stormed from the lab, slamming the door behind him.

How could she be so unreasonable? If Medea had let him know about the comet in advance, he could've sorted through the books and selected a number of potions. This was all her fault. *She* should be the one to lose a finger!

How could she think he'd remove his own? Pain wasn't the issue—it was *his* body, his most precious possession. Even if the finger could be regrown later . . . Nikolai shook his head. It felt like sacrilege.

He'd just have to get another test subject on his own. Plenty of Medea's gateways went to large cities. A Mundane transient or tourist wouldn't be missed. Hell, he didn't even have to bring them back. He could just take a finger.

He smacked into the gateway room door when the knob didn't turn as expected.

No. She hadn't, had she? He cast Magic Sight, and a bright green ward appeared. The lattice pattern spread over the hinges, the seams, even the wood itself.

He stormed back to the lab, taking a moment to compose himself before entering. Medea crumbled leaves into a cauldron, which emitted a puff of acrid smoke, causing her to cough. As usual, she refused to acknowledge his presence by looking up. He tried to keep the anger from his voice, but his words came out clipped. "Why is the gateway room sealed?"

"You know why. Patience or Sacrifice. Make your choice."

He wanted to scream. Couldn't she see how serious this was? Easy for her to scoff at waiting another two decades. Magic roiled in his hands, begging to be unleashed. He'd make her bleed, set fire to her pretty blonde head and watch her die screaming, crack her open like an egg and—

"You are wasting time. Figure out a solution to your problem."

Nikolai stalked away. He couldn't trust himself not to do anything rash, not right now. Plenty of time to kill Medea when victory was assured. If he had the invulnerability potion, he could do it. Why else would she try so hard to keep him from making it? He wouldn't let her stop him. Focus on the problem. Focus on the problem.

What could he do, besides sacrifice a piece of himself? He could always take a finger from one of the prisoners without replacing it. No. Medea would punish him for that, just as she'd blinded him for reading the letter. How though? Would the punishment be worth the risk? Medea wouldn't kill him over something so minor, he was sure of it. She'd want him to learn a lesson—which meant she'd repay him in kind by taking his own finger and cursing it against regrowth.

No—she'd want the punishment to be greater than the choice he refused to make. She'd take a hand, maybe even an arm, making him wish she'd *only* taken a finger. He could imagine her berating him. "Should have given up the finger when you had the chance, now you get to lose your whole hand . . ."

The only way to avoid taking his own finger was to take one from a prisoner, and the only way to do *that* was to regrow the digit after removal. How fast could he learn such a complicated healing spell? He had roughly eleven hours, factoring in some wiggle room. Could he do it that fast?

In his bedroom, he yanked open the desk drawer and pulled out his wand. Fuck the "no wand" rule—he had a time limit. On to the library. The damned master grimoire had better give him something good. He picked up the pen and scribbled "limb regeneration." He rolled his eyes as the page filled with references. Of course *healing* spells showed up, but if he wanted to look up curses, *noooo*.

For the first hour, he practiced wand movements and incantations, not just for Regrowth, but Sleep and Paralysis as well. He didn't need a repeat of the Irishman who'd nearly escaped. He pored over anatomical diagrams for another hour before returning to the lab. Medea was blessedly absent, and he resisted the urge to contaminate her potions. Always better to delay revenge until you were back on good terms with the target.

Regrowth spells were tricky. You had to know the human body inside and out. Images in textbooks weren't enough—he needed practical knowledge. He searched the ingredient shelves until he found a jar of human fingers stored in formalin. A shame the potion required fresh. He pulled out a dissection tray and spent three hours acquainting himself with the internal structure.

He had saved the bulk of his time for practice. He grabbed a cleaver and assorted knives from the dungeon and left the hovel. The finger needed to be replaced perfectly on the first try. He considered using animals in the forest as test subjects but rejected the idea after studying the anatomy books. As similar as animal anatomy could be, regrowing a human finger on a rabbit foot wasn't the same, and he didn't want to inadvertently learn it wrong. He needed a human body.

Thankfully, there were plenty in the graveyard. Did healing spells work on decayed tissue? He hoped so. He started with the mausoleum. The first casket contained a desiccated body. Probably not the best sample. The second split upon opening, unleashing a torrent of putrid sludge. He narrowly avoided the splatter, but the inside of the mausoleum was so fouled he had to vacate and shut the door.

Exhuming coffins from the ground was much harder. It took all of his concentration to move the dirt, and he had to take a mana potion to prevent fatigue from setting in. Thankfully, Medea's graves were relatively shallow, as if she'd intended them to be accessible. He found enchantments on the coffins, and when he cracked them open, the bodies inside were remarkably well-preserved.

Nikolai picked a corpse and dragged it to a flat rock, placing its hand on top. Using the cleaver, he hacked off fingers in varying places, examining each cut to see which would be the easiest to repair, then set to work regrowing tissue. Bone healed quite nicely, but the nerves, tendons, and blood vessels were harder. His first few attempts looked fine on the outside but were stiff and unresponsive when flexed. Several corpses and many fingers later, his success rate improved significantly. It was a shame he couldn't use any of the regrown digits, but the potion specified fresh, and with only one shot he didn't want to risk using a bad sample.

He practiced for as long as he could, then headed to the dungeon. Several prisoners shrank back as he strode purposefully toward them. He paced the cell block, looking for the prisoner with the smallest hands, then shot Sleep through the bars. With a wave of his wand, the cell opened, and the body floated toward the restraining table.

God, he'd missed his wand. While Medea's focus exercise had given him marginally better control over telekinesis, it was nothing compared to what he could do with his wand. Her insistence he go without it was just another ploy to keep him weak. The same went for her stupid "lesson" about patience. It was obvious she didn't want him to have an invulnerability potion. With it, he might be a real threat.

He cast Paralysis on the sleeping man to ensure there would be no flinching. With the cleaver, he neatly severed the finger and placed it in a waiting basin, then set to work regrowing bone and tendons. When he got to the blood vessels, he realized an artery was missing. Blood poured from the wound, obscuring the tissue.

Nikolai closed his eyes and felt around with his magic. There. The artery had snaked back into the palm. Ever so gently, he tried to tease out the blood vessel with his wand, but the errant artery didn't want to cooperate. Unlike shooting spells at sparring partners, this magic required a level of precision he wasn't accustomed to. It was like trying to thread a needle with his mind.

He almost laughed—that was just the sort of exercise Medea would make him do. Boil water, Nikolai. Stack rocks, Nikolai. Thread a needle, Nikolai. But no wand! Never a wand. Preposterous, all of it. In a moment of irritation, he yanked the vessel forward.

There is a delay between when our brain issues a command and when our body executes it. A command cannot be rescinded once sent, and new commands arrive after the first, delaying their effect. As a boy, Nikolai had once stepped into a crumbling apartment, invited by a man who claimed to have food. That was the first time he clearly saw into anyone's mind, and in an instant, he knew the man meant to kill him. Nikolai had registered his mistake and tried to stop, but his feet moved doggedly across the threshold, urged on by the previous command. For an agonizing moment, he'd been no more than a passenger angrily issuing commands to a body that refused to heed them.

He felt the same disconnect now.

While pulling on the artery, he realized he was going to use too much force. But try as he might, he couldn't stop his hand from completing the action, and the vessel broke. The piece closest to him came out, and the portion inside the palm slunk even further beyond his reach.

He stopped, horrified at what he'd done. The bit of artery on the table stared up at him accusingly. Next to it, his hand clutched the wand Medea loathed. What had she said about wands? They were lazy and made you less focused.

Gingerly, he set the wand down and leaned against the table. What could he do? The magic was too complicated to perform without a wand, wasn't it? He ran a hand through his hair. No, obviously it wasn't. Medea cast everything without a wand. He just needed to focus. He could do this.

He pulled a chair to the table and sat. He wanted his complete concentration. What had Medea taught him in the forest? Bare skin made it easier to sense with magic. He grasped the bleeding hand in his own, gently pressing his fingers on either side of the area where the artery hid. He closed his eyes and dove in with his mind.

It took a moment to get his bearings, but studying the anatomical diagrams had given him a map of how things should feel. The artery was too short. Pulling it forward now wouldn't help. He'd have to heal it where it was.

As he focused his will on germinating the artery still inside the palm, he palpated the artery on the table with his fingers. *This* was what it should be like, he just had to make it over *there*. One hand felt the artery; the other guided his magic.

Was this what Medea had been trying to teach him in the forest? She'd asked him to sense the blight in the roots, then replicate the effect on the plants holding him. They'd practiced for weeks, but he could never quite grasp the concept. It was simple replication. Why hadn't he been able to do it before?

The artery elongated up the half-formed finger, sending out little branches as it went. Nerves followed and then skin. When he opened his eyes, he didn't need them to know the finger was perfect.

A test would be prudent regardless. He applied the restraints before removing Sleep and Paralysis from the test subject. The man's eyes flew open, his breath quickening when he realized he was on the stone table.

"How is your finger?" Nikolai asked. "The pinky on your right hand. Can you move it? Does it hurt?"

The man turned a horrified gaze to the blood on the side of the table. His body trembled, but when his hand clenched, the pinky flexed along with the other fingers.

"What are you going to do to it?" the man rasped.

Nikolai grinned. "Nothing. It's already done." He held up the bowl, tilting it so the man could see the severed finger.

Back in the lab, Nikolai collected his ingredients, copied the instructions for the potion, and rummaged through the cabinets for an extra cauldron and burner. When he had everything he needed, he went to his room to brew the potion. As much as he longed to see Medea's face when she realized he'd overcome her little hurdles, it was more important to keep his success a secret. Given all she'd done to keep him from making it, she'd probably take it away if she knew he'd succeeded. He set up the cauldron in the back corner of his room and positioned the furniture to block it from view.

While the potion itself wasn't difficult to craft, the timing had to be perfect. He steeped the leaves of several different plants, removing them once the water darkened. The next step had to be completed during the time of the comet. He laid out the severed finger and a jar of freshwater planarian worms. The worms had to be diced and inserted into a cut on the finger, infusing the finger with their qi—whatever that was. The directions warned not to do this in advance, for the worms rapidly regrew once cut. Dagger ready, eyes on his pocket watch, Nikolai waited.

A knock sounded at his door.

Fuck fuck fuck.

"Coming!" He rushed across the room and called out through the door. "What is it?"

"The comet will be here in five minutes. If you want to make your potion, come to the lab now."

"I'm not coming." He tried to sound sulky and defeated.

"You left bodies all over the yard outside. Regardless of your failure, you are still required to clean up after yourself."

He was screwed if she made him do it now. "I'll do it in a bit. I'd rather not see the comet I can't use, if you don't mind." Would she pick up the feigned bitterness in his voice?

A pause. "I doubt it would be visible from here, but very well, if that is your choice. It can wait until the morrow."

He pressed his ear to the wood and listened for the soft retreat of Medea's footsteps. She wouldn't bother him again, not with her own potions to make. He smiled and returned to his work. Who needed patience and sacrifice when you had persistence and cunning?

30

YOXTL'S BARGAIN

Nikolai woke in a good mood. After dressing and completing his focus exercise, he checked his reflection in the mirror and plastered a scowl on his face. Let the old woman think she'd bested him.

He froze on his way to the laboratory. Two voices emanated from behind the library door. Nikolai slunk over and put his ear to the wood. No music this time, but Medea was speaking with someone. With utmost care, he turned the doorknob, wincing at the slight creak.

He followed Medea's voice across the empty foyer to the fifth alcove. Who the hell did she have in here, and what were they doing? He peered around the edge of the bookcase.

Goddamnit. It was just Yoxtl. The spirit stood atop the center table, surrounded by papers. Medea scribbled furiously, pausing now and then to reread her notes.

"Fascinating," she exclaimed. "What about weapon enchantments? Poison, Bleed . . .?"

Yoxtl shook its head. "No reason to rely on magic for that, not with the local flora. I do have several antidote spells." The spirit smiled as Nikolai rounded the corner. "Good morning, mortal!"

"Morning, Yoxtl. What brings you here?"

"Earning my keep."

"It's giving me spells it learned watching the Aztecs," said Medea. "I'm surprised to hear you ask, given this was your idea." It was just one faux pas after another with this woman.

He settled into an armchair and steepled his fingers. "First of all, it's customary to greet people and ask how they're doing, even if you don't care. Secondly, it's rude to call Yoxtl an 'it' when he's standing right there."

"I don't care what's 'customary.' It's silly." Her eyes remained focused on the paper in front of her. "As for Yoxtl, spirits are 'it' by default unless they choose otherwise. Some take a gendered form to appeal to mortals, but they can just as easily choose more than one, like Ahsonnutli and Hapi, or flit between the two, like Loki."

Oh, good, she'd stopped. For a second there, he worried he might have triggered another lecture.

He looked at Yoxtl. "And what are you? He? She?"

"Yoxtl," it said with a smirk.

"Did you make your potions for the day?" asked Medea. "Do your water boiling?"

"I'll do it later." He waved away the question and leaned forward to snatch a sheet off the table. "Any good spells?"

"The translation disk is *right* there."

He grabbed the edge of the disk and maneuvered the arm so it was over the table. The first several sheets were nothing but spells for growing maize—increasing crop yield and kernel size, preventing blight, repelling pests. Worthless. Where were the offensive spells?

He rifled through sheets until he came to magic that didn't pertain to plants. There was a spell to ward off lameness by treating the knees with ash. Useless. A spell for enchanting a toad. Placed in someone's home, it would croak every time the occupants tried to speak. Fun. A death curse. Cast on oneself, it caused whoever had slain you to be stalked by a jaguar until it dispatched them. Nice. The forearm of a mother who died in childbirth had magical properties and could be used as a makeshift wand.

He looked up from the paper. "A magic forearm? *Really?* I think Yoxtl's having a go at you."

"Just what I've heard," the spirit said haughtily.

Medea's pen paused. "Part of studying magic is sorting out fact from fiction. Belief is a powerful force. It can alter a man's behavior to the point where it doesn't matter if the magic works or not. If an item is taboo, or believed to be filled with dark magic, people will react accordingly. The same is true for things deemed beneficial."

"Are you going to test the forearm?"

"Not today." Medea pointed her pen at Yoxtl, indicating it should continue. The spirit dictated in another tongue while her pen scratched away.

He scanned several more pages. Plants and agriculture. Not much in the way of offensive spells. He laughed and remarked to himself, "I can see why they were wiped out."

The recitation and scratching ceased simultaneously. He looked up to see Yoxtl and Medea staring at him, faces unreadable. What the hell?

"Clarify," said Medea.

"The spells—there's nothing good here. I can see why the Aztecs were wiped out."

Medea leaned forward, propping her elbows on the table and lacing her fingers together. Fuck. Definitely a lecture this time. She opened her mouth, then closed it again and shook her head, though she looked close to bursting.

"Never mind. I don't have the time or the energy to delineate the numerous stupidities in that particular statement." She waved her hand, and a huge volume slammed into his stomach—*De finibus bonorum et malorum*, by Cicero. "If you're going to sit here, do something useful, like practice your Latin. Otherwise, get out and see to your potions. I'll meet you in the forest when I'm finished."

Nikolai stood and placed the book on the table. He had better things to do than study Latin.

"Wait," said Medea. "Yoxtl, tell Nikolai what happened to the people who survived battles with the Spanish."

The spirit turned its amber eyes toward him. "They died of disease."

"Nikolai, what magical school is used to combat disease?"

Not this again. Why couldn't she give it a rest? "Healing."

"You may go."

Nikolai smiled as the vines raced toward him. He let his mind drift into the soil, searching for a plant stricken with blight. As he'd done with the artery, he focused on the blight and targeted the vines wrapping him, willing the same condition to manifest.

Black spots appeared. The vines began to wither and brown. Why had he ever found this difficult? He pushed the necrosis toward the roots until the plants fell away limply. He kicked them aside.

"Well done," said Medea. "I knew you'd get there eventually."

He beamed. Coming from Medea, the words were glowing praise, and she wore an expression she'd never directed at him before—pride. He wanted to photograph that look and frame it. At times like this, he almost liked her. Sometimes she was the perfect master—stern but fair, a relentless perfectionist who pushed him to try harder—not to mention a good deal better looking than Petrov. Then she'd go and do something like ask him to cut off his own finger, reminding him who she truly was—a bitter, manipulative old woman bent on holding him back while she drained his youth. Today, though—today she was playing nice, and the vindication he received from her acknowledgment of his performance was glorious.

"Now let's see how fast you can do it," Medea said. "Try to necrotize the shoots before they hit you."

The onslaught began before she'd finished talking. Soon he could barely stand for all the puncture wounds, but he kept at it, until at last he could necrotize most of the shoots before they'd had a chance to break through the soil.

His pride swelled, then faltered as the all-too-familiar fog descended over his mind, stripping away the day's progress. Shoots bit into his flesh, but he lacked the will to fight back. At last he collapsed, shaking with disappointment and self-loathing, and his traitorous brain gave voice to the dark thoughts.

"Make it stop," he pleaded. "I won't kill you. I'll be good, just make it stop." Some small part of his mind screamed in fury that he would say such things. Begging and admitting defeat were beneath him. Was this the real goal of her curse, not to drain his youth but to warp him into a shadow of himself?

He looked up, expecting to see Medea gloating, but she stood rigid, her jaw clenched.

"I can't—I won't," she said quietly.

"Why?"

"It's not my place to say . . ."

Anger bubbled to the surface, breaking through the fog. "You did this to me. You can damn well undo it!"

Her mouth fell open. "You think *I* did this to you?"

"Who else? I don't see anyone else on this godforsaken island!"

"To what purpose? Why would I even *do* such a thing?"

"Oh, I don't know, maybe to keep me from learning too fast?" He bit back the accusation that she was draining him.

"That makes no sense. Why? Why would I even train you then? I would have left you where you were. You asked me for this!" She gestured at him accusingly. "As I recall, you spent a good week pestering me when I told you no."

"Maybe I shouldn't have. Why do all your apprentices end up dead?"

"I told you why. And they don't all end up dead."

"I don't believe you."

She crossed her arms. "It's not my job to convince you that the lie you believe is false."

"Look, if it's not you, just tell me what it is. You promised to help me become the best I can be. How can you do that and keep whatever this is to yourself?"

Her mouth opened slightly, and for an instant he thought he'd won, but then it snapped shut and Medea shook her head.

"This is your own puzzle to solve. You brought it on yourself." She turned her back on him and set a brisk pace out of the forest.

"What's that supposed to mean?" He flung the words uselessly at her back. *"What's that supposed to mean?!"* Despair washed over him. He plucked vines and thorns from his body, tears streaming down his face. He couldn't believe he was crying. *Really* crying. That was something other people did, not him. Fear and despair were Useless emotions. Yet here he was, plagued by thoughts that weren't his, begging for help from the very person he needed to kill. The potion remedies hadn't worked, finding old apprentices had been a literal dead end—there was only one option left.

"Yoxtl!" he bellowed.

The spirit instantly appeared on a branch above. It had probably been watching the whole time, waiting until he was vulnerable enough to call it.

"Yes?" Yoxtl crooned.

"Can you help me, and what's the price?"

Yoxtl leapt down, landing softly in front of him with a grin. Its black fur glowed with an eerie blue luminescence. "A soul."

"I know better than to part with that." Malaise or no, he would not promise his soul.

"It need not be yours, mortal. Help me procure a few souls, and I shall tell you the remedy."

Nikolai wiped the tears from his face. "What do I have to do?"

Nikolai straightened his uniform and entered the hospital. Yoxtl perched upon his shoulder, an arrangement he didn't enjoy but tolerated nonetheless. At this point, he would do almost anything to be rid of the curse. The spirit assured him it was only audible or visible when it wanted to be, and they made it through the front doors without any questioning looks.

They passed the lobby without incident and entered the first ward. Rows of beds lined either side of the immense room. Nurses bustled about, carrying meals or medical instruments, while patients slept or sat up reading newspapers. Yoxtl jumped from Nikolai's shoulder onto a passing nurse's white cap, then onto the first bed. It leapt from bed to bed, completely unnoticed, searching for an appropriate target.

"No. No. No. Nope. Not him." Yoxtl barely looked at any of the patients before dismissing them as unsuitable. "Ugh. Why did you have to bring me to a hospital with so many Christians?"

Did the spirit expect him to answer? He'd look like he was talking to himself. Nikolai moved to a sleeping patient and pretended to take the man's pulse. "You requested a place where people were dying," he whispered. "Next time, be more specific. Why can't they be Christians?"

"Because they're reserved. Converting people is a lot easier when they aren't set on something else."

"I don't follow you."

"That's unsurprising. You mortals are slow." Yoxtl grinned over its shoulder, then jumped to the opposite row of beds. "None of these people are dying!" it complained when it was halfway down the line.

Nikolai walked ahead and exited the ward. "Maybe the sicker people are in private rooms," he said when Yoxtl joined him.

He set off at a brisk pace, avoiding hospital personnel as Yoxtl dashed through closed doors, checking the contents of each room before popping out again. They passed surgeries, but Yoxtl needed the patients to be conscious. He was beginning to think the trip was a lost cause when Yoxtl poked its head through a door and proclaimed, "This one."

Nikolai opened it to find a semiprivate room with two beds, one occupied by an elderly man. He closed the door and drew the curtains while Yoxtl batted at the man's nose like an unruly cat. When the man's eyes fluttered open, the spirit shimmered and took the form of an ethereal young man.

"Greetings, my child," said Yoxtl.

"Wh—who are you?" the patient croaked.

"I am the great god Yoxtl, come to take you away to the hereafter." Magic flowed through Yoxtl's words, heightening their impact. *"All your life, you resisted the temptation of false religions. You have done well, my son. Pledge your eternal devotion to me, and you may join the rest of your family."*

"Sadie? I'll get to see Sadie again?" The old man squinted at Yoxtl.

"Yes, she is here with me." The spirit morphed into the figure

of a young woman, then spent entirely too long fawning over her supposed soon-to-be dead husband.

Nikolai rolled his eyes at Yoxtl's performance. The spirit was laying it on pretty thick, though he did have the old man in tears by the end.

Yoxtl morphed back into a young man. *"Sadie and everyone else you've ever loved are here with me. Let my priest give you the final rites, and you may join them when you pass on."*

That was Nikolai's cue. He withdrew a stone of polished jade from his pocket and bid the man open his mouth. As he placed the stone under the man's tongue, he said, "By Yoxtl's will, I bind thee. May he take you into the afterlife and guard your soul ever after." He touched the man's brow. "When you pass, Yoxtl will guide your soul to his side. Let no false gods tempt you, for you have seen the Truth with your own eyes."

The man nodded. Despite his frail body, there was now a fierce determination behind his eyes.

"Good-bye, my child," said Yoxtl. "Until we meet again."

The spirit shifted back into a fox and trotted down the corridor.

"Your performance was completely over-the-top," said Nikolai. "Why can't I just use the stone on someone who's sleeping?"

"The stone signifies a pact and marks them as mine, in a spiritual sense, but it's not infallible. If someone were to come along and perform last rites, it would undo my work unless the human truly believed. Belief is a powerful thing—if they truly believe they will join me in death, then they will, regardless of the stone." Yoxtl paused and sniffed the air hopefully. "There is another not far from here."

A knot of people clustered around a small figure bandaged head to toe. Dim light combined with the green walls to give the room a sickly air. Next to the bed sat a catatonic woman, her face streaked with dried tears. Behind her, a man stood with his hand upon her shoulder, steadying himself as much as comforting her. A nurse went through the motions of checking tubes. Her body language said it all—there was no hope to be had.

Nikolai perused their minds. There'd been some sort of accident involving farm equipment. The child's injuries were too grave, the bleeding too severe. His gaze strayed to the mother and lingered. Mothers didn't do well when their children died, not when they were this young. Her mind was a screaming void of anguish. He'd seen it before. She felt so much that she felt nothing at all.

This would kill her.

"Distract them," said Yoxtl. "Get them out of here so I can talk to the kid."

Nikolai left the room and beckoned Yoxtl to follow. He opened a few doors until he found a storage closet, then entered. Yoxtl popped through the wall a moment later.

"What are we doing in here?" it asked.

"I wanted to speak with you. The child—that's nothing a healing potion won't fix. It might not make him a hundred percent, but it would stabilize him."

"So?"

"So, didn't you say souls get more powerful over time? Why take the soul of a child, when you can have the soul of an adult?"

"A lot can happen between now and then. The parents are Christian. It's a miracle the child wasn't baptized in the first place. What if he decides to convert later?"

"What if you convert the parents too? Sure, it's a gamble, but you could end up with three adult souls, instead of one child."

Yoxtl frowned. "That's a long time to wait."

"As Medea keeps pointing out to me, time means nothing to immortals. Are you really too impatient to play the long game?"

The spirit eyed him curiously. "Why do you *care*?"

He disliked the emphasis Yoxtl put on the word, even more so because he didn't quite know himself. It had nothing to do with the kid, he was sure of that. The mother, on the other hand . . .

Nikolai shoved the thought away and leaned against the wall, arms crossed. "I don't. But it's a problem I can fix, so why not? What's the point of having power if you don't use it?"

Yoxtl's gaze held his a moment longer. Was his telepathic shield good enough to keep the spirit out?

"Aren't *you* philanthropic today," it said at last. "Fine. But I want one of the parents to convert first."

"No. You said belief matters—let them see the miracle first." Nikolai removed his white coat. His European suit was formal by American standards and would serve better for this. "Any chance you can make me look older?"

"You don't know Glamor? What the hell kind of wizard are you? That's the most basic—"

"Can you do it or not?"

"Yeah, I can do it." The spirit muttered something under its breath and gave Nikolai a sidelong glance.

As they walked back to the room, Nikolai changed his posture and gait to that of an elderly man. The religious aspect would be harder to fake. The Soviet Union pushed atheism after the revolution, so what little he knew came from movies or peripheral exposure in Ireland. How anyone fell for this drivel was beyond him, but he attempted to mimic the same benevolence and subtle air of superiority he'd seen in priests.

He paused in the doorway, waiting for the nurse to leave while skimming her mind for pertinent information. After she'd gone, Nikolai entered, Yoxtl trailing at his heels.

"Mr. and Mrs. Cunningham?" he asked.

"Yes?" said the father. The mother continued to stare at the bed.

"I'm Father Featherline. One of the nurses said you might need my services."

At this, a broken sob erupted from the mother. She thought he was here to give the boy his last rites.

"I'm afraid you mistake me, Mrs. Cunningham, I'm here to pray for the boy, but not in that way. I believe I can help heal him."

"What do you mean?" asked the father, eyes narrowing.

"I belong to a little-known religion from the Far East. Priests of my order are gifted with the ability to heal. Normally it would take several of us to heal wounds as grievous as this, but if you consent to help me with the prayer, I think we can do it."

"How dare you!" spat the father. "My son lies here dying, and you're trying to shove some mumbo jumbo down our throats?"

"Stu—"

"Let me handle this, Cheryl." He dismissed his wife with a wave.

Yoxtl shook its head mutely.

Nikolai turned to the wife. "Mrs. Cunningham, would you like me to heal your son?"

"Get out." The man took a step toward Nikolai.

Cheryl was suddenly out of her seat, clutching at her husband's arm. "Stuart. *Stu.* What can it hurt to try?"

Stuart turned to his wife. In a softer voice he said, "The harm is he's giving you false hope."

"Please, Stu. If he can help, why don't we try it? I couldn't live with myself if we didn't at least *try*."

Stuart sighed. "Alright." He shot a glare at Nikolai over his wife's head.

Nikolai approached the bed. "Please stand and hold hands over the boy. I will start the ritual."

"Ridiculous," muttered Stuart.

As if it was any more ridiculous than consuming the body of Christ. Nikolai removed the jade stone from his pocket and placed it on the boy's chest. He subtly jerked his head at Yoxtl, indicating it should get on the bed. The spirit flew onto the boy, the couple's hands clasping through it. Stuart looked away, refusing to acknowledge what they did, but Cheryl only had eyes for her son.

Nikolai chanted nonsense about invoking the power of the god Yoxtl. He bid the god appear before them and bless them with his light. Yoxtl morphed into a blinding blue orb centered on the couple's hands. As they stared at it, entranced, Nikolai unstoppered a healing potion and attempted to tip it into the boy's mouth.

"What are you doing?" asked Stuart sharply.

"It's all part of the ceremony," said Nikolai. He cupped the flask to shield the contents.

"Is that blood?" asked Stuart. "It looks like blood."

"Of course not." Nikolai moved before the man could protest further and tipped the flask toward the child's mouth. The boy coughed, spraying blood all over the bedding.

"You're killing him!" Stuart grappled for the flask, and Nikolai gave him a telekinetic shove into the wall.

Shut up and let me work. He sent the thought toward Stuart, and for a wonder the man obeyed.

Nikolai carefully unwrapped the bandages from the boy's head, revealing a zigzag of stitches and swollen flesh. He dipped his finger in the potion and ran it along the child's lips. The boy's eyes fluttered open.

"Drink this," said Nikolai, helping the child sit up.

The boy took a sip and grimaced. "It tastes terrible," he croaked.

"Yes, it does. But it will help you get better. That, and the power of the great god Yoxtl." The spirit better do something showy soon, or they were more likely to chalk up the healing to the potion rather than divine intervention.

Yoxtl seem to be thinking along the same lines, for the orb of blue expanded over the child's body and suffused it with light as the potion worked. The parents gasped as the child's wounds knitted closed and the swollen, discolored skin smoothed and returned to normal. The mother made to touch her son, but Nikolai grabbed her wrist.

"Not yet," Nikolai cautioned, motioning her back. "Our faith in the good god Yoxtl is what heals him, and the child still has internal injuries. I will let you know when it is safe to break the spell."

He pulled back the covers and stripped the bandages from the child's body. The more healing they saw, the stronger their faith would be. They exclaimed as ragged flesh became whole and healthy. When the effects of the potion dwindled, Nikolai cried, "Enough! This is the most we can safely do. Your son needs rest now, and nourishment."

Cheryl grabbed her son in a tearful embrace. Stuart watched them with a bewildered expression. "It worked. I can't believe it worked . . ." He looked at Nikolai. "Who *are* you?"

"I am but a humble priest of Yoxtl."

"Yoxtl—I've never heard of that god."

"Myself either, until I traveled far into the East and discovered a small village of people both happy and healthy. They suffered not from disease or injury, for their priests could heal all."

"The Lord truly works in mysterious ways," muttered Stuart. "We prayed for a miracle, and He sent you."

"Noooo!" wailed Yoxtl. "Not YHWH again. DO something, mortal! Make the windows shake, make stuff fly around —*anything* to display my displeasure."

Was the spirit really so weak it couldn't perform such magic itself? Nikolai focused on the couple and cast Gust. Confined in such a small space, the wind swirled around, tugging at the curtains and sending the child's chart flying across the room.

"Fool!" cried Nikolai, pointing an accusing finger at Stuart. "You've angered Yoxtl by attributing his gift to someone else."

"What? I . . ." Stuart ducked as everything caught in the wind flew at his face.

"Take back what you said," said Nikolai. "Take it back quickly before Yoxtl undoes the boon he's granted you."

Cheryl covered her son with one hand and jabbed her husband with the other. "Take it back, Stu!"

"I'm sorry! I'm sorry! I take it back." Stuart fell to his knees. "We bow to your greatness, oh, Yox . . . er . . ."

"Yoxtl," said Nikolai.

"Yoxtl!"

Nikolai stopped channeling Gust, and the room settled. He glared at Stuart. "Never do that again. You've seen the power my god holds. Our god. He's yours now too. But you must forsake this Christian god of yours, or he may deem you unworthy and take back what he has given you."

Stuart nodded and went to embrace his wife. He kissed her, then looked up at Nikolai. "Thank you. I didn't believe it first but —well, thank you."

Unseen, Yoxtl flew onto the bed and locked eyes with the boy. "I'm not as bad as all that," it said. "I just need your parents to understand—need *you* to understand—you're mine now. I'd like to check on you from time to time, if that's alright. Make sure you're doing well. Unlike the Christian god, I *do* care about my followers."

Yoxtl sniffed the dried blood caking the boy's head and took one long lick. "Now I can find you wherever you are. If you ever have need of me, call my name: Yoxtl."

The spirit leapt from the bed and walked out the door. Nikolai gathered up the jade stone and bid the parents farewell. They searched the rest of the hospital but only found one more target soul to bind.

Afternoon sun peeked out of fluffy clouds as they trekked back from the hospital. The trees on either side of the road had already lost most of their leaves. A gentle breeze did its best to detach the stragglers and send them down in a flutter of yellow and orange. Nikolai inhaled the crisp autumn air, his feet crunching over the carpet of fallen leaves. Yoxtl ghosted over them without a sound.

"Two souls! Terrible."

"Two more than you had before, and three potentials on the way."

"Potential doesn't do me any good, but I can work on the kid. With a little more power, I can make him god-touched." The spirit grinned up at Nikolai. "I could have a real priest again."

"How's that blood thing work? Tracking spell?"

"It's called a blood binding, and yes. Spirits can teleport with ease. Unlike you humans, we have no true physical form to break down and recreate, but we need something to latch on to, a person or a place."

"Can you teleport off the island then? Even with the wards?"

"Yes, though I don't know if they'd let me return. I'll have to get Medea to identify me to them before we do this again."

Nikolai stopped walking. "Again? I don't think so. I fulfilled my end of the bargain. Tell me how I get rid of this curse."

"You don't. You're not skilled enough."

"You lying little—" He aimed a kick at the spirit. All that work for nothing!

"Ah-ah-ah!" The spirit danced out of range, then spun and walked up the road backward. It grinned. "I said I would help you, not cure it. The effects can be mitigated. All you need is a dapper frog."

"A dapper frog? What kind of help is that?"

"The indirect kind. If Medea did curse you—"

"Of course she did!" Nikolai snarled.

"Then helping you directly would violate the geas she placed on me."

Coward. "You said it's only supposed to work on souls. Why are you worried about it?"

"I *felt* it. Like a hundred hooks digging into my essence." The spirit shuddered. "A human shouldn't be able to do that."

They came to a bridge. Yoxtl vaulted onto the railing and sat on its haunches, tail twitching. Light glinted off the creek below. A heron took one careful step at a time as it stalked prey in the reeds.

"If I can figure out how to remove the geas," asked Nikolai, "will you give me a straight answer?"

Yoxtl shook its head. "A geas can only be removed by the one who cast it. Soul magic is the most powerful and complicated magic there is."

No wonder Medea kept it locked up. Unlike telepathy and everything else he wanted to study, which she kept promising to make available "after he'd learned the basics," soul magic could only be learned by those above master rank—the rank at which apprentices normally left. Maybe that's why Thomas stuck around. What had he found in that section of the library, and was it the reason they'd had a falling out? Odds were, immortality lay in that direction. As Nikolai had done with his dueling partners, Medea kept the best magic for herself.

Thankfully, he didn't need to get into that section of the library—Yoxtl seemed to know all about soul magic. Most spirits probably did, given their obsession with souls. No wonder Medea forbade the spirits on her island from talking to him.

He leaned on the railing and mimicked Yoxtl's stare over the water. The heron made a stab. Its beak came back with a wriggling silver fish, which it gulped down before resuming its search for prey.

He needed to control Yoxtl. Soul magic aside, the spirit could be Useful, what with its ability to detect spells invisible to Magic Sight; Yoxtl had noticed his curse with ease. He could have it search the island for hidden magic. The blocked-off cave would be no trouble for a creature that could walk through walls. What he needed was something to leverage the spirit into obeying his commands.

"When I have those souls," said Yoxtl wistfully, "I can make myself more convincing. People on the brink of death are easy. They're scared, and they long for *something.* The young, the healthy, the well-to-do—they're harder to persuade."

Delicious desperation tinged the spirit's voice, the hunger there a siren's call. Yoxtl might be weak now, but given enough followers, who knew what kind of powers it might possess?

He kept his tone casual. "Then don't persuade them. Focus on the downtrodden. 'Religion is the sigh of the oppressed creature . . . It is the opium of the people.' I can't remember the full quote by Marx, but he saw it. Focus your efforts on those who have the most to gain. There are far more of them."

"YHWH has those souls locked up tight."

"Yeah, well, YHWH isn't out performing miracles. He's operating on goodwill earned nearly two thousand years ago. I think he could use some competition, don't you?"

Yoxtl seemed to wither in on itself. "I don't know—he doesn't take kindly to spirits who steal from him."

No wonder Yoxtl's people died out. The spirit thought small and took no unnecessary risks. How fortunate that it had Nikolai to make decisions for it.

Nikolai put his back to the water. He couldn't sell the idea too hard, nor seem too interested. "How did YHWH get followers to begin with? Performing miracles, right? Burning bush, curing leprosy—all that?"

"He had prophets—mages of extraordinary ability for their time, who he coaxed into spreading his message. That way he didn't have to expend any of his own magic. They did it all for him. The kid—I could give the kid magic—"

"But he'd need mana from you," Nikolai pointed out. "I had several witches in my dueling club. Always having to ask permission before casting spells." He chuckled and shook his head. "Quite sad, really. Nothing compared to a real Magi. Well, we best be heading back."

Before he could withdraw his arm from the railing, Yoxtl placed a paw on top, eyes pleading. "You could help. With your magic, you could perform all kinds of miracles for me."

"Casting spells in front of Mundanes is illegal. Why should I stick out my neck for you?"

"I can give you your heart's desire."

He arched an eyebrow in feigned disbelief and let the silence stretch.

Yoxtl's paw pressed more firmly against his arm. "I can give you immortality."

"And how exactly do you plan to accomplish that?"

"With your soul—"

"No. I didn't consider it before. What makes you think I'd consider it now, given what I saw today? You promise things you can't deliver—eternal paradise, rejoining loved ones. Don't insult my intelligence. Are the souls you collect even sentient once you take them? From what I can tell, you cast aside their consciousness and drain them for power."

"I can choose whether my souls remain separate entities within me or dissolve into raw ethereal power. But that's not what I meant. I speak of soul magic. Help me collect enough, and I can bring you back from the dead if ever you are slain. It would be my blessing to you for helping me."

He maintained his air of disinterest. "I see. And why didn't you bestow this 'blessing' on any of your followers?"

The foxish face was unreadable, but it paused before answering. "Resurrection is taboo. When YHWH did it . . ." Yoxtl shook its head. "It goes against all our rules. You break the rules for me, I'll break the rules for you."

Interesting. He had considered spirits to be independent agents, dissociated from one another. This made it sound like they had their own form of governance. Did Medea know?

"I'll consider it." His tone made it clear he wouldn't. He extracted his arm from under Yoxtl's paw and started up the road.

The spirit darted in front of him. "Help me, mortal."

"After the 'help' I just received? No thanks. I need something a lot better than 'dapper frog' to trust you."

"What do you want? I can't do any advanced magic in my current state."

He made a show of thinking it over. "Information. First, I want to know what really happened to all of Medea's apprentices. Did she drain them to keep herself young?"

"And second?"

"I want to know where she's hidden magic. Books, artifacts, spells—anything she doesn't want found. There's a cave on the beach she's blocked off, you can start there."

"I can do that," Yoxtl said brightly.

The spirit moved to trot alongside him, obedient as a dog. Nikolai couldn't help but smile. They crossed over the gateway threshold. In the common room a stone-faced Medea awaited them.

31

DIGITS

A jolt ran through Medea's body, the interruption like fingernails on the slate board of her soul. The stones she'd been hovering above the gravel pit pattered to the ground. Bad enough to be interrupted, but the ward told her one of the test subjects was near death, making it all the more irritating. Years ago, after a suicide attempt, she'd put health tracking wards on the test subjects. Not that she cared about their well-being; she just didn't come across people who met the criteria very often, and such encounters were distressing. She'd be damned if she was going to let one of them die and force her to restock.

She floated over the low wall and touched down lightly. The sensation of homey earth and grass against her bare feet after levitating offered no pleasure to her today. She took a deep breath and headed for the dungeon, reaching along the thread of magic to see what healing she'd have to perform, and recoiled at the puffy, sweltering body.

Bacteria flooded the circulatory system. Fever wracked the brain. The liver and kidneys fought valiantly to keep functioning despite the overwhelming inflammation and lack of blood flow.

Though she knew bacteria couldn't follow her through the ward, she still shuddered and wiped her hands on her dress.

How the hell did he become septic? Where did it start? She pulled back, checking the exterior. The skin on one arm swelled tight, pus oozing from open sores. Even through the ward, the stench was so thick she could almost taste it. She held her breath —not that it would help, as it was all in her head—and followed the damage down. There! A missing finger, and the remaining digits were necrotic. Nikolai had taken a finger after all.

She spun halfway through the common room and headed for his door. If he thought he could get away with this, he'd soon learn that actions had consequences.

"Nikolai!" She pounded on his door, mentally increasing his punishment every second he didn't answer. She should take his hand. No—his arm, or better yet, his tongue. He talked far too much anyway. "Come out this instant!" She banged again. Where *was* he?

Fuck, it was Nikolai's day off. He might not be home for hours, and the test subject would likely die in that time. Either she'd have to endure cleaning up Nikolai's mess or she'd be inconvenienced with finding a test subject.

She slammed through the outer doors. The cheery sun and perfect weather mocked her. Today was supposed to be peaceful. A time for meditation and relaxation. All ruined. She unleashed her rage on the garden beds, tearing up weeds root and stem with her bare hands and flinging them toward the ocean. There was something soothing about physical exertion, something she used to get with magic, back when she could still reach the point of mana exhaustion—no longer. She worked until her fingers were mottled green and brown.

The ward jolted her again. Fuck. She had to stabilize the test subject.

NO. The dungeon didn't have to be kept at capacity. She

would *not* clean up Nikolai's mess. He needed to see what he'd done. He needed to *fix* it. And he needed to learn some goddamned healing spells!

Didn't he realize that tearing apart an opponent required intimate knowledge of how the healthy body functioned? Without the ability to heal, he'd never survive a real duel, let alone be immortal. Why couldn't he see that? Was it a gender thing? Some cultures devalued what they saw as "woman's work." Was it like that in Russia? His superiority complex appeared to extend equally to both sexes, but then people were rarely aware of their own biases.

She swore as another magical wave rippled through her. No, this was a good notification—Nikolai had returned. She flung the last of her weeds aside and stormed into the hovel.

"Where have you been?" demanded Medea as soon as they entered the room.

She stood with her hands on her hips, cheeks flushed and hair disheveled. Streaks of earth clung to her dress at knee-height, and her chest rose seductively as she tried to catch her breath. The whole picture put him in mind of the last time he'd fucked Shailyn—on a grassy hill under a burning tree. Shailyn had been in a similar state when they'd finished, dirt stains and all, and it was easy to imagine Medea in her place, begging for more. Nikolai shelved the fantasy fodder for later. What the hell was she upset about now?

At the sight of Yoxtl, her eyes narrowed. Would she forbid the spirit from talking to him?

"Uh, I should be going," said Yoxtl. The spirit scampered across the common room and through the door.

Medea watched it go and returned her glare to him. "Where were you?"

He crossed his arms. The woman had some nerve. "It's none of your business what I do on my days off."

"It matters when you're needed here. Did you or did you not remove a finger from one of the test subjects?"

Shit. Had he messed up the regrowth spell? But he'd tested the finger! Something must have happened, or she wouldn't be asking. Time for a half truth.

"I cut one of them," he said, "but I didn't think I could regrow the finger, so I gave him a healing potion."

"You expect me to believe you started to cut off a finger and immediately changed your mind?"

She had a point. That didn't sound like him at all. "It occurred to me you might take something of mine in retribution. Like my hand."

Medea scoffed. "You're not wrong. Come with me." She led him to the dungeon.

A putrid stench wafted up the stairwell, as though something had died below and begun to rot. He raised a sleeve to cover his nose. With each step, the olfactory assault increased. Medea shot him a knowing look before striding toward the cells. At the tables he hung back, as if by standing apart he could distance himself from blame.

"Come here," she snapped.

He joined her beside the cell and fought the urge to retch. Even breathing through his mouth didn't help. The prisoner slumped in a corner against the wall, skin puffy. One arm curled across his lap; the other, blackened and purple, hung loose at his side. The finger he had painstakingly regrown had fallen off. The remaining fingers looked as though they would soon follow suit.

He opened the cell and entered, searching for the lost finger. "Here!" he exclaimed, holding it up for Medea to see. "I told you,

I didn't take his finger, and I *did* heal him. I have no idea why he's like this."

Medea approached the prisoner and held a hand to his forehead, bidding him do the same. "Feel that?" she asked.

"He's burning up."

"See how the skin is discolored? Not just the arm. See how the lips are bluish? That's called cyanosis. It happens when there is poor blood flow—in this case, sepsis. Do you know what that means?"

"Uh, the root is Greek for 'putrefaction.' His body is rotting, but why?"

"Look at where it started, and you tell me." She crossed her arms and waited, her frown extra bitchy.

What was she fishing for? They both knew it started with the finger. Had a blood vessel not connected properly? Had it bled out under the skin? But that wouldn't explain an infection.

When he didn't answer, she prompted, "What did you do, prior to cutting his finger?"

"I took him out of his cell and strapped him to the—"

"Before that. Before you came down here."

"I practiced on corpses in the graveyar—" Oh, shit. He hadn't cleaned the cleaver. It would have been swimming with bacteria from all those test cuts.

"What was your mistake?" She knew. Of course she knew. She just wanted him to say it.

He clenched his jaw. "I didn't clean the knife."

"You didn't clean the knife." Medea gestured to the prisoner. "Sloppy work yields sloppy results. Now you get to practice healing. Go upstairs and gather two blood replacement potions and five cleansing potions. And a stool. This is going to take a while. It would be much faster if you knew how to do things *properly*."

They worked on the prisoner for the rest of the day. Medea made him do the bulk of the dirty work. He forced the potions down the man's throat and removed the dead tissue. The whole arm had to come off. As he cut it free, several blackened fingers dropped to the floor like burnt sausages.

Medea didn't seem bothered by the smell. When he asked why, she remarked she'd altered her shield to keep out the stench, but she refused to share the technique. Despite his best efforts, he vomited several times, and she forced him to clean that up too. He was used to dead bodies, but cold and hard, not like this. Medea tsked at his physical reaction and made several disparaging remarks about his desire to become a necromancer.

When the dead tissue had been removed and the prisoner filled with potions, Medea instructed him to regrow the man's arm—a preposterous request, given he'd only studied fingers. Limbs were a whole different level. From what he had read in the library, limbs began in an embryonic state, like a flipper, which the caster coaxed into its final form over a period of weeks. "I can't. You know I can't."

Medea shook her head in disgust. "Attend me."

The stool and bucket flew into position next to the prisoner and Medea plopped down. Eyes closed, she weaved her hands below the stump. Pus and putrid clumps of tissue leaked from the wound into the air between her hands. When the trickle of vile fluids ceased, she deposited the muck into the bucket and returned her hands to the stump. They pinched and plucked the air, bare bone extending from the wound. Layers of tissue grew over each other, as if she crafted each layer from scratch, holding it in place with her mind before adding another, not unlike her focus exercise. Sometimes she teased the tissue into a slightly different position. It put him in mind of a sculptor molding clay.

The steady growth was far faster than it would have been with the embryonic healing method. Sweat glistened on the prisoner's face and chest, but his muscle tone and weight remained stable. Nikolai frowned. Healing required the body's own resources, and the man had to regrow a whole limb. Even with the potions they'd given him, the prisoner should be wasting away. Where did Medea get the raw materials for such a rapid healing?

"Why isn't he losing weight?" he asked.

"I thought you had no use for healing magic?" There was a challenge in her tone.

He wouldn't allow her to bait him. If she couldn't be bothered to explain, he couldn't be bothered to watch.

He shifted his attention to the other prisoners. He never had found out why they were here. No time like the present. He dipped into their minds one by one, but all he found was misery, hatred, and longing for death. All except number four, who was having an extremely graphic fantasy involving Medea, the dungeon worktable, and a number of knives.

He'd have to prime them. "What made you decide to throw this guy in here?"

Medea kept her eyes on her work, now down to the man's wrist. "Subject, not guy. And you're supposed to be paying attention, unless you'd like to do this yourself?" She paused and shifted as though offering him her seat.

"No."

It might be enough. Those who'd heard him would be thinking of how they ended up here. That is, if they even realized what they'd done to earn Medea's wrath. It's not as if the drunks from the Spotted Sow knew why she'd taken them.

Subject one—Medea had come to his house at night. Dragged him off. Subject two was unconscious. Subject three had been taken from a prison. But for what crime? The man wasn't thinking of it. Subject four, still fantasizing, had ignored the prompt. The rest were similarly unhelpful. Did none of them know why they were there? Perhaps that was part of her torture.

"There. Good as new." Medea stood and smiled at her handiwork. Her eyes slid to the prisoner's face and the smile faltered, as though she'd only just recalled who she'd been working on.

"I can't tell you why he's here," she said, "only that he deserves to be. They all do."

"Even that one?" Nikolai nodded to the lone woman.

Medea scowled. "That one is worse than the rest, for she knew what her husband did and, rather than stopping him, aided his efforts. *Repeatedly*." Medea raised a clenched fist. The woman spasmed and fell screaming to the floor, where she writhed, back arched. After a time, Medea dropped her fist and the woman stilled.

"Is her husband here too?"

"He died a few years back. Stabbed himself with a chicken bone. That's when I placed wards to monitor their health. I no longer feed them solid food. A spell passively summons the required nutrients into their bodies." She collected the stool and nodded to the bucket brimming with putrid liquid. "Carry that."

"Can't you just magic it outside like you do with the trash?"

"I'm trying my best not to magic *you* outside. You neglect your duties, damage my property, refuse to even *consider* completing an assignment that entails a minor sacrifice, and when I try to show you advanced healing, you stare into space, probably diving into the minds of this filth!" She kicked the leg of the man she'd just healed. "You want to be the best? Act like it!"

32

DAPPER FROG

"This is a terrible idea." Even standing in his own kitchen, Harper looked as though he'd rather be anywhere else.

"Agreed, but it's the best I've got." Nikolai had waited until arriving to broach the subject—easier to dispel Harper's misgivings in person—and hadn't explained all the details yet. First he needed Harper to agree.

"Can't you just . . . I dunno, persuade Medea to remove the curse?"

"She denies placing it. I told you, the woman is crazy."

"And your solution is to do something even crazier?" He eyed the box in Nikolai's arms with trepidation.

"If it mitigates the symptoms, yes." He put on his best pleading face, the one Harper couldn't resist. "I need this. I need your help. Please tell me I can count on my best friend."

Harper sighed and shook his head. "Alright, what do you want me to do?"

Nikolai grinned internally at the victory and set the box on the counter. "When the ladies arrive—"

"Ladies?" Harper said sharply. "What ladies?"

"The curse likes to hit in the middle of sex, so I ordered two of them to double my odds of triggering it."

Harper stared at him, aghast. "*Ordered?* Are you telling me you hired two prostitutes to come to my flat?"

"I needed professionals. Women who would arrive on time and leave once paid, not stay and fuss over me." Despite expecting an uncomfortable afternoon, he enjoyed watching Harper squirm.

"Goodness, Nikolai. My neighbor already has it in for me. If she sees a couple of prostitutes knock on my door—"

"Then maybe she'll stop worrying over the constant parade of men. Look, I need the prostitutes to make this work. I'll tell them to come get you once I start acting funny. Make the ladies leave, then give me the box. There's gloves in there so you can hold them up, in case I'm too out of it."

"You want me to wear *gloves*, but you're going to *lick* the damn things?!"

There was a gentle knocking on the door. Perfect timing.

"That'll be them. Please, Harper, just do this for me. Please?"

Harper groaned but didn't argue further. Nikolai slid the box along the counter toward him and went to answer the door.

"Welcome, ladies! Please come in." He smiled and offered to take their coats.

They shed their long overcoats to reveal summer dresses. One woman turned a suspicious eye toward Harper. "You said there'd only be one of you."

Nikolai laughed. "He's my valet. I sometimes fall ill—nothing contagious, I assure you, but he's here to assist me if it happens. This way, ladies."

He directed them to the bedroom, where he spent time boasting about his sexual prowess. Neither woman believed him, of course, smiling politely as he raved about how he'd show *them* a good time. He hated to look a fool, but the more he built up the encounter, the more likely the curse was to hit. They'd know the truth soon enough.

A threesome was more challenging than he thought it would be, though he performed admirably, tongue buried deep in one while a hand worked the other. Fingernails bit into his scalp as the first woman neared climax. He turned his full attention to her— she would remember him as the client who proved her wrong. Him, Nikolai, the greatest lover who ever—

Like clockwork, the fog descended and he slumped to the floor like the Useless waste that he was. The women were only humoring him. He'd paid for their services, hadn't he? A liar paying for lies. He curled on the rug next to the bed, vaguely aware of the women talking over him in hushed voices. The door opened and closed.

"Nikolai?" Harper's concerned voice spoke near his shoulder. "They've left. Let's get you up."

Firm hands grasped him under the arms and hauled him into a sitting position. Medea was right, he was trash. Harper should drag him into the hallway and leave him like the garbage that he was. He stared blankly at the box on the rug. It wouldn't work. Nothing would work. He slumped over and Harper had to right him again.

"Hang in there, Nikolai. Just give me a minute." Harper opened the box to reveal two sacks and a pair of gloves. He donned the gloves and removed the larger sack, which wriggled as he picked it up.

In the library, Nikolai had written every variation of Yoxtl's clue he could think of into the master grimoire. Nothing relevant came up for "dapper frog," so he searched for "frog" and "toad." This yielded a number of books. There were many frogs and toads with toxic or medicinal properties—poison dart frogs, cane toads, giant monkey frogs, corroboree frogs . . .

Two stood out as contenders, both native to Yoxtl's home

region. The first was the cane toad. While "cane" referred to sugarcane, it could also be interpreted as the walking variety, which was used in "dapper" dress. Poison dart frogs were another possibility. While their name did not suggest dapper, they were vibrantly colored and could be considered well-dressed compared to other frogs.

Both were incredibly toxic.

The experiment would no doubt make him ill, and he had prepared a variety of healing potions and antidotes just in case. If the poison mitigated the effects of the curse, it would be worth it. He could always isolate the active ingredients later. Right now he just needed to know if either poison worked.

Harper extracted the cane toad from the bag and grimaced as the fat, ugly thing struggled to break free. Something dark squirted between his fingers and splattered against his cream-colored pants. Harper shrieked and nearly dropped the toad.

"It *pooped* on me!"

He held the animal up to Nikolai's face. Nikolai stuck out his tongue and Harper dragged the amphibian over it.

His tongue erupted in fire. He grabbed the bedsheet and tried to wipe away the pain. Why was it so hot in here? He fumbled to loosen his collar but found only bare skin. Oh right, he'd undressed for the ladies. Lights danced before his eyes, beautiful in their brightness. Everything was wonderful!

". . . Nikolai! Nikolai! Wake up! Oh God, please don't let him die."

He opened his eyes to a blurry mass of pink and gold.

"Oh, thank goodness," exclaimed Harper. "Can you hear me? How do you feel? Your heart—it won't stop racing. You vomited and fell over. I didn't know what to do. I tried to get a potion into you, but you kept retching."

He tried to sit up, but his head pounded him into the floor. "I felt . . . it worked for a second there."

"Like heck it did! Didn't you hear anything I said? You almost died! Drink this."

Something pressed against his lips. He took a sip and coughed. So sore. It had worked—hadn't it? No, the high had merely driven the malaise away for a moment. Already he could feel the nagging doubts plucking insistently at his mind. He was worthless and stupid and . . .

He locked eyes with Harper. "The frog now. I need to try the frog."

Harper flung up his arms. "Are you mad? No!"

"Please, Harper, I have to get rid of this thing. I have to."

"At least wait until you've healed up. You should see yourself. You're beet red and shaking. If you collapse again and I can't get a potion into you . . ."

"I can't have this curse interfering with my life. Harper, please help me. You're the only one I trust." He bit his lip and tried his best puppy-eyed expression. Reaching for Harper's hand was out. If his motor coordination was as shot as he thought it was, he didn't want to fumble and reinforce Harper's belief that he was too ill to try again.

"Don't you dare lay this on me! You think I can't tell what you're doing?"

"Please?" Harper loved him. He'd do it.

Harper bowed his blond head and crumpled. "Why do you do this to me?" He reached for the second sack but made no move to open it. "Are you *sure* about this?"

"Yes."

Unlike the toad, the frog tasted peppery. The world swam before him. Colors. So many colors! Harper melted into the floor. Always so brightly colored and glittery, that one. Nikolai tried to scoop him up before he could seep through the carpet, but the bright colors slipped through his fingers.

"No, Harper, where did you go?" He grabbed the floor but came back with nothing.

A red candle appeared, such an angry hue. It shouted at him, but he couldn't make out the words so he turned aside. No time for that. He'd been looking for something. What was it?

He groped forward with his hands. Silver beams of light shot from his fingertips and radiated out in a blossom of color. He swayed his hands back and forth, watching the light dance. He laughed and ran his fingers along the wall. Colors trailed behind them.

An angry noise tugged at his attention. The red candle snuffed out the glittery candle. Pain lanced through his body and the colors dispersed, replaced with agony. His limbs pounded and he tasted blood.

Nikolai's health ward screamed at Medea. Just *once* she'd like to have a free day without a ward going off. Apprentices were equipped with health and location tracking wards, ensuring she didn't go too far while sparring and allowing her to find them in case of an emergency. They were *supposed* to be a rarely used precautionary measure, yet this was the second time Nikolai's had gone off.

The question was why. As much as she wanted to keep him alive, if he was drowning in the pools again or if he'd engaged in risky behavior, well, actions had consequences. She reached along the magical thread.

Poison coursed through Nikolai's body. Given the recent attempt on her life, the two were probably connected. Whoever the assassin was, they were clever. The man she'd dueled in Safe Harbor had probably been a decoy. Poisoning Nikolai was the perfect way to lure her away from the island, which meant the assassin knew how her wards worked. What trap did they have planned, and should she walk willingly into it?

If she did nothing, Nikolai would die, and she couldn't have that, not when it wasn't his fault. Where was he? Somewhere in London, but not close to the gateway. By the time she got there he'd be dead—unless she teleported.

So *that's* how the assassin planned to get her.

Teleportation required one to break up and reassemble the body. The spell was beyond the ability of most casters, demanding great focus and will to hold oneself together in the ether. Those who failed disintegrated into nothing, but that was not what worried Medea. The process left one sick and groggy and stripped away bodily enchantments. Her protective spells would be gone. Could she even remember them all, let alone recast them in time to ward off an attack? She'd have to disable her opponent fast and hard, before they could take advantage of her weakened state, *and* she'd have to do it while stabilizing Nikolai.

She felt along the ward. Odd—Nikolai's body had healed a bit. Had he solved the problem on his own? Still worth checking on, but it gave her time to use a gateway. Much safer.

She set a brisk pace to the gateway room. London assaulted her with its polluted air and unrelenting din of passing cars and people. She strengthened her shields, muffling the worst of it, and strode up the avenue looking for a cab.

The ward blared against her senses. Nikolai was dying, and he was dying *now*.

Heart racing, she closed her eyes, shielded her external senses, and felt along the magical thread to his position. She flew apart, yet held herself together. That was the key—to retain the idea of your body, grasping it close with your soul, while allowing the physical pieces of oneself to move freely through space. An instant later, she slammed her body back together.

Teleportation sickness nearly brought her to her knees. Every inch of her body screamed. Her gorge rose, but she managed to swallow it back down. Thank god she hadn't eaten yet today. Shields up. Assess the threat. She couldn't appear weak, not now.

There he was, her opponent—a young man Nikolai's age. She didn't recognize him, but that meant nothing, and anyway he had an illusion over his head. No doubt he'd made himself look like someone Nikolai knew in order to gain his trust. Nikolai fumbled against a wall, hallucinating.

Before the assassin could say a word, she threw him against the wall, bound and gagged him with her will, and ripped the illusion from his head. Flaxen gold hair and blue eyes turned to curly brown and brown.

"Who are you?" she demanded.

The man's eyes widened but he said nothing. Oh, right, the gag. She released his tongue.

A loud thump, followed by several lighter thumps, sounded behind her. She tore her eyes away from her enemy. Nikolai convulsed on the floor in a pool of sick. The sight did nothing to allay her nausea. Stomach acid stung the back of her throat and she bolted from the room, fumbling through the large apartment until she found a trash can, and heaved into it. Jelly-legged, she wobbled to an armchair and collapsed, shoving the trash can between her knees. Damn teleportation sickness.

Breathe. Stabilize the boy. Interrogate the prisoner.

Thoughts in order, she cast Stasis on Nikolai and examined the damage. Dealing with poison once it permeated the body was never fun. Always best to prevent it from entering at all. The assassin had been thorough, using multiple poisons to attack a number of Nikolai's systems, while amplifying the effect of each. She'd have to kill and regrow whole swaths of tissue. The blood vessels were so constricted that if she released the Stasis, he'd immediately go into cardiac arrest. She cast a few cleansing spells on Nikolai. A proper healing would take a more concentrated effort. Time enough for that later, after she'd dealt with the threat.

When she was certain the teleportation sickness had passed, Medea rose to confront her attacker. The big baby sobbed from his position on the wall, as though she'd crucified him or something rather than just held him in place. If he thought he had it bad now, he was woefully mistaken.

"Who are you?" she demanded.

"He's dead," the boy wailed. "He's dead and it's all my fault!"

"He's *not* dead, no thanks to you. Who are you?"

"He's . . . he's not dead?" The boy looked behind her, at Nikolai's still form. "Then you have to help him!"

"I *am*. He's in stasis. I'm going to ask you one more time, and then I start removing body parts. Who. Are. You?"

"H-H-Harper." The boy took a shuddering breath. "Nikolai's friend. Surely he's mentioned me? We went to the Academy together."

"Nikolai doesn't discuss his personal life with me. And people don't usually wear illusions to disguise their appearance around friends."

"I always wear it. Ever since the war." He laughed nervously. "Earned me the nickname Goldilocks. Heal Nikolai—he'll tell you."

He seemed sincere, but she'd been wrong before. Maybe he did know Nikolai but found out about the apprenticeship and decided to settle some age-old debt. No, he would have issued the *Servitus aut Mors* if that were the case—unless he found a way around it. Unlikely. Had someone approached him and asked him to lay the trap? She scanned the apartment and several nearby but could sense no magical presence.

"Who put you up to this?" she asked.

"Nikolai did. I told him it was a bad idea, but—"

"You expect me to believe he asked you to give him two vaso-constrictors back to back?"

"Vaso . . . what? It was just an experiment that went horribly wrong, that's all."

Experiment? Nikolai did this to *himself*? But why? What the hell had he gotten himself into now?

"The poison. Where is it?"

"There, in the sacks." The boy glanced over her shoulder, toward the floor. "Though I think one got loose. I'm afraid I was a bit distracted."

She floated a sack over. Careful not to touch it, she peered inside. *Bufo marinus.* The cane toad's toxin was mildly hallucino-genic, and some idiots sought the temporary euphoria despite the risk. Nikolai could be stupid, but she hadn't thought he was *that* stupid.

"Is *this* what you two do on his days off?" she asked, voice rising. "Take hallucinogens for fun? If that's how he plays, he can damn well endure the consequences."

She tossed the bag back in the box and released the boy. He slid to the floor and scrambled to his feet.

"What do you mean?" he asked.

"I mean I'm going to cancel my healing spells and remove Stasis." Just like that, another apprentice gone. She hated to see all that potential go to waste, but she would not prop up someone who seemed so dead set on getting themselves killed. Immortality had to be *earned*.

"No, please don't!" The boy ran in front of Nikolai's body and threw out his arms.

"You really think that's going to stop me?"

"He wasn't doing it for fun. He had a good reason!"

"The same reason every young boy has, I'm sure. What is it this time, 'expanding your mind'?"

"I—I can't tell you."

She crossed her arms and gave him her best scowl, which she'd been assured was quite severe.

Something hardened in the boy's eyes. "I *can't.*"

A true friend. It never ceased to amaze her that men like Nikolai could inspire such loyalty. Couldn't they see through the facade?

"Look, Harold—"

"Harper." The boy shifted and rubbed his arm. "He told me you were bad with names."

"Harper. I believe in *consequences.* While I am perfectly willing to heal my students for any injuries they sustain during training, or as the result of an assassination attempt on me— which I thought this was—I am *not* willing to heal someone senseless enough to poison himself for no good reason. So tell me, what was Nikolai's reason? And before you answer, consider this: if I remove Stasis now, his heart will stop."

The boy shot several nervous glances at Nikolai. His mouth opened and then closed again. She took a step forward, hoping it would spur a decision.

"Wait! He had a clue—'dapper frog'—that was supposed to help solve his, er, problem."

"Dapper frog?" She frowned. What on earth did—*Ohhhhhh.*

She called a pillow from the bed and sat next to Nikolai. "Would you mind getting me a glass of water? This is going to take a while."

Nikolai groaned and opened his eyes. He didn't recognize the bedroom, though the decor was Harper's taste. He sat up and immediately regretted it. The world spun. His fingers clutched the bedsheets as he tried his best not to vomit.

Harper bustled in with a tray and a smile. "You're up!" He set the tray on the nightstand and felt Nikolai's forehead. A mop of dark brown curls adorned his head.

"Why am I in your bedroom? And where's your illusion?"

"I forgot to put it back on, and the other bedroom was, uh, dirty. I had Medea put you in here. Are you well enough for soup?" Harper uncovered a white bowl and steam billowed forth, carrying the scent of beef and vegetables.

Nikolai clutched his head. "Medea was here?"

"She burst in just before you collapsed. It was awful. You were twitching all over, then you went rigid and stopped. If it hadn't been for her, I don't know what would have happened. Why didn't you tell me she had wards on you?" Harper dipped a spoon into the broth, carefully blew on it, and raised it to Nikolai's mouth.

Nikolai waved the spoon away. "Because I didn't know. What kind of wards?" Medea had to be using them to track his movements. So that's how she knew he'd been nosing around the cave.

"She didn't tell you? They let her know if your health gets low. She thought I'd poisoned you. When she found out what we'd been doing—"

"You told her?!"

Harper absently rubbed his arm. "I didn't have much choice. She was furious. Almost stopped healing you. Oh, before I forget." He reached into his jacket and withdrew a folded sheet of paper. "This is for you."

Nikolai took the letter—a lecture of course. Medea railed against him for his lack of judgment, and in particular for conducting the experiment without a healer—*"If you'd* bothered *to learn healing spells, it wouldn't be an issue . . ."* He skimmed the rest. It was more of the same. Learn healing, lack of foresight, blah blah. He crumpled the paper and threw it into the wastebasket.

Harper shook his head. "I have to say, from talking to Medea,

I don't think she's the one who cursed you. She seemed rather concerned, at least until she found out you were licking toads."

Poor Harper, always so trusting and gullible. "Of course she seemed concerned. She's not done draining me, or whatever it is she's doing. That's why she's got wards tracking my health. Probably to make sure she doesn't finish the job too fast."

"I don't know, Nikolai . . ."

"You don't know her like I do. Look, I didn't want to tell you this before, because you'd only worry, but the woman has a dungeon full of people."

"What?"

"I know she seems reasonable, but she's got it in for me, like she's had for every other apprentice."

Harper looked at him imploringly and scooted closer. "Then leave. We can figure out the curse once you're safe."

"You really think that's going to stop Medea? She tracked me here, didn't she? The only way for me to best her is to get rid of this curse. Then I'll have a fighting chance. I managed to make an invulnerability potion—that should give me an edge in a fight— and I've got someone looking into where she hides her magic."

Harper didn't look convinced. "How can she be hiding magic?"

"I don't know, but she does things with magic that no one else can. There's a cave on her island, and I can *feel* something back there, something powerful, but I can't get to it. When I tried, the curse stopped me, and afterward, Medea blocked off the cave."

"Maybe she just didn't want you nosing around."

"She's hiding something." Just like Petrov. Two years, and the bastard had a room full of black magic hidden in the shop the whole time. He would not be denied again.

Harper tugged one of his dark curls down his forehead. "Everyone's hiding something."

"Are you going to go back to blond?"

"I have to. It's my stage look." Harper shrugged, trying to make it seem like no big deal, but Nikolai knew the truth—he was terrified. "It's really no different than makeup. But maybe, around friends, I could start taking it off." He shot Nikolai a pleading glance.

"You can always be yourself around me."

Harper sighed and stared at his lap. "I know. Even after all these years . . ." He shook his head and closed his eyes, then ran his hands over his hair. The brown curls disappeared, replaced with flaxen gold. When his eyes opened, they were blue again. "I feel safer like this. I know I shouldn't have to hide, but . . ." He took a shuddering breath.

Nikolai leaned forward and placed a hand on Harper's shoulder. "You're safe now. And you know if anyone messes with you, you can come to me, right? Nazis or bad critics, I'll kill anyone who threatens you."

Harper chuckled, thinking it a jest.

"I do have a favor to ask." Nikolai reached for the bowl of stew and took a bite. Heavenly. "Did you tell Medea about the dapper frog?"

Guilt was written all over Harper's face. "I'm sorry, Nikolai, I had to."

"It's fine. Can you let me see it?"

Harper winced. "You're not going to like how you look."

"Just visualize it, please. I can go from there."

As soon as Harper nodded, Nikolai plunged into his mind. Such an odd thing, that someone would allow him access so. Didn't Harper realize how vulnerable it made him? The thought of what Nikolai could do made him giddy. But Harper was a friend, he would stick with what he needed to know.

Medea glared at Harper, and he could sense his friend's residual fear at the encounter. Harper glanced behind him, treating Nikolai to a view of his own body splayed in a puddle of vomit.

"Dapper frog?" said Medea. Her expressions were fleeting, but plain as day—confusion, comprehension, then an almost imperceptible nod of the chin. Yoxtl's vague clue made sense to her. He was on the right track.

"Thank you, Harper."

"What did you find?"

"The clue is real. It's just not a literal frog."

Harper pursed his lips. "Maybe it's a plant. Know any botanists?"

Nikolai smiled. "As a matter of fact, I do."

33

CONFRONTATIONS

Nikolai waited until he was deep in the woods beside Herr Bergmann's cottage before taking his frustrations out on a nearby tree, splintering the bark with Lance until the trunk was scarred with gashes. He itched to burn the forest to the ground. The irony wasn't lost on him.

How many trees had he torched in the jungle after Medea deserted him that day? All of them? Surely some must be left.

He had approached Bergmann about plants with names or properties similar to "dapper frog," which he claimed he'd found in a badly translated scroll. Bergmann rose to the challenge, enthusiastically digging through his collection of books until he found a species that matched. Frog's Fancy—a bromeliad, so-named for the frogs that laid their eggs in the water that collected between the leaves. An incredibly rare plant, slow growing and only known to occur in one small area of Mexico.

And Nikolai had torched them all.

Medea had brought him right to the plants, spent a full day priming his frustration, then intentionally deserted him, knowing full well how he'd react. Manipulating someone into destroying their own salvation—he had to hand it to her, it was the kind of poetic move he'd make against an enemy.

Nikolai stormed back to the gateway, and from there, to the temple. Finding the path they'd taken to the trees was difficult. The undead creature he'd summoned had destroyed much of the surrounding jungle. It took some time to locate the path Medea had cut through the overgrowth, and the wilderness was already attempting to reclaim the space. Using telekinesis, he hacked his way through the dense growth, scoring bark as he went to mark the way.

Hours later, he arrived at the burned cluster of trees. Rain had put out the fires he'd started, but not soon enough. Charred frog corpses littered the ashy ground. While most of the trees still stood, his salvation, the Frog's Fancy, had been all but obliterated. In total, he found four plants on trees outside the burn area. With utmost care, he took one leaf from each plant before casting Protection on them, not knowing if a spell designed for humans would keep the plants safe. He'd have to research other spells and wards to ensure the area was protected.

Back in the laboratory, he searched the counter for the Frog's Fancy leaves he'd collected on his trip with Medea. That had been his first trip to a garden, and the leaves were buried beneath endless clippings from subsequent excursions. Four leaves from today; thirty-two from his first trip. Spread out like this, it seemed a decent amount, but there was no telling how fast he'd go through them. They needed to be rationed with utmost care.

He carefully wrapped the leaves in cloth and stowed them in his pouch.

Medea stared at the pile of books—books she'd left out in the hope that Nikolai would have the sense to look through them. A pen spun in place on the table, rhythmically slowing down and speeding up with nudges of magic. Tino scampered across the table, dodged the pen, and climbed the stack of books.

"What am I going to do?" She asked the gecko, not really expecting an answer. He wasn't the best conversationalist. His creators had been chatty enough without a familiar adding to the din. Still, it felt good to express her frustration to someone.

"I have to get through to him somehow. Healing is possibly the most important school of magic there is. Why can't he see that? I thought the finger thing would force him to at least *look* in this section, but I don't think he did, given what I saw in London. His friend said he'd made potions in case anything went wrong. Potions!" The pen pinwheeled off the table.

Tino stared at her blankly.

She leaned back and summoned the pen to her fingers, twirling it between them.

Nikolai was competitive. Could she use that? Tell him healing had been one of Thomas' specialties? Would that make him take the school more seriously? She frowned. No, he'd probably argue that Thomas would've been more powerful if he'd studied something else.

Why were people so unreasonable? Present them with data and they dug in their heels and refused to budge. It made no damned sense. Nikolai operated under the faulty assumption that certain magical schools were more powerful than others, specifically in combat. If she proved that wasn't the case, would he listen? Or would it only make him more resistant?

The pen in her hands twirled faster. Like so many young boys, Nikolai was obsessed with flashy, high-damage things. Even if she restricted herself to healing spells during sparring and he saw how hard it was to kill an opponent who could negate any injury, he'd probably take it as a challenge to learn "better" offensive magic. He'd said it himself that first day in the library—the best defense was a good offense.

The only way to get through to him would be to use healing magic offensively.

Medea sat up and rested her chin on her hands. Not just offensively. She'd have to be careful not to use any spells that could be interpreted as damage, not healing. And she'd have to hurt him— nothing that would prevent him from continuing training, but something that would serve as a permanent reminder of the lesson. Nikolai might not like it, but it was the only way. He'd thank her in the long run.

Nikolai watched the ocean churn below as a salty breeze toyed with his hair. Yoxtl stood beside him, fur eerily still despite the wind.

"Well?" he asked the spirit. "Did you find anything?"

"I approached the other spirits, but unfortunately, they know I'm helping you and refused to talk."

"Why?"

"They're loyal to Medea. Maybe they hope to obtain her soul one day, or she feeds them magic. I don't know. We spirits, we usually don't help humans unless there's something in it for us."

Good to know. If nothing else, he could count on Yoxtl to be pragmatic. What were the spirits hiding? They desired one thing, souls, and there was only one way to get them on the island. Yoxtl had shown surprise at the strength of Medea's soul, even taking age into account. She must have made a bargain—her apprentices' souls in exchange for power, possibly even immortality.

But why train the apprentices first? Why train them at all? Was it merely to maintain the facade? Was that why she chose dark apprentices, so she could claim they'd attacked her and she'd killed them in self-defense?

He turned to Yoxtl. "You said souls get more powerful with age. What else increases their potency?"

"Casting magic. The more you use it, the more powerful you become. Why?"

"Just curious."

That's why she trained apprentices first, why she insisted they perform monotonous exercises like boiling water, and why she'd gotten so upset when he hadn't complied. Everything she did was to increase the value of their souls before making the sacrifice. She couldn't risk students fighting back, so she shunted them into Useless magical schools and cursed them to ensure they couldn't learn too much on their own.

Not a bad bargain. After he killed her, he'd have to make the same deal with the spirits.

"Incoming," said Yoxtl, before darting over the cliff edge and winking out of sight.

Nikolai turned to see Medea making her way toward him, her frown more pronounced than usual. He plastered a benevolent smile on his face.

"We need to talk," Medea said when she reached him. "Walk with me."

That didn't bode well. Did she know what he'd been discussing with Yoxtl? Fuck. She probably had a ward for that too. He followed her back to the meadow where they usually sparred. Once there, she sighed and pinched the bridge of her nose.

"When you accepted this apprenticeship, you told me you wanted to be powerful, immortal, the best. I vowed I would do everything I could to make you stronger—"

And now he knew why. Did the spirits give her a deadline? Was that why she was perpetually frustrated?

"—and yet I have consistently failed in one regard." Medea took a deep breath before continuing. "You still do not understand the necessity of healing magic. You continue to rely on potions for what you should be doing on your own. You will never become truly great if you do not learn this. It is no mistake that my best apprentice was a grand master in healing."

Sneaky bitch. She played on his competitiveness toward Thomas, as if he wouldn't see right through her.

"Oh?" he said with disinterest.

Her expression faltered. "Yes. He was—I mean . . ."

"You know what *I* think?" He stalked around her slight frame. Her sudden lack of confidence made her seem even shorter. "I think he's only your 'best' because he toed the line and did whatever you said. That's why he lasted so long. You couldn't bear to part with an apprentice who was your best *footstool*."

She spun to keep him in her sights. "I—what? No!" The frantic note in her voice was like blood in the water.

"You couldn't stand to kill your favorite pet. Is that why he left? He found out what you'd done to the others?" Before he realized what he was doing, he dove into Medea's mind, surprised to find it completely unguarded.

Compared to most memories he'd seen, Medea's was strikingly devoid of detail. She gripped the back of a chair, but he couldn't tell where she was or even what she was wearing, so focused was she on the texture of the wood beneath her fingers—and the emotion.

The emotion! A tidal wave of *feelings* undulated through the memory.

Behind her stood a man. Nikolai couldn't see him, only feel his presence. The man's warm breath on Medea's neck sent a shiver down her spine.

"You lied to me." The sultry voice made her feel too many things at once.

"Thomas, I . . ." Her grip on the chair tightened. She couldn't fly apart, not now.

"You *lied*!"

"I didn't!" There was a plea in her voice.

"A lie by omission is still a lie," he spat.

Her words fled before a storm of emotions. Thomas had every right to be angry. She'd hoped he would get over it, move on, but even gifting him with immortality hadn't curbed his desire. Blood welled in her mouth as she bit the inside of her lip. The pain of all these feelings had to be dulled somehow—

Nikolai slammed flat on his back. Medea loomed above, face a mask of pure loathing.

"How *dare* you!"

The grass rose and curved toward him, blades hardening into tiny wooden spikes. Her fury was the least of his concerns. What he'd seen—what she'd *felt* . . . Her emotions were muddled, but he could pick them apart clinically, as he'd done with so many others, and one particular emotion was clear—love. She was in love with the bastard.

Nikolai pierced her with his gaze. "You fucked Thomas."

Her eyes widened and she shrank from the words.

He necrotized the grass and stood. "A little biased of you to call your lover your 'best apprentice.' And here I thought you didn't like men." He tsked. "But it's about control, isn't it? He was the model apprentice, doing *everything* you said."

She blanched. "I would never . . . with a student. It's—it's a conflict of interest."

He laughed. "So *that's* why he was with you for seventeen years. If I show you how good I am in bed, will you make me immortal too?"

She slapped him. "You forget yourself!"

"What did you lie to him about? He wanted something from

you. What was it?" She'd given him immortality. What else could he want? What else was there?

"None of your damn business!"

"It's my business if it affects my health. You think I don't know what happens to your other apprentices?"

Her body trembled. "You have no idea what you're talking about."

"Don't I? Why did you really come out here, Medea, because it sure as hell wasn't to teach me healing spells."

"As a matter of fact, it was!" Some of the fight came back into her eyes. "And if you *ever* attempt to read my mind again, I will kill you. Do you understand?" She glared up at him.

"You're the one who left your mind unguarded." He laughed. "I thought you'd at least have *some* protection."

"I do! I just . . . forgot to recast the spell after I teleported to save you, you *ungrateful shit*."

"You think I can't understand when you insult me in Latin?"

"Shut up. Just shut up! We are going to spar. I am going to use healing spells. You can use anything you like. Even your wand—don't think I don't know you have it up your sleeve."

The bitch had just doomed herself and didn't realize it. "Anything I like?"

"Yes."

"And you're only going to use healing spells? No shields? What do I get if I win?"

Medea stepped the standard dueling distance away and spun to face him. "No shields, and you won't win."

"Then you won't mind placing a wager. If I win, you teach me immortality."

"Wagers are stupid, but fine. I accept. If I win, you commit to becoming a master healer."

"Done." This was going to be easy. What was she going to do, lob bandages at him? And besides, he'd rattled the hell out of her.

She'd be unfocused and sloppy. He called forth his wand, then grinned maliciously and withdrew the speed dagger from his pouch, wagging it to be sure she saw it. Let her try to block spells now.

"You *did* say I could use anything," he crooned.

"I did. It won't help. In fact, it will illustrate my point better, so thank you."

Yeah, right. "Ready whenever you are, *Master*." He made an overly theatrical bow.

"Begin."

"LanceaLanceaLanceaLancea."

The lancing spells fired from his wand like a Gatling gun, so fast he scarcely made out the ripples in the air before they rammed into Medea with a gong.

"You shielded!" he accused her.

"I didn't."

"I heard it!"

"I blocked."

"Bullshit!" he spat.

"What did I tell you, the first day we met? It's been what? Nearly a year, and still you cast in the slowest way possible." She crossed her arms and leaned forward. *"Stop using incantations."*

He clenched his jaw and aimed his wand again. He didn't speak but sent a litany of spells winging toward her—Lance, Bleed, Fear, Lightning, Fireball. He soon realized that although the spells cast instantaneously, they didn't move through the air with any greater speed. Medea easily redirected Lightning and deflected Fireball with a gust of wind. Bleed and Fear were caught in hand but seemed to have no effect.

Lance though, Lance she couldn't block completely in time. A red welt bloomed on her arm before it healed.

He began his onslaught anew, casting Lance only. Her body reddened as the spells were blocked, but only just in time. One

broke through, punching out a section of flesh from her arm.
Medea casually made a motion around the limb and a blueish,
water-like substance enveloped it. The arm steamed and the flesh
started to heal.

He aimed for her torso. Not head—not yet. Another Lance
took her in the abdomen. The bleeding stopped almost immediately as the flesh knitted itself closed. How did she have the raw
materials for such rapid repairs?

He cast Amputate at her neck and foot. She blocked the first,
but the second sliced her foot clean off. Blood gushed from the
stump. A moment later it stopped. The severed foot flew to the
stump and reattached itself.

"Do you see it yet, dear apprentice? The value of this?"

Nothing Nikolai did seemed to have a permanent effect. Soon
he felt the strain of mana fatigue. He took a potion and renewed
his assault through gritted teeth.

"I'll concede that healing is Useful," he said. "I don't want to
specialize in it. If you'd bothered to teach me any dark magic,
you'd be dead by now."

"You are mistaken, and it will be to your detriment."

Belatedly, he saw the change that had taken place in her since
the start of the duel. The uncertainty, the fragility, the desperation
—all had vanished, as though a switch had flipped. He'd been
hoping to catch her off balance, but only the master duelist stood
before him now.

Lance, Bleed, Amputate, Fear. Nothing worked. He wasn't
losing, but he wasn't winning either.

"Healing magic may keep you alive, but waiting for someone
to run out of mana is no way to fight. I want to *kill*. It's not like
you can use healing to defeat anyone!"

"I was waiting for you to say that." Her voice was resigned,
but a hint of a smile twisted the corner of her mouth. "I am sorry,
but if you don't learn this, I have failed as your instructor."

Three spells winged toward him. They bypassed his shield with a whisper and lightly touched his chest. There was no pain, only warmth, like a lover's caress. His limbs began to swell.

"You said you'd only cast healing spells."

"Those *were* healing spells."

His skin stretched painfully tight and his head filled with cotton. Agony radiated from his chest as the buttons on his shirt popped off and the wand slipped from his fingers, now swollen sausages.

"I am sorry it came to this." Medea's voice was close, but he couldn't make her out, only shadows. Had she blinded him too? "I hope that in time you will see the necessity of it."

A spell tickled his face and it became hard to breathe. He tried to gasp and felt his lips suck against his teeth without relief. Nikolai clawed uselessly at his mouth, only to discover it was no longer there.

He lashed out with his magic. The world darkened and he couldn't think beyond the burning in his lungs. He collapsed to the ground, thrashing.

Medea's voice, right next to his ear. "In the hands of a master, any spell can be dangerous."

Pain stabbed his neck, then all was black.

34

CONSEQUENCES

Nikolai jerked upright to the familiar trappings of his room. His hand moved instinctively to the puncture wound on his neck but encountered smooth skin. Medea had healed him. Nevertheless, something felt off. He glanced at his body—no longer swollen. Nikolai touched his face and bumped into something foreign. He tugged at it. A straw? He rubbed his hand over his mouth and jerked back from the wrongness.

No no no. He rushed to the mirror and stared in horror. NO. NO NO NO NO FUCK NO.

A mockery of scar tissue marred his once-handsome face. Instead of a nose, he had a bulbous protrusion without nostrils. His mouth was simply gone, as if someone had smeared clay over the area and left it to dry. A tiny incision had been made in the center for the straw.

His breath quickened, whistling in and out. Spots appeared before his eyes and he gripped the desk when lightheadedness threatened to topple him.

Relax. He had to relax. It would be fine. Medea was just trying to make a point, that was all. She'd always healed his scars before. He might be ugly for a week or two, but she would fix it. Breathe. Nice and steady. Okay, good.

He brought the straw back to his mouth, trembling hands defying every attempt to reinsert it into the hole. The hole. God, he had a hole for a mouth. Don't think about it. Breathe. Relax. It wouldn't do to hyperventilate now.

When he finally got the straw back into place, he noticed the desk contents—his wand, a letter, and about twenty bottles. He picked up the letter.

Dear apprentice,

As per our sparring wager, I would like you to familiarize yourself with the healing section of the library. I expect a full summary of the spells I used to heal myself, as well as the two I used against you. With this knowledge, you should be able to return your face to a reasonable state of normalcy.

Best wishes,
Medea

P.S. Please enjoy the meals I've prepared for you. They can be found in bottles on your desk. Wash them and return them to the kitchen when you are done.

He punched the wall beside the mirror. Three quick jabs until his fists came away bloody. Reasonable state of normalcy? What the fuck did that mean? Did she think this was some kind of joke? That his face was inconsequential? He'd show her. Lips and nose were simple compared to a finger. He'd fix his face, then he'd fix her.

He stormed through the common area and flung open the library door. If he hadn't needed the contents of the healing section, he'd have been tempted to torch them. The master grimoire, once so stingy with its answers, filled pages upon pages when he asked it for facial reconstruction texts.

Ignoring Medea's rule about keeping books in the library, he brought the most promising book back to his room and propped it up below the mirror. From his desk he withdrew a bottle of vodka and a dagger. Not the speed dagger—for this, precision was required.

The scar tissue had to be removed before he could do anything, but where did it end and his true countenance begin? He lifted the vodka to his face, irritably shifting the straw into position, and took a drink. The straw flew from his mouth as he began to sputter and cough. His cough pushed painfully at his cheeks, unable to escape through the tiny slit she'd left him. He leaned hard against the chair until the coughing fit ceased.

His mouth obviously needed to be dealt with first. He tried to part his lips, stretching them as far as the scar tissue would allow. Here went nothing.

He inserted the blade of the dagger into the hole in his face and drew it to the right. Blood spewed down his chin and chest. Without pausing, he cut again in the opposite direction until there was a crooked, gaping slash.

He took a swig of vodka and cursed as it dribbled from his makeshift mouth. He spat out blood, heedless of where it landed, and looked into the mirror. Before his eyes, the tissue began to knit itself together at the cut.

"No no no omf!"

His mouth sealed over, only this time there was no slit for breathing. He stabbed a new hole in his face and inserted his finger to keep the hole open. The skin grew back, but it didn't stop at his finger. Instead it fused, binding finger and face together.

Cut cut cut and his finger was free. Even as his mouth knit

itself shut again, he stared in horror at his finger, which spawned more tissue of its own. This shit *spread*?

He slammed his palm onto the desk and hacked at his finger, but the dagger wasn't meant to slice through bone. He bolted through the common room, lungs screaming for air, and grabbed a cleaver in the kitchen. One good hack and his finger was off. The wound hurt like hell, but it stayed open, which meant he could regrow it. Another stab to his face allowed him to breathe, but it wouldn't last long. What the fucking hell kind of spell was this?

The straw had worked, but his finger hadn't. Maybe the spell only interacted with skin. He grabbed a wooden spoon. No— wood used to be living, and the last thing he needed was a fucking plant fused and growing from his face. He tossed the wooden spoon and grabbed a metal one, inserting the handle into the hole.

There was no mirror in the kitchen, but the back of a metal pot served well enough. The skin regrew until it had closed around the spoon handle, then stopped. Tentatively, he removed the spoon, and this time the hole remained open. Okay, so cuts caused rapid regrowth that could only be stopped by an inorganic barrier.

He tried again, this time cutting a wide slit and then inserting a saucer. When the process looked complete, he carefully tugged the saucer free and scrutinized his work. It wasn't a proper mouth. There were no lips, no clear delineation of anything, but at least it remained open. He repeated the process to create makeshift nostrils, and he could finally breathe easily.

The rest of the day was slow and painful. Piece by agonizing piece, he sliced off bits of tissue and attempted to block the regrowth. He was able to get his nose back to a reasonable size, but there was no definition to it, nor to his chin, or anywhere else. If anything, his clumsy attempts to fix things only spread the spell further across his face. Taking a healing potion made the regrowth faster. No matter what he did, he could not call back his hand-some face.

He needed Medea. No doubt she wanted him to kiss her ass, apologize profusely for doubting her skill, and beg for forgiveness. Fine. Whatever it took to get his face back.

Knocking on Medea's door was easy. Not slamming his fist against the wood—*that* was difficult.

"Wait at the bottom of the stairs," said a voice through the door. He descended the narrow staircase and watched Medea's door with fire in his eyes.

———

Medea hid in her room. Doors had been opening and closing downstairs all day, but she dared not go down. Nikolai would be angry at what she'd done, and it was best to give him space. That's what people needed when they were emotional—space. She'd been tempted to leave the island but had stayed on the offchance he might need help finding something in the library. The healing section, after all, was immense.

Still, she was no fool—the boy had a temper. Last night she'd placed wards all over the house to alert her if he attempted to destroy her possessions. So far, all had been quiet. Maybe he was taking it better than she thought. Then again, he probably hadn't realized yet how hard the task would be.

Without fleshweaving, a true reconstruction would take years of study. The practical form would be easy enough to fix, but the fine tuning, the detail which made the human face so distinct to other humans—that would be much harder to replicate.

Long ago, she had a client seeking a similar reconstruction. The man was adept at healing and had successfully removed battle scars all over his body, but his face remained a problem. The closer he got to perfection, the worse people reacted. They thought him a changeling or some other malicious creature in disguise, and he was under constant attack. Prior to seeking her help, he'd scarred his face a second time in an effort to look more human. Perfect might be the enemy of good, but for faces, the opposite appeared to be true.

The stairs creaked and she braced herself for a dramatic pummeling on the door, but he knocked politely, putting her at ease. She rose and asked him to wait downstairs. Apprentices were always trying to catch a glimpse of her room for some reason. After a moment, she exited and peered over the landing, hoping to see progress, however slight.

Nikolai had never looked this slovenly, not even in the early days when he was in the throes of the curse. His hair stuck up at odd angles and his shirt was partially untucked. Dried blood streaked his chin and chest, and there was a trail of it between his room and the kitchen. A wide gash crossed his face. Good. He'd figured out how to enlarge the opening and keep it from filling in.

"Yes?" she said. Maybe he needed help finding a book.

"You —in. I can't do this —y —ysel—."

Oh dear. She hadn't counted on that. The lack of lips made him impossible to understand. Maybe it would be easier if she were closer.

"I can't understand you. Hold on, I'll come down." She stopped two steps from the bottom so they were roughly the same height. "Again."

Nikolai repeated himself, but the results were no better. This was untenable.

"I'm going to restore some of the tissue you removed. Try not to cut it off again." She weaved the flesh back into place—not pretty, but functional lips.

His hand leapt to his face. Excitement turned to disappointment as he explored her work. "I said, you win. I can't do this by myself. Can you please fix my face now?" There was polite deference in his tone.

"I thought I made myself clear in the letter. You are to fix this yourself. It's the only way you'll learn."

"I've learned. You're better than me and healing magic is necessary. I understand now."

She sighed. "No, you don't." Half a day and already he'd given up. "Nikolai, this is something you must learn to fix yourself. If you cannot, then the scars will serve as a reminder—"

"I don't need a fucking reminder. I need my *face*." The sudden vitriol was startling. His next words came out clipped. "People judge based on looks. I can't go through life looking like *this*."

"You can always craft an illusion in the meantime. No one would know."

"Fuck illusions!" he spat. "*I'd* know! You think I want to see this shit every time I look in the mirror?"

So stop looking in mirrors, she wanted to say, but that would have been rude and he was already on edge. As difficult as his face was to read, there was no mistaking the magic building inside him. He was losing control. Such a thing was more common in teenagers who lacked a firm grasp of their magic. In so many ways, he was still just a boy. What could she say to reassure him?

"I'm sure your personality can more than make up for—"

"ARE YOU FUCKING KIDDING ME?"

Trying to act the friend was only making things worse. Very well, she'd keep things professional. She straightened herself. "I have already set you a task. Do not ask me to help you with this again. I swear this to you—I will never remove your scars, not while they serve to—"

The dreaded words, so often spoken by strangers, erupted from Nikolai's mouth. "I challenge you to a *Servi*—"

Before he could finish, she closed off his throat and launched herself at him with a hiss. "Shut your mouth! Shut your mouth, you stupid boy!"

Nikolai's eyes widened. His mouth worked convulsively, trying to issue the challenge at the behest of her spell. Realization passed over his face, and the eyes that locked on to hers burned. His wand hand reflexively twitched in a gesture that would have called the wand from its holster, had it been there. The other hand rested on his hip pouch.

If only she could let him pass out from lack of oxygen and hide in her room, she could pretend this whole conversation never happened, but then their working relationship would be over. She couldn't lose another apprentice. Not this one. He was too valuable, magic like she hadn't seen in centuries. But if he was unteachable, if he wanted to kill her, then there was nothing to be done.

Nikolai made no move to attack, but there was no mistaking the look he gave her, even as his face turned crimson from lack of air. Good, he still had that much control. He was just angry. Murderously angry, but then she *had* poked him in a soft spot, not realizing how deep his desire to be handsome ran. She bit the inside of her cheek and sealed off Nikolai's mouth before opening his throat.

She couldn't stay now. Her presence was only making things worse and she couldn't risk triggering a *Servitus aut Mors* challenge.

"You need time to cool down. You *can* fix this yourself. Everything you need is in the library. Will it take time? Certainly. But I have the utmost confidence in your abilities." She tried to give him an encouraging smile. "I will give you two weeks here alone. Then I'll come and check up on you, see if you have any questions. How's that?"

The look he gave her wasn't encouraging, but he nodded.

35

PRIORITIES

"Greetings, Mr. Lewis," said the attendant. "How was the show?"

"Excellent as always," said Harper, beaming as he stepped into the lift.

"And will your manager be joining you for a business meeting tonight?"

"I'm afraid not. Seems to have taken ill, poor chap. I'm sure it's just something he ate."

Jonathan was sick through both shows. Harper hoped it wasn't anything serious. He'd tried to insist on bringing Jonathan home, but the man wouldn't hear of it. Too stoic for his own good. One of these days he'd convince Jonathan to move in with him. There was nothing suspicious about having a flatmate in a two-bedroom place.

"Your floor, Mr. Lewis."

Harper thanked the lift attendant and stepped out. His mood faltered as he rounded the corner and caught sight of his neighbor.

"Greetings, Mrs. Perkins." He nodded and forced a smile.

The old woman glared at him and closed her door with a snap. Last week she'd grilled him over his "parade of male visitors," as

Nikolai had called it. As much as he hated to deny his friends a
safe place to rendezvous, he might have to.

Maybe Nikolai could have a chat with her. Mrs. Perkins liked
him, though he showed up every other week with a new woman
on his arm. Harper shook his head at that.

He was so preoccupied, he almost missed the tie on the doorknob. The place was dark and no noise came from the spare
bedroom. Had his guests left and forgotten to remove the tie?

"I need a powerful illusion."

Harper nearly jumped out of his skin. The voice came from
the shadows—familiar, but strangely distorted. Pale light filtered
in through the shutters. He could just make out a figure in one of
his chairs.

"Wh-who's there?" Harper tugged the lamp chain next to the
door, but it didn't come on.

"Nikolai."

"Nikolai? Why on earth are you sitting in the dark?"

"I didn't want you to see me—yet."

Harper laughed nervously. "*I'm* supposed to be the dramatic
one, remember? What's going on? Why don't you want me to see
you? And since when do you want anything to do with illusions?"

"I need to disguise something. Glamor won't do. It needs to
be strong enough to fool all but the most powerful Magi."

Harper approached the chair. "Sure. Anything you need. Can I
ask what it's for?"

In answer, the lamp next to the chair sprang to life.

Harper gasped. Nikolai's nose was misshapen, the skin on his
face an angry red. His lips, once so enticing, were a mockery, as if
a child had worked in clay to create something they thought
passed for realistic. Nikolai gazed at him levelly, daring him to
voice his opinion.

"Oh, my goodness! Nikolai, what *happened* to you?"

Cold fury tinged Nikolai's voice. "Medea decided to punish

me. It's not something I can fix." He gestured to his face. "This was the best I could do."

That was his attempt to *fix* it?

"Nikolai, this can't go on. No apprenticeship is worth what she's doing to you."

"I'm dealing with it."

Harper wanted to ask how, but Nikolai cut him off.

"I need your help. Can you hide my face?"

Harper knelt beside the chair, examining the wreckage. "Can I touch it?"

"You can do whatever it takes to fix this mess." His friend had never sounded so bitter.

"Okay, okay." Harper traced the outline of scar tissue, turning Nikolai's face this way and that. The skin was raised—definitely noticeable to the touch, even if it was concealed.

He took a breath to ask the delicate question. "This illusion—I'm assuming you want it to feel real? For kissing, and er . . ."

Nikolai's face blanched. "Yes. Can you do that?"

"You came to the best for a reason!" Harper flashed his most confident smile, even as his stomach tied itself in knots. The face wasn't some extraneous body part like a toe or arm. People paid attention to it.

An invasive tickle ran up the base of Harper's skull, and Nikolai sagged in the chair. "You don't think you can do it."

"I didn't say that."

"You were thinking it. Sorry for prying. I had to know. If you can't fix this, I don't know what I'll—"

"Hey!" Harper tugged Nikolai's chin to face him. "If anyone can fix it, I can. Have a little faith in me."

They worked for hours, Harper testing out different strategies and Nikolai applying them. His friend grew frustrated at the slow pace. Nikolai lacked even a basic understanding of illusion, owing to his staunch refusal to learn it at the Academy. He wanted an illusion that plastered a sense of handsomeness on his face. Harper patiently explained it wouldn't work for day-to-day interactions. Beauty was subjective. What if the illusion showed someone two different faces on two different days? The illusion had to be objective and stable.

Harper worked to help Nikolai create an image of his old face, imposing it over the scarred area. People's perspective of their own appearance was rarely accurate. Nikolai dipped in and out of Harper's mind, looking at his face through Harper's eyes, modifying the image until it was perfect.

"Now remember," Harper warned his friend, "you have to work to maintain the illusion. Practice daily. Hold it as long as you can. It doesn't take much mana to maintain, but make sure you keep some in reserve. If you get too distracted, it may drop."

Nikolai rubbed absently at his face while staring into the hallway mirror. "It still feels wrong."

"That's because you cast the illusion and know the truth of what it hides." Harper ran a finger over Nikolai's lips. "Feels fine to me."

"There's only one way to make sure."

Without warning, Nikolai's hand shot out and pulled Harper's face to his, their bodies pressing together. Nikolai's kiss was rough and hungry. Better than he'd ever imagined. Throughout their Academy years, he'd had a bit of a crush on his friend, but Nikolai wasn't like him, and Harper had pushed past it. No sense pursuing someone who didn't feel the same way. The kiss was gasoline on a fire, igniting all his old passions.

When at last Nikolai pulled away, Harper was left breathless. He sagged against the wall.

Nikolai lounged next to him with a devilish grin, sexier than any man had a right to be. "How did it feel? Real enough?"

Did he know how he set Harper's body afire? Surely not, or he would never have done that.

"I'm sorry, Nikolai. I wasn't paying attention."

Nikolai laughed. "Excellent! As long as you felt nothing amiss. Of course, we could try again to be sure . . ." He reached a hand behind Harper's head.

God, he wanted it, but Nikolai wasn't like that, and anyway he was with Jonathan. "No, no. That's quite alright." Harper tried to inch away.

Nikolai's eyes followed him greedily. What was he—

"What's going on?"

Jonathan stood in the hallway. Though he was pale and trembling from his illness, his bright eyes were full of hurt.

Heat rose in Harper's cheeks. "Jonathan, this isn't what it looks like—"

Nikolai swept toward Jonathan and clasped his hand. "Jonathan! So good to finally meet you! You handle Harper's mundane affairs, is that right?" Nikolai glanced over his shoulder at Harper, the question clear.

"That's right," said Harper. Jonathan was Mundane, and though they were dating, he was unaware that Harper's shows involved real magic.

"Harper was just helping me with a little problem," Nikolai continued. "Tell me, does my mouth feel real?" He grabbed Jonathan's hand and brought it up to his face. What was he doing? Playing the mentally unbalanced friend angle?

"What?" asked Jonathan, confused by Nikolai's bizarre behavior.

"My mouth, does it feel real?" Jonathan tried to tug his hand free, but Nikolai held it fast, rubbing it over his lips. "We've only just fixed it. I'd kiss you too, only I can smell vomit on your breath and we hardly know each other."

Jonathan shot Harper a pleading glance.

"Uh, Nikolai, Jonathan has been sick all evening. I think he needs to lie down and rest. Maybe you should be going."

"Certainly. My apologies." Nikolai released Jonathan, who fled to Harper's side. "Pleasure to meet you, Jonathan. Oh, and Harper—I'll take care of that neighbor on my way out." He winked and was gone.

Nikolai knocked on Mrs. Perkins' door. Already the high he'd gotten with Harper was fading. Watching the conflicting emotions play across his friend's face was exactly what he'd needed. Scarred and hideous he might be, he could still make people desire him with hopeless abandon. He would have liked to play longer, winding Harper's longing and loyalty even tighter, but Jonathan's arrival had spoiled the game.

Unlike some of Harper's previous lovers, Jonathan didn't have enough backbone to pose a threat to his relationship with Nikolai. Harper seemed enamored with the man, worrying about him all night while trying not to burden Nikolai with his own problems. Not wanting to destroy his friend's budding relationship, Nikolai had salvaged the situation as best he could. Tonight they'd laugh over Harper's strange old classmate and later, when they did other things, Harper would taste Nikolai while kissing Jonathan.

A bent old woman with grey curls answered the door. Her face announced her displeasure at the late call but brightened when she saw who it was. The illusion was holding.

"Good evening, Mrs. Perkins. I wonder if I could come in and trouble you for a moment?" The nosy woman had intruded on Harper's mind all night. *This* was a problem he could solve.

"Oh, yes. Please come in, young man."

Mrs. Perkins led him into the sitting room. The place stank of mothballs and cat. Several felines lounged on the sofa. She shooed them away and asked him to sit.

"I can't stay long, Mrs. Perkins. I just needed to have a quick word."

"What is it? It's not about that filthy man down on the end, is it?"

"*Harper*, and yes."

"Do you know what he does in there? Well, I do!" She jabbed her finger toward the wall bordering the hallway. "Men coming and going at all hours. He says they're in show biz, like him, but I know what's really going on. It's unnatural!"

He raised an eyebrow. "As opposed to what *I* do in there?"

"You?" She blushed. "Oh, well—you're a strapping young man. It's quite normal for young men to . . . but then of course I can't say the same for the girls you're with . . ."

"It takes two to tango, Mrs. Perkins."

Perception was everything. Who you were, what you cared about, whether or not you were a good person—none of that mattered if people's perception of you didn't match. Nikolai had honed his social mask over the years. He rarely dropped it in front of others, for when he did, they invariably became unnerved, if not downright terrified. He couldn't fathom why. It was the same face, albeit devoid of any feigned emotion.

On the plus side, it came in handy when he wanted to scare the absolute shit out of someone. Careful to hold tight to the illusion covering his scars, he discarded his mask and watched with amusement as Mrs. Perkins registered the change.

"I want you to leave Harper alone."

She shrank back, clutching at her necklace. When she hit the kitchen table and could go no further, she stared at him wide-eyed.

"No more dirty looks. No threats to turn Harper in to the landlord or the police. You even mention your suspicions about him to another person, and I'll kill you and feed you to your cats."

He'd made his point—both her body language and her mind

told him that. Still, he couldn't resist the urge to show off in front of a Mundane. One by one, five knives flew from a block in the kitchen and hovered around her head like a crown, the same pattern he used with the focus exercise.

Nikolai could almost hear Medea's exasperation at his choice of placement. *The skull is difficult to penetrate. You should aim for the neck and other arterial locations.* God, even when he was away from Medea, he couldn't get her stupid voice out of his head. He was struck by the sudden desire to defend his choice on the grounds that it was intimidating and looked cool. What did Medea know about perception? Nothing.

Mrs. Perkins gawked at the whirling blades and wet herself.

See, Medea? Intimidating!

"I'm glad we understand one another." The knives clattered to the floor. Mask back on, he was once again the polite young man. "Do try to enjoy the rest of your evening, Mrs. Perkins."

Control was a better fix than sex, and Nikolai rode a high of competency back to the gateway. The scars were hidden. Man or woman, he could make people love him—or quail before him. He was a god. One with the ability to aid his allies and subdue his enemies.

And Medea was most certainly an enemy.

Dropping his own mask made everything so clear. Medea was like him, just more skilled. She'd had a millennium to practice, after all.

The whole thing had been a honeypot. All of it. How did the most powerful Magi in the world retain her position? By presenting herself as a trainer of great skill. She would lure the best and brightest to her, before they'd grown strong enough to become a real threat.

Rebuffing potential apprentices had been a masterstroke. Weaklings would give up. She had nothing to fear from people like that. The most ambitious Magi would be undeterred and only they would she train.

Except she wouldn't train them properly. She lied, telling them up was down and down was up, that dark magic was weak and healing was strong. If they fell for her ruse, their magic would be crippled and they would never gain the power necessary to challenge her. But not everyone was fooled, and it was them she gave to the spirits.

It was well played. Medea had outmaneuvered him at every turn. The mask she presented was designed to make him drop his guard. At times he had almost believed she meant him well, despite all signs to the contrary. Did she not take great pleasure in torturing him during lessons? How often had she smiled while stabbing him with vines? She'd even manipulated him into burning his own cure. Her heart was cold. Decent people didn't have dungeons.

Petrov had underestimated him and so had she. Compared to Medea, he was nothing. He would never defeat her, outsmart her, find her secrets. His face was ruined. The illusion would hide it for now, but that was a temporary fix. He would never look the same again. Damaged and broken, hideous . . .

He twitched at the intrusive thoughts and withdrew a vial from his pouch. He'd prepared a tincture of highly diluted Frog's Fancy, but this was his first opportunity to test it. Why bother? It wouldn't work anyway. He should just drop it and be on his way. The bottle started to slip through his loose fingers.

A piece inside of him screamed, and his fingers curved around the bottle. Might as well try it. No need. He stared at the bottle for what seemed like ages, locked in indecision. At last, if only to quiet that small part of him that wouldn't let up, he raised the bottle dispassionately to his lips.

Minty flavor tingled over his tongue and the foreign thoughts died. Irritation bubbled to the surface. The malaise had almost made him drop the damned bottle. Yoxtl said the Frog's Fancy would only mitigate his symptoms, not cure him. He'd either have to take it continuously—impossible, given his limited supply—or he'd be battling with himself to take his treatment every single time.

Fuck this stupid curse and fuck Medea. Whatever it took, he would crush her.

THE DIVE

Nikolai returned to the hovel with clarity of purpose. Killing Medea had always been part of the plan. Had she proved to be a competent instructor, he would have spent years as the diligent apprentice, carefully disposing of her only when she ceased to be Useful. Whether or not he enjoyed her company was irrelevant. Medea couldn't be allowed to train future Competition, and that was that.

But Medea hadn't been a competent instructor. From day one, he'd been struck down by her curse. She refused to teach him telepathy or anything else decent, wasting his time with Latin, gardens, and boiling water while restricting books to prevent him from learning on his own. And now she'd ruined his face.

Hatred wasn't a requirement for murder, but it did sweeten the pot. Every apprentice who'd tried to kill her had failed, but he was better than the rest. Despite all her efforts to block him, he'd crafted the invulnerability potion and found a way to mitigate the curse. What he needed now was a plan.

Every other apprentice had tried to kill her and failed. She was too powerful. As with Petrov, she was hiding something. Whatever it was, he would use it against her.

Nikolai strode into the forest and called loudly for Yoxtl. When the spirit finally appeared, it yelped and did a double take. "What happened to your *face*?"

Nikolai winced, hand instinctively flying to his mouth. Had his illusion dropped?

As if in answer, the spirit said, "I can see through that."

"Never mind my face. Tell me about the cave."

Yoxtl studied him. "You're on a war path."

"And?"

"And it's not a good place to be where Medea is concerned. What makes you think you'll succeed when everyone else died?"

"Because I'm better than the rest and I'm going to use her own magic against her. Now tell me what you found."

"Why? So you can get yourself killed? You're of no use to me dead, mortal."

"I'm killing her with or without your help, so if you want to increase my odds of survival, you'd better start talking. Otherwise I'm going to have to get creative, lure her into a trap—"

"Alright, alright!" The spirit shook its head. "But first I want your word you'll help me build a following."

"Done. Tell me what's in the cave."

Yoxtl leapt onto a tree stump and sat, ringed tail bristling. "*Under* the cave. Of course, what I can tell you is limited, thanks to the geas."

He was going to strangle the spirit if it gave him another riddle. "Medea bound you not to interfere with my training. Why would whatever's under the cave count?"

"*Hypothetically speaking*, when a master hides something from an apprentice"—Yoxtl paused, choosing its next words carefully—"well, maybe they think he's not ready yet, or it would be dangerous in the wrong hands."

"I see." Giving Nikolai access to a forbidden magic before Medea deemed him ready might constitute interfering with his training, activating the geas. Yoxtl could answer him, but only in hypotheticals and generalities. "Is it safe to assume that a master would lay traps for their apprentice?"

"No, since the goal is to keep the student out, not harm them, and such things are kept in inaccessible places."

Nikolai paced in front of the stump, errantly rubbing at his scar tissue. Petrov had kept his secrets hidden in plain sight, knowing Nikolai had no reason to look. He shook his head at his formerly trusting self. He knew better now. Medea had blocked the cave entrance with solid rock. He had to find a way to get through. There had to be spells that created explosions. No. Medea probably had wards up to detect a magical attack on the cave. Thankfully, he wasn't opposed to using Mundane tools.

"Go on. Hypothetically, how would an apprentice reach . . . whatever their master was hiding? Would dynamite work, or would that damage whatever's inside?"

Yoxtl cocked its head and stared off into space. "The other day I was swimming off the coast when I came to a trench. I followed it toward the island, for the water was warm. Eventually the water became hot—too hot for a mortal to survive—but I kept going, for I felt that if I reached the end, I would find something wondrous."

Of course! Medea would expect people to enter from the cave and work their way down, not approach through a scalding underwater trench hidden in the ocean. She might not even know about it. If he could approach that way, he could make off with her prize without disturbing whatever wards she'd set up in the cave. All he needed was a way to breathe underwater and survive the heat.

"Thank you, Yoxtl, that was enlightening." Nikolai left the forest and made his way back to the hovel and the library.

Nikolai lived in the library for the next few days. It gave him no small amount of pleasure to eat there while loudly proclaiming to the empty room that he was doing so. He summoned *pirog* and *kokoreç*, licking fruit filling and grease off his fingers in between turning pages. Occasionally a stray bit of fruit or offal would make it onto an open book. He'd wipe the page clean, but a spot always remained as proof of his transgression.

The scalding water didn't concern him, as he had the invulnerability potion, but breathing underwater proved more complicated than anticipated. There was a potion that allowed the body to absorb oxygen through the skin. Unfortunately, carbon dioxide still had to be expelled through the lungs, which meant "breathing" water in and out and enduring the sensation of drowning the entire time. If the potion stopped working, he'd have no way to tell if he was really drowning until it was too late. The pain he could handle, but he'd also have to "breathe" the scalding water, and the invulnerability potion might not protect the inside of his lungs. Nikolai brewed one potion as a fail-safe and hunted for better solutions.

Shields looked promising. The grimoire brimmed with books on how to customize them, many of which contained excessive margin notes scribbled in Medea's own hand. The woman did love her shields. Creating a shield that could both repel water and allow gas exchange looked incredibly complex. Thankfully, Medea's excessive scribblings proved easier to follow than her lectures. Had he not planned to kill her, he would've started asking for notes on her more complicated lessons.

As with the finger regrowth, Nikolai threw himself into mastering the shield. He submerged off the coast for hours, each day diving a little deeper until he felt the weight of the water pressing in on his shield. Moving while completely shielded took some getting used to, but after a few days he managed to counteract the currents that tried to pull him in other directions.

Medea's tracking wards were another problem—he couldn't find them. After searching fruitlessly for hours in front of a mirror with Magic Sight, he sought help from Yoxtl.

"They're buried in your skull," said the spirit. "That's why you can't see them. And Magic Sight doesn't work with mirrors. Sorry, but I can't remove them without triggering the geas."

"You don't need to remove them, just make them visible and I'll handle the rest."

Yoxtl leapt onto his head and stuck a paw through his scalp. He expected the invasion to be disconcerting, but it hovered on the edge of pleasant, like a lukewarm bath you knew would feel better if only it were heated a few more degrees. The spirit carefully teased out two threads, steering them toward his cheek. "If you cut them, she'll feel it."

"I figured. Don't worry, I have another plan."

Nikolai entered the dungeon and walked along the row of cells. He chose the youngest prisoner and cast Sleep, then carefully extracted the wards and attached them to his decoy. On his way out, he pried loose one of the luminous crystals from the stairwell and pocketed it. He spent the rest of the day in the lab crafting an excess of healing and mana potions.

The next morning, he strode purposely to the cliffs. Sunlight glinted off the calm water—perfect day for a dive. As he shed his clothing, Yoxtl appeared at his side.

"You sure about this?" it asked.

Touching that the creature cared. "I'll be fine."

He removed the belt from his discarded clothing and secured it around his waist. To the belt he attached the illumination crystal from the dungeon, tied in a bit of cheesecloth, and his pouch, brimming with potions. Mana potions he planned to take regularly to fuel his shield. Healing, water breathing, and invulnerability potions he was saving for emergencies. He withdrew a vial of

Frog's Fancy and took a long draught. The curse wouldn't stop him today.

"I'm not sure this is a good idea. Mortals are so fragile. Even if you make it all the way in . . ." Yoxtl shook its head.

"I have shields and a pouch full of potions."

"Give me your hand." Yoxtl's grave expression didn't fit the normally jovial beast.

"Why?" he asked suspiciously.

"I'd like to shake it before you go. Isn't that what humans do?"

Nikolai turned away and stretched his arms. "That's not really necessary. I'll be back in no time."

Something tore into his ankle. Beads of blood welled across his skin in parallel lines.

Yoxtl did its best to appear nonchalant, licking its paw and running it over its ear.

"Did you just scratch me?" Nikolai demanded.

"Something to remember me by, mortal. Good luck!" With that, Yoxtl bounded away.

Nikolai waded into the water. Salt stung the fresh wound as he swam to the area above the trench and set to work crafting his shield. An amorphous bubble sprang to life around him. He willed the remaining water out and started the process of respiration. Oxygen in; carbon dioxide out. With another nudge of will, he was off.

During practice, the chill water in the surrounding ocean had gradually fogged his shield with condensation. Here the water was warm, ensuring a clear view. An entire ecosystem had sprung up around the isolated heat source. Fish wove in and out of coral, flashing disks of color forever on the move. A small shark patrolled, and the fish darted to avoid it, though it didn't seem interested—at least not now. On another day, he might have lingered to watch the dance of life and death. He swam on, into the gaping maw of the trench.

Light dimmed as the overhanging walls of the trench swallowed him and his shield. The illumination crystal sprang to life, but it did little to pierce the eerie darkness, extending its light only a meter or so beyond the shield. Life covered the walls of the trench—green living stones, crabs, anemones, and odd tubes with feathered red tongues. Drably colored fish darted out of his path.

The trench narrowed, pressing in on both sides until it splintered into two fissures. He shined the crystal down each, but it was impossible to see which led in the right direction. As he had with the temple in the jungle, he opened his mind and searched for magic nearby. For a time, he could make out nothing over the magical signature of the island itself. He relaxed further, straining his senses, until at last he felt a familiar pulse against his awareness. He followed the magical rhythm down the right fissure.

The lifeforms of the fissure seemed to shrink in response to the claustrophobic space. Shrimp and mussels now lined the walls, though the occasional creature swam past, blind and alien in its foreignness. Heat radiated through the shield as he progressed down the fissure. Sweat dripped off his body, landing on the interior of the shield with a sizzle. The shield wavered. He pushed more mana into it and downed a potion.

A wall of rock halted his progress. Magic pulsed just beyond, his heart keeping time with the rhythm. He crawled along the rock, searching for an opening. At last he found a tight crevice near the bottom. If he compressed his shield near-flush with his body, he might be able to slip through.

He drew in his shield, leaving an inch buffer against the unbearable heat. Into the crevice he squeezed, gritting his teeth as the shield's surface seared his chest. At last he was through. He expanded the shield as much as he could in the cramped cavern beyond.

At a glance, there was nothing unusual about the cavern. Red-feathered tubes and ghostly white shrimp dotted the rocky walls. Sweat steamed the inside of his shield. Whatever heated the hot pools in the cave above, it was close.

He didn't need Magic Sight to sense the raw power before him. The center of the cavern thrummed with magic, invisible to the eye yet blinding in its intensity, its steady pulse never wavering. Power, glory, immortality—all could be his if only he could harness the magic here. He moved toward it, a moth to the flame.

The shield wavered as he approached. He pushed mana into it, thickening his layer of protection. Just a little further.

CRACK.

Water poured in with a hiss, desperate to fill the void created by his shield. He cried out as the water pooling at the bottom scalded his feet. He redoubled his effort to fortify the shield. The breach sealed and he fumbled for another potion, even as he continued to push the bubble forward.

Fractures like lighting forked over the shield. Mana. He needed more mana. Another crack sent scalding water down his back.

He lurched toward the magic. If he could just get close enough to absorb it somehow, everything would be all right. A healing potion helped contain the damage, but he needed invulnerability. Potions, potions . . . He sifted through his stash. Why hadn't he thought to put the invulnerability potion in a different-shaped vial?

One after another he pulled vials out, letting them topple to the growing puddle at his feet. Mana. Healing. Healing. Mana. Come on! Where was invulnerability? Blisters formed on his arms and the shield stank of cooking flesh.

At last he found it. He tore open the stopper and gulped it down. As his hand dove back into the pouch for the breathing potion, the shield failed.

Fiery pain enveloped his body. The breathing potion in his hand cracked and burst, leaking green fluid into the surrounding water. He slurped at the water, searing the inside of his mouth. Had he gotten enough? No way to tell. His skin though, his skin wasn't forming new blisters, and the pain subsided to a dull ache. The invulnerability potion worked.

Nikolai cast Magic Sight and the roiling magic appeared in all its glory. He dove into the middle, biting back a scream as the unbridled power threatened to shatter him. Whatever magic this was, he would master it. He wrapped the pulsing magic in his will and attempted to fuse it with his body.

Pain lanced through him, chased by the tremors of mana fatigue.

But he'd just taken a potion! If his mana drained completely, the invulnerability would fail. His lungs spasmed and darkness tinged the edges of his vision. Was he drowning, or did it just feel like it? Either way, he was out of time.

He paddled for the crevice in the rock. If he could make it halfway through the trench, he could squeeze through the over-hang at the top and surface in time. It seemed to take twice as long to go half as far. He'd barely gotten past the crevice when white-hot pain seared his body. The invulnerability potion had failed.

He could no longer distinguish between the misery in his lungs and that of his skin. He swam forward, skin sloughing off in ribbons and floating into the deep. A curious fish tugged a piece still attached to his arm. He made to swing at it, but the beast darted away.

He paddled faster, muscles screaming. Injuries could be healed. All that mattered was getting to the surface before he drowned. He kicked frantically upward, head slamming into the roof of the fissure. Or was it the side? Impossible to see which way was up in the blurry seascape. His lungs spasmed again.

The world faded, and Nikolai with it.

37

DEATH CURSE

Medea sipped her tea and tried to concentrate on her book. It was no use. All week she'd ruminated on the Nikolai problem. Being back in Haven wasn't helping. She hated sleeping at the Hanged Man, with its stuffy room and itchy blankets. Downstairs should've been a reprieve, but she was constantly reminded of her wayward apprentice. After so many luncheons together, her brain had formed an association between this place and Nikolai.

The townsfolk avoided her more than usual. Even the innkeeper, usually in good spirits, had barely spoken a word to her since she'd arrived and served her orders with downcast eyes. It wasn't until a tearful girl, Shay-something, accosted her in the street with wild accusations that Medea realized the villagers thought she'd killed Nikolai.

She couldn't wait to go home but dreaded that too. Nikolai's time was almost up. She hoped he'd used it productively, but the realist in her doubted it was so. One way or another, they were going to have it out, and if he couldn't shape up, she wasn't sure what to do.

Breaking her vow to train him was out of the question, but he could always decide to walk away. As if that would ever happen! Even if it did, he would no doubt come back to haunt her after training under some lesser master. He'd challenge her, she'd kill him, and then she'd be right back where she started.

Medea shook her head. Already planning his death as if it were a sure thing. Was this what she'd been reduced to? She'd always had few peers and fewer friends, but it seemed she was destined to remain an outcast among her own kind. She suddenly wished her tea was spiked with brandy.

Rather than summon it herself, she flagged down the innkeeper. He approached cautiously, his demeanor excessively formal.

"Oh stop it," she said. "I didn't kill the boy. Can I get some brandy?"

"You didn't?" The innkeeper visibly relaxed. "Thank the gods. Ever since you came back, rumors have flown. Everyone's been asking me if I've seen him."

"Nikolai's fine. Or was, when I left him behind. The boy has far too much confidence and not nearly enough sense."

To her chagrin, the innkeeper slid into the seat across from her and started talking local news. Petrov had been discovered dead in a secret room filled with black magic. The dueling club had fizzled out and the local youth were getting restless. Medea wanted to remind him about the brandy. He seemed to have forgotten, and now she was trapped in pointless conversation.

Come home.

Medea jerked out of her chair, assessing and reassessing her mental barriers. Ever since Nikolai had entered her mind, she'd worried about what other spells she failed to reapply after teleporting to London. A telepathic message should have knocked at the outskirts of her boundaries. This message had bypassed them completely. Who had the skill for such a thing? The voice, if telepathy could be called a voice, wasn't one she recognized.

The innkeeper looked up at her with concern.

"I need to go." She whirled away from the table, spurred as much by the desire to extricate herself from unwanted socialization as by the strangeness of the calling.

Harsh words pelted Nikolai's awareness. He tried to open his eyes and found they'd been reduced to puffy slits. Two voices, both muted, sounded faintly in his ears.

"I tell you, it wasn't that. I was just coming to get you . . ."

"Don't lie to me!"

He'd been on the receiving end of Medea's irritation often enough to recognize her voice, even through the haze. A small part of him wanted to listen, but his body dragged him back into unconsciousness.

When his head cleared again, the voices had been replaced with the subtle shifting of movement. Nikolai attempted to speak and a hundred tiny blades scraped against his throat. All he could manage was a groan.

"Nikolai?" Medea sounded concerned. Another ruse. "Can you hear me?"

"Y-yes." He tried to shift to get a better look at her, but his body didn't respond. "Can't . . . move," he rasped.

"You were badly burned." Medea was no more than a blurry red shadow. "I've paralyzed you and shut down most of your pain receptors while I heal you. What happened?"

"I—"

"You were testing shields underwater," Yoxtl interrupted, voice urgent. "She can't hear this. Don't say it was the curse! I spent a long time convincing her it wasn't."

Nikolai covered his pause with a cough, the pain of which set off a true coughing fit. "Shields," he croaked. "Testing shields."

"So I've been told." Medea's tone said she found this dubious. "But why did your shields fail?" Her shadow stopped moving. The answer, for whatever reason, mattered immensely.

"Mana. Ran out."

"I see." The shadow moved again. "I had worried it might have been your affliction. You need to work on your mana pool. I don't know what else I can do to persuade you of that."

How much healing would she do? Would she fix his face or allow his entire body to remain scarred as another sick lesson?

"Medea?"

"Yes?"

"Face first. Throat."

"As soon as I'm done with your chest."

"Face," he insisted. "Please."

There was a pause and he thought she would refuse—lord knew she hated to have her work interrupted—but the shadow moved over his eyes. The pain in his throat subsided to a dull ache, and the laboratory came into sharp focus. He lay on the center worktable. Medea's hands wove the air above his scarlet chest. Yoxtl was curled on the back counter, pretending to sleep.

His limbs were bloated beyond recognition and covered with weeping, angry blisters. The skin ranged from taut red to crackly black, with gaping chunks of flesh missing. Someone had haphazardly thrown a towel over his crotch. He didn't want to know how bad the damage was there. As long as Medea fixed it, that's all that mattered.

"Not pretty, is it?" she said. "How did you even get in this state? In some places, it's as though you've been burned by fire, while the rest of your body is simply *cooked*. A man with your condition needs to be more careful. It's a miracle you survived."

"With my condition," he said bitterly. "Tell me, how am I supposed to live my life with my *condition*? Shall I take no risks, ever, in case it strikes? How can I do *anything* with this hanging over me?"

His voice rose. Yoxtl stared at him wide-eyed. Medea simply looked resigned. A tiny part of him cautioned this was not the time, he was at her mercy and needed her help. Piss Medea off now and he might be scarred for life or left to die. He didn't care. He was beyond caring.

"I don't know," Medea said, "but it is not my concern."

"Not your concern? It started the day after I moved here! You claim you have nothing to do with this, but that's one hell of a coincidence. Why should I believe a word you say?"

"Because I am not a liar!" A jar flew into Medea's hand. She wrenched the lid open and furiously dabbed a foul-smelling ointment on his chest.

"You might as well be. You do nothing to dispel my ignorance. I almost *died* tonight. It might not have been the curse—yes, I know it's a curse—but it *could* have been. I suppose that doesn't matter to you. What's one more apprentice to the great Medea? I know you don't care about me, but I thought at the very least you would honor your duty as my mentor."

"I have! Time and again! Though you seem keen on ignoring my advice. Still you view some magic as better than others. When I scarred your face, did you turn to the library as I had urged you? No. Yoxtl tells me you crafted an illusion to hide your failure from the world. You learned *nothing*, and I'll not heal that for you. Stop blaming me for your own ineptitude!"

"*Me?* You act as if the curse were my fault!"

"It *is* your fault! All of it! Your impatience, your greed, your insistence on coming here. That's what brought you to this."

Her careful knitting of his flesh stopped. To kill him, she need do nothing more than allow him to die. Maybe there was a way to convince her otherwise. He set his jaw and met her eyes squarely.

"I'm obviously not the apprentice you want. When you're

done healing me, I'll leave. All I ask is that you remove the curse before I go." He stamped down his thoughts of revenge. Though confident in his ability to detect a telepathic intrusion, he would take no chances.

She shook her head and began healing again. "The curse is not mine to remove. I will not interfere with someone else's magic, especially given the circumstances under which it was placed. Really now, I grow quite weary of you blaming me for your own error in judgment."

"What error in judgment?" Could the woman be any more vague? She acted like Yoxtl under the geas, tiptoeing around a topic for fear of triggering the spell, but for Medea it seemed self-imposed. Unfathomable, but he could work around the constraint. "What do you mean, you won't interfere with someone else's magic?"

"It's not all magic, but curses in particular. If someone has one, they likely did something to deserve it, making it unethical for me to remove." She paused and absently rubbed her face. "And sometimes the curse itself is indicative of a heinous crime."

His mind raced. Who could have cursed him, if not her? Someone in Haven. Ethne? She wasn't the type. Mr. Gallagher? Perhaps he'd found out Nikolai was banging his wife. But the man had no skill. Shailyn? Even less skill. His mind drifted to the last time he'd fucked her—under the tree he'd set on fire in a moment of rage. Shit. A lone hawthorn tree, he was sure of it.

The Irish said it was bad luck to harm a hawthorn tree, for they belonged to the fae. And he'd knocked over a milk saucer left as an offering. He'd never given any credence to the superstitions before, but now he knew spirits were real. Had he pissed off a spirit? Is that why Yoxtl could see the curse?

"Yoxtl. Yoxtl! Stop pretending to sleep. You're not fooling anyone."

The spirit opened its amber eyes and yawned. "What?"

"If I pissed off a fae—whatever spirit that is—could you help me make amends?"

Medea laughed bitterly and shook her head. She went to the cabinets, opening and shutting them again with undue force until at last she returned with another jar, which she slammed onto the table next to him.

Her mouth opened. Then closed. Then opened again. Finally, she blurted out, "What did you do the day we left Haven?"

"I put in my last day at the shop. I went home and packed."

"That's not all you did." There was venom in her voice.

Had she known or simply guessed? In either case, there was no point in lying about it anymore. Time to see what truth would buy him. "I killed Petrov."

"Yes, you did." Her hands went back to work.

"What does Petrov have to do with—" But he stopped, for Yoxtl had fallen over in a fit of laughter.

"It was the Petrov guy," Yoxtl burst out between laughs, "*he* cursed you."

Had he? Nikolai replayed Petrov's final moments in his mind. "Petrov didn't have *time* to curse me. I struck quickly, without warning—"

"I bet you did," muttered Medea.

"—so he'd have no chance of fighting back."

"He didn't need time," Yoxtl said, glancing at Medea as though checking to see if this would violate the geas, but she focused resolutely on her healing. "It's called a death curse. You cast it on yourself. If someone slays you, the curse ensures your killer faces justice."

"It's the kind of thing you want to check for and dispel *before* attempting to kill any reasonably talented Magi," said Medea.

Nikolai closed his eyes. The world as he knew it reordered itself. Petrov! He'd never thought much of the old man. Even when Medea mentioned Petrov was good at curses, he hadn't put two and two together. The curse on him was so masterful, so complex, it could only have come from Medea.

Except it hadn't. It came from an old man in a dingy shop. One who had never amounted to anything.

"My head hurts."

"Oh, good," said Medea, "maybe it's finally working."

He frowned at her. "It's too bad Petrov never bothered to show me how to cast spells like that. Then maybe I wouldn't have killed him."

"It's too bad he took on such an ungrateful, impatient ass for an apprentice."

Medea finished with his torso. His arm levitated and a chunk of flesh detached, dropping to the floor with a wet plop. She winced and stepped to the side, then began her work on the underside of the arm.

"I knew Petrov for many years," she said. "He always found me good items, even if he didn't see them as such. You could have waited and finished your apprenticeship with him first. It's not like I was going anywhere. But no, you had to be impatient. Worse than that—impulsive! Did you even stop to consider the consequences of your actions before killing him?"

"I had two years left. Unlike you, my time *is* limited. I plan to make the most of it."

"And how much of your time here has been fruitful, given the effects of the curse?"

"Less than I'd like," he admitted. His time on the island felt infinitely longer, thanks to all the half-started, broken-up lessons.

"Did it not occur to you that I would have spoken with Petrov on your behalf, had you but asked?"

"No. And I didn't think you'd wait for me."

Her hands cupped his arm. The tissue underneath softened and changed color. "As you keep pointing out, time is not something I lack. Two years is nothing to me. I'd already given my vow to teach you. Unlike your word, mine means something. If Petrov hadn't budged, I would have allowed you to join me in two years."

Damnit, she was right. He'd been so caught up in the moment he hadn't even considered if there were other options— but there was no use thinking about what might have been. It was done. The only thing that mattered now was moving forward.

He studied Medea as she worked her magic. Her perpetual frown intensified with her concentration, but she was still easy on the eyes, even more so now that she wasn't trying to kill him. Of course he still owed her for the face. And she still couldn't be allowed to train future students. But for now, he could set those things aside.

"There. I think I'm just about done." Medea stepped back, her eyes roving over his body. "I'm going to release you now and reactivate your pain receptors. Let me know if I missed a spot."

He gasped as his body flooded with sensation, then screamed at the fiery burning in his crotch. His hands clasped it through the towel and he nearly rolled off the table.

"Sorry! Sorry!" Medea's magic halted his fall and the pain vanished as quickly as it had come.

"You healed everything . . . but that," he panted.

Medea hugged herself. "It's not something I touch with my magic."

"It's just a body part, like any other."

"No, it's not. It's a—" She shook her head. "You'll just have to take a potion."

"And leave myself scarred?" She couldn't be serious. Scarred face and cock, he'd never get laid again. "I don't think you realize how important it is."

She laughed ruefully. "Well do I know the importance men place on *that*." She closed her eyes and leaned against the table, nails biting into the wood, breath measured. After a moment, she addressed Yoxtl. "Could you?"

Nikolai sent a pleading glance to the spirit. His fate hung on the next words.

"I don't have the magic for it."

The air left the room. Was this his life now, truly? It couldn't be.

A golden beam shot from Medea's hand to the spirit. Yoxtl's fur stood up and crackled as though beset with electricity. An attack? But Yoxtl smiled and its amber eyes glowed intensely.

"Come get me when you're done," said Medea. "I'll finish the rest." She paused at the door, tone harsh. "It will be covered when I get back, understand?"

Nikolai nodded and the door snapped shut. Yoxtl leapt from the counter to the table, buzzing with enthusiasm.

"What did she cast on you?" Nikolai asked.

"A nice bit of soul magic. Wizards can lend mana to one another, but as a spirit, I require a different currency." Yoxtl cackled. "She carved off a tiny fragment of her soul just to avoid touching your manhood."

"She did *what?*"

"Let's see what I'm working with." Off flew the towel.

Nikolai let out a string of curses. His rod was blotchy and red, misshapen as a melted candle.

"Please tell me you can fix that."

"Are you sure you want me to? It looks ready to fall off. I think your chances with Medea might be better if it did."

"Yoxtl . . ."

The spirit grinned, savoring his discomfort. Nikolai refused to be goaded.

Yoxtl sighed. "You're no fun." A silver light suffused Nikolai's flesh and it began to heal.

"No, it was bigger than that."

"Sure it was."

Despite the jests, Yoxtl's healing appeared sound. Nikolai turned his thoughts to Medea. Why hadn't she left him disfigured? She could've used healing as a bargaining chip, doling it out a little at a time to keep him in line. Instead, she flatly refused to heal his face but restored the rest of his body, even offering a bit of herself so Yoxtl could fix something she inexplicably wouldn't. It didn't make any sense. *She* didn't make any sense.

"Yoxtl, what do you think of Medea?"

"Why do you ask?"

"I'd like another perspective."

"First time for everything, I guess." It shot him a grin. "Look, you have ulterior motives, therefore so must she. Lying is as natural to you as breathing. You can't fathom someone with power defaulting to truth, because in your mind, truth is for the weak."

"I suppose . . ."

When the curse first hit, he thought she'd been poisoning him, as he poisoned Petrov. She definitely hid things, as Petrov had, but the curse made him suspect she wanted him drained or dead. That had proven to be false, yet he still had difficulty disentangling it from his perception of Medea. Why else would she be hiding things? Why refuse to train him in telepathy?

Yoxtl rolled its eyes. "I'll never understand the mental loops you mortals go through to justify your beliefs. Did it ever occur to you that she might have your best interests at heart? That she might be up-front about everything?"

"But she's not! She hid the curse from me—"

"A secret she felt was not hers to tell. But more than that, you killed an acquaintance of hers. Why shouldn't she keep silent, when she feels your punishment is justified?"

He'd assumed she was like him. Why? Because she was a master duelist who used black magic, murdered countless people, and had a dungeon. Yet her memory of Thomas had overflowed with emotion, which meant she *couldn't* be like him. Aside from anger and irritation, emotions were something he faked. She *felt* them.

That didn't mean anything, though. Most people weren't like him, not in that way.

"She likes hurting people, and me in particular. She has a *dungeon*."

"Hurting you is part of the training. As for the prisoners, she grew up in a time when criminals were severely punished. Crucifixion, branding, quartering, stoning, amputation—these would be the rule, not the exception. Is it that odd for Medea to keep prisoners of crimes she considers abhorrent?"

What had she said about immortality? She knew her morals were different due to her age, and so she didn't seek to impose her values on others. Maybe she wasn't as bloodthirsty as he'd thought.

"She still hides things from me, just like Petrov did. The cave, most of the library. She hides in her room half the day. What does she do up there?"

"I don't know. Why don't you ask her?"

"Why would I? She'd only lie and *oh my god you're right*."

Asking had never occurred to him because he assumed she would lie. For all he knew, she was knitting up there. Or napping —though probably reading.

The past year replayed itself in a different light. Had Medea ever been overtly dishonest? No. Failed to answer a question? Yes, but only about immortality, and she'd been transparent about why.

It was like peering into Harper's mind all over again. He'd allowed the lens of his own worldview to color his interactions with Medea, prescribing motivations that weren't there. If anything, she was honest to a fault. Truth was her self-imposed geas.

Something Petrov said came floating back. *That woman and her damned integrity.* In Medea's memory, Thomas was angry with her for hiding the truth about something. What had he flung at her? *A lie by omission is still a lie.* The accusation had landed because truth was something she valued, and being accused of lying struck down to her core. His accusation that she'd used telepathy had done the same. No wonder she'd been so upset. Only one thing didn't fit. Why would someone who valued truth and knowledge to that extent block access to books and restrict lessons?

"Done!" said Yoxtl brightly.

He looked down. Everything had been returned to normal. "Thank you, Yoxtl. And for talking to me."

"No problem. Don't forget to cover that before she comes back in." The spirit laughed as it went to fetch Medea. Nikolai rose and snatched the towel, sitting back on the table just as a knock sounded at the door.

Medea cracked the door but didn't enter. "Are you covered?"

"Yes."

She peeked cautiously into the lab as though expecting to catch him in a lie. Her body relaxed at the sight of the towel in place.

"You really know how to boost a man's confidence, you know that?" he said, laying back down.

She ignored the quip and bustled in with an armful of clothes, which she dumped next to him.

"I'm going to activate your pain receptors. Tell me if anything hurts."

His whole body ached, but here and there, something screamed. He identified the trouble spots and Medea tackled each in turn.

Here she was, helping someone who'd killed an acquaintance, simply because she'd given her word. The newfound theory demanded testing.

When all his pains had been resolved, he invented one on his arm. Medea leaned over the limb, probing with her mind, unable to locate the problem. He insisted it was there, right there, didn't she sense it?

If she didn't care how he felt or enjoyed causing him pain for the sake of it, she would give up easily. Thirty minutes later, after attempting multiple spells, opening his flesh and sealing it back up again, Medea still persisted in trying to locate the problem.

"Thank you," said Nikolai. "I think it's feeling better now. Whatever you did just then helped."

She slumped on a stool and rubbed her eyes. "Good. I was starting to worry I'd have to amputate your arm and start fresh."

"Uh, no. It's *definitely* feeling better now." He sat up, careful to keep himself covered.

"Well, then, I'm off to bed. Make sure you eat. Oh, and Nikolai—"

"Yes?"

"Your healing assignment still stands."

When the door shut, he reached up to feel his face. The scar tissue around his mouth and nose remained. He slid off the counter and began to dress.

Yoxtl raised its head from where it was curled up like a cat on the laboratory counter. "'Oh, just a little to the right, Medea. You almost got it there,'" it mocked. "I would've laughed if she *had* decided to chop off your arm."

"I had to be sure."

"Mmm-hmm."

The spirit placed its head back down, tucking nose under bushy ringed tail. Nikolai was struck with the strong desire to buy it a pillow.

"Thank you, Yoxtl. For pulling me out of the water. I'm assuming you put a blood link on me."

"I did. You're welcome."

Nikolai moved to the door and paused with his hand upon the knob. "I don't suppose you could fix my face?"

"No. That would go against the geas."

Figures. No time like the present to find answers. Nikolai headed to the library.

38

TRUTH AND TRUST

Nikolai pored over healing texts to no avail. Medea had tasked him with determining which spells she'd used in their last sparring match. One spell, cast three times, had caused him to swell. The other had scarred his face, causing the tissue to regrow excessively when damaged.

Two weeks after his foray into the trench, he was no closer to discovering what she'd used. He'd begun with the most advanced books. There were spells for reattaching limbs, repairing dead tissue, and treating burns. It was, he grudgingly admitted, Useful to know such things. But he could find no offensive spells, nor any spells that could be used offensively.

One night, in a sleepy stupor, he accidentally grabbed a healing book for novices. He almost put it back when he realized his error—laughable to think Medea would use beginner magic in combat, but he sat down with it anyway, flipping through for anything Useful.

And there it was—Blood Rejuvenation. Designed for victims suffering from blood loss, it stimulated the body to produce blood faster. Medea had cast it on him three times, tripling the volume of blood being produced. With no outlet, his body had swollen, causing lightheadedness and a faint heart. She'd stabbed his jugular before he'd passed out to release the pressure.

When the book didn't yield the second spell, he yanked down several more introductory tomes. At last he found the spell she'd used to scar his face.

In a manual for beginning healers.

In a footnote.

As a cautionary tale on bad spellwork.

On the surface, it was a standard healing spell. When cast upon an open wound, it told the body to build up tissue. The problem was that whoever designed the spell—apparently one of the author's apprentices—did such a bad job that the spell didn't take into account whether there was a wound to heal.

Cast upon healthy skin, the tissue multiplied for several minutes. Anything caught in the affected area would overgrow. The author cautioned that the spell could only be used if one were to magically draw out an area of effect first, ensuring the spell stayed within the boundaries and well away from undamaged tissue.

Nikolai leaned back in his chair. Basic spells. He had been laid low by two basic spells. Not only that, one of them was *bad.* Medea's words came back to him, "In the hands of a master, any spell can be dangerous." Would he have considered using such spells offensively? Not in a million years. Yet Medea had, and to great effect.

His eyes roved the library. How many spells were contained in these books? Hundreds of thousands? Millions? How many had Medea committed to memory, on the off chance they might be Useful one day? He could read all day every day for decades and not scratch the surface. No wonder she was insulted when an apprentice thought they could kill her.

As he had.

No—he could still kill her, just not using magic. There was more than one way to break a person. He could—

Nikolai slammed his fist on the table. Damnit! He was doing it again. He needed to be smarter, consider his options. Revenge was sweet, but he needed to think long-term.

Medea was a neutral party. Unlike himself, she had no greater aspirations. She was perfectly content to sit alone on her little island, researching new spells and reading. Her knowledge of magic was second to none, and she loved to talk about it. Maybe the best course wasn't to kill her. She could be a powerful ally—maybe more. Thomas had gotten there. It wasn't impossible.

What about after his apprenticeship? Masters were allowed unrestricted access to the island. He would be allowed to use her laboratory, dungeons, and library, so long as he kept them in good order and replaced any ingredients used. Continued access to the library alone would be worth it.

Still, she *could* train others. He drummed his fingers on the table. He'd have to do something about that. It's not like she was jumping at the chance to take on new people. He'd have to deal with what, one person a decade? He could tackle the problem as it arose.

For the first time since his scarring, he was optimistic. He closed the book and returned it to the shelf, then sat down to finish Medea's assignment, along with a carefully crafted apology.

Medea willed the nails out of the board and pulled it off the wall, stacking it neatly with the others. The gap behind wasn't large enough for the tank she had propped against the bathtub, but she could fix that. The annoying part would be running a second set of pipes to the house.

"What are you doing to my bathroom?" Nikolai leaned against the doorframe. His scalp sported a regrowth of dark fuzz.

"I'm putting a water tank back here. You continually run out of mana because you refuse to do the boiling exercise. From now on, if you want hot showers, you'll have to heat your own water. I'll no longer do it for you."

He grinned. "That's not much incentive. I grew up in the Soviet Union in the middle of a war. Hot water is a luxury. But for you I'll make the effort."

What the hell did that mean? And why was he smiling so much lately? It put her on edge. Some people were overly nice to disguise when they were up to something.

He approached and peered at the wall. "What do you mean you do it for me? If there's no tank back there now . . ."

She pointed to the pipes. "See these? They run to the ocean. There's not much fresh water on the island, so I draw up water from my boil site, desalinate it with a spell, and run it through pipes all the way to the house."

He said nothing. When she looked over, he wore an odd expression. Maybe he was constipated.

"Do you need to use the toilet?" she asked. "I can come back later."

"Your boil site. Where is it?"

"Under the cave. How else would it get hot water?"

"You boil . . . the ocean?" He stared at her with uncomfortable intensity.

She avoided his gaze and focused on removing more boards. "Yes. The more often you do the boiling exercise, the larger your mana pool grows, which means you can heat more water before running out of mana. I told you when you get better we'd increase the size of the pot."

The board came loose and she set it aside. "I've been doing this for centuries. Small pot, large pot, tub, uh . . . I can't remember what I used after that. At some point I started heating a nearby lake. That worked well at first, but when I was finally able to heat the whole thing, everything died—the fish, the plants—all rotten. It was disgusting. The ocean is perfect. There's always cooler water moving in so I never run out, and apprentices seem to enjoy the hot springs above the area." She looked at him pointedly. "When they're not drowning in them."

Nikolai slumped against the doorframe. Was he ill? One hand ran errantly over the fuzz on his head. It looked to be a pleasant sensation and she wanted to touch it, but one didn't just touch other people's hair, and anyhow he seemed to be having a moment, though she couldn't for the life of her understand why.

"You boil the ocean?" he muttered. "From here? *Nonstop?*"

"You make it sound like a difficult thing, but the process was incremental. Do you look at a master work of art and think the artist learned their skills overnight? No. I timed the boil with my heartbeat, and now I don't think about it any more than I do breathing. It's important to build good habits, *especially* if you plan to become immortal. Because one day you'll wake up and five hundred years will have passed, and if you're not going to be judicious with your time, why have it?"

"Medea, I—" His hand clenched into a fist, and for a moment she thought he would hit something, then he sat on the toilet and shook his head, laughing softly. "Why did you accept me as an apprentice? I mean, I know I manipulated you into it, but there had to be some other reason."

He didn't sound at all like himself. Was the curse active? No. The insidious thing encircled his soul as tightly as ever but wasn't currently permeating his brain.

She made to lean against the tub, only the narrow rim was uncomfortable, and the water tank was in the way. She gave up and levitated in a sitting position. Where to start?

"Because I'm bored. Immortality is . . . long. It gets lonely.

I'm used to being alone, but when you get to my level, well, there's no one to talk to. Every Magi I meet—it's like trying to make conversation with an infant. Their grasp of magic is immature to the point where we might as well be speaking different languages.

"And sparring—I love sparring! But no one even comes close. You know what I think when another apprentice tries to kill me? Well, two things. One, 'Not again.' Two, 'I hope this lasts more than a minute.' Five minutes would be a miracle. I handicap myself, you know. I'll pick a magical school and say, 'Today I'll only fight with this.' I tell my students it's for their benefit, and they do benefit from it, but in truth it's more for me. But now even that's not challenging.

"And it doesn't matter anymore because magic is dying out, and I'm the only one who seems to notice. You're an anomaly in that you were born with a bit more magic, but in a few generations, I doubt I'll see anyone with a quarter as much. I'll be the only true Magi left. Sometimes I wonder if I'll kill myself when the loneliness gets too great, but I probably won't. There are always more books to read, things to learn. But it gets so hard . . ."

"What?" Nikolai stared at her, aghast.

Oh, no. He probably hadn't wanted a detailed answer. Like when people asked, "How are you?" but it was only a greeting. And now she'd gone overboard and shared too many things.

She dropped to her feet and made for the door. "I'm sorry, I'll leave you—"

He grabbed her wrist as she passed. She glared at the touch and he relinquished her.

"Sorry. Don't leave. You said magic is *dying*?"

"Yes." She rubbed the wrist where he'd touched her, then the opposite wrist, making them even. "It's been going on for some time, but it's accelerated this last century."

"How do you know it's dying out? I'm not contradicting you!" he said at her look. "I just want to know."

She nodded. "It's good to ask for evidence. The short answer is I can feel it. I have wards in place to retain ambient magic on the island, but when I leave—"

"You feel like shit."

"Yes." Medea smiled. He felt it too! Most apprentices were too weak and unskilled to notice.

"I thought it was—never mind what I thought it was. Are you saying that how it feels here on the island, that's how it should feel everywhere?" He looked perturbed—not that Nikolai ever truly looked bothered by anything, but perturbed for Nikolai.

"Yes. Pockets of magic remain. My island, the temple, some of the older Magi towns. But in most places, especially the big cities, it's like there's an overwhelming . . . emptiness. People go about their business, and no one feels it but me."

"Have you mentioned it to anyone?" he asked.

"Who would I tell? Individuals don't matter. The Collective hates me, though I daresay I'll approach them once testing is complete."

"Testing?"

"I don't know what's causing magic to vanish. I had been hoping to run experiments, maybe even with an apprentice, but then I took you on, and you seemed so . . ." Selfish? Apathetic? She couldn't think of any inoffensive way to end the sentence, so she just let it hang.

"I'll help you," he said quickly.

Of all the people she thought would take her seriously, she never thought Nikolai would be the one. "Okay."

He smiled and stepped to the side. She was halfway out the door before she recalled why she'd been in the bathroom in the first place. She whipped around and returned to the wall. Her mind dove into the space, pushing it outward on all sides, until the gap behind the wall was large enough to fit the water tank.

―――――――――

Nikolai watched Medea from the door as she casually ripped apart the space-time continuum or whatever the hell she did to make the massive gap behind the bathroom wall. Since he'd decided against killing her, observing Medea's power had become infinitely more enjoyable. Allies *should* be powerful.

He needed to work on cultivating their relationship. The past year, he hadn't been his best. For whatever reason, Medea had made him forget Harper's lessons about winning people over. Again and again he'd let his mask slip, resulting in outbursts and snarky comments. If he wanted her as an Ally, he'd have to wear a different mask.

Medea valued truth and so he'd give it to her—in limited quantities. She had to trust him, especially if he wanted to get as far as Thomas. But more importantly, if Medea was right about magic dying—which she probably was—she'd need his help. The woman wasn't exactly good with people, and the Collective, regardless of their opinion on her, were stubbornly opposed to change.

She stood with her hands on her hips, studying the gap as the tank floated into place. It clattered against the pipes and listed to one side.

No time like the present to start building trust. "By the way . . ." He paused to ensure she was listening. "I've decided not to kill you. I know that sounds like a line, but I wanted you to know."

A range of emotions played across Medea's face, and she mumbled something about the Botanist.

"What was that?" he asked.

"What?"

"You said something about the Botanist being right."

"I did? Oh, well, the Botanist told me the reason all my apprentices try to kill me is because I allow them access to too much information too soon. You said you've changed your mind, so maybe it—"

Motherfucker. "Is *that* why you blocked off the entire library?"

She crossed her arms. "I didn't block off *everything*, but yes. I've never done that before. But it seems to have help—"

Herr Bergmann! He should kill the bastard. Medea watched him with some alarm, and he found his fist poised to punch the door. He relaxed his arm.

"No. It *didn't*. Medea, listen to me. It didn't work. It made me angry. It made me think you were hiding things, like Petrov hid things. It—"

FUCK. He didn't want to admit to the mistake, nor his motivations for the dive, but the truth would help her, and so he told Medea why he'd been in the ocean and his plans to kill her with her own magic. She listened with increasing alarm, her frown intensifying as she stared off to the side, eyes darting.

"So you see," he said, "it didn't help. It only made things worse. Listening to Bergmann—the Botanist—his kind are all about restricting spells. Of *course* he would tell you to do that."

"It seemed reasonable advice at the time." Medea shook her head, then frowned. "Why are you telling me all this?"

"I've . . . made errors in judgment of late."

She raised an eyebrow. "Of late?"

"Don't start, this is hard enough as it is. I'm not normally one to—"

"Yes, yes, I understand." She waved a dismissive hand. "I suppose I'd better release my wards on the library. Study whatever you like. I know you'll gravitate toward the darker stuff, but at least I can ensure you learn it right."

Trust. It went both ways. Before he could change his mind, he spoke the dreaded words.

"I would prefer if you chose my . . . academic path." It was the hardest thing he'd ever done, putting his life's trajectory into someone else's hands, but he'd sought Medea as a mentor for a reason. She was the best. She'd vowed to make him stronger, and a vow from Medea meant something.

She stared at him like he'd grown two heads, then blurted out, "What the *hell*?"

"I may be a slow learner, but I do learn. Don't make me regret it."

She grinned. "You know what your first task is, right?"

He sighed. "Yes. I'll go boil water."

THANKS FOR READING!

If you'd like to receive an epilogue with Medea and Yoxtl (from Yoxtl's point of view), please sign up for my newsletter:
https://www.subscribepage.com/t7a2d4_copy
You'll also get a short story from Nikolai's time at the Academy, detailing "the bread incident." I email once a month with book recommendations, interesting facts, and cool extras like deleted scenes (though not all in one email, that would be a lot).

If you enjoyed Dark Apprentice, please leave a review wherever you buy books. Even just a line or two is fine. It helps other readers know my work isn't a steaming pile of shit.

If you didn't enjoy Dark Apprentice, why the heck are you still here? Are you just a die-hard completist? (If so, I feel you.) That said, it would also be helpful if you left a review. I don't expect my work to appeal to everyone, and your honest review ensures others won't suffer through as you did. Life is too short to read stuff you dislike.

AUTHOR NOTES

Medea is autistic. There's so little decent representation that I want to cry every time I see it. While autistic characters aren't unheard of, few are labeled as such, either because the creator didn't realize they were writing an autistic character or because the powers that be decided they "wanted to reach a broader audience" or "didn't want to risk getting it wrong." It forces us to headcanon characters as autistic with little chance of verification.

Unfortunately, there's no way for Medea to know she's autistic, so it can't be mentioned within the story (not this early in the series anyway). I didn't want a "Dumbledore is gay" fiasco after the books were done, nor did I want autistics to have to wade through the social minefield of asking, hence these notes. Knowledge of autism is not necessary to enjoy the story, but it does add nuance and give one a better understanding of certain events.

Nikolai is written to be a psychopath, more formally known as Antisocial Personality Disorder. Accuracy is important to me. I studied firsthand accounts from psychopaths, and my beta readers included a psychopath and a psychologist who works with ASPD clients. I obsessed a bit over getting it right, to the point where the psychologist had to remind me that humans are individuals and will display the characteristics within their neurotype to varying degrees—something that I know from an autistic perspective but had trouble applying in this case. What can I say? I overthink things.

Unfortunately, my goal to depict an accurate, unmasked

psychopath was somewhat derailed by the fact that neurotypicals respond terribly to that shit. (Psychopaths reading this are probably thinking some variation of "duh" or "what did you expect?".) I blogged about it on my website so I won't get into it here, but in the end I had to take some creative license, toning down Nikolai's thoughts and using outward behaviors to fake emotions he wasn't having, effectively masking him to tolerable level.

Nikolai does fall into the murderous psychopath trope, which isn't great representation. Most psychopaths aren't killers or even violent. They're just people who process emotions differently. Like autistics, they have to mask near-constantly to avoid being ostracized, and there are a lot of damaging misconceptions about them. For an interesting read, check out Life as a Nonviolent Psychopath:

https://www.theatlantic.com/health/archive/2014/01/life-as-a-nonviolent-psychopath/282271/

It's an interview with James Fallon, a prominent neuroscientist who accidentally found out he was a psychopath, much to his surprise and no one else's.

YHWH is "Yahweh," the oldest known spelling of the Jewish/Christian god. Yoxtl, being a spirit, would use the oldest version of the name. It's not like they call each other "God" because they're all gods to their own followers.

Yoxtl is a fabrication. I didn't feel comfortable using an Aztec god, as I needed Yoxtl to fulfill a specific role, so I created a spirit that would have existed nearby.

I try to include references to real-world magic whenever possible. The books on Petrov's shelf are mostly real (the names that sound the fakest are probably real), as is Nikolai's description on how to make a wand (including getting permission from a tree). All but one of the listed Aztec spells are real (I made up the death curse). Yes, the magic forearm is a real thing. Families had to guard the bodies of women who died in childbirth because someone might steal an arm. At least they were dead. The same can't be said for albinos living in present-day Africa, which you can google if you're in the mood to be horrified.

I will say that weaving magic into the real world is harder than it looks. Technological advances played a big part in which cultures subjugated others. Adding magic into the mix would've leveled the playing field considerably, and history wouldn't have proceeded as it did.

What I have now is a magic system that progresses like technology—people make advancements based on prior knowledge and experiments, so different areas of the globe would have had access to different types of spells. Medea almost touched on this when she chastised Nikolai about the Aztecs. Unfortunately, I had to cut the segment as the book was already long and the conversation had little to do with the current plot.

Found a typo? Report it here:
https://forms.gle/L3QBaFZp38QTCjXN9

g goodreads.com/valneil
BB bookbub.com/authors/val-neil
f facebook.com/valneilauthor

Lightning Source UK Ltd.
Milton Keynes UK
UKHW012024300621
386418UK00002B/329